By the same author

Dark Lantern
A Very Civil War
Out of the Shadows
The Widow
Three Sisters

The House on the Hill

CAROLINE ELKINGTON

Copyright © 2021 Caroline Elkington
All rights reserved
www.carolineelkington.net

For Tessielou, with love.

One

He watched her from shrewd eyes, white as a frosted bone. His grey hood and black cape pulled close around him, affording him little protection against the bitter January morning.

She moved nimbly across the yard, skipping over the frozen puddles in her pattens, holding her skirts bunched in fingers, blue with cold, her breath making opaque clouds.

As ever, she took no notice of him. He could follow her at will, indulging his curiosity, without fear of discovery. He waited impatiently for her every morning without fail and if she was late, he fretted, imagining she might not appear. He paced and fidgeted, keeping a watch on the kitchen door, he flexed his neck and pretended that he was interested in other things to help pass the time.

The sky was a misted silver, the colour of a bruised snowdrop. The distant hills smudged into it, their edges melting, and no matter how hard he squinted he couldn't bring them into focus. The elms, their limbs drawn with a scratchy quill, crouched crookedly in the lane, the last ones in the avenue just a faint blur of smoky grey.

The door to the barn clattered open, disturbing the hens inside, making a few of them let out startled complaints. The sound of the scraps bin opening, the splash of water, a snatch of a cheerful song and the early morning creak of wings stretching and the ruffling of feathers, rustling like a taffeta gown. Two stout-hearted chickens wandered out into the yard and idly pecked the iron-hard ground; they curtsied and scratched to no avail, curling their yellow claws away from the icy cobbles and with a disappointed shake of their heads, returned to the barn and the warmth of their nesting boxes.

After a while, she came out again, holding just a pair of eggs in her hand, her cheeks pink from the cold, as though someone had pinched their childish curves with spiteful fingers.

She stood for a moment and frowned at the eggs and then with a resigned shrug, she picked her way across the yard to where the geese were kept in a lean-to pen against the wall and let them out and then on to the pigsty to release the two pigs into their enclosure. The yard was suddenly alive with happy grunting, gooseish fluttering and honking. The day had begun.

He noted the steam rising from the pigsty and the five hissing geese forming an orderly queue to the orchard, where they were always hopeful they'd find some rotting apples still hiding in the crunchy, frosted knots of grass; disappointed, they'd then troop across the field to look despondently at the frozen pond for a while before returning to the yard for their breakfast. They were bad-tempered creatures but there was something absurdly military about them, they carried themselves with stiff dignity like elderly sergeant majors marching to the beat of a regimental drum.

From the church came the sound of the churchwarden unlocking the door so that he could prepare for the Sunday service and somewhere outside the nearby village, a cow lowed, a melancholy sound, resonant with her despair.

He could hear all kinds of noises now, as the world awoke, the clattering of pails and the barking of dogs. The sounds, deadened by the mist were echoless and smothered. The scent of woodsmoke reached him as fires all around the valley were stoked and the chimneys issued ashy sighs and scattered gilded sparks into the milky-white. Standing in the lee of the hay-barn, he was only waiting for her to return to the kitchen, as she always did. Then he'd watch the door for a few minutes before leaving. Peering in through the smeared windows was beneath him and he refused to do it, so what happened inside the farmhouse went unseen and he was unable to provide a more detailed account for his master.

She stopped to stroke the yard cat behind its ears, and it wound itself about the hem of her petticoat, striped tail arched; he could hear it purring and he shrugged his bony shoulders because cats were such devious beasts. She seemed to have a soft spot for anything living, animal or otherwise, which to his mind, was an inherent weakness. His master seemed to think it would be beneficial for them; he supposed his master found it eminently exploitable and therefore worthwhile for his scheme.

He returned home across the fields and up the densely wooded hill to Galdre Knap and tapped on the leaded panes of the library window.

His master's manservant let him in.

* * *

She banged the kitchen door shut rather too hard, the latch rattling in protest and her grandfather let out a sharp click of disapproval as he hunched over the fire, trying to gather some warmth into his aching old bones.

"Slow down, for pity's sake, Hetty. You'll have that door off its hinges."

"Sorry, Old Pa, I was in a hurry to get out of the cold. Hens didn't want to go into the yard."

"Can't say I blame them. Any eggs?"

"Only two. Enough for breakfast, at least. Slowing down though. I pickled several dozen when they were plentiful."

"Pickled eggs for breakfast? *How are the mighty fallen.*"

"We were never mighty, dearest. And pickled eggs are perfectly tasty and good to eat, so you'll have them and not complain."

"It's not what I'm used to," lamented the old man.

"We've plenty of dried apples and dripping for your bread and saltings and cured bacon, we've got jars of honey from our skep and beets and parsnips and carrots from our garden. And flagons of cider. We won't starve that's certain. Anyway,

Grandmama taught me to forage and make do — we'll get by. We always do, despite your incessant worrying."

"You shouldn't have to live like this. It's not right. It should be my job to take care of you, to keep you safe."

Henrietta Swift put a little of their precious lard into two dishes and cracked one egg into each added a pinch of salt and then placed them in the small brick oven set in the wall beside the fireplace. She took two oatcakes she'd baked the day before from the wooden cupboard by the sink and put them to warm on the iron rack in front of the fire, then she wiped down the table and set some cutlery and platters out. She poured some spring water from the pail into the kettle and hung it on the bar over the fire and lit another tallow candle as the daylight was still dimmed by the mist.

"Extravagant," said her grandfather.

"We have to be able to see what we're eating. Stop complaining, you old grump. You'll see, we'll be as fine as fivepence."

He stuck a gnarled finger up under his outmoded full-bottomed wig, which perched at a rakish angle on his head and constantly slipped down over his rather finely carved forehead and he scratched absentmindedly, "It just doesn't sit right."

"What, your wig? I'm not surprised! That old thing must have arrived with the Ark. I wish you'd at least allow me to wash it."

"Wash it! Ruin it, more like! You keep away from it. I was wearing this when I married your grandmother. If it was good enough for her it should be good enough for you, Miss High and Mighty."

"That was sometime in the last century, Old Pa!" She laughed at his disgruntled expression; the perceptive but much faded blue eyes and beetling, whiskery brows showed his displeasure, "And I'm fairly sure that Grandmama would have burnt it by now."

He was silent and stared into the flames for a while and she knew that her words had conjured up a likeness of his wife in his still lively mind.

"And what's more, you would have let her, because she scared you!"

He smiled, reluctantly, "You have no respect for age and wisdom. I'm nearly ninety years old and should be treated as though I might know more than you. You're a mere slip of a girl!"

"I'm two and twenty! And hardly a slip!"

"You're just fine as you are but you should be married by now, my child — not wearing yourself out looking after me. God only knows why you didn't accept Edwin's most gratifying offer!"

"Because I would have been Mrs Henrietta *Scroggs* and, more to the point, I don't, and never ever could, love him. He believes that he's far above me in consequence and cannot see why I might refuse him because he thinks he's such a splendid catch! Well, I'd much rather stay here and muck out the pigs than be married to such a supercilious prig."

Her grandfather laughed and shook his head, "You're just like my Anne. She was a thorn in my side too."

"You're an old fool," said Hetty.

"No respect," muttered her grandfather. "What's *that?* Don't we have any proper tea left?"

Hetty had warmed the teapot and was spooning dried leaves into it from a small wooden box. "It's raspberry leaf tea. It's all we have for now and it tastes jolly good. My, but you're in a peevish mood this morning. You know, if you like I could ask Mrs Warren if she has any used tea leaves, we could have?"

"Don't you dare! The shame of it! Raspberry leaves will do just fine. I don't know why you're making such a fuss. I was only asking."

"Yes, Old Pa. Mr Randall said he'd pop round to have a chat with you and maybe a game of chess this afternoon, if you're up to it."

"Of course, I'm up to it, I'm not yet in my dotage. Anyway, it doesn't take much to beat the churchwarden at chess — he's a nincompoop."

Hetty opened the oven door with a thick cloth, took out the baked eggs and put them on the table, "You'll go straight to hell if you talk about him like that. He's a good man and you know it, but you despise a good man because it shows up your own shortcomings. Come and eat your breakfast like a good fellow."

He gave her a frosty look but did as he was told.

* * *

The library was warmed by a substantial fire in the hearth and dozens of the finest beeswax candles burning lavishly in their sconces. It was one of only a handful of rooms that were used in the house; with such a small household, only two servants, there was not much call for the main rooms to be kept warm and lit — it was all the present staff could do to maintain the cosier rooms as it was. But neither of them would ever dare to suggest that more help was needed. Given their own personal deficiencies, they were fortunate to be employed at all and they trod carefully, glad of sanctuary, food on the table and a place to lay their heads. A last resort it may be but residing at Galdre Knap had its advantages. They knew better than to dwell upon the disadvantages.

Finn closed the window and coldly observed the beast hop from chair to table to chair.

"What news do you bring, Crow?" asked his master.

The indignant jackdaw, perched on the back of a high-backed carved chair, scratched its head with its claw and stared unblinkingly at him.

I'm not a damned crow.

Torquhil Guivre smiled, "I mean it as a compliment. Crows are clever creatures."

But jackdaws make crows look as feeble-minded as sheep.

"You're from the same genus, you insult your own relations."

Crow, whose real name was Lonán, tapped his beak against the chair back and allowed his thoughts to fall silent.

"So, what did you see? Anything to report?"

The same as ever. She works. She sings. She talks to the stupid beasts and caresses them.

"Interesting. Any sign of the grandfather?"

He stays inside. His legs are weak.

"And the suitor?"

He still sulks. She caused him pain.

"To his pride, nothing more. He cannot feel deeply and thinks only of himself and his own standing in the county. He's unworthy."

She's just a farmhand. Why would he even care?

"She wasn't always so, and he can still see her as she was before circumstances brought them to this. Roland Swift, her grandfather, was once a force to be reckoned with in the district; he owned all the land as far as a man can walk in a day. He was a good landlord, a man of principle. Admired and trusted. It was his reprobate son who brought about their downfall — and, added to that, an unfortunate outbreak of influenza that devastated the county." Torquhil Guivre glanced at Finn from dark, hooded eyes, "Many families were decimated, and the world would never be the same again for some."

Crow looked across at the manservant, silver-haired, bent and old before his time. Even a jackdaw could see the scars.

Finn, listening to only half a conversation, tried to imagine what the other half might be like, but it was hard to conjure up what a jackdaw might be thinking. Finn was a prosaic man not much given to flights of fancy and often wondered what quirk of fate had landed him here, in this godforsaken house on the hill, where nothing made sense and, for the sake of his sanity and his future, he asked no questions. He obeyed orders and kept himself to himself. In truth not much more was ever asked of him, but he knew he had a roof over his head and a square meal or two every day and in his state of health, that was all one could expect. His master was a mystery to him, and he was content for him to remain so. But he had to keep a wary eye on that bird though — it'd steal the pennies off a dead man's eyes.

No, I wouldn't. Not copper. Maybe silver though.

Finn didn't like the way Crow looked at him sometimes and often felt like wringing his scraggy neck but no sooner had the thought come into his head, but the wretched bird would take to the wing and find somewhere high to perch, or he'd sit on his master's shoulder and make his *tchack-tchack* call as though he were laughing at him.

Crow cocked his grey head to one side.

Thick as a goose.

"Why a goose?" asked Torquhil Guivre.

Ever had a chat with a goose?

"Not that I can recall."

Then you probably have. They're so stupid they just wait about until they get fat and then they get eaten.

"The farmers clip their wings so they can't fly. They have little choice in the matter."

I'd let no man clip my wings. I'm free.

"As free as a bird. But are you really? Why aren't you tumbling down the sky with the rest of your jackdaw family."

Silence.

"None of us are truly free, Crow. We all have our masters and must obey them for very different reasons. So, if you have nothing more to impart, I shall allow you to get back to your spying duties."

Crow dipped his head in acknowledgement and fluttered to the windowsill. Finn opened the casement and was glad to see the bird hitch his glossy wings and flit away into the mist.

Finn turned back to look at his master, waiting for orders.

Torquhil Guivre looked back at him steadily, "He's useful. Exasperating but useful. I need eyes in the village so that I can anticipate the mood. I have to take care."

"Yes, sir. I understand."

"I'm sorry about the mess he brings," said Torquhil Guivre indicating the grey splatter on the chair. "He's a wild thing and his standards are low."

"It's not that so much — it's the way he stares at me. It's — unnerving."

"He does it on purpose. Don't let him unsettle you — that way he wins. He likes to play games. It's in his nature — mischief maker and thief. His character has been so since ancient times and is unlikely to change. He amuses me."

"A daw with a sense of humour. It's not natural."

"Some birds are dull creatures — wood pigeons for instance, and — geese. Jackdaws are the tricksters of the bird world, and they take great delight in fooling humans. Don't let him see your anxieties or he will be tempted to play upon them."

"Yes, sir."

Laughter lit the sloe-darkness of Torquhil Guivre's strange eyes and Finn watched without blinking, as an embroidered salamander eased its way over his master's shoulder and disappeared under his long black hair. The exotic, floor-length banyan he habitually wore, of midnight blue satin, every inch embellished with weird and wonderful flora and fauna, caught the candlelight, and gleamed as though alive. Sometimes Finn would notice the eyes of the creatures that adorned it follow him around the room.

When he spoke of such things to Mrs Ashby, she shrugged her plump shoulders and told him he should keep away from the cider. She mostly stayed in the kitchens, away from the main part of the house and, tight-lipped, spent her days gutting fish, pounding herbs and chopping vegetables, filling the place with delicious aromas. She was grateful for the position; no one else would give her employment and since her husband had decided to get himself trampled to death by a herd of irate cows, she'd been forced to take her renowned skills as a cook and try to earn a living from them. After several false starts, she'd practically given up all hope and begun to imagine herself in the poorhouse in Cirencester. No one wanted to employ a female of her advanced years, with a deformed leg and only one good eye. The day Finn had knocked upon her door she'd been at her wit's end and the offer to work at Galdre Knap seemed heaven-sent. She'd heard the whispers of course; the locals were very free with their opinions about Mr Guivre. She hadn't thought twice; she'd briskly accepted and packed her bag, leaving behind her rented, one-roomed cottage, and cast a glance to the heavens in thanks.

When she'd arrived at the house on the hill she would admit to being momentarily taken aback. It was not at all what she was used to, and she soon developed a crick in her neck as she eyed all the wonders to be seen. She didn't have a nervous disposition and after thirty years spent with a husband who regularly beat his dogs, his cows and his wife, she was sanguine about someone, however odd he may appear, who was ready to give her a chance at a life without ill-use. She was blessed with a good-nature, resilient sense of humour and the patience of a heron.

Finn drove her to market every week in the cart and she'd carefully buy their supplies and tolerate the sidelong glances from the villagers. Only one stallholder refused to sell to her and muttered darkly about her mysterious employer. If she strayed too near to him, she caught the words that she was undoubtedly meant to hear, "Ungodly." "Foreigner." "Depraved." And she smiled serenely, thinking that the belligerent farmer's produce wasn't worth having anyway — his turnips were wooden, and his beets wizened. He soured his own soil with his bile, and she felt sorry for him.

Finn carried her basket for her as she had to use a cane to walk, and he heard the farmer's vitriol but ignored it. He liked to keep his head down, stay out of the firing line. If he thought the cook were in trouble, he'd say something, but she always seemed perfectly able to deal with the jibes.

Occasionally Mrs Ashby would bump into Miss Swift at the market and the young lady would always stop for a chat. She hadn't seen her so much recently and assumed that it was because money was in short supply and she and her grandfather were having to live off the land to make ends meet. She made up a batch of Banbury Cakes and a beef and ale suet pudding, which she knew would be hearty and filling for the old man and on their way home from the market she asked Finn to call in at Friday's Acre.

Miss Swift was busy digging up some parsnips from their kitchen garden, her skirts tucked into her waistband on either side, like any good farmworker; she was so intent upon her task she didn't hear Mrs Ashby approaching.

"Best after a good frost," said the cook.

Hetty straightened up and put a hand to her aching back, "Mrs Ashby! How lovely to see you. Yes, indeed, parsnips are always the sweeter for a frost. I'm going to make soup."

Mrs Ashby shook her head, "Soup? Does Mr Swift *like* soup?"

"No, he doesn't. He thinks it's only fit for bairns. He says it's not food any grown man should be forced to eat, not while he still has some teeth left in his head."

"I should think not! So, it's fortunate then that I made rather too much suet pudding yesterday — it'll give him something to chew on. A nice bit of beef in it. And some Banbury Cakes for his sweet tooth."

Hetty didn't say what was on her mind because she liked Mrs Ashby and knew she was only being kind, but she didn't like the idea of her unknown neighbour supplying them with charitable gifts albeit most likely unbeknownst to him. It made her feel a little uneasy, but she took the basket and thanked her enthusiastically, praising, as always, the cook's magical culinary skills.

"Come in and have a word with Grandpapa. He'd be happy to see someone other than me."

Her grandfather did indeed greet Mrs Ashby with unmitigated joy, Hetty thought, just as though being stuck with only his granddaughter for company all day was a great trial. She rolled her eyes at him expressively, but he gave her one of his old-fashioned looks and continued to welcome Mrs Ashby rather too fulsomely. Mrs Ashby's round shiny face flushed pink with delight and she settled down for a chat beside the fire, quite forgetting poor Finn still sitting outside in the cold.

Hetty quickly made some raspberry leaf tea and unpacked the basket, the aromas of the tasty gravy in the pudding and the cinnamon in the cakes making her mouth water.

"Would you like a Banbury Cake with your tea, Old Pa?"

"I'd never say no to one of Mrs Ashby's cakes! Best Banburys in the county."

Mrs Ashby allowed herself a little preen because it was the truth and there was no denying it. She wasn't a vain woman because she'd had a lifetime of being told that she was worthless, but when it came to her cooking, she knew her true worth. Nobody could take that away from her.

"So, how's life up on the hill?" asked Mr Swift, taking a bite out of a flaky Banbury Cake and letting out a sigh of pleasure.

"Oh, not so bad. Mr Guivre is a good master. He never complains about what I spend and if I need any new pots or pans, he's always amenable. No thank you love, no cake for me, I've had my fill of them!"

"I'll take Mr Finn out a cup of tea," said Hetty and left them to their gossip.

Finn was glad of the hot drink and even unbent enough to exchange a few words on the weather and to ask if she was having a problem with jackdaws.

Hetty looked baffled, "Jackdaws? Why, no, I can't say that we have. They don't bother me anyway. I like their chatter and their squabbling — it's good company when I'm in the garden."

"They're sinister beasts and they steal things. I'd hide your jewellery if I were you."

Hetty laughed, "I don't have any! We don't have much to steal anymore." She said this without an ounce of self-pity, just her usual forthrightness for which her grandfather often chided her, believing it to be a disguise for some inner regrets.

She patted the horse's head and murmured something reassuring to it and then smiled up at Finn, who was finishing the last drop of his tea, "Thank you for bringing Mrs Ashby, she'll cheer Grandpapa up. He's always bad this time of year. Grandmama died in February, in the snow. It makes the cold weather even harder for him to bear."

He nodded but said nothing, he wasn't so fond of the winter either as the influenza epidemic had taken his family from him. One much beloved wife, one son, three daughters, an aunt and two cousins. All of them, just gone, as though they'd never existed, in less than a fortnight. He never allowed himself to love anything anymore. That's when, at his lowest ebb, he'd been unexpectedly offered employment at Galdre Knap and he'd accepted it immediately. Anything to get away from the memories that haunted him. The offer came in a letter, which he'd had to ask the churchwarden to read to him. Mr Randall, deciphering the beautiful looping hand, had been rigid with disapproval. His feelings about Mr Guivre were widely known — he was outspoken about him having forsaken the Church. It didn't seem to matter to him that he'd never met the man and therefore was just responding to hearsay. Although Finn agreed with some of what he said, he was contrary by nature and felt an urge to defend his prospective master against the unfounded allegations. In the end, he just tended to keep quiet.

Mrs Ashby left the farmhouse still talking to Mr Swift, who remained standing in the doorway, his shoulder against the jamb for support. She was still calling back to him as she climbed into the cart.

"Good cakes, Old Pa?" murmured Hetty as they waved goodbye.

"She has magic in those fat fingers of hers. Best cook in the whole of the South I'd say."

"No wonder Mr Guivre snapped her up. No one else would give her work because of her lameness and her blind eye. It's curious is it not? Finn is damaged too. He was devastated after losing his family and everyone feared for his sanity, but Mr Guivre took him in regardless. I cannot see how someone who would do that could be thought to be beyond redemption."

"Unless, he had ulterior motives."

"Oh, what tosh! You're such a doomsayer!"

"I have good reason to be."

Hetty sighed. Some days it was difficult to rouse him out of his permanent state of apathy and considering there wasn't much to entice him, other than endless hours sitting beside the fire with nothing to occupy his mind, she couldn't really blame him for feeling hard done by.

"Well, cheer up! We have suet pudding for supper!"

Two

Mr Edwin Scroggs blamed everyone but himself for his proposal being rebuffed. Henrietta, of course, was principally to blame, for not realising what an honour he was bestowing upon her. There were many more adequately qualified females in the county who would be grateful to receive his regard. It had disappointed more than half a dozen hopeful young ladies when he'd declared himself to Miss Henrietta Swift. He'd fully expected to be accepted with unadulterated joy, perhaps even a maidenly show of tears but instead she had put out her hand as though to stop him in mid-flow and turned away her face. He'd faltered, uncertain, his words left trailing in the air like smoke, but he'd quickly rallied and continued until she'd furiously stamped her foot, which had brought his offer to a premature conclusion.

"I don't understand, Henrietta. What can you mean by this odd display?"

Hetty had hardly been able to meet his eyes, "I'm so sorry, Edwin, but I simply must stop you. I am *profoundly* grateful for your flattering addresses, but I cannot marry you."

"But why not? I had thought that we had an understanding. You have said nothing before this! Given me no hint of your feelings!"

"*Precisely*, Edwin. Would you not have thought, that if I had found your attentions desirable, I might have shown you some small sign of my affections being engaged?"

Mr Scroggs was incensed and paced the tiny parlour with small impatient steps. "But I was so *certain* that you felt the same way. How could I have been so mistaken?"

"Because Edwin, you forgot to ask *me* how I felt. You were so sure of my capitulation — "

"*Capitulation!* Is the idea of marriage to me so *abhorrent*?" interrupted the affronted gentleman in some distress.

"Oh, goodness, no. You don't understand! I *cannot* leave Grandpapa. He's far too old to be left alone and a husband would quite naturally expect a wife to move into his own house and not to come encumbered with an infirm and rather cantankerous old gentleman. He couldn't possibly stay here by himself, and I wouldn't wish him to either. I am deeply conscious of the honour you have done me by singling me out for your consideration, which I am sure many a sensible female would covet, but — I'm afraid that I cannot contemplate accepting your most gratifying offer. My answer must therefore be no, but — I say it with the deepest regret."

* * *

A week later Mr Scroggs felt compelled to call in at Friday's Acre again, but very much against his better judgement, in order to find some kind of solace; he desperately needed a balm for his wounded spirits, to hear from Henrietta's own lips how she thought him far too good for her. He needed reassurance. He needed her to justify her foolish decision and eradicate some of the humiliation he felt after her rejection. He needed her to understand that there were not many men who would take on such a liability: a female with no dowry, a shameful history, and no beauty to speak of, especially if one took into consideration the shocking colour of her hair.

But, as luck would have it, she was trying to catch a pig. So, the encounter didn't go well. To his chagrin, he found himself following her around the farmyard and into the orchard as she chased the determined and vociferous runaway. He mostly talked to the back of her head, as she tried to corner the beast and she was only able to reply in short, breathless and rather ill-tempered gasps. Eventually he gave up and left her to her pointless pursuit of the pig.

Crow watched with interest from the chimney. Some humans never ceased to astonish him. This man was so ridiculous with his stiff-legged walk, mean little mouth and short, useless beak. Crow just couldn't help himself — he swooped down from the roof, sailed up and over the man as he was mounting his horse and left him a generous present upon his hat. He circled the yard a few times and clacked his beak with joy at the sight of Mr Scroggs swearing profusely and shaking his fist at him.

The triumphant jackdaw returned to the orchard where Hetty had finally caught hold of the pig and was tugging it by its ear back to the sty. He waited until she'd successfully confined it and then dropped down and perched upon the wall beside the back door and waited for her to pass by.

She was trudging back across the frosted cobbles when she looked up and spotted him. She stopped in her tracks and stared. He stared back at her. She tipped her head to one side and looked amused. He cocked his head the same way. She laughed.

"Greetings, Mr Jackdaw. What can I do for you?"

Crow hopped a little closer to her along the wall.

"Are you hungry? I have some bacon rinds if you fancy them?"

He clacked his beak.

"Wait there and I'll get them," she said, and dashed into the kitchen. A few minutes later she emerged with a handful of the rinds, thoughtfully chopped into small pieces and, approaching him cautiously, she made a pile of them on the wall and then took a few steps back.

He hopped sideways until he reached the tempting treat and quickly gulped down several, one after the other. He wasn't really that hungry as he was fed well at Galdre Knap, but it would have been churlish to refuse. Bacon rinds, after all, were the Food of the Gods. She seemed to be a pleasant, harmless sort of human although she was rather strange to look at, with her bright orange crest and drab plumage.

"Isn't it funny, I was only talking about jackdaws to someone just this morning. And here you are. He seemed to think I should hide my shiny belongings to keep them safe!"

Don't listen to Finn. He'd be suspicious of a duckling.

"I like Finn, he seems trustworthy."

He wants to murder me.

"He has such kind eyes, if a little sad. Oh, dear, listen to me chatting to a jackdaw as though we regularly take tea together. I simply must get on. There are more scraps if you get hungry again. I'll save some for you instead of putting them into the soup," she said and then disappeared back into the farmhouse.

Crow swallowed some more bacon rinds until he felt a little sick and then flew back up to his perch beside the chimney, where the stones were warm from the fire. He wondered why his master wanted him to watch this particular female. She didn't seem to be anything special, but Crow became a bit twitchy when his master's eyes darkened and he appeared to be distracted by something trivial, like a speck of dust on his sleeve. He wouldn't dare question his motives again and he'd dutifully watch the girl and report back, but he felt it was beneath him. It was an errand more suited to a jay or a magpie, they were such sly birds.

* * *

Torquhil Guivre fitted the key into the lock and turned it. It was an ancient door, and the key was ill-fitting and seldom worked first time. The lock made a series of clicking noises, like a flint striking flint, sharp and snappy. He waited until the clicking ceased and then he lifted the latch and pushed open the door and, with what seemed like a small sigh, he picked up his lantern from the floor and went along the passageway, down the stone steps and passed through the arched entrance into the undercroft and then another doorway. He paused for a moment as the door closed quietly behind him and waited for his eyes to adjust to the gloom.

The smell of damp clay and chalky limestone was overwhelming and the pressure of the hill above, bearing down, compressing the air, and intensifying the darkness, caused the blood to pound in his temples, inducing the usual dull headache.

At the end of the low passageway, he ducked under the low stone lintel and held up the lantern to illuminate the cell and then he slipped through the perforated septal slab that was held in place by two giant sarsen stones and disappeared into the darkness beyond.

* * *

Mrs Ashby filled the deep dish with some leftover pork and apple, onions and sage, topped it up with a little stock, then folded the thick potato crust over the top, crimped the edges and cut slits in the middle to allow the steam to escape. She dusted the flour from her hands and wiped them on a cloth and then put the pie in the brick oven. She then turned to look at Finn who was in his usual place beside the fire.

"There now, there's supper done. That should please him. He likes a bit of pie. Funny, when he's so very thin. Looks like he don't eat much at all. Looks like I starve him. Not good for my reputation — I'd best make him more puddings. Maybe a Shropshire Pudding? I've got some stale bread and a good pound of butter from old man Warren and a couple of eggs left over. That would fatten him up a bit. Brandy, I'll need brandy. Where is he anyway? Still down there? Must be cold under the hill and him with not an ounce of fat on him to keep him warm. And wearing that peculiar nightgown! Are you listening Finn?"

Finn was listening, with half an ear; he was accustomed to Mrs Ashby's lengthy monologues and allowed them to wash over him like a balmy summer wind. He enjoyed the gentle, undemanding flow of words; it reminded him of his late wife — it was comfortable and reassuring. He was happy to sit in his chair by the fire, his feet up on a stool and drift gently in and out of his half-sleep, Mrs Ashby's seemingly inexhaustible lists of ingredients weaving their way into his dreams. His back was aching, sending sharp stabbing pains down his leg and his right hip never allowed him to rest easily in bed. He was old at two and sixty and had so little to live for, now that he was entirely alone, that it was better if he napped, like a cat, whenever he could, to shorten the day and save his limited energy for his duties, which he had to admit were mostly pleasant and few and far between.

"Wearing that peculiar nightgown," repeated Finn, sleepily.

"I *knew* you weren't listening. I don't know why I waste my breath. I might just as well talk to myself. Poor Mr Swift, he's that worried about his granddaughter. He thinks she's wasting away working on the farm and looking after him. Says it's no life for a pretty young girl like Miss Henrietta. Not that she's what I'd call pretty, mind. Not with that hair. Didn't get it from her mother that's for sure. Golden hair she had, and her father — well, I suppose he *may* have had red hair, but it was always hidden under his wig, so we'll never know. A wastrel, that lad, if ever I saw one. They did their best for him too, gave him everything; he had no cause to behave so wickedly, leaving them mired in his debts. He wanted for nothing. Every opportunity a boy could ever desire and then he just threw it all away. Ruined their lives and now that dear old fellow must suffer the humiliation of living in one of his tenant's farms and Miss Henrietta has to care for the pigs. Not that she ever complains. Such a sweet, cheerful thing she is. Finn, are you paying attention?"

"Sweet, cheerful thing," said Finn without opening his eyes.

"You think you're so droll, don't you! What do you think he's doing down there?"

"Brewing beer, hopefully."

Mrs Ashby cast him a look of reproach and opened the oven up to take peek at the pie. "Not long now, it's looking nice and crispy and brown. I'd say another twenty minutes.

You'd better go and give him fair warning. Brewing beer, indeed."

Finn heaved a sigh and sat up, "It's a long way. All those stairs."

"There'll be a good supper waiting for you when you get back."

"All right, I'm going. You'd think he'd have some sort of system with bells or something, he's that clever."

"His mind is on other things. More important things."

Finn shrugged, "We don't know that. We don't know what he's thinking about or doing. He's not exactly chatty, is he? I mean, what do we know about him? Other than he just appeared out of nowhere; I mean nobody saw him and Miss Guivre moving into the house, did they? His clothes! They're outlandish and more than likely foreign, that's for certain. You've seen his bedchamber. And his study or whatever you want to call it. Hardly a gentleman's sort of thing, is it? And, of course, there's the small detail of him talking to that damn Crow. I wouldn't believe it had I not seen it for myself."

Mrs Ashby shook her head, "It does seem a trifle odd, if what you say is true. But then I talk to the chickens."

"Yes, but you don't think they answer you though, do you!"

"No, I suppose. Still, he gave us both work when no one else would."

"Yes, but why? Why did he take us on when we're both past our prime and practically unemployable? Because no one else would work here at Galdre Knap, or for such a strange person as Mr Guivre. That's why. We were both desperate in our own ways and he knew that and had us over a barrel."

"Oh, I think you're being a bit harsh. I believe he has good motives."

"So, why's he watching Miss Swift then? What's that about? It just don't sit right. She's not old or desperate. Why should he be so interested in her? As you said, she's not even much to look at. That hair — it's like a beacon. Nice girl though. Kind. Brought me tea. Thoughtful. Always stops to chat. Her grandfather's a good man too. No, I just don't see what he can be up to. He's got some sort of scheme going on, but I have no clue to what it might be. A dark horse, that one."

"Will you stop yammering and go and fetch him! I'm taking that pie out soon and if you don't hurry it'll be cold by the time he comes all that way and sticks his fork into it. What will he think? You've been a'chattering on like a skylark."

Finn struggled to his feet, "I'm going, I'm going!"

Fortunately for his tired old knees, Finn met Torquhil Guivre coming up the stairs from the cellars and so he wasn't forced to traipse down the long dark corridors to the very bowels of the house and then all the way back up again just to announce supper.

Torquhil Guivre washed his hands under the pump at the sink and after drying them he went to stand by the fire to warm himself.

Mrs Ashby busied herself setting the table and wondering if any other lords of the manor ate with their staff in the kitchen; she thought probably not.

"There's pork and apple pie, sir."

He nodded and took his place at the head of the table.

She exchanged a glance with Finn, "It'll warm you up. The marrow in your bones must be frozen solid."

"It's a bitter day, indeed."

Mrs Ashby took the pie from the oven and placed it upon a bread board on the table; she then dished up a serving for her master and put it before him. He murmured his thanks and waited until she'd served Finn and herself before beginning to eat. She often thought he had the finest manners she'd ever come across despite his other strange traits.

Conversation was desultory despite Mrs Ashby's best efforts. One could only discuss the merits of fresh herbs or whether the addition of nutmeg to buttered spinach was worth the extra cost, for a limited amount of time before becoming ill-at-ease. She got barely any acknowledgement from Finn, and Mr Guivre supplied only the slightest of responses, just enough to politely keep the cook happy.

She knew he wouldn't talk about himself, and she had very little to say about being his cook other than to chat about recipes. Finn wasn't interested in anything other than having a good moan about the things that grieved him, which were legion, and as Mr Guivre seldom left the estate, and although she didn't know it, he knew only what Crow told him about his neighbours. Her words of wisdom were doomed to fall upon stony ground. None of them could talk about their families. She wasn't even sure Mr Guivre had a family. He'd never mentioned anyone, not relations nor friends. It was very frustrating. Her husband had not encouraged her to talk; he had disapproved of garrulous women. In fact, he had disapproved of most things and made that disapproval known with awful regularity. She now wondered why she'd stayed with him but had no answer that sounded remotely acceptable even to her own ears. She'd been paralysed with fear: fear of the unknown, fear of him and, ultimately, fear of loneliness. She'd promised herself that once free from his tyranny that she would never be daunted again and then, quite unexpectedly, his much-mistreated cows had set her free.

She eyed her employer discreetly and couldn't help but wonder at his exotic attire; he would certainly stand out in a crowd if he should ever be in a crowd. His long straight hair was as dark as a rook's eye and his complexion as white as a winter moon; the only colour was his robe, which was embroidered with extraordinary birds and beasts in rich jewel-like hues, magenta and turquoise, emerald green and scarlet, silver and gold. It was like nothing she had ever seen outside Galdre Knap and she wasn't at all sure that it was suitable clothing for anyone, let alone a gentleman such as Mr Guivre. Finn said he could see the animals moving but she never had, nor did she want to; it was quite bad enough as it was. She smiled as she thought about what her husband would have said if he'd seen her employer.

"Mrs Ashby?" said Torquhil Guivre.

She started guiltily, "Oh, I was just thinking about my husband!"

"There must surely be more pleasant things to dwell upon."

Without asking him, she spooned some more pie onto his plate in an attempt to rescue her reputation as a cook; he would have to just try to eat more, nobody should be that thin. "There are, sir. I feel very fortunate."

Torquhil Guivre looked at her for a long moment in silence, until she began to shift about a little awkwardly.

"What do you think of Miss Swift?" he asked unexpectedly.

Taken unawares, Mrs Ashby floundered, "I — I think — I don't rightly *know* what to think, sir! She — seems to be good sort of girl. I've never heard anything bad about her — or Mr Swift. They have dealt with their misfortunes with great dignity and have always been ready to help others. What can I say? She's hard-working and kind. She looks after her grandfather as though born to it — not a job for the faint-hearted, taking care of a testy old man. She loves animals — she talks to them." She was slightly astonished by her own daring.

"Does she? I've been reliably informed that's a sign of madness."

Finn cleared his throat uneasily and wiped a crust of bread around his plate to mop up the gravy; he didn't look up.

Mrs Ashby would say afterwards that she could have sworn Mr Guivre smiled a half-smile, but she couldn't swear to it.

"I'd like you to prepare the Chinese Bedchamber if you please, Mrs Ashby and you may hire a girl from the village to help you because we are expecting three visitors, one of whom will be arriving on Friday and the others, before that."

"Yes, sir, of course. Visitors?"

"And, once you find suitable help, would you also make ready the adjoining room, the Green Bedchamber and I'm sorry to overwork you but also the Indian Bedchamber at the end of the main corridor and also the Lilac Bedchamber. It's a good deal of extra work, I understand — but with some assistance, I think you'll manage in your usual capable fashion. I have every faith in you, Mrs Ashby."

That lady blushed with pleasure and pursed her lips, "Well, I don't know about that, I'm just the cook — "

"No, indeed, you are so much more. Anyone who didn't see that would be a fool."

"Why, much obliged, sir! I think I'll hire that Agatha Giffins, from Foxhill Farm — she's a strong lass and willing too. I'm sure they could do with some extra pennies. Seven children and counting!"

"Whatever you think. Pay her well. And let me know if there's anything else you need." He turned his gaze to Finn, "I wonder if you would be so kind as to deliver a letter to Mr Swift, Finn? First thing in the morning."

Finn nodded, "Aye, happy to."

"We'll need sufficient supplies to feed four extra mouths, Mrs Ashby, can you manage that?"

"Good gracious, course I can! Market tomorrow — I can go with Finn. Can I ask how long the visitors will be staying, sir?"

A moment's silence made her think she'd been too forward, but he eventually replied, "I think we had better suppose they will be staying indefinitely."

That checked Mrs Ashby in mid-thought. Indefinitely? They'd never yet had guests come to the house even for a cup of tea, let alone additions to the household who might be staying for ever. Mrs Ashby tried to catch Finn's eye, but he was studiously avoiding looking at her. Four more people to cook for! Beds to make, rugs to beat, furniture to polish and spiders and mice to vanquish! So much work to do and not long before the house would be busy with newcomers. It was all rather exciting and worrying, at the same time. She'd better start making lists.

"Meant to mention it before, sir, but we could do with a groom or stable-lad," muttered Finn, keen to reap some rewards for himself while his master was feeling so generous. He was getting too old and stiff to manage the stables all by himself, despite there only being the one horse for the cart at the moment. If Mrs Ashby was going to get some help, then so was he! "And maybe another horse for general riding. Or two."

"If you think that would be useful, then by all means. And perhaps a couple of lads to help you with the heavier work?"

After Mr Guivre left the kitchen, his staff sat in dumbfounded silence while they tried to process the news. Then Mrs Ashby began officiously clearing the plates away and tidying up, rattling the china and clattering the cutlery. Finn took his clay pipe out of the box beside the fire, filled it with tobacco and lit it with a spill. He took a moment to puff on it, sucking in the smoke with little kissing noises and expelling it in a thin stream and then examining the bowl of the pipe with interest and giving it a poke with his gnarly thumb.

"That'll get chins a'wagging, then," he remarked offhandedly.

Mrs Ashby sat down again in her chair as though her legs had suddenly grown too weak to hold her up, "What can it all mean? Who *are* these people? Why so sudden?"

Finn shrugged, "No doubt we'll find out on Friday."

Mrs Ashby scoffed, "*Friday!* I'll find out well before then! All the best rooms to be cleaned! The *best* ones, mind! And the Chinese Bedchamber! It must be someone important. That room's only fit for royalty. So much work! Lor, I hope Agatha don't turn her nose up at working here. If she's heard the gossip she might just refuse to come."

"They need the money. She'll come all right. He pays well above anyone else because otherwise he wouldn't get no help up here, would he?"

"I suppose. Just the same, it's going to be quite a change. We won't know if we're coming or going."

"Maybe it'll keep that damn Crow away. That would indeed be a blessing. Things might just get more normal round here."

"I wouldn't count on it," intoned Mrs Ashby prophetically.

Three

Mr Swift held the letter in his hand and frowned at it, "Who on earth would write to me?" he wondered aloud.

Hetty stopped shelling the hazelnuts she'd carefully gathered and stored away since the autumn and looked up at her grandfather, "Who is it from?"

He turned the letter over and over, examining it closely, "I have no idea. It's addressed very clearly to me. In a good hand."

She resumed her shelling, "Are you going to open it then, or just sit and caress it in growing confusion?"

Mr Swift glared, "It's not often I receive a letter. I am making the most of the anticipation."

"Well, it's been almost ten minutes now and I'm becoming impatient! And I am tiring of listening to you wonder who it might be from. Open it for pity's sake!"

"It's not really surprising that Mr Scroggs made himself scarce," muttered her grandfather.

"I rejected *him!* He practically begged me to change my mind — before telling me what a favour he was doing me because no man in their right mind would find me an attractive proposition."

"The man's clearly unhinged," said Mr Swift gruffly.

"He cited my hair as a major stumbling block — saying it was the colour of carrot and swede mash, which I thought was a very — *vivid* image. He also feared our children might have been cursed with the same appalling colouring. But he suggested that I could always powder my hair or wear a wig to conceal my shame."

"He should be horse-whipped."

"My hair *is* a dreadful affliction. I do wear an old coif with lace lappets if I go to the village, to stop people staring and children calling me names. They can be surprisingly unkind. Papa was redheaded so I suppose I must take after him."

There was a dissatisfied growl from the old man, "You in *no* way take after that — *person*. You are nothing alike. You're the spit and image of your grandmother. You only knew her when she had that glorious silver hair; as a young girl she was exceedingly striking. Her hair was the first thing I noticed about her. She was leaning on the church gate and the sun was behind her and made her hair into a glowing halo and she smiled at me, and I lost my heart to her there and then."

"And she never gave it back," said Hetty, a little misty-eyed. She'd heard the story many times and it always affected her in the same way; although her grandparents had been such very different people, they were perfect together, each complimenting the other with their opposite temperaments. He was terse and exacting; she was imaginative, perspicacious and really quite mischievous and yet, despite being so dissimilar, their love had been deep and enduring and when she had died from what seemed to be, at the start, merely a chill, everyone thought that Mr Swift was sure to follow but his granddaughter had given him a reason to live. He had lifted himself out of his terrible grief in order to take care of Hetty and now here she was, not many years later, looking after him. It hardly seemed fair that such a selfless man should have to endure such indignities in the last years of his life.

Watching the expressions crossing his face, Hetty wished she could protect him from the painful memories, knowing that regrets haunted him. He seldom expressed his innermost feelings, hoping to spare her any added anxiety — and so they tiptoed around each other, each only concerned for the other and careless of their own sensibilities. It was like a merry-go-round.

"You'll find someone, Hetty, my love. Someone who will understand you and shield you. There's someone out there, just waiting for you."

She smiled at him and rolled her eyes, "I'm not looking for anyone. I have you and that's all I need. Now will you *please* open that wretched letter!"

After giving it one last close inspection, he broke the seal and spread out the sheet of paper. He peered at the signature and looked up at Hetty with wide eyes. "'Pon my soul!" he said.

She made an agitated gesture with her expressive hands, "Good gracious, Old Pa! What *is* it?"

He read the first lines of the missive, "You're not going to believe this! I am all astonishment! It is hard to comprehend," he glanced up and saw his granddaughter advancing towards him, a martial glint in her eye and held up his hand to stop her, "It's from our mysterious neighbour on the hill! Mr Guivre, if you please! You may *well* look thunderstruck! I have never been so lost for words."

"You seem to have *plenty* of words! If you could use a few of them to explain why he is writing to you, I would be exceedingly grateful!"

"Patience, my child, patience. He hopes that I am in good health and asks about the farm — and here he mentions you —"

"Me! Why does he ask about me?"

"I do not yet know, as your constant interruptions are preventing me from reading the contents."

Hetty sat back down in her chair and crossly buttoned her lip and waited, tapping her foot impatiently.

"Ah, and here we come to the crux of the matter. Well, by Jove! This is beyond belief. He appears to be offering you employment at Galdre Knap."

She gasped, her face flushing hotly and then immediately blanching so that the band of freckles across her nose stood out distinctly against her chalk-white complexion.

"If I understand him correctly, he's suggesting that you might work for him — that we both move into his house and make it our home. He needs a nursemaid come companion and believes that you have all the necessary requirements for the job."

"But he's never even met me!" exclaimed Hetty.

"He writes that he has heard good reports and urgently and unexpectedly requires assistance. Oh, and here he mentions the salary he's willing to pay you. It appears that the rumours are true — not only must he indeed be very wealthy, but I fear he must also be quite mad. He says that he would need us to move into Galdre Knap this very week! Quite mad."

Hetty stood up and began to pace about the tiny kitchen, making little indignant puffing sounds, "Of all the — what is he — does he think that we're so *desperate* that we would even *consider* such a ridiculous proposal! He must think we're in dire need of his charity. Well, he can *keep* his money! It's absolutely mortifying. I wonder if Mrs Ashby or Finn have had anything to do with this? I know that Mrs Ashby likes to bring us pies and cakes but I'm hoping that she doesn't think that we're on the verge of destitution! I think we manage extremely well."

Her grandfather was still contemplating the letter in his hand, "He says snow is coming on Friday so we must make up our minds quickly in case the hill becomes impassable."

"Fiddlesticks! He cannot possibly know that. What a ludicrous man."

Mr Swift gave her a long considering look, "He says that he'll send Finn with the cart for our belongings on Tuesday and pick us up on Wednesday."

"How presumptuous!"

"Hetty — ? "

"No! Don't look at me like that! We cannot consider it! I would rather stay here and starve."

"You may wish to starve but I do not. I would rather live in comfort for the limited time I have left on this earth, and I would much rather know that you were safe and comfortable — it would put my mind at rest."

Hetty buried her head in her arms and leant on the table amongst the shattered hazelnuts, "That's unscrupulous of you to use that argument! I cannot countenance it. I *will* not. I don't want to work for *anyone* — least of all *that* man!"

"You're beginning to sound like the locals. Narrow-minded. Frightened of newcomers. Wary of the unknown. I had not thought you so parochial. I thought I had taught you well, but I see that you're as bad as those bigoted folk who won't sell their produce to Mrs Ashby."

She raised her head and looked at him with tears in her eyes, "Old Pa! It's not true. I just — it *frightens* me — the thought of change. I am used to Friday's Acre now — it's our home. The idea of having to leave and start all over again — it would be too much for you."

He laughed softly, "Oh, Hetty! Is it really *me* you're worried about? I have been in many worse situations in my life. Losing my darling Anne, Julian's destructive behaviour, poor Beth giving up on life, the loss of our ancestral home and estates — having to let down all my tenants and face a future where I couldn't provide for you and keep you safe — to have to watch you become little more than a farmhand when you could have achieved so much more."

"Well, if you mean I could have married Mr Scroggs then it's *you* who are mad! That would never have made me happy. Nor would it have made *him* happy, I can assure you! And it could hardly be considered an achievement — marrying someone who will always believe that by making you his wife that he has bestowed upon you the greatest honour possible and therefore you should be deeply and eternally grateful to him. What a life that would have been! You would not have wished me to live like that. This man, this Mr Guivre — what do we know about him? Nothing but gossip and none of it exactly encouraging."

"Mrs Ashby says he's an excellent employer. And you will admit that the very fact that he gave her a job when no one else would — that must surely count in his favour."

Hetty sat in silence for a moment, trying to gather her thoughts and make some sense of them.

Galdre Knap was, according to Mrs Ashby, equipped with every luxury; her grandfather would be warm and secure, they would have the company of Mrs Ashby (and her famous cooking) and Finn. And the generous salary would mean that they would not have to struggle and worry.

"Mr Randall won't want to play chess with you anymore — not in that man's — Mr Guivre's house. He would be afraid for his soul."

"Is that your only objection?"

"The chickens and pigs and geese and the bees —"

"We can take them with us. He says he has room for all our livestock."

"He seems to have thought of everything."

"He has certainly been very thorough. You know, I get very little satisfaction from beating Mr Randall at chess. It serves no other purpose than to supply me with gossip about the village, but I can live without that."

She cocked her head to one side, "Are you trying to tell me that you think we should accept?"

"I think the offer is curiously providential. I believe we would be foolish *not* to accept it."

Hetty was fiddling with the hazelnut shells, sweeping them all up into a neat pile on the table as though it was all that occupied her mind at that moment. She popped one of the shelled kernels into her mouth and chewed upon it thoughtfully, her brow furrowed.

Mr Swift waited, knowing that if he pushed too hard that she, just like her grandmother, would immediately lean in the opposite direction. Anne had dug her heels in at the most unexpected moments and he had learned over the years to feign indifference so as not to antagonise her and hope that she would eventually come to her senses.

"It doesn't say who I would be companion to?"

"No, but it does say *this!*" and he jabbed his finger at the suggested salary written very clearly in the letter.

Hetty peered closely at it, "Good gracious! That's a King's ransom! He *must* be deranged. What can he be thinking?"

"He's quite obviously in desperate need and you have come up to snuff."

"But how does he *know* that? Who would have told him such a thing?"

"Perhaps Mrs Ashby? She thinks very well of you."

Holding a bowl to the table, Hetty crossly swiped the nutshells into it, "Perhaps. I shall ask her. It seems very odd, the whole business but — if you really think we should accept — then I shall, of course, do what you wish."

"That would make a nice change," said Mr Swift blandly.

* * *

Finn dropped Mrs Ashby at the market and then had delivered Mr Guivre's letter to Friday's Acre; he hadn't waited for a reply because, guessing what the letter might be about, he thought there would have to be lengthy discussions before a reply could be written. When he returned to pick Mrs Ashby up, he found her chatting merrily to Agatha Giffins, who, it had to be said, was looking overjoyed; he was surprised to see her solidly square face quite lit up and animated, when she was usually rather placid with slow movements and a plodding walk, reminding him of one of the older milk-cows coming in from the meadow. She was only seventeen years old, but he thought Mrs Ashby was correct in her thinking that the girl would be delighted to have a reason to leave home and, in doing so, make her sister envious.

As the cart drew alongside them, Agatha looked up and beamed at him, "Mr Finn! I be goin' to Galdre Knap to be a chambermaid. Me Ma's never goin' to believe it! She goin' to be that proud! Reckon I'll be the favourite daughter now — not Bessie no more!"

"Glad to hear that, Aggie," said Finn, clambering down from the driver's seat so that he could help Mrs Ashby load the baskets of provisions into the cart. She appeared to have bought up most of the produce at the market and by the time he'd loaded everything, his troublesome back was aching.

"Go home and tell your Ma, Aggie," instructed Mrs Ashby, "Finn will pick you up tomorrow morning early so that we can make a start on the bedchambers. Bring old aprons for dirty work if you have them and we will provide you with ones for best. And coifs, you'll need a few coifs to cover your hair — the house is that dusty!" She delved into her pocket and pulled out some coins and tipped them into Agatha's eager hand, "Here, this is for any expenses. Don't keep Finn waiting tomorrow, he gets testy else."

"Oh, I won't! I probably won't be able to sleep at all! I'll be up afore the cock!"

"You'd best get all the sleep you can! You have a great deal of hard work ahead of you."

"Yes, ma'am," said Agatha and dropped a little curtsy.

Mrs Ashby laughed and shook her head, "Lor, Aggie! I'm not gentry! No need to curtsy. Get along with you now, we'll see you first thing."

Agatha Giffins stumped away across the small village square, waving cheerily to them as she went and shouting greetings to the stall holders, most of whom were farmers and farmhands she knew well. She wondered what they'd all say if they knew where she would be working the very next day. She thought some wouldn't be best pleased, but she didn't care one jot. She was going to the house on the hill, and she was going to see the strange Mr Guivre and get paid an enormous wage so that her siblings would be beside themselves with jealousy and her mother would not keep going on about stupid old Bessie and how pretty she is. *Pretty* hadn't got a job at Galdre Knap! *Pretty* wasn't ever going to be paid enough to send Ma something home every month to help out and *pretty* wasn't going to eat Mrs Ashby's cooking every day! Agatha chuckled to herself with glee.

Mrs Ashby watched her lumbering progress through the market, "I pity her poor family now! She's going to be cock-a-hoop. Still, she's a dependable worker and won't be much trouble. She may be lumpish, but she's blessed with a good heart."

Finn said nothing and handed the cook up into the cart; he was tired and just wanted to get back to the house and his chair by the fire. His toes were numb with cold, and he still had to talk with old man Warren, who knew a thing or two about horses and might know of a local lad who could take over the stable duties. It was going to be a long week. And, if Mr Guivre was right, snow was coming so he'd have to make sure there was plenty of wood for the fires and so many other chores he couldn't bear to think about them. He sighed and wondered what the days ahead would bring.

* * *

Torquhil Guivre stood on the observation deck of the tower, which occupied the south-west facing corner of Galdre Knap, and from where he could watch any carriages approaching the house from the village and beyond and usually, on a clear day, he could see further out to the softly folded range of hills that bordered the county. In three days' time, those hills would be covered in snow and the avenue would be as good as closed to any kind of vehicle and all but the strongest horses. The house would be cut off from the village and very difficult walking would be the only option.

The sky was still pearl-grey, and the view blurred by the persistent mist, the ground unforgiving with frost. A careless scattering of jackdaws flew over the twisted chimneys and turrets of his house, and he listened to them cackle as they disappeared into the wood on the crest of the hill.

He waited, his eyes on the sky.

There, he was. He watched the bird tuck his wings close to his sides and dive down towards the tower, at the last moment stretching them out and pulling backwards to slow his rapid descent, then with a quick flick and a hunching of his shoulders, he dropped down onto the edge of the balcony.

Crow rearranged his feathers and made some minor adjustments to the angle of his tail.

Finally, balanced to his satisfaction, he turned his white eye upon his master.

Rumour has it that there will be snow?

"On Friday."

In preparation, we've been out to the fields, making the most of this weather, although it's hard on the beak. Not much to eat out there now. Might have to visit Friday's Acre for some more bacon rinds.

"Miss Swift will be here tomorrow, with her grandfather."

So, they are decided?

"It was never in doubt."

I was certain she'd refuse. She seems to be — a determined sort of human.

"I'm sure that she did, at first, but Mr Swift has her best interests at heart, and she could never refuse him. He knows that this will be the ideal solution for her — for both of them. Ideal for everyone."

Despite the snow?

"There are always drawbacks. They can be overcome."

I admire your confidence. How can you be so sure?

Torquhil Guivre's face was a mask, "It has been foretold."

Crow shivered his feathers.

Well, that's that then. No escape. We're doomed.

"You exaggerate as usual. I'm sure we shall deal very competently with what's to come. Anyway, we have no choice. We'll know where we stand on Friday."

I hear the geese will be coming too.

"At least they'll give you something to torment."

But they're not fair game. They're so stupid they don't understand they're being tormented. There's no fun in that.

"I'm glad you have some scruples, at least."

Now, if they were wood pigeons —

Crow cackled loudly.

Torquhil Guivre allowed himself the slightest of smiles — the corners of his thin mouth turned down when he was amused, as though he were repressing his response.

He looked out at the monotone landscape, where no form had edges or substance, everything flattened and lifeless and yet filled with a strange kind of frosted enchantment. This weather was a prelude to what was on the horizon. He was about to bring inevitable suffering to Galdre Knap and there was nothing he could do about it. His only hope appeared to be a girl with fiery red hair and a heart filled with enough warmth to weather the storm and perhaps bring some kind of resolution.

You truly believe it's the redheaded farmhand?

"I have no doubt in my mind."

She seems so — ordinary.

"And yet, she is extraordinary, or so it seems."

Hard to believe.

"She doesn't yet know her own potential. The knowledge is locked away. We must tread carefully so as not to scare her. It could be too overwhelming for her, and we might lose her and her gifts."

She can't hear me.

"She cannot hear anything yet. She is as good as blind and deaf until the key is found."

Crow extended one wing as far as it would go, flexed it and then had a good scratch under his chin with a claw.

It takes skill to do this.

"I can imagine."

So, Friday is the day.

"Yes, it's been set in motion now and cannot be halted," said Torquhil Guivre gravely.

Isn't that just grand.

"I want you to keep an eye on them and let me know if you suspect anything might be amiss. I have some serious concerns for them until I can get them here and ensure their safety."

Crow dipped his head and clacked his beak.

Your word is my command.

Four

Are we to pack *everything?* Will we need to take our kitchen stuff? Pots and pans? I think I'll take my baskets. I like my baskets. I'm used to them. Your baskets become a part of you. They each have their own character."

"We have so little left anyway, Hetty, I shouldn't worry. They will have everything we need at Galdre Knap. Mrs Ashby said the house is well-stocked. It's exciting is it not?"

"No. It's frightening."

"You'll get used to it. You got used to Swift Park after living your early years at Fifield House. You got used to Friday's Acre after living most of your life at Swift Park. You will get used to Galdre Knap after a while. You just need to give it time and be patient. Of course, it will be uncomfortable to begin with and everything will seem strange. But we'll settle in, and you won't have to dig roots for our supper anymore. That will give me some peace of mind."

"I know Old Pa. That's why I agreed."

"You're a good girl, Hetty. This is going to be the answer, I am sure of it. I can feel it in my bones."

Hetty wasn't so sure, but she did think it would be a better life for her grandfather and was determined that he should be comfortable in his old age. He deserved it. He had borne all of life's vicissitudes with equanimity and had done everything he could to protect her from the harsh reality of their much-altered existence. It was now her turn to repay that kindness and selflessness by ignoring her own misgivings about this new twist in their fluctuating fortunes. Something was niggling at the back of her brain though and she couldn't quite pin it down to make sense of it. Something just didn't feel right. She felt uneasy, as though she were perched upon the edge of a precipice with churning darkness below, concealing unnamed terrors and, creeping up behind her, everything that she wished to escape.

There was no other lifeline. The only solution was to keep going and hope that the capricious wind that had chosen to blow them in this direction, ultimately had benevolent intentions. She doubted it though.

* * *

Mrs Ashby and Agatha made a good team. The elder of the two, keen to instruct and the younger very eager to please. They tackled the daunting amount of work to be done with varying amounts of relish. Having shown Agatha where everything was and explained which rooms were to be cleaned, Mrs Ashby retreated to her kitchen and left her new recruit to it. Agatha was slow and steady but had endless endurance, she could keep going all day without complaint and as long as she was given regular meals and some praise, she possessed the same qualities as a loyal and selfless horse, she would work until she dropped, and, somehow, enjoy every minute. Mrs Ashby was practically rubbing her hands together in glee as the house was swiftly restored to something close to its former glory; soon it began to smell of beeswax and lavender-scented linen instead of dust and damp mould. Even Finn was looking slightly more cheerful than usual, with two new horses in the stables and a keen young stable-lad, Sam, recommended by Mr Warren, making himself busy about the place; along with another new recruit, Jacob Hall, a stout-hearted fellow from the village who could turn his hand to just about anything and didn't seem to mind working for a person such as Mr Guivre. Galdre Knap was suddenly bustling with unaccustomed activity and seemed to come alive. Those who lived in the cottages at the near end of the village remarked upon the change and noted the illuminated windows giving the house an altogether more welcoming aspect. They looked at each other in bemusement and shrugged, even though rumours had been circulating for the last few days, as Sam's proud mother boasted about her son's splendid new job and Jacob Hall's grandfather bemoaned the fact that his grandson had stooped so low, accepting employment from such a suspicious character.

Mrs Ashby gladly redoubled her efforts in the kitchen, providing sustenance for six instead of three and those six, soon to become a veritable multitude who would be grateful for her cooking.

She bottled and pickled, conserved and salted, preserved and cured; whatever happened, she was not going to be caught unawares. Galdre Knap would not be short of food, her people would be well fed. Once Agatha had finished the cleaning, she was put to work making lavender bags from the bunches of dried flowers hanging up in the stillroom and then to making soap for their guests so that the house was soon redolent with the scent of damask rose water.

Eventually everything that needed to be done had been done and Mrs Ashby was finally satisfied.

There was then a brief lull in the hectic activities, when she was able to take stock and make sure that nothing had been forgotten. She wondered if they might need a porter or another housemaid, perhaps a dairymaid, but when she'd mulled it over with Finn and Agatha, they'd been adamant that they would be able to cope without further assistance. Finn said that he was in charge of household security so a porter would be unnecessary, and Agatha said she'd been taught all the skills of a dairymaid and a laundry-maid by her mother and was eager to try her hand at anything. Finn suggested, in his habitually tranquil manner, that they should see how they went on and should the need arise at a later date, they could always hire extra staff. He said they'd probably be better off not filling the house with yet more strangers because it would be hard to keep an eye on them all whilst they were being trained. Mrs Ashby happily agreed.

* * *

Torquhil Guivre removed himself to his study and read his books and wrote notes and studied maps and stared out of the window. He watched the night sky for the telltale signs and listened out for Crow's impatient tapping on the window. He watched the servants coming and going and was impatient for Friday. Impatient and yet — ambivalent. He nodded his consent when asked by Finn about anything; no matter what it was, he acquiesced. There was no point in debate, it was best to just agree and suffer any consequences afterwards.

* * *

Hetty watched with mixed feelings as Galdre Knap came into view. The last of their belongings were bouncing about in the back of the cart and she, her grandfather and Finn were all squashed together on the driving seat. She hadn't dared look back over her shoulder as they left Friday's Acre as it would have only accentuated her loss. As usual, she felt a great tearing sensation inside her chest and thought it must be her heart being ripped from beneath her ribcage. Her grandfather glanced at her as they passed through the gate onto the lane and she somehow mustered up a smile, but it was false. Of course, he wasn't fooled and patted her knee in sympathy.

She knew that he was excited to start this new life and be in the vicinity of a man whom he sincerely hoped might be both educated *and* entertaining. He had quickly tired of Mr Randall's prosaic conversation and yearned for a companion who would stimulate his thoughts and perhaps enjoy a robust discussion about matters other than the sad state of the hymn books. Matters such as politics and world affairs, The Americas and Europe and Enlightenment and the triumph of reason over tradition. He longed to argue about Voltaire and Rousseau and Samuel Johnson and have someone vanquish him at chess. Above all, he was tired of sitting in a chair beside the fire while his granddaughter struggled, gathering acorns and chestnuts for them to eat and hoping a neighbour might leave them a woodpigeon on the doorstep for their supper. It wasn't any way for a young girl to live. He wanted more for her, and his instincts were telling him that he would find what he sought at Galdre Knap.

* * *

The Swifts were welcomed at the front door by Mrs Ashby and Agatha in her best clean apron and a crisp new coif. The cook thought that familiar faces would help Miss Swift get over any fears she may be having about the rather sudden change in her circumstances.

Finn had only told her that morning who the other guests were to be, and she'd been greatly relieved. She liked them and knew Miss Swift to be a kind soul and not afraid of hard work. Much to her chagrin she still hadn't managed to discover who the honoured guest was going to be. She had tried to subtly winkle it out of Mr Guivre at mealtimes, but he'd been maddeningly resistant to her blandishments, and she'd found out nothing about whom they were expecting on Friday.

Hetty was, after her initial reluctance, all agog to see the inside of the house and it lived up to all her expectations and more. As they were ushered through the grand entrance hall and up the extraordinarily beautiful staircase, a work of art in itself, with its smoothly polished shallow treads and intricately carved banisters, she tried to take in everything at once. The staircase curved elegantly up to the first floor and the anchoring wall was hung with enormous portraits and landscapes that Hetty recognised as being painted by some exceedingly skilled artists. She remembered the artworks and treasures that had adorned Swift Park and thought she recognised some of the same artists.

The corridors were graced with even more impressive works of art and plinths holding what looked like extremely precious vases and statues. The rugs covering the dark elm floorboards were Persian and richly patterned in strong warm hues. Hetty was getting dizzy from the strain of trying to see everything as they passed and decided that as it was too much to assimilate in one go that she would wait until another, less stressful time, to try to appreciate the splendour of her new home.

Agatha showed her into the allotted bedchamber and watched Hetty's face in delight as she tried to absorb what she was seeing.

"It's the Green Bedchamber, Miss Swift," explained Agatha helpfully.

Hetty smiled, "Thank you, Miss Giffins — I have never seen anything like it! It's — magnificent!"

"You haven't seen the Chinese Room or the Indian Room yet! They be even more like a mad dream! If I had to sleep in them, they'd give me nightmares! And you'd better call me Aggie like everyone else does or Mrs Ashby will think I'm gettin' above myself!"

Hetty laughed, "All right, then, we can't have that! I will gladly call you Aggie. Oh my, look at that bed, there's enough room for a family of six in it! I shall probably get lost in there and never find my way out." She examined the four-poster with its rich green velvet hangings edged in gold braid and golden tassels and a counterpane that looked as though it had been made from leaves all sewn together and embroidered with perfect satin stitches; it was like a forest floor and nestling amongst the leaves were beautifully rendered acorns and toadstools. The huge rug on the floor was moss green with gold and amber and the walls were hung with paper that had been painted to look like a beech wood. The effect was quite extraordinary, and she couldn't help but think of the beautiful beech woods that cloaked the hills around Swift Park and wondered if this was just a coincidence. The likeness was uncanny, but she supposed that woods were pretty much alike anywhere in the country. The memories from her previous home made her shiver.

"Look, all your bags are already here an' I unpacked them for you and put everythin' away in the press. I hope that was all right?"

"Oh, perfectly fine! I don't really have much anymore so it won't take up much room. Thank you for doing that for me."

"Well, I thought you'd be right tired after all the excitement. An' it is part of my duties as housemaid and abigail. Would you like to rest before comin' down to meet Mr Guivre?"

Hetty turned a little paler and felt a surge of panic rising, "Perhaps, I ought to just have a wash and see to my hair and then go and face — meet him." She cast the maid a sideways glance, "Is he — is he very — ?" she faltered.

Agatha grinned, "I've only seen him in the distance, Miss. But Mrs Ashby says he dines with her an' Mr Finn in the kitchen normally. He hasn't while I've been here, he takes his meals in the study."

"Oh, that seems a trifle odd. I mean, dining in the kitchen! Still, perhaps he likes the company. I wonder if I should change my gown?"

Agatha looked Hetty over and thought that she looked very nice; her extraordinary hair was a little disordered from the journey in the cart, but her gown, although clearly old and unfashionable, was a pretty shade of harebell blue and the simple white kerchief tied about her shoulders looked fresh and clean.

"I think you look lovely, Miss. Would you like me to help straighten your hair? I'm quite good with hair because I used to do my sister's all the time until she got too grand to let me."

Hetty, who was a little shaky with nerves started to decline the offer and then changed her mind, "Do you know, Aggie, that would be really nice. Thank you. I shall just wash my face and hands."

Agatha proved to be a great help and also rather a calming influence and after very capably redoing her hair she showed Hetty along the corridor to the Indian Bedchamber where her grandfather was waiting for her.

He was closely examining the Indian wallpaper, "Hand painted," he announced, "Gold leaf. Look at these colours: Malachite green and azurite blue, I suspect. The very best pigments. Such detail — it's exquisite."

Hetty looked over his shoulder at the extraordinary scenes of elephants and tigers, monkeys in palm trees and panthers and even cows, many-armed gods playing strange musical instruments and Indian lovers embracing — it was bewildering and rather shocking.

"Goodness gracious, you'll never be able to sleep in here — it's far too fascinating! I have a beech wood in my bedchamber, just like at Swift Park."

He gave her a curious look, "And, as you know, I have always longed to visit India."

"You don't think — ?"

"I really don't know what to think."

Spying a rather preoccupied couple half-hidden by the trunk of a palm tree, Hetty laughed, "I'm not sure this is a suitable room for an old man! Heaven knows what Grandmama would have said!"

"She wasn't as strait-laced as you might think. She was fiery and passionate. Her hair told you as much. She only pretended to be prim because, as a grandmother, she knew that it was expected of her."

"All my illusions are shattered!" declared Hetty, grinning.

He turned to study her for a moment, "And don't forget that you are just like her, right down to her hair and her temperament."

"Thank you. I'll take that as a compliment."

"It was meant as one."

Hetty put her arms about him and gave him a long hug, hoping to convey her love for him but also to gain a little comfort for herself.

"Come," she said briskly, "We had better go down and face our host. Are you ready?"

"As I'll ever be. Chin up, my love, we shall prevail."

One quick glance at each other outside the door of the study and then Finn was ushering them into the room.

"Mr Swift and Miss Swift, sir."

"Thank you, Finn," said Torquhil Guivre quietly and he rose to greet his guests.

Hetty crossed the room behind her grandfather and tried desperately not to stare as Mr Guivre introduced himself.

"Mr Swift, I am so glad that you are here at Galdre Knap, I wish you a warm welcome and hope in time it will become as much your home as it is mine. Miss Swift," and here he paused fleetingly as his eyes met hers for the first time, "I am delighted that you have accepted my invitation. I hope it has not been too much of an inconvenience?"

She took his outstretched hand and looked up at him, smiling slightly, and trying to ignore the strange tingling sensation she felt in the tips of her fingers as their hands touched, "Not at all, Mr Guivre. We cannot thank you enough for inviting us into your home. I only hope that I can truly be of assistance in some way."

"I'm absolutely certain that you will make a huge difference. Please, come and sit and I shall try to explain my reasons for needing you here."

They took the proffered chairs beside the fire and arranged themselves comfortably and waited. It seemed to take a few moments for their host to gather his thoughts and then he addressed Hetty.

"On Friday, I am expecting another visitor," he said and Hetty was sure that as he spoke his eyes became even more shadowed, "She is the sole reason you are here, Miss Swift. Her name is Eirwen, and she is my little sister. There is a long story attached but I will not bother you with it at the present time. She is in dire need of care and, more than anything, a companion she can trust. I have only just found her again after she disappeared two years ago, and I mean to keep her safe here and hopefully to help her recover."

"I see," said Hetty, "May I enquire what ails your sister, Mr Guivre?"

Another pause, "That is rather difficult to explain. She suffers from a variety of — afflictions, none of which are yet fully understood. I have no wish to alarm you, but they are mostly thought to be disorders of her mind, although sometimes they have drastically affected her physical well-being too."

"I see," said Hetty uncertainly, "How old is Eirwen?"

"She's sixteen."

"Oh, goodness, she is so very young."

"I have not seen her since she was fourteen years old, so I am not yet sure of her present condition."

"Is she dangerous?" asked Mr Swift, coming straight to what he thought was the salient point.

Torquhil Guivre shook his head, "I cannot answer that, I'm afraid. When I last saw her, she was biddable and understood a good deal of what was going on around her. I've no idea what may have changed in the intervening years and the reports I've received say that she's become — less amenable. Obviously, if there are any signs of her becoming a danger to herself or anyone else, I shall take rigorous precautions. I do assure you that I would never knowingly put anyone in harm's way."

"I'm relieved to hear it," said Hetty, who was feeling a little apprehensive at the sound of her charge.

"There's no reason to be nervous, Miss Swift. I shall not allow you to ever be alone with my sister if I think there may be any chance that you might be harmed."

Hetty couldn't help a slight wry chuckle escaping, "I wish I could say that I found that reassuring, Mr Guivre, but the very idea that one cannot be safely left alone with a child of sixteen makes me wonder if perhaps she should be receiving some serious medical help."

He squared his shoulders, "The best doctors in the country have already examined her and concluded that, as it's all in her mind, there's nothing they can do to alleviate her condition. All they can suggest is dosing her with laudanum until she becomes insensible and therefore less of a problem."

"That is *outrageous!* What a barbaric idea! There must be a better way — there *has* to be."

Mr Swift knew immediately that his granddaughter's innate sense of justice had been stirred into life like the embers of a fire; even as a small child she would become indignant and then progress rapidly to pugnacious if she thought anyone was being unfairly treated. She had always flown to the defence of anyone she thought needed her protection and it had often got her into some serious scrapes, one particular time ending with a bloodied nose, of which she had been inordinately proud, even while the blood was still dripping down her face and spoiling her gown. She had explained that her assailant was in a far worse state and had run home to his mother in tears and anyway he shouldn't have been tormenting the scruffy little mongrel in the first place. They had been forced to adopt the dog because Hetty said, her eyes shimmering, that otherwise the poor little beast would die all alone and unloved. It had been a poor decision as the creature had been much misused in its short life and its nature never fully recovered despite all the love Hetty lavished upon it; it always remained timid and would cower beneath her skirts if there was too much noise or disturbance. She named him Hercules, hoping to give him courage.

"I truly believe that Henrietta will be the best person to help your sister," said Mr Swift.

"You don't know that, Grandpapa!"

"We shall see, my love. You see, I haven't forgotten Hercules."

Hetty smiled, "*Dear* Hercules."

"Hercules?" asked Mr Guivre.

"A rescued puppy with some challenging traits. Hetty never gave up on him despite receiving a bloody nose for her part in its liberation."

Torquhil Guivre looked at Hetty, "A champion of the downtrodden, Miss Swift?"

"I don't choose to be — I just become very — agitated and cannot help myself." She turned a delicate shade of pink; she had never enjoyed being the centre of attention and this was somehow even more disturbing because her grandfather's immediate future depended upon how she answered, and she had no idea what this stranger before her was expecting from her and how he would react. She was beginning to feel responsibility weighing down upon her shoulders.

"I don't want you to worry about anything," said their host, "I'm not going to throw you out into the snow if things do not go according to plan — I'm just hopeful that you'll be able to help Eirwen in some way. That is all. There are no definite expectations and there will be no judgement."

"I would like to know why you have chosen me to be your sister's companion. You don't know me and have no idea if I might be suitable or not."

Mr Guivre's eyes flickered as he looked from young girl to old man.

"Let us just say that I have heard glowing reports, Miss Swift."

"But even so I would still be reluctant to entrust a loved one to a complete stranger." As Hetty spoke she saw something close down in Torquhil Guivre's strange face. His hooded, downward slanting eyes became even more shuttered. It was like looking at the blank surface of a standing stone.

He had chosen to wear a costume that was not quite as startling as his usual exotic attire: a floor-length coat of black velvet, the only embellishment were silver fastenings fashioned like lizards and a simple white neckcloth. Hetty thought he looked quite restrained. After the descriptions she'd heard, she'd expected something more outlandish. As she surreptitiously studied him, trying to make sense of her new employer, she thought she saw one of the silver lizards blink its glittering eye and she frowned and shook her head, thinking that she must be more distraught than she'd thought.

Roland Swift saw the quicksilver expressions of astonishment followed by incredulity in his granddaughter's eyes and saw how she swiftly tried to disguise her startled response. He had no idea what had caused her reaction, but he was fairly certain that it was something he was not able to see, having not been gifted with the same abilities. She had never understood just how expressive her face could be — it was a mirror to her thoughts. Even the sudden changes in her skin tone gave away a good deal. And her eyes, almond shaped and a warm cobalt blue, were constantly changing as she assessed and tried to understand the unfamiliar world around her. And he also saw that it had not gone unnoticed by their host, who was silently observing her.

Even he would readily admit that his beloved granddaughter was by no means a fashionable beauty, being on the short side, with more than just a dusting of freckles, which most people belonging to the *haut ton* would consider unsightly and would have had her apply lemon juice to fade them. And then, of course, there was that conspicuous inherited hair, those ginger curls that practically glowed, but which she defiantly refused to disguise unless there was a chance they might attract too much attention and bring insults down upon her in a public place. Despite all of this, it was her innate vivacity that one remembered; it left a lasting impression upon everyone who met her.

"Perhaps I just have a feeling about you — about your abilities," said Mr Guivre equably.

Hetty frowned, "I'm sorry, I didn't mean to question — "

Torquhil Guivre raised one hand, "Allow me to just establish from the beginning that I want you to feel free to talk to me about anything. In the circumstances, I think we must be candid with each other and not stand on ceremony. And you must both promise to ask for help or let me know if you need anything."

"I'm much obliged, and I will do my very best."

"Of that I am certain, Miss Swift. I understand that you play chess, Mr Swift? I would be happy to pit my poor skills against you if you would like?"

"That would indeed be a pleasure, Mr Guivre, but I wonder if I might suggest that as we are to reside together, we immediately ignore convention and you call me Roland and I am sure that Henrietta would rather you called her by her given name, would you not, my dear?"

Hetty, who would much rather not be called Henrietta, a name she had always felt unwieldy and even a trifle absurd, smiled uncertainly, but said, "Of course. Please do call me — Hetty."

"Of course. I'm afraid my name doesn't trip lightly from the tongue. There are names that can be something of a curse to their bearer. Mine is unpronounceable for most people."

"I think it's rather beautiful. Like a warm breeze on a summer's day." Hetty bit her lip thinking she sounded foolish and wished she could control her tongue.

"My granddaughter is very fond of reading and has a fertile imagination," explained Mr Swift.

Torquhil Guivre made a gesture that encompassed his study, "Please do make use of the books in here — and there is also the library, of course. They are both entirely at your disposal."

Hetty, who had been forced to leave behind her much treasured books at Swift Park when they moved to Friday's Acre, was overjoyed, but, wary about showing too much unladylike enthusiasm, she merely smiled her thanks at him.

"Well, you've quite made her day!" declared Mr Swift with all the joy she felt unable to express.

"Hopefully it will make Galdre Knap more like home for you and, in the same vein, as the dining room is a rather chilly and formal room, perhaps the library, which has a suitable table, might be more appropriate — more homely."

"We are just happy to be eating Mrs Ashby's cooking to be perfectly honest!" said Mr Swift with a chuckle.

"I don't blame you. She not only deserves her reputation as a cook, but she also copes well with adversity, which, as she's captain of the ship, is an invaluable attribute. I think you'll find her helpful, and Finn, although sometimes a little terse, has a wide range of capabilities. Once Eirwen is here and settled we'll learn to manage everything, and we'll know what will be required on Friday."

* * *

Later that evening Hetty sat upon her grandfather's bed, an even more impressive construction than her own; she kicked off her shoes and tucked her legs up underneath her and watched as he arranged his few belongings on the side table against the wall.

"What did you think of Mr Guivre, Old Pa?"

"We must learn to call him Torquhil, my dear! Why, I believe he is one of life's oddities, but I also think that deep down he must be a good-hearted fellow if he is going to so much trouble for his sister. He could just as easily have her locked away in some faraway asylum and never think of her again. There are not many men who would take on the responsibility of looking after someone like Eirwen, who, by the sounds of it, is bound to be a nuisance and seriously disrupt his way of life. I think most people would turn away."

"Yes, I suppose you're right. What did you think of his attire? The silver lizards on his coat?"

"They were very finely wrought. Expensive, undoubtedly. A little too ostentatious for my liking. I am starting to think he may have spent some time abroad — perhaps in the Far East, for he has very eclectic tastes."

"He must be at least five and thirty, so why is he not married? Did he inherit his wealth — for he certainly isn't short of a shilling or two. Did you see those beautiful paintings? And look at our bedchambers! They are quite extraordinary. Did you look *closely* at the lizards?"

"Why are you so obsessed with the fastenings upon his coat Hetty?"

"No reason. I just thought they were rather — odd."

Five

And so, Friday finally arrived.

Hetty was delightfully warm and comfortable in her bed, buried under a mound of counterpanes, and she stretched luxuriously, but even before she opened her eyes, she knew that something was different.

She sat up and pulled back the hangings that were drawn around the bed and peered out. Her bedchamber was still in darkness because the shutters were closed, so she hopped out of bed and tiptoed across the floor as quickly as she could because it was so cold. She unlatched the wooden shutters and folded them back against the wall. It should have been light outside, but the sky was heavy with mushroom grey cloud; it looked ominous, and she recalled Torquhil's warning about snow. She hoped that Finn, Sam and Jacob had managed to collect all her animals and get them safely up the hill to their new home. It would take several journeys as the cart wasn't very capacious. One of the pigs was inclined to be malicious if he was manhandled; she had warned them, but nobody ever understood the vagaries of one's own animals as well as one did oneself. She hoped they'd remember to catch the yard cat they'd inherited with the farmhouse; he could be awkward too unless food was involved. She really must give him a fitting name now that he would be living in such a grand house. She'd seen a mouse on her first day so she felt that he would be welcomed despite his rather unfriendly demeanour. She chuckled to herself, thinking that she seemed to specialise in adopting disagreeable animals. She had always liked a challenge.

She found her clothes on top of the blanket chest and pulled on her stockings and petticoats, adding an extra one to keep her warm and was just about to wash in the bowl of cold water when Aggie arrived bearing hot water in a large pitcher.

"You weren't goin' to use that cold water, Miss? That won't do at all! You *must* let me do my job or I'll be out on my ear."

"Yes, Aggie. I'm so sorry, I didn't think. I just wanted to get dressed and prepare for Miss Guivre's arrival."

"Well, I'm here now. I can give you a hand."

"You know, since we left Swift Park, with all its comforts and luxuries, I have looked after myself and become quite used to it."

"You may be used to it, Miss, but this is what I do an' I *like* doin' it what's more. So, I'm goin' to pour the water out for you an' you're goin' to wash an' then I'm goin' to help you do your hair and get dressed."

"Yes, Aggie."

* * *

As Hetty skipped eagerly down the main staircase the first snowflakes began to fall. At first just an easily countable number, drifting aimlessly down as though they were trying to remember something important or were questioning their reasons for falling.

By the time she was sitting in the library at the breakfast table, the snowflakes had stopped wandering without purpose and were in earnest about their descent. As her grandfather and Torquhil entered the room she could no longer see the distant hills through the blurring mass, and it was making her dizzy watching them zigzagging past the window.

"Good morning, Mr Guivre! You were right! It's Friday and it is indeed snowing, just as you predicted! I do hope Miss Guivre is able to make the journey in this weather. Do you think it might discourage them?"

Torquhil glanced out of the window, "They're already on their way."

Hetty raised her eyebrows, "But how would you know that? Are you some kind of soothsayer?"

He turned away and pulled out a chair for Mr Swift. "It's snowing," he said cryptically and changing the subject began to talk to her grandfather about the intricacies of chess.

She followed them to the table and sat down, looking puzzled. There was so much she didn't understand, and she had a need to know everything so that she knew where she stood — she wasn't at all keen on surprises.

There were no footmen to attend them and although Finn hovered for a while, having brought in the dishes, he soon disappeared back to the kitchen, and they were left to their own devices. Torquhil didn't seem to find anything strange about that, so Hetty soon found that she was able to relax and enjoy the meal, instead of worrying about keeping the servants waiting as she usually did.

She was able to help herself to whatever food she chose and just the right amounts. She ate some delicious bread rolls, still warm from the oven, and home-made butter, cheeses and some baked ham, which was quite the best she'd ever tasted; she then tucked into a large bowl of porridge with cream and honey and finished with several slices of toast and quince paste. She had been offered tea, coffee or chocolate to drink and the unexpected choice had rendered her momentarily speechless so that her grandfather had been forced to supply the answer for her and she was able to savour her first real cup of coffee since leaving Swift Park — roasted dandelion root was just not the same. She found it all quite delightful and kept eating until she thought she might very well burst. She felt self-conscious but didn't seem to be able to stop sampling the wonderful food.

She looked up and caught her host watching her and guiltily put her last piece of toast back onto her plate.

Torquhil smiled his peculiar half-smile, "Mrs Ashby would be gratified to see such a hearty appetite. I must say that I do find the modern affectation for ladies who pick half-heartedly at their food rather vexing; when someone has gone to all the trouble of making it, the least they could do is to enjoy eating it."

Hetty picked up the slice of toast again and took another bite of it while thinking that his face was vastly improved by that crooked smile; it made him look almost ordinary. Not in the accepted meaning of the word of course, but it stopped him looking quite so forbidding and — unconventional. She idly wondered why he didn't tie his hair back instead of allowing it to hang down onto his shoulders, falling across his face and making him look more eccentric than was really necessary. And despite his words he clearly didn't eat enough himself because he was so gaunt that she felt a sudden urge to feed him suet puddings to put some meat on his bones. She blushed at the ridiculous thought and turned her wandering attention back to her delicious breakfast, eyeing the dish of cinnamon-scented stewed apple with greedy interest.

Her grandfather kept up a steady flow of conversation, having been starved of male company whilst at Friday's Acre; he was making the most of his new companion. Hetty was glad to see him so animated; she hadn't liked him dozing beside the fire and wasting away his days. She knew that he would do much better if his mind was stimulated and her usual chatter about chickens and crab apples was not enough to keep him interested even though he would never say so.

Her eyes kept straying to the window and the snow falling steadily outside and she found herself fretting for Eirwen and those who were in charge of transporting her to Galdre Knap. It wasn't going to be an easy journey even though the road was still passable and the settled snow barely an inch thick as yet.

Finn had lit a fire in the library, and it was quite cosy, with the candles giving a warm light and the richly embroidered furnishings, the glorious tapestries upon the walls and the shelves crammed with gilded, leather-bound books. There was a terrestrial globe and, on the other side of the room, what she thought might be a celestial globe. She was fascinated and asked if she could take a closer look.

Torquhil made a small gesture of consent or approval and she rose and moved towards the celestial globe, which was fashioned from ornate gold, and embellished with sea-serpents and bearded gods.

She heard a chair being pushed back and felt his presence beside her.

"It's mechanised," said Torquhil, "And this one is an armillary sphere which also has an astronomical clock."

Hetty examined the skeleton sphere of bronze rings with its indecipherable hieroglyphics engraved with such delicacy and skill onto every surface and was filled with the kind of wonder that gave one gooseflesh.

"Do you understand the workings of it?" she enquired, whilst trying to define the rather odd sensation she was having, coming to the conclusion that it was the thrill of seeing such rare scientific instruments.

"Yes," he said almost apologetically, "I'm afraid I do. I've always been interested in astronomy. It was made in Switzerland. And this one, is the oldest one I have. It's known in German as an *Erdapfel* — which means earth apple."

"Earth apple," mused Hetty, "What a lovely name."

"They are strangely beautiful," agreed her companion, watching her profile as she studied the globe closely.

"And this one?" asked Hetty pointing at an oddly angled metal structure with a spinning disc.

"That is a torquetum. It is used to measure celestial bodies."

Hetty looked up at him with laughing eyes, "Were you named after it?"

Torquhil Guivre's brows drew together, "I don't believe so."

She straightened up and looked at him quizzically, "I asked only in jest!" But before he could respond her eye was caught by the scene outside the window. "Oh!" she cried and dashed to the casement to kneel on the window seat. "It's falling so thickly now!"

"If you are ready, we had best go to the hall to welcome Eirwen. She will be here any minute," said Torquhil.

Again, Hetty wondered about his certainty because there was no way he could know when his sister would be arriving.

As they entered the hall, there came muffled sounds from the driveway, men shouting and a horse whinnying, the rattle of metal and the slamming of carriage doors. Finn ambled into view and went to stand by the front door, his eye upon his master, waiting for a sign.

Torquhil Guivre nodded, and Finn lifted the latch and pulled the heavy door open, the snow swirling eagerly in through the opening, and he stood just behind the door to allow the visitors to enter unimpeded.

The master of the house moved forward and stepped out into the snow. Hetty tried to see past him to get a sight of what was coming.

She could just make out the looming dark bulk of a travelling coach and the snow-covered horses through the hectic snowstorm. There were several men bustling about, their heads down to keep the snow from their eyes, their collars up and their hats already white. Then there was a tall thin female stepping down from the carriage, turning back to assist someone down the steps. Torquhil was at her side and holding out his arms.

Hetty watched as a frail-looking figure was handed down to him by one of the helpers. She was now standing right on the threshold, the snowflakes flicking into her eyes and landing in her hair. She opened her mouth and let one settle upon her tongue, she could feel the crystals melting and could discern an elusive taste, like the scent in the air after rain falls on dry earth.

Torquhil Guivre mounted the steps carrying his sister in his arms. Hetty stood back to give them room. As they passed her, she felt a sudden icy blast hit her and shivered. The men outside were busy unloading the carriage and, advancing towards the door, was the other passenger.

Hetty, realising that Torquhil had taken Eirwen straight upstairs to her bedchamber, stepped forward to greet the visitor as there was no one else to do it.

"Welcome to Galdre Knap. I'm Miss Henrietta Swift, Eirwen's companion. Do please come into the warm and I shall send for a nice hot drink for you. You must be freezing!"

As she entered the hall, the lady stopped and threw back the hood of her cape, revealing iron-grey hair and a long face with eyes like currants, a beaky nose and small, prim mouth. Hetty thought she looked rather dour and girded her loins in preparation for what was bound to be an awkward time.

"I am frozen to the marrow, Miss Swift, I doubt I shall ever be warm again. I cannot feel my toes anymore and to tell the truth, I am ravenously hungry! We set off at dawn from the last coaching inn and the snow has chased us all the way here. I thought we would overturn at one stage, where the road had become so rutted — the coach tipped right over but miraculously righted itself. I felt we were to be killed or injured for sure and left lying in a frozen ditch all night. But here we are, safe and sound, as you can see."

In the tiny pause she left as she drew breath Hetty quickly managed to get a word in, "And I am *so* glad! I was exceedingly worried for you. This weather must be quite dreadful for travelling. Come into the library, there's a good fire and I will send for some breakfast for you, unless you'd rather go straight up to your bedchamber? Is there anything you would particularly like Mrs — ?"

"Mrs Waverley. I am Miss Guivre's nursemaid. I'd be happy with anything warm. Porridge would be fine and some tea, please. A nice hot cup of tea. I have an exceedingly strong constitution and will not require a nap to recover!"

Hetty glanced at Finn who was lurking by the door to the kitchens, and he nodded and disappeared down the corridor.

Her grandfather was still loitering in the hall and Hetty introduced them and suggested that he could keep Mrs Waverley company and he seemed to be delighted at the prospect.

"This way, Mrs Waverley," said Hetty briskly and led the way into the library.

The nursemaid looked about her as she moved across the room towards the welcoming fire, "What a bizarre room! What are all these devices?"

"It seems Mr Guivre is very interested in the stars and the planets and scientific things in general. I suspect he's something of an intellectual as everything here seems to be for the purpose of improving his mind — he has a vast quantity of books and strange astronomical instruments."

"Yes, so I see. He looks to be as peculiar as his unfortunate sister."

Hetty couldn't help asking, "*Is* she so very peculiar? I've not had the pleasure of meeting her yet and Mr Guivre has told us very little."

Mrs Waverley fixed her with a very direct stare, "I would say that she is not at all — *usual*. She is most assuredly of unsound mind and can be quite a handful when she's at her worst. The doctors at the asylum where she's been confined for the last few months were obviously more than glad to be rid of her. They were unable to tell me much apart from complaining about her uncontrollable behaviour and regaling me with some of the inexplicable incidents that occurred while she was with them. I have now spent three days travelling with her and must admit that she makes my other charges seem quite obliging in comparison. But the doctor said that she responded well to regular small doses of laudanum — just enough to keep her calm. It was difficult to administer in a bounding coach, but we managed. I had no choice but to call upon the men to assist me. She has been asleep for the best part of the journey. Once I realised that it was better for everyone."

"Oh dear," said Hetty, feeling decidedly uneasy, "How very disturbing that must have been for Eirwen — and you. Still, the journey must have been distressing for you all, I'm sure. You'll soon settle in here, I'm sure; Mrs Ashby, the cook, is renowned for her restorative cookery. You'll feel as fine as fivepence in a day or two."

"I feel perfectly fine now, thank you, Miss Swift — no more than a trifle chilly. I come from resilient Highland stock and am seldom put out by anything."

"Oh, you're Scottish? I thought I could detect a hint of a brogue."

"Indeed, I am and proud to be. We are a belligerent people and those qualities come in handy when faced with such hardship. We know how to endure without complaint."

Not knowing quite how to respond to this, Hetty was delighted to see Finn arrive at that moment bearing a tray laden with breakfast for Mrs Waverley. The aromas were almost enough to make her hungry again. He was followed by Agatha with a pitcher of steaming water that she set upon the side table.

"If you'd care to wash your hands, Mrs Waverley?" said Hetty and she turned away discreetly to set the dishes out on the table in readiness.

After making use of the hot water, the nursemaid sat down at the table and shook out the napkin into her lap, "I will be perfectly all right with Mr Swift if you wish to go and see to your charge. I am sure she could do with some sustenance when the last dose of laudanum wears off — she has refused food for two days."

Hetty took her at her word and begging her pardon she went to find Torquhil and Eirwen.

* * *

She knocked on the door of the Chinese Bedchamber and waited. After a moment the door opened and Torquhil gestured for her to enter.

"I didn't know if you might need me. Mrs Waverley is settled at her breakfast with Grandpapa for entertainment, so I just thought — ", she began, speaking softly.

"You did the right thing. I've managed to get Eirwen onto the bed but other than that I haven't been very successful.

She's still wearing her clothes and shoes and seems to be much impaired by the effects of being heavily drugged."

"Yes, Mrs Waverley said that they'd had to resort to laudanum."

"A necessary evil. She's become alarmingly fragile. She's not usually this slight. It's disturbing to see her in such a state."

"It must be dreadfully upsetting for you. Poor girl, how she must have suffered." Hetty went to stand beside the bed and looked down at their patient. "She's no more than a child."

She reached out and pushed a wet tendril of hair away from her forehead and was shocked at how cold Eirwen's skin felt.

"She's freezing! It's imperative that we get her out of these clothes and into bed at once! Please would you build up the fire? I'll undress her. Oh, and we'll need a warm woollen nightgown. You'll find one in the linen press over there." Hetty wasn't even aware that she was ordering the head of the house around as though he were a servant; she was just determined that her charge should be warmed up as soon as possible.

Twenty minutes or so later Hetty pulled the covers up to Eirwen's chin and stood back, feeling slightly better about her condition. The girl was breathing evenly, and her pulse was steady. She had managed to dry her hair by rubbing it gently with a cloth and braided it to keep it neat. She'd been astonished by its length — it very nearly reached the girl's ankles — and was pure silvery white, as though she had somehow aged prematurely, but her skin was as flawlessly smooth as the finest porcelain, though stretched tightly across the sharp bones in her face.

The fire was snapping and crackling into life and Torquhil stood beside it and observed Hetty as she finished her task of settling his sister.

Hetty looked over her shoulder at him, "You're not telling me everything," she said, "I sense that this is not just a case of — some kind of lunacy. I think there is more to her condition than first appears."

Torquhil was gazing at Eirwen's still form, his face expressionless, "As I said, we do not yet have a diagnosis for whatever this is — this — affliction. The doctors who examined her before she disappeared were confounded and could not agree upon a diagnosis — some were convinced that it was an inherited illness, others that it's a form of moon madness and the most respected of them all declared that she just needed to have a baby to cure her. That was when she vanished from their care and I've had endless experts investigating her disappearance, but until two months ago there had been no news of her — not one word. Then, just when I had all but given up hope, a letter came." He paused and turned to nudge a log back into the fire with the toe of his boot, "A letter that finally convinced me she'd been found. She was removed to a local asylum and kept there so that she couldn't harm herself or anyone else. I fear that it was a brutal place, as they generally are, and it has taken longer than I would have liked to secure her permanent release."

Out of the side of her eye Hetty thought she saw something move in the shadowy corner of the room, but turning to have a look, saw nothing but darkness.

"You cannot blame yourself. She's here now in the best place for her. You've already done more than most brothers would. My bedchamber is adjoining hers and I'll sleep with the door open. I'm a very light sleeper. If necessary, I shall have a truckle bed set up in here."

Her companion said nothing, and she wondered if she'd been too presumptuous in talking to him in that manner, but he *had* said that she should be honest, so she was just doing as she'd been told. She waited, expectantly.

He seemed to be looking just past her, into space, not focused on anything in particular.

"Thank you," was all he eventually said.

The snow continued to fall resolutely from the obscured sky, just as though there were an infinite supply, and it had no particular plans to cease its singular business.

Hetty had naturally seen snow before, many times, but this was quietly and unnervingly relentless.

"Will Mrs Waverley be staying?" she asked.

"She will. I thought it might be helpful to have a nursemaid here, if only for a while until we can fully understand Eirwen's needs. I know you have some expertise in caring for your grandfather and, apparently, your grandmother before him, but Mrs Waverley is used to dealing with those with troubled minds. I don't know her personally, but she came highly recommended by some of the doctors and a trusted friend."

"I shall be glad of any advice," said Hetty "Grandpapa is no trouble to look after at all and Grandmama was too ill to put up much of a fight. She was a very unusual grandmother and taught me all her skills as a herbalist and forager before she became too unwell to continue."

"So I understand."

Hetty cast him a questioning glance, "Gracious, you sound as though you've had spies watching me!" she laughed. "They must have been terribly bored! I've led the dullest life imaginable."

"Have you? I wouldn't know," responded Torquhil with the merest glimmer of a smile.

She cocked her head like an inquisitive bird, "I think you're teasing me. Of course, I realise that you haven't spied upon me because there would be no need when you could just have visited us at Friday's Acre and asked anything you wanted to know — I have no secrets."

"I think we all have secrets, Hetty. It's only human to want to keep some things to yourself."

"Really? I have a fearful job trying to keep things to myself! If I cannot find anyone to talk to, I chat to my chickens — they're extremely good listeners and make sweetly encouraging noises as though in sympathy with me. It's very soothing. Do you not think it's damaging to keep things to yourself? Secrets can fester and eat away at your soul."

"That's an interesting concept. I'm not sure I have a soul."

Feeling a little shocked but trying not to show it, Hetty said, "You do not believe we have souls, Torquhil?"

"I will only alarm you if I answer that truthfully."

"You have given me your answer then. Mr Randall, the churchwarden, was right to fear for my spiritual welfare! He was exceedingly anxious about the idea of us coming to live at Galdre Knap."

"I cannot blame him," said Torquhil quietly.

"Well, I have seen nothing yet to persuade me that you are beyond redemption!"

"What if I am not seeking redemption?"

Hetty's brows snapped together, "But, surely everyone wants to be saved? We are all in need of someone to care about us enough to want to rescue us. You have rescued Eirwen. And, in so doing you have also saved Grandpapa and me, even though it may not have been wholly intentional."

"Saved you from what though?"

She laughed, "From eating acorns and a life of smallness and tedium."

"I fear you've seen the last of boredom for a while, Hetty. You may be pleading to have it back by next week."

"I don't think so. Grandpapa is so excited at the thought of having someone to play a game of merciless chess with and I'm beside myself with joy at the idea of being allowed free rein in the library and to be able to help Eirwen in any way I can. I've felt quite useless recently — as though I were trapped in aspic. I need to be useful and keep myself busy or as Grandpapa will no doubt tell you, I tend to get into mischief."

Torquhil's eyes flickered away from her and Hetty, following their direction, turned to see that Eirwen was staring at them from pale aquamarine eyes.

Six

"She's awake!" cried Hetty moving quickly to the bed. "Good day, Eirwen. My name is Hetty, and I shall be looking after you while you get well again. Look, Torquhil is here too. You're safe now at Galdre Knap."

She took the girl's limp hand in hers and found it was still cold to the touch, she gently chafed it to try to warm her.

"Oh, you are so dreadfully cold! Torquhil, could you please find the other quilt in the blanket chest? Don't worry, we'll soon have you warm again."

The girl just continued to stare, unblinking.

Torquhil found the extra quilt and Hetty spread it over the bed, "Would you like something to drink? Or perhaps you're hungry? Would you like some chicken broth? Mrs Ashby makes the very best broth."

There was no response.

She looked back at Torquhil, "Perhaps if *you* talked to her — ?"

"It won't make any difference. She was — often like this. Just silent and still."

"But there must be something we can do?"

"We have to wait. It'll take a while for the laudanum to completely wear off. She seems to be particularly susceptible to its sinister charms. Then we shall see how she really is."

"All right, I think I'll fetch some broth. It won't hurt to try, at least. I'll just run down to the kitchen and talk to Mrs Ashby and check on Mrs Waverley and Grandpapa. Will you remain here until I get back — ?"

"Of course. Whatever you wish."

With one last look at Eirwen, Hetty hastened from the room, glad to have decided on a course of action. Being uncertain made her anxious and she'd much rather be doing something to keep busy. If she'd still been at Friday's Acre, she'd have been preparing the next meal for her grandfather, peeling and chopping, crushing herbs and spices and occupying herself with the day-to-day tasks that she had fortunately never found mundane. Her grandmother had taught her from an early age that a knowledge of the natural world would stand her in good stead in later life. She had never questioned the fact that it might have been considered a little unusual for a lady of her grandmother's quality to be so interested in the properties of various roots, fungi and leaves in the woods. She had happily trotted after her, holding a basket that was almost as big as she was, eagerly watching as the old lady gathered flowers and plants, seeds and berries, fungi and oddly twisted roots. It had been an adventure and she'd been thrilled to have her grandmother's attention all to herself. She had learned so much from her but had not yet had the chance to put that knowledge to good use.

* * *

In the kitchen she found Mrs Ashby hard at work mixing something dark and sticky in a large bowl and Finn noisily knocking the snow off his boots at the back door. He took off his hat and bashed it against the door jamb, "Sam and Jacob are coming in for a hot drink in a minute. All the animals are fed and secure. Good workers those lads."

Mrs Ashby looked up and glowered at the snow on her kitchen floor, "I've just cleaned that! Take off your boots! How are things going upstairs, Miss Hetty?"

Hetty shrugged, "I'm not really sure yet. It's all a bit puzzling. I was going to try to get Miss Guivre to take some of your wonderful chicken and barley broth. I can't seem to get her warm and I shall need a hot brick for her feet please."

"Finn, can you see to the brick? Aggie can take it up when it's ready. The broth is in the pantry — it just needs heating up. It'll do her good if you can get her to try some. By all accounts she didn't look too well when she arrived, but the journey must have been hard on her. Poor wee thing." She tipped some golden powder into the bowl and stirred it in.

"Ginger," said Hetty, sniffing the aromatic air in delight.

"Gingerbread. Good to keep away colds."

"Oh, Grandpapa loves gingerbread!"

"He shall have some for his supper then. And this new lady? Mrs Waverley? I caught a glimpse of her as she came in. Aggie has prepared the Lilac Bedchamber for her which is right at the end of the long corridor at the back of the house. She'll be able to find some peace and quiet there. I thought she might appreciate the lilac, being an old maid."

"She's married though!"

Mrs Ashby rolled her eyes, "That's just a courtesy title to give her importance. Makes her seem more respectable."

"Well, I never," said Hetty. "But how can you possibly tell?"

"That woman's never been in any man's bed," muttered Mrs Ashby.

Hetty glanced at Finn, but he was busy taking off his boots. "*Mrs Ashby!* What a thing to say! She seems to be a very competent female. Surprisingly talkative but perfectly composed, which in the circumstances is impressive. Apparently, the coach very nearly overturned!"

"Yes, so the coach driver said. He said he'd never seen the like — a big travelling coach like that, just righting itself. The men came in for something to eat to sustain them for the return journey."

Hetty disappeared into the pantry and came back with a skillet into which she'd ladled some broth. She placed it carefully on the hearth near the hot embers. She fetched a small earthenware bowl and perched it on the iron grill, then she sat down on the stool by the fire to make sure the broth didn't boil over.

Agatha ambled into the kitchen carrying a crumpled bundle of linen that she took through to the laundry room and returned a few minutes later at the same sedate pace, "There, that's a good job done," she announced cheerfully, "Everythin' is ready now." She eyed the skillet of bubbling broth, "D'you want me to take that up for you, Miss?"

Hetty smiled at her, "Thank you, no. I'll take it up," and, as soon as it was hot, she poured it into the bowl, grabbed a spoon, some of the bread made for breakfast and put it all on a tray.

"Butter?" said Mrs Ashby.

Agatha passed her the butter and Hetty set off for the Chinese Bedchamber, pausing in the doorway to call over her shoulder, "Finn? Please would you check on Mrs Waverley and Grandpapa and make sure they're all right?"

Finn grunted and Hetty trod carefully up the stairs with the tray, trying hard not to spill the broth.

She nudged the door of the bedchamber with the toe of her shoe and Torquhil opened it immediately and took the tray from her.

It was clear that nothing had changed while she'd been downstairs; Eirwen was still staring. She looked like a wax doll before it had had its face painted. She was the colour of mist and looked just as insubstantial.

"Right," said Hetty, as he put the tray down on the chest next to the bed, "If you could help me sit her up a bit so that I can give her some of the broth?"

Torquhil gently lifted his sister while Hetty arranged the pillows behind her. She could see that it took no effort to move the young girl; she was so delicate, like a tiny bird, with bones made from air. When they had her perfectly positioned, Hetty laid a cloth across her chest and perched on the edge of the bed with the bowl of broth.

"Eirwen, I've brought you some delicious chicken and barley broth that I think will be very good for you. I simply need you to open your mouth so that I can spoon some in," and she demonstrated opening her mouth like she would to a baby. She scooped up some of the liquid and held the spoon up to Eirwen's mouth, but her lips stayed stubbornly closed and her eyes blank.

Hetty touched the immobile lips with the edge of the spoon. There was no response. She tried again and still there was nothing. She glanced up at Torquhil who was hovering just behind her.

"Perhaps if *you* tried? She knows you and that might help."

She stood up and made room for him to sit down in her place.

He looked thoroughly awkward, as though he'd never had to even consider such a thing before and was thrown by being asked. Hetty swallowed nervously and wished she hadn't suggested it. She felt embarrassed watching him and had to turn away to the window and pretend to study the snow, which was still falling with alarming single-mindedness. As the snowflakes passed the window, they looked grey against the pale distance, and she tried to follow one all the way down to the ground, but it got lost in the melee. After a minute or two she peeped back at the bed and could see that Torquhil was gently pulling his sister's chin down with one long finger in an effort to get her to open her mouth but to no avail.

Hetty was just about to suggest that he might as well give up when, with a sudden and explosive movement, Eirwen smashed the spoon out of his hand and it landed halfway across the room, leaving a trail of broth across the rug.

What was shocking to Hetty was that the girl's face didn't alter at all; it remained empty and unaffected by her own violent action.

She must have let out a startled gasp because Torquhil glanced up at her, "I think the laudanum must be wearing off," he said with considerable restraint.

Hetty went immediately to retrieve the spoon and mop up the mess and then instinctively went to Eirwen and stroked her forehead soothingly, just as she had always calmed her chickens when they became agitated after a fox had been near the henhouse. She would stroke the top of their beaks between their eyes, and it put them into a stupefied state and when they awoke from their trance it was as though the fox had never happened. She stroked Eirwen in the space between her brows in softly soothing movements and she didn't really know why, but she began to hum a simple and repetitive melody. She was aware of Torquhil beside her, sitting perfectly still but his presence didn't impinge upon what she was doing.

After a few minutes, Eirwen's eyelids fluttered, closed, opened again and then closed and her breathing deepened slightly and Hetty allowed her shoulders to relax.

"She's asleep," she whispered and straightened up. She took a few steps back and found a chair to collapse into. She watched the girl's face not daring to look away in case she missed any sign of life.

Torquhil stood and crossed the room to the fireplace. He looked from his sister's face to the young woman perching on the edge of the armchair, in apparent readiness.

"That was masterly, Hetty."

She didn't look up, "My hens like me doing that if they're upset. We must get her to eat and drink though. She cannot go on without sustenance. She's already fading away. We cannot allow it to continue."

"You've found a way to calm her perhaps later we'll find a way to encourage her to eat. It's something of an improvement."

"I won't be satisfied until she begins to respond properly. This stillness and sudden violence is frightening and very discouraging. Still, it's only the first day. We must be happy to have her here in comparative safety. It has to be better than the asylum! Family must always be preferable to those who work in such terrible institutions."

He made no reply.

She bit her lip, "But — of course, you had no influence over where Eirwen ended up. It was out of your hands. Anyway, she's here now and we shall give her the very best care. It's an odd comparison, but some of my hens were rescued from a nearby farmer who hadn't treated them well and everyone said I might as well wring their necks because they'd never recover and start laying again. But they were so very sad and trusting — I could not just make them into stew! And now, they are as fit as fiddles again."

Torquhil Guivre looked at Hetty from hooded eyes, "Hopefully you won't want to make Eirwen into a stew either."

She laughed and cocked her bright head, "I think you're making a joke! How unexpected."

"You're suggesting I'm humourless."

Smiling impishly, she replied, "Not at all. Although I'd started to form the impression that you might be a rather serious sort of fellow."

"That was your first impression?"

"No," she said, cautiously.

He had an unsettling habit of not responding immediately to her comments or questions and she had to force herself to be patient and not try to fill the echoing pauses with mindless nonsense. She was more accustomed to talking to chickens and doting grandparents who didn't seem to object if the content of her conversations was a little wanting. She waited.

"First impressions can change," he reflected.

"People's first impression of me is generally the colour of my hair. I can see that's all that registers."

His eyes travelled to her hair, the colour of flame, brighter than polished copper. "I hadn't noticed," he said, not meeting her challenging gaze.

Hetty laughed out loud, "Thank you. You're a terrible liar. I'm used to the colour now. My father was a redhead and also my grandmother, although I never saw her with anything but white hair. So, it runs in the family."

"Do you have siblings?"

"My only sister died at birth, so it's just me."

"I'm sorry to hear that. Your parents are both gone?"

Hetty sighed and looked out at the snow, blinking away unexpected tears, "My father was a great trial to everyone, apparently from the day he was born. You could blame the red hair or just the sad fact that he was a selfish, reckless fool.

My mother always suffered from delicate health after losing my sister and she wasn't able to withstand my father's more ridiculous ideas and had to watch as he squandered what would have been his inheritance and stand by as he ruined his own father. He lost everything. And Grandmama — it took a terrible toll on her. She took to her bed in the end and just drifted away. She was such a — magical person."

"Yes. So I've heard."

Hetty raised her eyebrows, "Really? You seem to have heard a good deal about me and my family, while I have heard very little about you apart from some absurd flights of fancy from the more imaginative locals. How strange though. Who would speak about Grandmama?"

A darkness fell across his eyes making the whites appear ink-stained, concealing any telltale emotion.

She gazed at him curiously, "I'm sorry — there I go again — questioning where I shouldn't — it's a regrettable trait. Are your parents — ?"

He paused, "They're both dead."

"Oh! I'm sorry. Are you and Eirwen actually brother and sister? You look so very different."

"We are blood siblings."

"How extraordinary. I sometimes wonder if my sister would have had red hair like my father or my mother's golden hair."

"We have the same pale complexion. Her eyesight has never been very strong though. When she was little, she would peer at things, unable to distinguish shapes if they were too far away. She seemed to compensate for that disability with acute hearing and her other senses are also extra keen. And before — this — her understanding was unconventional but otherwise sound."

"Do you know what happened to her to make her like this?"

"Not specifically. It happened gradually. She began to disappear as though she were becoming lost inside herself, until she seemed no longer aware of the real world around her.

She was still here. We could see her, but all that was left was this outer shell."

"What did you do?"

"We took her to the top physicians in London — Paris, Berlin, Vienna — wherever there was a doctor who professed to know something about such disorders, we travelled there. Their diagnoses varied from blaming hysterical female complaints to full-blown insanity, to the stars not being aligned or the moon waxing or waning. One gentleman in Vienna quite seriously assured me that it was the work of Faeries and gave me a spell to rid the house of their malevolent presence. I quickly learnt not to trust anyone professing to be a so-called expert. They are not interested in the patients, only in money and fame. Some of them were more unhinged than my sister. It grieves me that Eirwen suffered at their hands and even though I'm not sure how much she actually remembers, it was an unpleasant experience for her." He paused, "And I allowed them access to her."

"But you were only doing your best for her. Nobody could blame you for trying anything you could to save her. What made you stop the search for a cure?"

"The last physician we saw was keen to try trepanation."

"I'm afraid I don't know what that is."

"Drilling holes in the skull to let the evil spirits escape. It is, apparently, an ancient medical procedure used by the Incas. Needless to say, we were soon on our way back to England — but without a cure."

"Merciful Heavens! It sounds utterly inhuman! The poor child. There *must* be another way. I wish my grandmother were still here — I feel sure she would be able to find a way to help Eirwen."

Torquhil said nothing.

"When you were talking about the doctors — you said *we*. You had someone else with you?" asked Hetty a little hesitantly — she had no wish to pry, but she needed to know everything about her patient if she was to help her.

He cast a glance at his sister, who was still sleeping, "Yes, I had to have help, I couldn't manage her alone. A physician from London insisted on accompanying us, mostly out of a desire to try to gain an understanding of her condition and he couldn't pass up the chance to talk with such revered medical men. And of course, a nurse had to come along as well, we needed a female companion."

She sensed he hadn't finished the story, so she waited. She was learning to be patient with this strange man.

"And a very good friend of mine came with us. He heard we were going to Vienna and loves the opera — I don't think he'd taken into account the weeks travelling in a coach with someone as troubled as Eirwen. He found it extremely stressful — as did we all, but he was even less capable of dealing with it."

"Still, it must have been reassuring to have some company on such a long and difficult journey. Then you came back to Galdre Knap?"

"Eventually. We stayed in London for a while, still hoping to find the help she needed, but in the end, we had no choice but to return home in the hopes that she might find the familiar surroundings reassuring. By then, she was almost unreachable. There were just faint glimmers of the girl she used to be."

"And your opera friend? What became of him?"

"Adam Deering. I haven't seen him since we returned from the continent."

"Is that usual?"

"He found it impossible to come to terms with Eirwen's rapid decline. If you had seen her before — she was so very different. It was a shock to see her deteriorate before our eyes and not be able to do anything to prevent it."

"I can only imagine how distressing it must have been." Hetty sighed and stood up. "I think that while she's like this, I'll go down and make sure that Grandpapa and Mrs Waverley are all right. I asked Finn to look in on them, but he didn't seem very keen. Would you like me to ask Agatha to come and sit with Eirwen for a while — if you have things to do?"

"I'll stay here while you do that. My main priority is Eirwen."

"I shall be back as soon as I can. Send for me if anything changes in the meantime."

He nodded briefly and Hetty went out, thinking that he may be eccentric, but he was certainly a loyal and devoted brother.

* * *

She arrived just as Agatha was coming out of the library, bearing a tray with Mrs Waverley's breakfast things on it.

Agatha smiled and rolled her eyes, "She said the porridge should have a pinch of salt an' the tea was too strong!"

"Oh dear, don't tell Mrs Ashby! It'll be pistols at dawn! I do hope they're not going to become foes — that would be most inconvenient. I'll be along in a moment, Aggie, when I've talked to my grandfather."

She ducked her head and stumped away to the kitchen.

Hetty found Mrs Waverley sitting beside the fire chatting to her grandfather about the finer points of making porridge. Mr Swift looked up at his granddaughter and without batting an eyelid managed to convey his innermost feelings.

"Mrs Waverley," said Hetty brightly, taking the hint, "We have Miss Guivre nicely settled for now, although we failed to persuade her to take any broth. I was thinking that I should show you to your bedchamber so that you might make yourself at home. Grandpapa can read his book for a while?"

Mrs Waverley was on her feet immediately, "A splendid notion. I expect I've been boring Mr Swift with my sermon on porridge! I think I might do a little embroidery until Miss Guivre needs me again. I find it very soothing."

"That's an excellent idea. She's sleeping at the moment and Mr Guivre is sitting with her."

"Well, I'm here to do my share of the nursing. It's what I'm used to, after all — I like to make myself useful."

Mightily relieved to hear this, Hetty thanked her and with a mischievous backwards glance at her grandfather, she led Mrs Waverley from the room.

The nursemaid was more than pleased with her bedchamber, finding it to be far superior to the accommodation she was accustomed to and took some time to admire the pretty flock wallpaper in shades of lilac and silver and the floral curtains and counterpane. She found the colours to be soothing and remarked that the beautiful plaster ceiling reminded her of decorative sugar work with all its intricate mouldings. Her bags had been emptied already and put away and all she had to do was find the sewing she was in the midst of and make herself comfortable beside the welcoming fire.

Hetty left her and returned to her grandfather who was looking through the shelves of books in the library.

"There are some quite remarkable books here, Hetty! There are many I've never even heard of and some that I should think are worth a small fortune. And such subjects too. I've never seen the like! They're going to keep me occupied for a long time."

"That's really good news. I'm sorry to have left you for so long with Mrs Waverley."

He smiled, "I didn't mind — until the porridge! She's a very loquacious female, but not without intelligence and a bit of spark. It sounds as though she's had quite a hard life, but she wasn't complaining. She said she was happy with her lot."

"Just not the porridge."

Her grandfather laughed and patted her shoulder, "I fear there may well be trouble brewing between Mrs Waverley and Mrs Ashby."

"I shall do my very best to avert any skirmishes."

"And the poor little girl? How is she?"

Hetty shrugged, "I really don't know, Old Pa. She's not showing any signs of recovering her faculties, but it's early days. She did at least open her eyes, but then unfortunately she dashed the spoon from Torquhil's hand. It was as though her action was involuntary. I hardly know what to make of it all."

He pulled a book down from the shelf and studied the gilded lettering on its spine, "You just need to trust in your own judgment, my love. Your grandmother always said that you would be able to do so much if you would only believe in your own abilities. She had absolute faith in you, you know. She said you hadn't been given that fiery hair for nothing — it was a gift that set you apart and made you special."

"It certainly set me apart!" she remarked light-heartedly, but he turned to look at her gravely.

"But you didn't allow it to keep you apart for long. You just kept trying, kept chasing after the other children until they gave in and let you play their games. Eventually you won their approval, and they forgot the differences. You have a strong heart and somewhere inside you is your grandmother's extraordinary ability to restore order to the world. She taught you how to use all that Mother Earth is willing to give you in order to help others. You just have to listen."

"Listen to *what* though?"

"To your grandmother's voice. She's speaking to you, but you just can't hear her yet."

"Goodness gracious, Old Pa! You're getting very mystical in your old age!"

"Well, I thought we had time. But I see now that matters are coming to a head and your skills are going to be needed sooner than I thought."

"What on earth are you talking about?"

"My darling girl, your grandmother — was a healer."

"You mean she made potions? Yes, I know that."

He carefully laid the book down on a table and took her hand in his, "I don't think that you do. You see, child, the skill goes with the red hair. It should have been passed from your grandmother to your father, but he — he didn't want it, he didn't believe in it. He denied what he was and well, you know what happened. So, she passed the knowledge down to you, but she only had limited time. It follows the hair, you see? It tends to stick to the female line but sometimes it strays a little off the beaten track and is forced to skip a generation. You have it, Anne made sure of that. She said it was in your fingertips."

"My — what on earth did she mean by that?"

"Have you never felt anything? Never suspected that you were somehow special?"

"*No!* Oh, this is — what are you *saying?* I really don't understand." She snatched her hand away and paced the room crossly, her heels pounding into the floor. "This is ridiculous! Red hair! Magical skills! Fingertips! It's such nonsense!"

He watched her from sad eyes, "She said you would reject the idea at first. But she told me that somewhere deep inside you would already know. You suspect. You are aware of your dormant potential — have seen signs of it already, but you dare not acknowledge it because it would challenge everything you have ever known."

Hetty put her shaking hands over her eyes.

"Why are you *telling* me this? It can't be true!"

He moved slowly to the nearest chair and sat down as though his legs were too weak to bear his weight, "She said I'd know when it was time to tell you. I think the time has come. I think this is why you were chosen to come to Galdre Knapp. From what I can gather, Torquhil doesn't know anything about this, but it seems that *something* prompted him to ask us here — we just don't know exactly what, as yet. Perhaps I should have told you sooner, but you were so happy at Friday's Acre with your garden and the animals — I didn't want to spoil everything too soon."

Hetty made a soft groaning sound from behind her hands, "Well, why do it *now?* You know I hate change! This is madness! I'm already having to deal with the move here and now — *now* — !"

"She said I had to ask you if your fingertips ever tingled."

Silence.

"Or if you had ever seen anything that you couldn't explain."

Silence.

"Or if you heard voices in your head."

"Oh, my God! She thought I was *deranged!*"

"No, you need to understand that she had the same manifestations. Henrietta, you must try to understand — to listen."

"Don't call me Henrietta! I know things are bad when you do that, and I *am* listening!"

Seven

Hetty was hunched into a tense knot on the window seat in the study and staring out at the snow. There was nothing but snow as far as her eye could see, white upon white, muffling, suffocating snow. It was enthralling and frightening at the same time, and she found it difficult to think of anything else while she was watching it fall, so she concentrated hard on watching it fall. She didn't want to think about anything. Her grandfather's words had been so unexpected, so disturbing, that she'd wanted to cover her ears to keep them out.

Of course, it couldn't be true. It was completely beyond belief.

And yet, even as she denied them, she was remembering her grandmother's words, the insistent push of her voice, the constant flow of plant names, recipes, uses and warnings, repeated over and over, like nursery rhymes. Sometimes in song, they'd sing the ingredients as they walked hand in hand through the woods. Even as Anne lay in bed in her final weeks, she still continued to drum knowledge into Hetty's eager young mind. For Hetty, the words held mystery and beauty, the traditional names of the plants and trees, the mixtures and potions, the pretty rhymes and the promise of cures for nagging ailments; it had been tantalising for such a curious child.

She had been neglected by her own parents: a father interested only in escaping his responsibilities and a mother whose ill-health, after losing her second child, had given her permission to ignore the boisterous child she already had, and who had found her mother-in-law's devoted interest in Hetty a blessing in many ways.

From the few words her grandmother had said about her mother, Beth, Hetty soon realised that there was little love lost on either side. They were forced to call a truce because of the child they shared. She thought her mother like one of the tiny, perfectly dressed and painted wooden dolls in the doll's house, which she could look at through the tiny windows but was never allowed to touch. She could only remember being permitted to embrace Beth a few times and was almost always pulled away by the nervously hovering nursemaid and promptly removed back to the nursery where she could do no harm.

For Hetty, losing her parents and moving to Swift Park with her grandparents, had been a stroke of good fortune, for it meant that she then was able to enjoy a life of being nurtured and loved, with no nursemaid or nursery to confine her, no father to be wary of or mother who would turn her face away from her.

The snow was about a foot deep and unruffled by any natural or human disturbance; it just fell and lay still and flat like linen laid out to bleach on the grass. The greys and greens, the browns and ochres had been shrouded like the dead, leaving softly rounded ghosts of trees and shrubs, the garden losing its shape and pattern and becoming another world altogether, a world of unfamiliar forms and structures, where one could easily become lost, the landmarks having been erased and the recognisable disguised.

Hetty thought it was bit like her life. Everything had changed; all things familiar had been removed and she now lived in a world where she was struggling to find her place. She was, although loathe to admit it to herself, lost and confused, and now her world had been turned upside down again and she was facing all kinds of new problems and she wasn't sure if she could face them.

She closed her eyes and leant forward, pressing her forehead against the windowpanes, the glass and leads painfully cold on her skin. She just wanted to wake up.

Taptaptap.

Hetty sighed.

Taptaptap!

She opened her eyes and found herself looking into the beady white eye of a jackdaw, its dark face pressed right up against the window.

Startled, she sat up, "Goodness! What a fright you gave me!" She took a closer look at the bird, "Oh, it's you again! Good day to you! What do you want?"

If I could roll my eyes, I would. It's cold out here and I want to come inside. I would've thought that was obvious.

"You look cold," said Hetty.

Taptaptap.

"You're very insistent! Are you asking to come in?"

The jackdaw flapped its wings and cocked its head.

Hetty opened the window and the bird quickly hopped through the opening and into the study before she could change her mind.

Whilst keeping a wary eye upon the visitor, she closed the window behind him and brushed away a few snowflakes that had fallen onto the window seat.

"Well, there you are! I'm not sure what to do with you now you're here but you're in the warm at least."

Some food would be welcome. It's getting hard to find out there.

"You can't stay long. I don't think Mrs Ashby would approve." She eyed the beast anxiously, "Especially if you cause any damage to the furniture!"

Food.

"Perhaps I should call Finn. He might know what to do."

He wants to strangle me. I'd rather have some food.

"On the other hand, Finn can be a bit irritable. I think I'd better go and get Torquhil."

Good idea. He can hear me. I cannot understand why you can't. You should be able to, all things considered.

Hetty was thinking she must be mad to have allowed a wild bird into the house however bad the weather outside and started towards the door, but she'd only got halfway across the room when the door opened and Torquhil came in.

"I was just coming to find you!" exclaimed Hetty with relief. "Is Eirwen all right?"

"Yes, she's still asleep and Mrs Waverley is sitting with her."

Torquhil glanced from the girl to the jackdaw perched on the back of a chair and looking at him expectantly.

"Ah, I see why you needed me. Good evening to you Crow."

Not a crow.

"He's not a crow, he's a jackdaw. I don't actually know if he's a he, but whatever he is, he's in your study, for which I can only apologise — I stupidly let him in."

To be fair, I beguiled her, but she didn't put up much of a fight.

"Don't worry, Hetty, he's a tame bird — "

Tame! I am still wild —

" — but he's inclined to be rather a nuisance. Nevertheless, you were quite right to let him in, sadly he's come to rely upon us for food and has lost some of his wild cunning and would otherwise starve."

Crow clacked his beak angrily.

"He also has some very poor habits so he mustn't be given the freedom of the entire house or Mrs Ashby will resign in protest."

"Perhaps he should be put in a cage of some sort?"

Crow took off with a snapping of indignant feathers and flapped up to the highest shelf he could find.

Hetty raised her eyebrows, "It's almost as though he understands."

"Isn't it! It must just be the tone of our voices. Crows and their kith and kin are very intelligent creatures but on no account to be trusted."

"That's what Finn said. He said I should hide my valuables."

The jackdaw hopped up and down, outraged at the unwarranted slur.

"Oh, I think your jewellery will be safe. He needs our food and warmth and won't want to be thrown back out into the snow."

Hetty laughed, "I don't have any valuables unless you count Grandpapa!"

"No jewellery? Nothing?"

She shook her head, smiling, "Everything was sold to pay my father's debts. I don't mind though because the colour of my hair was impossible to marry with any kind of ornament without an ugly clash. The same with overdecorated gowns or anything but the plainest materials. Queen Elizabeth I was able to wear every colour and jewel under the sun by all accounts and still look regal with her red hair but then she *was* the Queen of England and I doubt anyone would have brave enough to tell her she was looking a bit too embellished."

Crow watched his master twist his face into a strange expression and remembered it was something he did when he was amused. It made him look different and vaguely untrustworthy. Crow preferred him the way he usually was — impassive.

Hetty thought Torquhil's crooked smile a little rusty, as though it hadn't been used very often; she thought it made him look younger and less forbidding, but it came quickly and was just as quickly gone again.

"May I ask what happened to your father?"

She lowered her eyes and seemed to find the pattern on the rug interesting.

"I shouldn't have asked."

Her head came up and she stuck out her chin, "No, it's all right. It's still hard to talk about though. Grandpapa will not speak of it. He — Father — was killed in a brawl. Over a paltry gambling debt. It was senseless. And ugly. But, in a way, I suppose, inevitable. After Mama died, he was just looking for a way to escape what he'd done to the family — he couldn't face us. He attended her funeral, but that was the last time we saw him. He took some of the heirlooms from Swift Park and probably sold them in order to continue his life at the tables. He was unrepentant. He never even said goodbye."

"Perhaps he didn't really think he'd be leaving for good. He may have believed that he'd see you again."

She nodded, "Yes, you could be right, of course. I'd like to think that. But from everything I've since learnt about him, I fear his reasoning was wholly selfish and he had no intention of ever coming back to us. But thank you for suggesting that."

"People do extraordinary things — things that would normally be considered out of character, when they become desperate. They forget where their real loyalties lie until it's too late. They may suffer regret, but by then it's too late to go back."

If I don't get some food soon, it'll be too late.

"Be patient, Crow."

Hetty frowned, "I beg your pardon?"

Awkward.

"I can see that the bird is getting restless. I suspect he needs sustenance. It must be difficult for the wildlife at the moment."

"I'll go and see what I can find for him in the kitchen."

Not a moment too soon.

Hetty glanced up at Crow where he was perched on the edge of the bookshelf and smiled at him, "I don't know how I shall break it to Mrs Ashby though! I'll have to tell her in case she comes across him by accident and has a seizure. I'll be back in a while," and she went out.

There was a moment's silence when neither man nor jackdaw said anything.

She's nice — for a human.

"Yes. We were fortunate — finding her so easily. If it hadn't been for her wastrel father it might have been a different story altogether, they wouldn't have moved to the farm. Fate has played a large part in our good fortune."

Crow hopped down to a lower shelf and then fluttered back to the chair, he shook out his wings and settled.

I'd have found her — eventually. That crest is easy to spot from the air.

"Perhaps, but time is of the essence. Eirwen is in dire need. We may only get this one chance."

Then you should tell her —

"I don't want to alarm her. It's not exactly an everyday dilemma. She must come to terms with the truth first and then she may be able to accept the rest."

Do you think she'll bring bacon rinds?

* * *

In the kitchen Hetty found quite a commotion. The room seemed crowded with people: Sam and Jacob had come in from the stables to warm themselves, Agatha was patiently and laboriously scrubbing out a burnt pan with sand and Finn was stacking logs in the hearth. Mrs Ashby was sitting at the table in a misty cloud of grey feathers, plucking a dozen wood pigeons.

She looked up at Hetty, "Make yourself useful and pass me the cleaver please."

Hetty found the lethal looking hatchet and handed it to the cook.

"Miss Eirwen?"

"Still sleeping. Mrs Waverley is with her."

"Is she indeed," said Mrs Ashby, pulling on some feathers rather vigorously.

"I was wondering — Mrs Ashby, if there were any leftover bacon rinds?"

Finn made a disapproving sound from inside the inglenook, "Damned jackdaw's back, is it? Don't encourage it."

"He was cold outside and needs some food. I can't let him just die in the snow."

Mrs Ashby nodded towards the larder, "I don't approve of wild beasts in the house but neither do I approve of them dying needlessly. Some sunflower seeds in the spice cupboard and suet in the big bowl in the dairy, if you mix it together it'll keep him going. I gave the last of the rinds to the hens." She tossed a naked pigeon into the pot beside her, "Just don't let him roam the house, he'll ruin the rugs and the furniture."

"You really don't mind?"

"The master seems to like the beast — who am I to argue?"

Finn cast Hetty a speaking glance and shook his head.

Before Mrs Ashby could change her mind, Hetty fetched the seeds and suet, softened the fat over the fire and then quickly mixed some together and found an old cracked dish to put it in. Sam and Jacob chatted amiably in the background about the jobs they had to do that day.

"Aggie, fetch me the jarred cherries and the mace and two onions. And the nutmeg. Oh, and a nice big slice of bacon off the flitch," ordered Mrs Ashby.

"What are you making?" asked Hetty.

"I'm just going to fry the pigeons in butter and spices, wrap them in the bacon and bake them and then serve them with the cherries and balls of force-meat."

"That sounds delicious. It's making my mouth water. I'd better take this to the jackdaw before he gets any crosser. He seems to be quite annoyed."

Finn threw a large log onto the pile, "He's always annoyed."

"Does he come to the house often?"

"Too often."

"I think I may have come across him before at Friday's Acre. I gave him some bacon rinds."

"They're pests, jackdaws."

Knowing that she wouldn't win an argument with him, Hetty patted him on his shoulder as she passed, "It's just while the weather is bad, Finn. I won't make him too welcome, and the minute the sun comes out, he can go back out."

"Good luck with that," said Finn grimly.

Hetty took the bowl of suet and seeds and an old rag to the study where Torquhil was still entertaining Crow.

She spread the rag out on a small table near the window and put the bowl on it, "There you are. Despite our fears, Mrs

Ashby has provided you with some suet and sunflower seeds. I hope you like it."

Seeds! Where are the bacon rinds?

"He'll be very grateful for that. A nice bit of suet will fatten him up and keep out the cold."

It sounds like you're going to eat me. No meat on these bones.

"Mrs Ashby was surprisingly amenable. She seemed to think that as you were fond of the jackdaw that it would be all right."

See? Jackdaw. It's only you doesn't know the difference, Master.

"I wouldn't say I was fond of him precisely, but I'm used to him. But I suppose one can get used to anything."

Crow clacked his beak.

Hetty smiled, "It's so funny the way he seems to react to what we say!"

The jackdaw shook his head and hopped down to the table and sidled up to the bowl. He pecked unenthusiastically at the seeds.

Food fit for wood pigeons.

"There, he seems very pleased with that," said Hetty happily.

I thought that the red crest meant she was like her grandmother! The old lady could hear me.

Hetty tiptoed past the bird, "I think I shall go back upstairs to Eirwen now."

"I just have a few things to do here, and I shall join you in a while," said Torquhil, quelling Crow with a frown.

* * *

Friday passed slowly, and Hetty was exhausted by the end of the day, but when she thought back to what she'd achieved, it didn't add up to much; it seemed as though she'd just run around all day, fetching and carrying, talking to herself and fretting while she sat with Eirwen. She'd learnt, to her dismay, that her grandfather thought her to be a healer with some sort of magical ability; she'd found that the strange young girl she was supposed to care for was cursed with a condition that nobody understood, and it was slowly removing her from this world and nobody could find a cure; she'd allowed a jackdaw into the house, and apart from that she'd achieved very little of any worth.

Mrs Waverley had finally gone to bed having talked ceaselessly for almost two hours and Hetty was sitting before the fire in the Chinese Bedchamber watching the flames in a stupor and listening to the sound of Eirwen's barely perceptible breathing.

She was wondering what she wasn't hearing and why it was so important.

Her grandfather's words had unsettled her because he had always been, since the collapse of their family, the one person she could rely upon; he never changed, he was always there, and he always told her the truth even if it was unpalatable.

Torquhil and Mrs Waverley had helped her prepare for the night ahead, getting Eirwen settled and trying to cover every possibility. Torquhil reminded her that he was only just down the corridor and was a very light sleeper. Hetty's bedchamber was joined by a small closet room, to the Chinese Bedchamber and she would keep both doors open so that she could hear if there were any changes in Eirwen's condition.

As it was, the night was uneventful and although she had trouble getting to sleep and woke a few times thinking she heard something strange, Eirwen slept right through until dawn.

At half past five in the morning Hetty, still in her nightgown, pulled a shawl around her shoulders and tiptoed barefoot into the other room. She had a long look at Eirwen and then knelt down at the hearth to stoke the dwindling fire. It didn't take long to encourage some flames and soon it was giving out some welcome heat again. She pulled her nightgown down over her knees and tucked it around her toes and just enjoyed the warmth for a moment.

The door opened behind her, and she turned expecting to see Agatha, but it was Torquhil, in a floor length coat of burgundy satin with gold frogging.

"Good morning, Hetty. You didn't call me in the night, so I assume there were no alarums?"

She saw him take in her state of undress and blushed, "No, it was peaceful and I'm sorry to still be in my nightgown, but I wanted to tend the fire as soon as possible and check on Eirwen." She thought he looked tired, with dark shadows under his eyes and a grey pallor to his face. "I can see you didn't sleep well."

He made a slight shrug, "I'm not a good sleeper even at the best of times." He went to his sister's side and stood looking down at her, "If we knew what to expect, it would help, but when there's no name for the sickness, and no prognosis, one can only guess and prepare for the worst. There's no point in asking the local apothecary or doctor — they would know even less than the medical men in London. We have no choice but to wait and hope."

Hetty was feeling a little anxious that all his hopes were resting on her and that she was bound to disappoint him.

The expressions crossing her face were, unbeknownst to her, very revealing.

"When she was little, Eirwen used to sit before the fire like that, her feet tucked up in her nightgown."

Feeling even more self-conscious, Hetty didn't know whether to stay there or to stand up with as much dignity as she could muster and leave the room. She was fully aware that in normal circumstances she shouldn't be in the same room as a man, especially as she was wearing only her nightclothes, but these were trying conditions and there must be some allowances made for such an odd situation. Anyway, she thought, there was no one there to see, so it hardly mattered. She just wished she didn't blush so readily — it made her feel even more embarrassed.

As though reading her thoughts, Torquhil moved away towards the door, "I shall go and find Agatha and you can put on some nice respectable clothes."

Hetty let out a little gasp, "Oh, that's too bad of you — there was no need to draw attention to my predicament!"

He smiled as he pulled the door open, "I'm afraid I have never learnt the finer points of etiquette. You'll have to teach me." And he went out leaving Hetty staring after him in astonishment.

Agatha arrived not long afterwards, in a state of disarray because she'd overslept and Hetty had to reassure that all was well.

Once she'd quickly dressed and Agatha had helped her with her hair, Hetty and her helpful companion set about washing their patient, brushing and braiding her hair and tidying the pillows and bedclothes. By the time Mrs Waverley arrived everything was looking shipshape, and Hetty was able to send her downstairs for her first cup of tea of the day.

"I've never known anyone drink as much tea as that woman," said Agatha with enormous respect.

The day drifted by in similar vein: bedside vigils, sudden flurries of activity, meals taken in a hurry and fleeting encounters with the others. And the snow continued to fall.

* * *

Then, at just gone six o'clock the following morning, Hetty was awoken by a sound; she couldn't place it for a second and then she was scrambling out of bed and rushing into the Chinese Bedchamber.

There she found Eirwen standing on her bed, emitting a high-pitched wailing so piercing that it rattled the windowpanes.

Eight

Hetty clapped her hands over her ears to block out the dreadful keening noise that gave her an instant headache. For a moment she didn't know what to do and stood as though nailed to the cold wooden boards and then she suddenly sprang towards the bed and grabbed Eirwen's arms, which were held stiffly down by her sides. The screaming grew even louder. Starting to panic, Hetty just followed her instincts, clambering up onto the bed beside her and putting her arms around the girl; she held her tightly, binding her arms, in just the same way she would have held a stressed hen. And she talked to her, in a firm but comforting voice.

"Eirwen, it's Hetty and I'm just going to hold you until you feel a little calmer. I want you to listen to me and try to understand — no one is going to hurt you, you're perfectly safe. You're at Galdre Knap and you're going to be all right, I promise. Torquhil wouldn't let anything bad happen to you, you're going to be all right," and she just kept repeating the words like an incantation, even when she heard the door slam open and with relief heard Torquhil say something that she didn't quite catch because of the deafening wailing.

She could feel the fragile body in her arms, feel the ridges of her ribs and the sharp edges of her shoulder blades, it was like holding the skeleton of a bird and she was afraid she might just snap into tiny chalky pieces.

Then she could feel Torquhil take the weight of her, and she was able to let go and watch as the screaming girl was lifted down and cradled gently on his lap as he sat on the edge of the bed.

Hetty's legs suddenly began to quiver uncontrollably and gave way and she slid down and sat beside him. He glanced at her over his sister's head as the terrible sound continued and mouthed something to her, "Are you all right?"

She nodded and tried to smile, but it went a bit wobbly, and she gave up.

Torquhil reached out his free hand and took hers in his and held it.

The wailing stopped just as though it had been cut with a knife.

Hetty gasped and looked up at her companion, startled. He was staring down at his sister's face, so close to his. Her eyes were open, and she seemed to be focused on him.

"Eirwen? Can you hear me?"

She didn't respond but the silence made Hetty breathe a sigh of relief, her ears were ringing, and she had stabbing pains behind her eyes.

She looked down at their hands, which were still joined together, and thought, rather illogically, that not even Mr Scroggs had ever held her hand.

Torquhil gave her hand a briskly impersonal squeeze and released it.

She looked anxiously at Eirwen, but the girl made no sound.

"Has she ever done that before?" asked Hetty softly, afraid she might spark more screaming.

"Never. In the beginning she would weep, for no apparent reason — but silently and sometimes she'd hit her head with her hands but nothing like this. I'm sorry you were alone with her. I came as soon as I heard her."

"Yes, I know. I couldn't think what to do, so I just hugged her tightly so that hopefully she'd know she wasn't alone."

"You did the right thing."

"But — why did she suddenly *stop* screaming?"

"That I don't know but it seemed to be — when we touched."

"But how can that be? Oh, I don't understand anything about this."

"Nobody does — yet, but I think this shows that somewhere inside there are still some remnants of my sister left unchanged. I feel that any reaction, however violent and strange, must be better than nothing."

Hetty, whose fingers were still tingling as though she'd been stung by nettles, said nothing. The sensation was so pronounced that when she looked at them, she quite expected to see glittering sparks flying up into the air and swirling in spirals. She was almost disappointed to find they looked just the same as always. She shook her head; she was starting to sound quite mad.

"Hetty?"

"It's nothing. I was just wondering exactly what she could sense. Grandpapa said — no, it's not true, it can't be — I — I can't seem to think rationally at the moment!"

"What did your grandfather say?" asked Torquhil.

"Oh, I'm afraid he's getting old and losing his faculties — it was nothing of importance."

"But even though you believe it to be nonsense, there may be a chance that it may be important. Mr Swift is a man of sound sense. I think we should consider everything, however hare-brained."

She couldn't look him in the eye, knowing that the words spoken out loud would probably make him laugh at her.

"I think he's become a little muddled. He told me that my grandmother, Anne, was a healer — and that I have inherited her gift."

"There's nothing odd in that," said Torquhil mildly.

Hetty took a deep breath, "He said I would hear voices and — feel tingling in my fingertips."

"And have you?"

She paused and chewed the inside of her cheek anxiously, "I haven't heard voices, thankfully, but when — we first met and shook hands, I felt a strange tingling in my fingers for the first time and again when I was looking at the torquetum with you and then — just now when you held my hand. It sounds quite insane but it's like being stung by nettles — it doesn't make sense. I like things to make sense."

Torquhil didn't respond immediately, he gazed down at his sister's face; she'd closed her eyes and seemed to be asleep again.

"Anne Swift was renowned for her skills. Even I had heard of her. But you sound almost as though you'd like to reject those gifts."

"No, that's not true. I loved learning about herbal remedies from her and I'm beginning to understand that I cannot escape the inevitable — like my father hoped he could. He only managed to avoid the fate he thought was stalking him by staying true to his basest instincts — he became a drunkard, a gambler and a thief, which, of course, proved to be a very different and final kind of fate. But he was not the type of man who could ever consider the prospect of becoming some sort of mage! It would not have sat well with his image of himself. He was filled with his own importance and thought that he was owed respect and an easy life just because of who he was. But such a sudden life-changing revelation is not exactly an easy thing to come to grips with when just a fortnight ago I was happily feeding my hens and picking chickweed and shelling hazelnuts for our supper without any thought of this terrible — *legacy* bearing down upon me. I now have a little more sympathy for his plight."

"What if everything was preordained? Everything in the past was leading to this, and everything that awaits you in the future will be altered by what you choose to do now. Perhaps coming to Galdre Knap wasn't merely an accident or chance. Perhaps it was always destined that the skills you've inherited would save Eirwen."

Hetty felt her mouth go dry and she swallowed nervously; she didn't like the sound of what he was intimating. She didn't like the idea of her life being controlled by someone or something unknown.

"But that would suggest you knew all about me, about my grandmother — *before* we met — that you asked us to come to live here because you believed I'd inherited Grandmama's healing powers."

"Would that make a difference? What does it matter what I knew? Surely it only matters that you can be part of the solution — part of her recovery? Look at her. She's imprisoned and fading away and I cannot reach her. I've tried everything. I've used every resource I have and when I had begun to believe there was no hope, I heard about your grandmother, but it was already too late. She'd passed away and your father too — there was only you left with the gift. But then I discovered you'd been kept in the dark about your healing powers and I didn't want to alarm you. We needed you."

Hetty closed her eyes for a moment to try to regain her balance, "I understand, and I don't blame you for doing everything in your power to cure her, but I should have been told the truth."

He gently stroked a wisp of silver hair from Eirwen's forehead and dropped a light kiss onto her smooth translucent skin, "But, if I'd told you, would you have come to Galdre Knap, or would you have continued to turn a blind eye to the gift your grandmother knew you possessed and tried to prepare you for? Coming here has precipitated your understanding and means that you can now make good use of those skills."

"But, you see, I know it's silly, but I feel as though I've been hoodwinked into it. I can see that Eirwen needs help, but I'm afraid that you're mistaken about me and will find that I don't have Grandmama's abilities and then all this has just been a pointless venture and Eirwen will be no nearer a cure. What if you're wasting your time with me?"

Torquhil gave her a considering look, "I want you to go and find Mrs Waverley and ask her to sit with Eirwen because I have something I want to show you."

He gently lifted his sister up and put her back into bed, pulling the counterpane up and tucking it in around her frail body.

Hetty stood uncertainly by the bed.

"Go. I'll stay here until you return with the nursemaid."

Hetty, surprised by the crisp authority in his usually quiet voice, turned and left the room. She ran downstairs and found Mrs Waverley and her grandfather in the library chatting amiably about the weather.

Her grandfather pointed to the window, "Did you notice, Hetty? The snow stopped falling a short while ago — just like that. When the screaming ceased so did the snow."

* * *

Accompanied by an infuriatingly unhurried Mrs Waverley, Hetty was desperate to run back upstairs to the Chinese Bedchamber to discuss the snow with Torquhil, but forced herself to walk sedately beside the nursemaid, who seemed entirely unaware of Hetty's need for haste.

They found Torquhil adding more logs to the fire, and he looked up when they entered the room, nodded at Mrs Waverley and seeing the expression on Hetty's face, stopped tending the fire and steered her firmly out into the corridor.

"What is it? You look like you're fit to burst."

"The snow! Grandpapa said it stopped snowing as soon as Eirwen stopped screaming." She looked up at him expectantly, "What can that *mean*?"

Torquhil shook his head, and in the dim light, Hetty thought his eyes were almost black. "It's a mystery to me," he said, "Why don't you go and get dressed and I'll change out of my night-clothes."

A short while later she met him at the top of the stairs; he was wearing a coat of plain black, black breeches and top boots — she'd never seen him look so restrained and would have remarked upon it, but he didn't give her a chance, leading her downstairs and to the study without another word.

Crow was asleep with his head tucked under his wing.

"Wake up, Crow! You have work to do," said Torquhil, closing the door behind Hetty.

This had better be important.

Hetty stood uncertainly in the middle of the room.

"It's stopped snowing," said Torquhil.

The jackdaw stuck his head out and folded his wing back into place.

I'm staying inside until it thaws.

"You can do what you like but I want to conduct an experiment and I need your help."

Are bacon rinds a part of it?

Torquhil smiled, "Possibly, if all goes according to plan."

That doesn't sound very promising.

Hetty was watching Torquhil talk to himself and wondered if it wasn't too late to grab her grandfather and run back to Friday's Acre and safety.

"Whatever happens, a little patience is required. And some restraint because I don't want to frighten Miss Swift."

"Torquhil? I don't wish to seem rude but — your talking to yourself is already frightening me."

"I apologise but it's hard to explain and I'm not convinced that this demonstration will help."

Hetty was watching his face and saw something there that made her check her fear and pay careful attention.

"A demonstration?"

"Allow me to just say a few words to explain first. This will be challenging for you, but I need you to trust me and I'm not sure that I've given you sufficient reason to have faith in me yet — "

"Your love for Eirwen is testament enough," said Hetty gravely.

He paused for a moment, "Then we shall proceed. Crow, just act as you usually would but without the habitual trickery."

Crow ducked his head and shivered his feathers.

You're asking a jackdaw not to be a jackdaw.

"Only for a very short while. It's important."

Oh, go on then but be quick, I'm hungry.

Torquhil turned back to a very confused-looking Hetty and beckoned her to come closer. She joined him near where Crow was sitting on the back of the ornate wooden chair. He held out his hand to her and after a brief hesitation and a speculative look, she put her hand into his.

Immediately she felt the tingling sensation in her fingers and tried to remove her hand from his grasp, but he held onto her firmly.

He kept looking into her eyes, holding her attention, "Lonán? Are you crow or jackdaw?"

Jackdaw!

Hetty gasped, her eyes opened wide, and she snatched her hand away from Torquhil's and stepped away.

Ah, I see what you did there. Cunning.

Torquhil waited silently, watching her intently.

Although the tingling was slowly fading, Hetty's heart was thundering in her ribcage as though trying to break free. The jackdaw had its head tilted to one side and was observing her with beady interest.

She closed her eyes to block everything out and tried to gather her fractured thoughts. She remembered her grandmother showing her how to make elderberry syrup when she had a bad cold and could hear the sound of her soothing voice, itself a balm, telling her that in order to fully understand what Nature had to offer, one had to use all your senses.

Hetty sighed and opened her eyes.

She held out her hand to him.

Their hands touched and the tingling began again.

"Just trust me," murmured Torquhil.

Never trust a man not bearing bacon rinds.

The hand in Torquhil's flinched but remained resolutely in his.

"You can hear him?"

She nodded, her face even paler than usual.

"I can only apologise again for that — but it's a necessary evil."

Thank you.

Hetty smiled a trifle wanly, "He's funny."

"Oh, please don't encourage him. An appreciative audience will just make him even more insufferable."

Hetty glanced down at their joined hands, "But why does it work like this? Is it only when we are connected?"

"I think that until you begin to believe in your own abilities you need some sort of interceding link with Crow."

"What if he and I were linked by touch?"

Crow let out a sharp protest of alarm.

"Yes, that might work. Crow come here."

A fluttering of feathers and a reluctant Crow landed on Torquhil's outstretched arm.

Hetty took a deep breath and reached out to the bird and touched her fingers lightly to his grey head.

Scratch in-between my shoulders. Hard spot to reach.

"Oh, goodness gracious!" whispered Hetty, wide-eyed. "I can *hear* him."

"I'm not sure if that's a good or a bad thing, but at least it shows you that things are not always how they seem. I'm hoping that it'll be like a door opening and once you see through into the other world, you'll be able to follow."

"The — *other world?* What does that mean?"

"It's *this* world, but at an angle — a little skewed, and it runs side by side with our world, border to border, like a wood beside a river. The river sometimes floods the wood, the trees reflect onto the river's surface, their roots take the water, the river takes the shade. They overlap but are separate and they weave in and out of each other's lives, feeding each other and enriching each other. It's nothing to be scared about, but one must treat it with respect, or it can become overbearing and will try to frighten you over to its side."

"I thought you said it wasn't scary! That sounds absolutely terrifying!"

"Don't worry, I won't allow anything untoward to happen to you."

Hetty frowned, "Has this got something to do with what happened to Eirwen? Has she become in some way lost in this?"

So, she is *like her grandmother.*

The gentle fingers stopped stroking his head and he pushed up to find their soothing touch again.

"Like my grandmother? What does he mean?"

"He means that your grandmother was in tune with the other world or The Borderland as she called it, and even came to understand it a little. She was able to learn from it without becoming lost in it or tainted by it. It can easily blight a person if they're not strong enough to withstand its intoxicating influence. She listened and learnt from what she heard and used it for the benefit of others. I don't know whether it was this tangent world that impaired Eirwen or whether it was something already inside her that just found its way out. I think Anne could have made a difference and I believe that her skills are, even now, entwined with yours and that makes them even more powerful. You just have to trust in them."

"It's difficult to trust in something you can't see."

"I can only assure you that it's true and ask you to believe me."

"Yes, that's as maybe! But although I can see you quite clearly standing here in front of me, how am I to know if what I see is genuine or if you're trying to bamboozle me or are concealing something from me? I see how you are with Eirwen, and I believe the love you feel for her is sincere, but how will I ever know for certain that you won't use deception to make me do what you want?"

"The bond you still have with your grandmother is powerful — those instincts you share will inform you."

Hetty knew that they already had, but she felt she should not give in without a fight. Those same instincts told her that although Torquhil Guivre was an unusual man, he had a good heart. Her grandmother had taught her to look at the outside of an acorn or an apple and to be able to see if they were rotten inside. She could tell, when she touched his hand and felt the strange sensation in her fingers, that he was trustworthy. Of course, she didn't know if he would remain so. Things change, people change. But she would make sure that she was prepared for any eventuality. She did not like to be caught unawares.

"I know you're right and I can see that despite appearances that your heart is good and Grandmama insisted that one's heart was the most important thing of all. And I can hear Crow, so I know there's truth in your talk of — other worlds or — borderlands and I remember everything Grandmama said to me."

Crow suddenly took off, flew a tight circle around the room and with skilled manoeuvring of his sharp wings and claws, alighted upon Hetty's shoulder without hurting her.

So, what about those bacon rinds then?

* * *

Hetty went to find her grandfather and having searched the house, eventually tracked him to the kitchen, where he was sitting comfortably beside the fire across from Finn, enjoying a pipe of tobacco and chatting about the problems of clearing snow.

"It's ultimately pointless work," Finn was saying, "Snow'll thaw soon. Always does. Futile to waste your time shovelling it from one place to another just to watch it all melt the next day. Might as well shovel air."

"But it means you can't get to the stables with ease."

"So much the better," replied Finn incorrigibly.

Mrs Ashby glanced up from peeling onions, her eyes watering, "All morning. They've been at it, all morning. Wrangling."

"Debating. Discussing."

"Arguin'."

Hetty could see that they were set for the afternoon and were enjoying themselves so decided to wait until a more convenient time to talk to her grandfather.

The back door opened and Sam, the young stable lad came bustling in, kicking snow across the floor and letting in an icy blast that made Mrs Ashby bellow at him whilst blowing her nose furiously.

"Honestly, anyone'd think you lived in a barn!"

"I *do*, Mrs Ashby!" said Sam with a cheeky grin. He received a disapproving frown for his troubles, and he showed Hetty what he had tucked under his arm. "Got yer cat, Miss! He was outside, stuck in deep snow an' howlin' like the very Devil!"

Hetty crossed the kitchen, and her yard cat threw himself gratefully into her familiar and welcoming arms, "Cat! I've missed you. Thank you, Sam, I'll keep him indoors I think while the weather's like this. He never was very happy getting his paws wet — a fair weather yard cat. I've seen several mice around the house, so he'll hopefully be able to get rid of them — he's a good mouser. He still hasn't got a proper name though."

"Even a cat deserves a name," said Sam.

"He's not the most amiable of creatures," admitted Hetty.

"He can be a bit prickly at times."

"Call him Thistle," said Agatha coming in from the scullery, with a pail of water.

Hetty turned to her, "Aggie, that's perfect! How clever you are!"

Agatha shrugged, smiling, "Thistles are right prickly, Miss."

"Yes, indeed. Right, Thistle, we shall have to find you a suitable bed although I doubt you'll take any notice of it. He always slept on the windowsill in the sunshine or Grandpapa's chair by the fire. He doesn't think much of rules."

"He's a fine-looking cat," said Finn.

"Just a plain old tabby cat, I'm afraid, with dreadfully poor manners," laughed Hetty.

"Sounds like Mrs Waverley," muttered Mrs Ashby under her breath.

Hetty stole a piece of pigeon from the pot beside the fire and found an old plate and put it down in the scullery for the cat. He seemed delighted with the rich treat and the air was soon reverberating with his contented purring.

"It's fortunate that Mrs Waverley is here as she can help with the nursing. I must say that she seems very willing," said Hetty quietly.

Mrs Ashby placed the peeled onion on the chopping board, lifted her knife and swiped it in two with one swift movement of the blade.

"Off with 'er head," said Agatha, tipping the water into the sink.

Hetty smothered a laugh and wondered if she could prise her grandfather away from this cosy little scene so that she could talk to him about what had just happened with Crow and Torquhil, but he seemed so content she couldn't bring herself to do it. She'd go to his bedchamber later and talk with him then. She wanted to share with him the extraordinary revelation that she could hear a jackdaw's thoughts, that Eirwen seemed to have something to do with the snowstorm and her beloved grandmother had somehow been involved with a mysterious "Borderland". Her forbears may have been willing to believe that the country was teeming with mythical monsters, hobgoblins and other evil spirits but she was an eighteenth-century woman and was not so easily gulled. It sounded like a preposterous faerie tale and although she had always believed in the magical things Anne Swift had told her, she did feel as though this was stretching her credulity to its limits, but there was no denying what she'd heard with her own ears. That was surely proof enough. That and Eirwen's strange behaviour, the freakishly relentless snow and a certain look in Torquhil's dark eyes, which had convinced her that she was not being hoodwinked.

Thistle wandered in from the scullery and wound himself around her skirts making satisfied noises and Hetty looked around her, at the motley group of people and the warm and welcoming kitchen and she smiled.

Nine

"When did you first find out that Grandmama was — peculiar?"

Roland Swift laughed, "Hetty, my love, your grandmother was not *peculiar* — she was exceptional in every way, and I first realised that the moment I set eyes upon her."

"Did it not frighten you when you realised?"

"Not in the slightest."

"Did she talk about me — about me being like her?"

"Frequently, but quietly and with such hope."

"When she spoke about hearing things, was she ever more specific?"

Her grandfather raised his shoulders in an apologetic shrug, "She did mention it. She was amused at the thought because you already talked to the chickens as though they were people! She was absolutely sure you could cope with the knowledge when you eventually found out and was positive that only good would come of it. She knew in her heart that you would find a way to use your gifts for others and said that although your father was never able to come to terms with what he learnt, she had unshakeable faith in *you*."

"That's quite a responsibility to bear. She might have given me a clue that I'd be able to hear jackdaws and be asked to save Eirwen from — I don't know what! I seem to be the last one to know."

"I think it was for your own protection. She began to wonder, after your father failed to fulfil his potential, if perhaps she'd waited for the right time before telling him then things may have worked out differently, so with you, she bided her time. In the end, she felt it was necessary to begin teaching you in earnest because she became ill and knew her time with you was limited. She didn't want to leave you unprepared. Up until then she'd been gently imbuing you with her knowledge like any grandmother might — passing down recipes and making sure that you knew the fundamentals."

Hetty's eyes shone with tears, "I wish she'd *told* me!" She was pacing the Indian Bedchamber as though penned in by the four walls, and her grandfather had little choice but to watch her try to work things out in her own mind and make sense of them in the best way she could.

"You were too young, and she'd learnt a salutary lesson with your father. You cannot blame her for being hesitant, she did her best for you, knowing what was on the horizon."

"Did she know about *this* — about Torquhil and Eirwen and Galdre Knap?"

"Not in so many words, but she knew that there was something coming — something that would change everything, and she knew that you would be required in some way. She told me that you would be the lynchpin — the person who held everything together — that it would be the goodness in your heart and your love that would make the difference."

Hetty stopped her fretful movements to glower at him, "Well, if I wasn't terrified before I certainly am now! I feel like a fish on a hook. I have absolutely no idea how to proceed."

"I believe that you must just have faith in everything that Grandmama taught you and above all, in yourself. You will know when something isn't right. She said when the time arises, you will know what to do."

"You said *when* the time arises — not *if*. So, am I to suppose from those doom-laden words that there's no way for me to elude my fate?"

"Yes. Of course there is. You can leave Galdre Knap and Eirwen behind and we can return to our old life at Friday's Acre. No one would think badly of you, and no one would try to stop you. You are not a prisoner here."

"Oh, *Grandpapa!*" cried Hetty, throwing herself onto his bed and burying her face in her arms and making muffled and furious noises into the counterpane.

"All you need to do now is kick your heels and you'd be just as you were when you were four years old," he chuckled.

More vexed sounds followed, and he just stayed comfortably in his chair and waited for the outburst to subside. He knew that Hetty had to quickly come to terms with her part in what was coming and although he felt desperately sorry and anxious for her, he realised that she would have to find the strength within herself in order to cope.

"But what if I let everyone down?" she wailed, "What if this is all a terrible mistake and we lose Eirwen because of me? What if — "

"What if you stop feeling sorry for yourself and start to think like your grandmother? What would *she* have done? Do you think she'd have just sat around moping?"

Hetty rolled over, angrily kicking her voluminous skirts out of the way, "Well, Grandmama was *perfect!* How can I compete with that?"

"She was far from perfect, and no one is asking you to compete, you foolish child! You have to find a way to use what she taught you and perhaps with Torquhil's help and knowledge together you can unravel this mystery."

She sat up and, sensing disorder, put a hand up to her hair and found it to be coming down in its usual unruly fashion, so she removed all the pins and allowed the lively copper curls to tumble over her shoulders.

Her grandfather inwardly sighed; she reminded him so strongly of Anne that it was like a physical pain to watch her sometimes. Even her movements held echoes of his wife: a hand gesture, the tilt of her head when she was listening intently, the quick smile and volatile temper that often seemed to go alongside the vibrant hair, but most of all, the way that when she loved, she loved with all her heart and soul, and while that reassured him, it also made him afraid for her.

Hetty slid off the bed and got to her feet, bashing the creases out of her skirts with an impatient hand, "I shall go and take over from Mrs Waverley. She must be needing yet another cup of tea by now." She walked to the door then stopped and returned to her grandfather and bent to kiss his papery cheek, "I'm sorry. I'm being selfish and thoughtless. It's a lot to take in all at once. One minute you're chasing an errant pig through the orchard and the next you're fighting unseen forces of evil. It's quite hard to comprehend. But I know you're right and I will try to make you and Grandmama proud."

He caught her hand and squeezed it, "You've already done that, Hetty. We couldn't be any prouder of you."

Hetty kissed him again, "You're going to say that she's watching over me, aren't you!"

He smiled, "I know she is."

* * *

Mrs Waverley and Agatha were standing beside Eirwen's bed, debating whether or not to call Hetty, so when she walked in, they were both very relieved to see her.

"Is anything wrong?" she asked.

Agatha rolled her eyes, "We was just wonderin' if the sounds she's been makin' are normal. Not that *anything* she does is normal."

"Oh? What sounds?"

Agatha looked at Mrs Waverley for permission and then demonstrated a high-pitched wailing sound. "Sort of like that, Miss but I can't quite get it as high as she does!"

"Did she wake?"

Agatha shook her head, "No, her eyes were closed, and she didn't move at all — did she, Mrs Waverley? She just made that scary noise." She eyed Hetty, "D'you want me to put your hair up for you?"

Hetty had forgotten the state of her hair, "No, thank you Aggie, I'll do something with it in a minute. Has Eirwen had anything to drink today?"

On finding that Eirwen hadn't been persuaded to take any water or cordial, Hetty decided that should be their next most urgent task and she and her companions set about trying to accomplish it, which they did after a good deal of tribulation. The triumph they felt after managing to get her to take a few dribbles of water was out of all proportion to the actual achievement, but Agatha was able to go off to help Mrs Ashby make the supper with a wide smile on her face and Mrs Waverley, declaring that she was a little weary, went off to put her feet up for a while. Hetty fetched a book from her room and settled down to read by the fire, wrapped in her grandmother's old shawl.

Torquhil arrived about an hour later to find Hetty asleep in her chair, her face half hidden in a tangle of bright hair; what he could see of that face was flushed pink from the heat of the fire, her book open on her lap.

He just stood and stared down at her for a long moment before turning away to look at his sister.

She was staring at him from unblinking eyes.

"Hail, little sister. You're awake." He approached the bed and reaching out, touched her cold hand.

As he watched her, her gaze slid towards the sleeping girl.

"Do you want to see Hetty?"

Hearing her name through her dream of being chased by a huge flock of talking chickens, Hetty stirred and suddenly sat up. "Oh no! Is she all right? I must have dozed off. I'm so sorry!"

He held out his hand to her and she jumped up, her book falling unheeded to the floor, and went to his side. They stood together and watched as Eirwen's gaze moved from one to the other and Hetty was reminded of a newborn baby trying to work out what it was seeing from innocent milky eyes.

Eirwen's eyes were a transparent blue, like a raindrop frozen on a windowpane, but gave the impression of being sightless although she seemed able to focus on their faces. The cold light from the window near the bed filled the room with an ethereal luminosity and cast its unearthly glow across the concave planes of her face. It was as though she were made from ephemera and might just disappear like mist, drifting away through the gaps in the windows to become one with the frosted air outside.

Hetty wanted to hold onto her and keep her anchored in their earthy, real world.

"We mustn't let her go," she whispered almost to herself.

"We won't. Somehow, we'll keep her safe," and he reached down for her hand and took it in his.

There was a sudden sharp sound, like the hiss of metal scraping ice. Hetty flinched and felt Torquhil's grip tighten on her fingers, not allowing her to pull away.

They looked to the girl lying so helplessly in the bed.

Her pale lips were open and moving. Her wide-apart eyes darting from side to side. A sibilant sound came from between her small, childish teeth, which were tightly clenched together.

"Eirwen?" said her brother leaning in closer.

Another strange sound like a hard indrawn breath.

"*Be….ware….*"

Hetty gasped and pressed her hand to her mouth.

"*Galdre….beware….*"

Eirwen's wasted frame began to tremble as though shaken by unseen hands.

Hetty released her hand from Torquhil's and threw her arms around Eirwen and just as suddenly the girl became motionless again, barely breathing and her eyes closed once more.

"Torquhil! *Do* something!" cried Hetty.

"There's nothing I can do."

"What did she mean? What should we beware of? Why was she warning us? Why did she say Galdre!"

Torquhil looked down at her, "The house."

"Yes," said Hetty impatiently, "But what did she *mean* by it?"

"Galdre is Old English for — enchantment."

"Yes, yes, it is a very enchanting house! But why should we beware?"

"Enchantment — as in an incantation."

"I don't understand."

"The house was named Galdre after an age-old spell song and Knap merely means crest of a hill."

"But, why?"

"According to legend, the house was accidentally built upon an ancient burial site. A chambered long barrow."

"Surely that is most unusual? To build on a sacred site?"

"You're right, it would normally be considered sacrilege to desecrate a holy site and they're usually avoided. But this one is buried within the hill, and no one knew of its existence until after the house had been planned and the builders were putting in the foundations, but they decided to carry on with the construction, despite the locals warning them. The build was, apparently cursed with accidents from the very start and they found it hard to keep their workers, but eventually it was completed, and no one spoke of it again and two centuries later it had been forgotten and families had lived here, and everything had been peaceful for all those years."

"That's — extraordinary and sounds rather far-fetched. I'm not sure that I believe in such things."

"And yet you have heard a jackdaw's thoughts and have seen how Eirwen is."

Hetty looked down at his sister and drew a deep breath, "Yes, and I have had such a stern lecture from Grandpapa about — about trusting my intuition and trusting *you* — "

"Would you find that so difficult?"

She glanced up at him and noted the shadows in his gaunt face and briefly put a hand on his arm, feeling sudden and extreme sorrow for him and this terrifying situation he found himself in, over which he had no control. He always seemed so calm and composed, as though nothing could disturb his serenity, and although she had seen his eyes alter in response to things that were happening around him, that was the only sign that he might be affected by events. She knew that she was entirely the opposite to him, all raw emotion and unthinking reaction and very little rational thought.

"No, it wouldn't be hard — I already — Well, perhaps trusting *myself* is going to be the hardest task of all because I don't have any reason to think highly of my abilities. But Grandpapa was very blunt about that, so I shall do my best. Even though you're quite unlike anyone I have ever met before, I do feel as though I can trust you, in spite of your more — unconventional qualities."

He smiled his crooked half-smile, "I'm much obliged, Miss Swift, how gratifying. That one's defects should be so readily disregarded!"

"I didn't say they were *defects!* Unconventional can be good too." She peeped up at him from under her lashes and thought that although she'd never met anyone as strange as him that she'd far rather be in his company than many of the ordinary people she knew — like Mr Edwin Scroggs or Mr Randall, the churchwarden. At least she'd never be bored.

He caught her look and raised his dark brows and she looked away, covered in confusion, hoping he couldn't read her thoughts.

"This long barrow," she said, keen to paper over the awkward moment, "Is it accessible or has it been completely buried?"

There, she thought, his eyes had turned obsidian-dark; it was as though even the whites had been stained with ink.

He turned away, "It's buried in the hill beneath the house and securely sealed."

"Oh, that's a shame. I would have liked to have explored it."

"That would be very unwise. Those who were here at the time of the building of the house were resolute that it should remain forever buried deep in the earth and forgotten."

Hetty moved away from him to the window and looked out at the snow-covered garden and distant hills, still barely visible in the overarching greyness.

"Perhaps that's when the trouble started. Perhaps that's where we need to begin our search for the truth about Eirwen's condition. If, as you say, there is something unnatural about Galdre Knap, then might there not possibly be a connection to whatever lies beneath the house?"

"You would probably find only a ransacked tomb and not much else. Most of the long barrows were robbed aeons ago by intrepid thieves who clearly didn't believe in fanciful curses. I fear that this — illness comes from within her."

A flock of fieldfares flew over the house and out towards the fields beyond the village, their steady, solid movements grazing the tranquil landscape and Hetty wondered what Crow would think of them and was sure that he'd have something derogatory to say about their intelligence or lack of it. Her grandmother had told her that the fieldfares came only in winter, and she had always wondered why any creature would want to suffer an English winter when they could be further south where it was warm, and food was plentiful. Anne had explained that birds were as peculiar as some human folk and there was just no accounting for it.

She sighed and turned away from the window, "Well, we shall see, shall we not? I believe Eirwen has somehow fought her way back to us from wherever she is, to warn us and we would be foolish not to heed that warning."

Silence greeted this statement and Hetty bided her time, knowing that there was no point in rushing him.

His eyes met hers and she noticed that some of the darkness in them had abated.

"You could very well be right," he said, "As you are having to learn to trust me, I must also learn to have faith. But as I have been focused solely upon her well-being for years now, to have to hand over some of the responsibility to someone else goes against the grain. The Guivres are a stubborn breed."

"I think I've already noticed that. But you are up against someone with hair the veritable *colour* of stubbornness!" She gestured to her tousled tresses with distaste.

He looked at her, taking in the despised mane, "It's beautiful," he said quietly, "You should wear it like that more often, instead of trying to bind it and tame it."

Hetty knew her cheeks were getting warmer, and she wasn't quite sure if it was from embarrassment or pleasure. Other than her grandparents, no one had ever complimented her hair before, and it gave her a strange feeling in her stomach, like excitement and hunger and fear, all mixed up together, like wild cats in a sack. Her heart beat a little faster and she wondered what on earth was wrong with her.

"Thank you," she murmured rather shakily, "That's kind of you, although I'm now seriously doubting your eyesight *and* your sanity!"

Torquhil continued to look at her for what seemed like an age to Hetty, "Don't make light of it. I meant it. You are beautiful — like the first day of Summer after a cold, wet Spring."

Hetty stared at him, unable to form words. He held her gaze and Hetty thought she heard a faint thrumming sound that slowly became more resonant, making the hairs on her arms stand on end. The sound slowly changed and became a steady rhythmical thudding, and she began to wonder if it was her own heartbeat beating too loudly in her ears and if Torquhil could hear it as well. It was as though the walls were vibrating and she looked around the room in some alarm.

"What is it?" asked Torquhil and she knew he couldn't hear it.

"That sound? Like a loud pulse — a swarm of bees — "

"I don't hear anything different."

Hetty's eyes opened wide, "But the floorboards — they're trembling — you must feel that! I can feel it moving under my feet!"

Torquhil crossed the room and took her by the shoulders, "I cannot feel anything Hetty. Perhaps you're imagining it."

But as he held her the noise subsided and she breathed a sigh of relief, "It's stopped now. The sound — the shaking — it's stopped."

"You're probably just tired and overwrought."

She shrugged herself out of his grasp and stepped away, "I'm not overwrought! I'm perfectly fine and I'm *not* imagining it. It's like the lizards."

That checked him, "Lizards? What do you mean?"

"The silver fastenings on your coat, I'm absolutely certain I saw one move." She observed his face closely, "And I thought I saw something moving in the shadows — "

"Strange things may appear to happen when emotions are under such strain. It can encourage unusual behaviour. Your imagination can sometimes play tricks on you."

"My imagination is not playing tricks on me. I could feel the shaking of the floor and hear the sound just as I could feel your hands on my shoulders. It was real." She could hear her voice rising and tried to calm herself, she didn't want him to think she was becoming hysterical, but she was finding his incredulity hard to bear.

A fortuitous knock on the door heralded the arrival of Agatha bearing a tray with some supper for Eirwen.

"Mrs Ashby's made some of her beef tea. It's got mace and cloves and onions and herbs an' all in it. It smells really good."

"It certainly does," agreed Hetty stiffly, glad of a distraction from the intense conversation with Torquhil. "Shall we try to feed her some now, while it's still warm?"

"I'll give you a hand, Miss."

As they busied themselves around the bed, Hetty noticed with some misgiving, Torquhil's quiet departure from the bedchamber.

"Bit moody, ain't he!" said Agatha, "Mrs Ashby says he's been very different this last week though."

"Having Eirwen here must be quite a trial for him. It's very worrying to see someone you love be so very poorly," said Hetty.

"If you say so, Miss."

Hetty frowned at her, "Aggie, what do you mean — ?"

"Oh, it was Mrs Ashby said the master was — how did she put it — a bit more talkative than usual."

"Did she indeed! And what did she mean by that exactly?" asked Hetty rather indignantly.

"I have no idea, Miss," replied Aggie with a decided smirk.

"Agatha," said Hetty with awful dignity, "That will be enough of that, if you please! Now, let's get on with giving Eirwen some supper before the beef tea gets cold."

Agatha was able to tell Mrs Ashby that Eirwen had taken a little of her precious tea and that Mr Guivre and Miss Swift were in the middle of some sort of quarrel when she'd arrived with the supper.

"What kind of argument?" asked Mrs Ashby under her breath so that Finn didn't hear her gossiping.

Taking her lead, Agatha whispered, "I heard Miss Swift's voice through the door, quite upset she sounded and then they was glarin' a bit and standin' quite close together."

Mrs Ashby pursed her lips and nodded pensively, "Early days, early days," she murmured.

Agatha's eyes widened with barely concealed excitement, "D'you really think — ?"

"Never you mind, Aggie Giffins! It's none of our business!" And the cook returned to stirring some herbs into the onion soup.

Finn, who had been idly eavesdropping from his place by the fire, thought that women were odd creatures, making up imaginary romances, when there were quite clearly some dubious goings-on at Galdre Knap that were far more noteworthy. The way women could be distracted by such nonsensical things, when there were obviously far more serious matters going on right under their noses, had always astonished him. He tapped out the tobacco from his pipe and returned it to its nook in the wall beside the hearth.

"I'm going up to my bed," he announced tersely.

Mrs Ashby and Agatha exchanged a glance and shook their heads.

Ten

Hetty sat with Eirwen for a while before retiring to her adjoining room; she was finding that she was still wide awake even in the early hours of the morning and thought what she was lacking was fresh air and the regular and tiring exercise of looking after the farm and her livestock, which were now well cared for by Sam and Jacob. Being inside the house all day long without her usual journeys back and forth to the orchard, walking to the market or to forage in the fields, or the physical activities of making bread, washing the laundry or churning butter, meant that she wasn't nearly as physically tired as usual — although she knew that her grandfather would say it was probably because she'd had a short nap earlier and taken the edge off her weariness.

Feeling a little chilly she went to her bedchamber to find her shawl, knowing there were a few hours to go before Mrs Waverley would arrive to take over the bedside vigil. Pulling back the hangings on her bed, she saw something on her pillow. Cautiously, she took a closer look, not quite trusting anything that just appeared at Galdre Knap and with Torquhil's words about curses and hidden tombs ringing in her ears, she was even more suspicious.

Whatever it was didn't move, which was encouraging, so she poked it with a nervous finger praying it wasn't a spider and when nothing untoward occurred, she gingerly picked it up and took it to the light of the candle.

In the palm of her hand was a small stone carving of a female figure, who was holding what looked like three apples in her hands. It was clearly ancient and worn smooth by time, but some delicate details were still evident and Hetty felt strangely sure that it was a benign and welcoming object. It felt warm to the touch, and she found that reassuring. Turning it over and over, she examined every part of it but there were no clues as to where it might have come from or what it might be. She put it carefully on the table beside her bed and sat and stared at it for a while, feeling oddly comforted by its presence.

The days passed slowly, and they remained in a period of stasis, as though the weather had frozen everything, inside the house and out. The minutiae of everyday life carried on, with delicious meals and fireside chats, trifling concerns and gentle laughter, the trivial disputes and the gently flourishing friendships. Hetty watched with relief as her grandfather steadily settled himself into the unfamiliar routines of his new home and was finally able to be grateful that they had come to Galdre Knap. She enjoyed hearing Finn griping about everything from the snow to his dwindling tobacco supplies; the sound of Mrs Ashby banging pots and ordering Aggie about; the aromas that flooded the house, of herbs and spices and roasting parsnips; Sam and Jacob's boisterous visits, their loud cheery voices nudging their way along the dark corridors and brightening the gloom; Mrs Waverley's steady, if somewhat humourless, support; the newly-named Thistle's heartening attentions and trouncing of the house's persistent rodent population, and then there was Torquhil — although, when she came to think of him, she wasn't quite sure what it was that made her look forward to seeing him. She found that when he entered the room, in that quiet way he had, that her spirits lifted and she thought it rather odd, as he was, on the whole, a sombre presence and not much inclined to frivolity or laughter. Of course, she could hardly blame him, with his poor sister lying in her bed; it was a painful burden to bear but he cared for her with obvious affection and without complaint.

It seemed to Hetty that they had made some small progress with Eirwen, managing between them to keep her health from declining any further. She hadn't shown any more signs of life since the day of the trembling floor, but Hetty was convinced that she felt a little warmer to the touch and pointed out to her brother that she seemed to have stopped losing weight so rapidly. She knew it wasn't enough though and wracked her brains to find a way to get through to her. She hunted through the books in the library, usually with Crow perched on her shoulder, so that he could chatter *ad nauseam* in her head, which she kept telling him crossly was very distracting. He, naturally, took no notice of her scolding. She sat for hours in Eirwen's bedchamber staring blindly at the snow-swathed landscape, willing inspiration to come to her. She even found herself talking to her grandmother's spirit when she was alone — as yet she had heard no response, but that didn't deter her. Somewhere there was an answer to this conundrum, and she was becoming more and more determined to find a solution — it was becoming something of an obsession.

Sometimes she felt as though Galdre Knap, wedged as it was onto the side of the hill, like the Ark after the Flood had subsided, was besieged by the snow and unseen foes, that they had pulled up the drawbridge and were hunkering down in readiness for a bombardment from an invisible enemy. She felt a little uneasy thinking of the concealed long barrow buried in such close proximity to the house and on the occasions when something inexplicable occurred she consoled herself with the thought that they had an army of their own, a trifle ramshackle but nonetheless, determined. She smiled at the thought of anyone or anything trying to get past Aggie; she would fell them with one blow from her sizeable fist.

* * *

She had listened all morning to Finn fretting about his low stocks of tobacco and thought that this at least was something she could certainly remedy without too much trouble.

She asked Mrs Waverley and Agatha to keep an eye on Eirwen for a couple of hours and finding her warmest flannel petticoats and borrowing her grandfather's old coat, which reached almost to the ground on her, she wrapped Anne's woollen shawl tightly around her, rammed Finn's battered old hat onto her head, and discarding her impractical heeled shoes, she pulled on a pair of boots that Sam had left by the back door that were too big but sensible and having warned Mrs Ashby that she was going out for a walk to Friday's Acre, she happily set forth into the white wilderness.

She saw that despite Finn's prejudice against shovelling snow, that Sam and Jacob had cleared a narrow path around the house to the stables and down to the edge of the formal gardens, so she was able to, at least, start her walk with some ease, tramping between the banks of snow with her usual vigour, until she came to the first gate, where the path ended, and the track began. No carts had been up the hill since the snow had begun falling, and apart from some boot prints in the pristine surface, there was no way of telling where the drive began or ended. She stood and looked down the hill, towards the elm avenue and beyond to where Friday's Acre nestled in its sheltering combe. She eyed the flat grey sky and thought it looked favourable. Her first steps after the gate were practically skips; it was such a relief and a joy to be out of the confining gloom of the house.

The snow scrunched underfoot, crisp and undisturbed, her boots cracking through the delicately frozen crust into the powdery filling below. The whole landscape was completely altered; all the familiar landmarks disguised, shapes smoothed and lost in uniformity; any recognisable clumps of trees or bushes had been ironed away, and the beauty of this unknown world made Hetty let out a tiny squeal of delight. Here and there she could see the spiky, criss-crossing tracks of birds and the sly narrow gait of a fox, the heart-shaped marks of deer and the energetic lolloping prints of some rabbits.

Friday's Acre was just over three miles from Galdre Knap and as Hetty had always been a brisk and frequent walker, following her grandmother across fields and through woods for hours; chasing her chickens and pigs when they escaped and foraging in the hedges and ditches for herbs and berries, she was used to, and greatly missed, a good invigorating walk through the countryside she loved.

She reached the foot of the hill and despite being rather breathless from the effort of walking through the deep snow, which was even deeper further down the slope, she pressed on into the very distinct avenue of elms, where the snow, hindered by the dense branches, had fallen sparsely and was slightly easier to traverse. She made good progress and was quietly pleased with herself. In order to cut the journey by a field or two, she took her usual shortcut. She slithered down a short bank and crossed into the meadow, which was bisected by the rivulet that had fed her animal troughs and kept the duckpond fresh.

Struggling across the vast plain of faceless snow, she headed to where she thought the rickety wooden plank crossed the deep ditch. The hems of her skirts were encrusted with snow and getting quite heavy, bashing against her legs and snatching at her ankles. She wished she could have worn breeches as it would've made the walking so much easier. Next time, she decided, she'd borrow a pair from Sam and never mind offending Mrs Waverley by ignoring convention.

She stopped for a moment to try to work out where the stream was, she could see where the line of bushes stopped so reckoned that the ditch was about twenty feet or so ahead and trod cautiously towards where she hazarded the bridge should be.

She couldn't see anything at all, the glare from the snow made her eyes ache. It all looked the same. Featureless and baffling. Frowning, she began to tentatively move along what looked like the edge of a ridge that she thought bordered the stream. Just when she thought she was on the right track, a solitary snowflake drifted past her. She looked up at the sky, which had dramatically changed colour since she'd last paid it any attention and was now an ominous dark mushroom grey and obviously laden with snow. She hadn't noticed it changing and borrowing some of Finn's pithy expressions, cursed roundly, thankful her grandfather couldn't hear her.

Within a couple of minutes, the snowflakes were tumbling past her in tight little flurries and the hills had disappeared from sight. It wouldn't be long before she lost all idea of where she was, so she decided to quickly retrace her steps and head back towards the avenue.

The snow dashed into her eyes and slid down her neck, cold and insistent, she began to shiver and had to clench her teeth to stop them from chattering.

"You idiot!" she berated herself. "You stupid *pea goose*."

There was nothing but shades of white on white, the fast-moving snowflakes threw her off balance and bewildered her. She pulled the shawl around her face to shield her eyes and tried turning her back to the squall but to no avail, it just seemed to follow her as though determined to persecute her. Having completely lost her bearings she could no longer tell in which direction Friday's Acre now lay.

She was too nervous to move in case she stumbled into the ditch. It wouldn't be long, with the snow falling so heavily, before she was no more than an amorphous bump in its smothering surface.

Beginning to panic, she was finding it hard to breathe steadily and her heart was racing. If she stayed out in such a storm, she'd freeze to death in no time.

She tried shouting for help, but her voice was just swallowed up by the muffling snow and she feared she was too far from any dwellings for anyone to hear her cries.

She had just opened her mouth to shout again when she thought she heard the faintest sound.

She snapped her mouth shut and listened.

Nothing. No sound at all apart from her own agitated breathing.

"Is anyone there?" she yelled.

No answer.

"I'm here! I'm over here! I can't see you!"

Then, there it was again.

A whisper of sound.

No more than a breath.

She cocked her head and closed her eyes and listened with every part of her being.

"Stay. Listen. I'm here."

She knew that voice.

Tears were trying to slide down Hetty's cheeks, but the snow stopped them.

"Grandmama!" she sobbed, "Don't go! Don't leave me! I can hear you!"

"Trust. My love. Trust. I'm with you."

Hetty could no longer make a sound, her throat had tightened until she felt she was choking.

She stood quite still and listened.

There, the merest disturbance in the air.

A barely discernible sound

Distant but coming nearer.

A fluttering.

An irritated squawk.

And Crow landed on her shoulder, digging his claws in hard to steady himself.

"*Crow!*" shrieked Hetty.

There's no need to shout. I'm right here. I'm not deaf.

"Oh, Crow! What are you doing here?"

I would have thought that was obvious.

"But, how — ?"

She's over here!

"Who — what — oh, no!"

I appear to be the only one with any sense of direction.

A dull thudding sound, the clink of metal and the sound of a horse blowing.

A large bulky shape loomed out of the all-enveloping white.

"Oh dear," said Hetty forlornly, looking up at Torquhil astride their sturdy cart horse. Crow took off and circled them making harshly impatient noises.

Hetty could just make out the shifting shape of rider and animal and then his arm reaching down for her through the grey blur.

She put her hand out and found it firmly grasped and she was pulled up and onto the saddle in front of him, her legs dangling down on one side. He hauled her close and adjusted his position to accommodate his passenger.

Relieved, Hetty snuggled nearer, out of the snow and buried her head under his coat. She could feel his warmth and felt the steady thump of his heartbeat under her cheek. She heard Crow's wings snap sharply and, following the jackdaw, Torquhil guided the horse through the storm. Hetty didn't care where they were going, she felt safe and secure.

She thought about what she'd heard. Her grandmother's voice reassuring her. Had she imagined it because she'd been so frightened? She didn't think so. It had sounded so real.

The giant horse plodded on and every so often Crow returned and Torquhil changed their direction a little.

After some fifteen minutes or so, she heard a change in the thudding of the great beast's hooves, and she knew with absolute certainty that they were in the yard at Friday's Acre.

Torquhil lowered Hetty down right beside the back door and she felt her way blindly to its familiar solidity and after a bit of a struggle with the stiff latch, she let herself into the kitchen and shut the door behind her, knowing that Torquhil would want to stable the horse.

She knew where everything was and found the stump of a candle and the tinderbox by the hearth and soon had light to see by and within a very short time had lit the fire as well and by the time Torquhil, carrying a pail full of snow, and a bedraggled Crow, came into the kitchen and slammed the door on the storm, the fire was kindled and burning well and Hetty was rummaging through the cupboards hoping to find something for them to eat.

She looked up when they arrived and watched Crow flap down onto the stool by the fire and Torquhil shrug himself out of his greatcoat and put the pail of snow on the iron grill in front of the fire to melt.

She turned her attention back to her search. In the pantry she found a small sack of wrinkled old potatoes and in a dark corner, a rather ancient wheel of cheese she'd deliberately left behind; it was as hard as marble, but she hoped it would still be edible.

She put the meagre pickings on the table and sighed, thinking of Mrs Ashby's fragrant onion soup they should have been having for supper. She remembered there was salt in a box in the hearth and some pepper in a stone pot. She could make a veritable feast from these ingredients she thought wryly. Picking out the best of the potatoes, she shoved them into the ashes of the fire and began to cut up the cheese with a blunt blade Torquhil found hanging from the beam over the sink. He cleaned it on a rag and as he handed it to her their eyes met.

"I'm sorry," she murmured, scarcely able to look at him, "I was stupid. I shouldn't have ventured out."

Silence. She waited.

"You weren't to know it would snow again. Earlier, when you set out, the sky did not look threatening."

"I still shouldn't have risked going out. I endangered your life as well."

"Hardly. I had Crow to guide me. And you had sensibly told Mrs Ashby that you were going out. Once the snow began, she came straight to find me, worrying that you might get caught in it. Even though Crow couldn't see much, he could sense where you were."

"Thank you, both! It really didn't feel like it was going to snow."

His eyes darkened, "No, there was no hint of it — until the moment you left Galdre Knap."

She frowned, "I don't understand — "

"This is Eirwen's doing," he said quietly. "She didn't want you to leave. She stopped you."

"But I *wasn't* leaving! I just wanted to collect my dried raspberry leaves to make Finn some tobacco! Oh, how *could* she? She might have — !"

"No, she knew I would follow you and probably knew that we would end up here."

Hetty opened her mouth to speak and then thought better of it.

Crow clacked his beak.

Hetty, overcome with confusion, took off her coat and hung it up to dry and then scooped some snow into a pot and hooked it over the fire to boil, fetched the salt and pepper and put it on the table and then found two broken and chipped platters.

"I'm afraid there's no cutlery, we'll have to eat with our fingers."

"I don't mind at all. While you finish this I shall go and find something to keep us warm. It's dark now. We'll have to stay the night." He took a candle from a wall sconce and lit it and went out of the kitchen.

Hetty looked at Crow, who was drying his wings beside the fire. Crow tilted his head to one side and looked back at her.

"I know what you're thinking! Oh, dear, this is just dreadful. He must be so annoyed with me. Although of course, he won't shout at me — which is what I deserve. And now — he has to stay in this pitiful little cottage! It's all my fault!"

It is but he doesn't blame you.

"He will, when he has time to think about it. I'm such a —" she stopped and stared at the jackdaw, her eyes wide. "*What* did you say?"

I didn't actually say anything as I can't talk.

"Crow! I can *hear* you! And we're not touching!"

Ah, I shall have to be careful what I think in that case.

"But this is — astonishing! Why can I hear you all of a sudden?"

I'm just a bird. How would I know?

"It's like I heard Grandmama! In the snow. Her voice! It's a miracle."

Did you bang your head by any chance?

Hetty glared at him, "Perhaps I don't want to hear you after all!"

You know you do.

She was still laughing when Torquhil came back into the kitchen, his arms full of rather musty old blankets.

She can hear me.

"You'd better guard your tongue then."

"You don't seem surprised," said Hetty.

"It was bound to happen eventually. You just needed something to wake you up so that you could hear other voices."

Hetty's eyes filled with tears, "That's what Grandmama told me — out in the snow. I heard her whispering to me. She said to listen — and trust. She said she was with me. She said to stay still."

"Very wise, or you'd have fallen into the stream. You were very close to it."

The tears fell onto the table.

Torquhil moved to her side and patted her shoulder a little awkwardly, "It seems she was there to keep you safe and because the fear blocked out all other distractions, you were able to hear her. And now the door is open and unfortunately you can hear Crow too. There are always bound to be disadvantages to any advantage."

Hetty laughed and the laughter turned to hiccupping sobs and she put her head down onto her arms and wept silently.

Torquhil looked at Crow.

Crow hunched his wings.

They let her cry and after a while she sniffed and Torquhil handed her his handkerchief. She mopped her eyes, gave a great sigh and went to take the potatoes out of the hot embers. She gave them a squeeze and pronounced them ready, hacked them open with the dull blade and stuffed some crumbled cheese into them. With a muttered apology she put the rustic supper in front of Torquhil and passed him the salt and pepper.

She then lifted the pot of hot water from its hook using the rag to protect her hand and put it on the table. She found her raspberry leaves hanging up in the pantry and stirred a handful into the hot water.

"There, raspberry leaf tea," she said, "Except there are no cups to drink it from." She gave a little gasp and dashed away into the pantry, and they heard a door creak open and then thump closed. She returned brandishing a small wooden ladle, its handle twisted and tied in a knot.

"How could we have forgotten to take this? Grandpapa made it for Grandmama when they first got married. He carved it from sycamore wood." She took it to the sink and poured some hot water onto it and gave it a good wipe with the rag, then placed it in front of Torquhil. "There, you can scoop out some tea and drink from that."

He picked up the smoothed ladle, running his long fingers over the shining wood, "This is a love token. That's a love knot carved into the handle."

Hetty blushed; she'd had no idea — to her it was just a spoon her grandfather had carved. Now she'd put a love token in front of Torquhil.

Awkward.

Hetty turned on the jackdaw and threw the rag at him. It missed and Crow clacked his beak and let out a cackling laugh.

Torquhil scooped some raspberry leaf tea and held it out to Hetty. She bit her lip but took it and gratefully sipped some of the tea. She handed it back and he took some tea for himself, sipping from the ladle.

"Quite delicious. Worth the journey."

Hetty thumped down onto her chair, "Oh, eat your potato!" she said crossly.

Torquhil smiled and did as he was told.

Hetty gave Crow some cheese rinds that he happily gobbled up and then he settled down by the fire and tucked his head under his wing.

They sat in silence for a few minutes, the crackling of the fire the only sound.

"Why would she — ?" Hetty began, uncertainly.

Torquhil shook his head, "She must have some kind of plan. I suspect you leaving Galdre Knap was not part of it."

"It's all too incredible. How can such a thing be true?"

"I know, it's beyond our understanding, but you must agree that there are things afoot that cannot be denied."

"We should be with her now. I don't like leaving her for so long."

"Mrs Waverley and Aggie are there, and they can cope very well. Anyway, I have a feeling that now Eirwen has manipulated us, she has what she wants and will be content for the moment."

"I cannot see why she would want us at Friday's Acre."

Torquhil glanced around the dark little kitchen, "It's very cosy here."

"Yes, it was nice living here with Grandpapa. We managed well. It was simple — life here — we were well-fed and warm and happy."

"And then I came along and spoiled your idyll, for which I can only apologise — although I will admit that I do not regret the outcome."

"But there is no outcome yet. There's only uncertainty and mystery and sadness. We shall not know — may *never* know what the outcome may be."

They ate their supper and Torquhil said it was one of the finest meals he'd ever tasted, which made Hetty roll her eyes.

Afterwards, she cleared everything away and Torquhil moved the table to make room for the settle, which had been pressed up against the far wall. He arranged it in front of the fire and padded it with the blankets to try to make it more comfortable. Hetty stood and looked at it for a long moment, told herself not to be so prudish and, with a studied air of indifference settled down at one end and covered herself with one of the blankets. Torquhil stoked the fire and made sure there were enough logs and peats for the night and sat down at the other end of the settle, stretching his long booted legs out in front of him.

It was a dreadfully uncomfortable piece of furniture, meant for pious folk to sit on and stay awake through dreary sermons and was certainly not meant for sleeping upon.

Torquhil suddenly stood up and looked down at Hetty, "I shall turn away while you take your skirt off, I can see it steaming in the heat from the fire. You'll catch a chill. We can spread it over the chairs so that it can dry properly."

She could feel the heavy wetness of the material against her legs and knew he was right. He walked away and she quickly kicked off Sam's boots, pulled off her stockings, slipped out of the sodden skirt and the top petticoat and lay them all across the chairs near the fire, then darted back to the settle and pulled the blankets back over her. Torquhil returned and sat down again. She tucked her legs up under her and tried to make herself comfortable against the high wing at her side.

She closed her eyes thinking she'd never be able to fall asleep in such peculiar circumstances.

The fire smelt sweet, of wood and peat and sounded soothing, like a lullaby.

To her complete surprise, she drifted, her head dipped, she lifted it, her chin sank onto her chest, and she was asleep.

* * *

At some point in the night, while it was still dark, she awoke and found she was very comfortable and warm.

She opened her eyes and for a moment couldn't work out where she was. Then, she saw the fire still glowing and the sleeping jackdaw.

She realised, without any feeling of consternation at all, that she was stretched out full-length on the settle, covered in blankets, her head resting on something firm but giving, unlike wood, and a protective arm curled down her back and around her waist, keeping her securely on the narrow seat. She stirred, her cheek cushioned against his thigh, and felt his fingers in her hair, stroking, soothing, as though she were a child, and gradually, she slipped back into the unthreatening land of her dreams.

Eleven

Hetty smiled contentedly in her sleep. She was dreaming of picking mushrooms with her grandmother, with Autumn leaves carried on a cool October breeze, falling around them, catching in their hair and dancing against the bright blue sky.

She felt someone remove a leaf from her windswept curls and gently smooth her hair away from her face. The wind had worked it loose from its pins and it was getting in her eyes.

She didn't want to wake up. Her dream was like an embrace.

Suddenly aware that she was awake, she remembered, all in a rush that she was at Friday's Acre after being caught in a snowstorm. There were no Autumn leaves in her hair.

With a start, she sat up and nearly slid off the settle, the blankets falling to the floor and her hair, which had indeed come down during the night, falling in tangles across her face. She pushed it back impatiently and looked around.

Torquhil was looking at her from the end of the settle and Crow, who was perched on the back of it, was poking his beak around under his wing.

With the imprint of Torquhil's breeches pressed into her scarlet cheek, she knew that she must look utterly dishevelled and lost to all propriety. She tried to straighten her clothes and then realised that without the blanket for cover, she was sitting there in plain sight in just her petticoats, with bare feet peeping out from under their rather grubby hems.

Meeting Torquhil's interested gaze, she took a steadying breath, "I — think a *true* gentleman would have made himself scarce so as not to embarrass a lady."

He continued to look at her, "I couldn't move without waking you and you were sleeping so peacefully with your head resting on my leg that I didn't want to disturb you — although you do talk in your sleep."

"Oh! I'm so sorry! You must be awfully stiff sitting in the same position all night. Did you manage to sleep at all?"

"When not listening to you complaining about leaves in your hair," he said with his half-smile.

"Oh," she said again and put a hand to her ungovernable mane. "I was picking mushrooms with Grandmama. In my dream. It was Autumn and leaves were falling — " She hesitated and frowned at him, "It was you — my hair — "

His eyes travelled to her hair, "It appeared to be troubling you. I was worried you might wake. You had a tiring day yesterday, you needed to sleep."

"Thank you — I — I've been a fearful nuisance."

"I should think your skirts should be dry by now and your stockings."

Hetty blushed, somehow the word *stockings* seemed rather too intimate for a farmhouse kitchen.

"It's stopped snowing," she said, in an attempt to cover her confusion.

"Yes, as soon as we were settled here, it stopped. I've no doubt that if we don't return soon to Galdre Knap it'll start again."

He stood up and stretched the cricks out of his back and went to the door, "I shall saddle up the horse and bring him around while you put your clothes on," and he went out into the snowy yard.

Her cheeks a furious pink, Hetty swiftly, but a little clumsily, pulled on her stockings and threw on her flannel petticoat and skirt. She wrapped the shawl around her and tied it at the back and tugged on her grandfather's coat. Encumbered by the bulky clothing, she was struggling to get Sam's boots on when Torquhil returned to say all was ready for their journey home.

Without a word, he crossed the small kitchen, knelt in front of her and helped her tug on the big boots, and when he'd finished, he held out his hand to her. She took it and allowed him to haul her up like a helpless fat sheep.

Crow stretched his wings and fluttered out of the door. Torquhil made sure the fire was secure and then they went out into the bright snow.

Sitting high up on the enormous cart horse, Hetty could see further out across the fields, but seemed unable to concentrate on their ethereal beauty because she was being firmly held in place by Torquhil's encircling arms. It was very distracting, but she found that when the hill finally came into view, she felt vaguely disappointed. She tried to fathom why this might be and discovered an interesting fact; she was enjoying the sensation of being held against him. This came as something of a shock to her as she had thought herself to be quite beyond feeling anything for any man let alone such a curious creature as Torquhil Guivre. Mr Edwin Scroggs had made her feel as though she were doomed to forgo any of the romantic feelings females usually were susceptible to and, persuaded that there was more than a kernel of truth in it, she'd been quite content to imagine a life caring for her grandfather followed by solitary spinsterhood in some lowly hovel, with some cats and chickens. She certainly never could have imagined that she might develop a tenderness for this peculiar man. She chewed the inside of her cheek and hoped he wouldn't discover her ridiculous secret. It would be too humiliating.

Crow swooped overhead.

A penny for your thoughts.

Hetty glared at him as he seemed to hover in the air in front of them for a moment before he flapped away cackling.

They made their way steadily up the hill to Galdre Knap and were pleasantly surprised to see a grinning Sam holding the gate open for them.

"Saw you comin'!" he shouted. "Glad you're back safe. That was quite a storm!"

He raised his cap as they plodded past and closed the gate behind them.

Jacob came out of the stables to lend a hand, helping Hetty down from the massive horse and leading the animal away to give it a good rub down.

They were welcomed back into the kitchen as though they were heroes returning from battle; Mrs Ashby gathered Hetty to her large bosom and squeezed her tightly, saying she'd made her a special dinner and Aggie couldn't stop grinning. They told her that Mrs Waverley was with Eirwen, and they'd had an uneventful night.

After a few minutes her grandfather tottered in and seemed compelled to give her a good scolding until Torquhil gently reminded him that it hadn't been her fault and she could hardly be blamed for the vagaries of some very unstable weather. Hetty looked up at him gratefully and then quickly busied herself removing her coat and shawl in case he read something into her expression.

Finn nodded at her which she took to be his version of an effusive welcome and then Sam and Jacob arrived and Mrs Ashby, over-excited by the celebrations, cut some wedges of brandy-laced plum cake and handed them around, much to everyone's joy and they chattered on for quite a while, everyone wanting to hear about her adventure in the snowstorm.

Torquhil left the kitchen without saying anything and Hetty sighed.

Then, with a comical start of outrage, Mrs Ashby suddenly noticed the jackdaw had sidled in, uninvited and was warming himself by the fire; before she could brandish a broom at him, Hetty scooped him up and took him, squawking indignantly, into the library.

"Mrs Ashby will make you into soup if you're not careful. Stay in here!"

After all I've done —

"I know! Thank you for rescuing me. I've never been so glad to see anyone in my whole life!"

You were quite glad to see my master.

"Well, of course! *You* couldn't carry me home!"

Crow cocked his head.

"What are you saying?" demanded Hetty.

I didn't say a word.

"Crow! If you — if you say *anything* to him, *I'll* be the one who wrings your despicable neck!"

The jackdaw hopped further away from her.

Ungrateful —

Hetty put her hands on her hips and stared at him coldly.

Oh, keep your petticoat on —

She took a menacing step towards him, and he flapped up onto the top shelf, out of reach.

"Soup!" snapped Hetty as she left the room and heard the defiant clack of his beak as she slammed the door.

* * *

The next time Hetty was alone with Torquhil it wasn't exactly an auspicious occasion. She'd secretly been hoping for some time alone with him but since the night at Friday's Acre he seemed, if it were possible, even more reserved and she wondered if he might suspect that she had had some sort of an epiphany in that dark farmhouse kitchen and was now embarrassed for her. The thought made her feel quite anxious, and she was determined to show that she was utterly unmoved by his remote and mysterious presence.

The night after the night at Friday's Acre, she had, under some flimsy pretext, taken her supper in the kitchen, leaving her grandfather, Mrs Waverley and Torquhil to dine together in the library, while Agatha kept watch over Eirwen. Hetty thought that this would show that she was entirely indifferent to Mr Guivre and his rather sinister charm. Then after a quick supper with Mrs Ashby and Finn, she went straight up to the Chinese Bedchamber where Aggie was ably mending some worn linen with neat little patches by the light of a branch of candles.

Hetty looked over her shoulder and admired her work, "Goodness, Aggie, I'm so envious — you have so many abilities! Those stitches look like they've been made by faeries!"

"Ma always said I was better than Bessie at sewin' — an' Bessie was so cross she put a frog in my bed! A *live* one! I very nearly squashed it when I got into bed! How she laughed!"

"Bessie sounds as though she can be quite a handful. Do you get on with her?"

Agatha shrugged, "Oh, she's no trouble really! In her mind I don't count because she's so pretty — far prettier than I'll ever be, as she never stops tellin' me — an' she knows there's no girl in the whole parish can hold a candle to her, so she's quite smug really — a cock is brave in its own midden."

"Have you considered that perhaps it's better to be practical and liked than merely pretty and envied? I could never be considered pretty because of my unfortunate hair and freckles — so dreadfully unfashionable! But anyway, Grandpapa says that beauty must always fade as will the memories of that fleeting beauty and he reminds me that my hair will one day turn silver and that one should remember that it's character and kindness people remember in the end. Sometimes I find it hard to recall what my mother looked like now, and she was possessed of the most beautiful guinea-gold hair and the face of an angel — but I remember *precisely* how my grandmother was, how she talked and laughed and the wonderful things she shared with me! I could *never* forget her generous spirit and warmth."

Agatha wiggled her needle into the material, fixing it in place, and folded the sheet tidily away into her sewing bag, "Oh, I expect you be right, Miss — " she sighed heartily, "but sometimes I'd quite like to be pretty for a day just to see what it's like. The boys in the village don't whistle at me — they call me names. It'd make a nice change for someone to think I wasn't like some kind of farmyard animal and was maybe pretty enough to kiss!"

"Aggie! You're still only a girl! One day some lucky young man will see that you're an absolute treasure and he'll just swoop you up in his manly arms!"

"He'd have to be as strong as an ox to lift *me* up!" laughed Agatha, undaunted.

"You wait and see!" said Hetty, "There's someone out there just waiting for you."

"Do you have a sweetheart, Miss?"

Hetty blushed, "Well, I suppose you could say I very nearly had one! He seemed terribly keen for a while but couldn't forgive the colour of my hair and some aspects of my nature seemed to irritate him beyond measure. Mr Edwin Scroggs."

Agatha rolled her eyes, "I know him! He's such a jaw-me-dead! You're well rid of him!" She eyed Hetty archly, "There's no one else what's taken your fancy then?"

Sensing a rather unsubtle ambush, Hetty shook her head, "None whatsoever! As you know, I rarely get the chance to meet anyone these days anyway. But, looking on the bright side, I suppose there's always Finn!"

Agatha let out a delighted hoot, "He'd be lucky to get another wife, he's that grumpy! You can do better than ol' Finn, Miss! There's bound to be a gentleman closer to home who might win your favour."

Hetty kept her face as expressionless as she possibly could, "I think I'm too set in my ways now. I'm perfectly happy looking after Grandpapa and Eirwen. I don't need anyone else."

As she said this, she felt suddenly chilled, as though someone had opened the casement and let in the bitter night air; she looked around, but nothing had changed in the room, there was no reason for a sudden blast of icy air. She shivered and went over to the bed to look at Eirwen, but the girl was lying just as she had been for the last few days, like an effigy on a tomb. Hetty took her hand in hers and held it. It felt very slightly warmer than usual but still seemed too cold to sustain life.

She thought about what her grandmother had said to her out in the snowstorm and how it had made her feel and she bent down and whispered in Eirwen's ear, "I'm here with you, Eirwen. There's no need to fret, I won't leave you." She watched the girl's face hopefully for any sign of comprehension and when none came, her shoulders sagged a little with disappointment. She leant forward again and lightly kissed her waxy cheek, her lips retaining the chill as she stood up and turned away.

A slight sound made her pause and turn back.

Eirwen's eyes were open, and she was holding out her pale bony hand.

Without taking her gaze from the girl she whispered to Agatha, "Please go and fetch Mr Guivre at once!" and she heard the maid mutter something under her breath and thunder from the room.

She moved back to the bed and took Eirwen's hand in both of hers, "Good evening! Can you please stay awake until your brother gets here? I wonder what woke you up this time? I wish we knew so that we could hold you here with us."

The door opened and Torquhil came in with long quick strides, his midnight blue coat swirling about his legs. Hetty sent him a warning look, "Your sister's suddenly woken up and is holding my hand, Torquhil!"

He approached the bed and Hetty moved over a little to make room for him but clung onto Eirwen's hand as though fearful of what might happen if she let go. He pulled the chair closer and sat down.

Eirwen's eyes travelled from Hetty to Torquhil, and she stared at him blankly.

"What happened?" he asked.

"I was talking to Aggie — about sewing and — " she faltered.

"And — ?"

"And my grandmother and — and — sweethearts — "

He glanced at her, "So, things a young girl might naturally be interested in?"

"Yes, although — and I have no way to explain — when I happened to mention that — oh, dear, that I would not be getting married because I had too much to occupy me already — I felt, what I can only describe as, a chilly gust of air — but the windows are not open!"

He continued to look at her, his expression unreadable, "That was all you said? You can't recall anything else?"

Hetty frowned, "I think my actual words were that I don't *need* anyone else," and she turned away to hide her embarrassment.

Torquhil said nothing for a while.

"I was only chatting with Aggie! We were just joking really."

"Yes, I see that — but of course, Eirwen doesn't know that. She only knows what she hears."

"But I don't understand! Why would such a light-hearted comment make her react that way?"

The dark eyes looked at her and she forced herself to hold his gaze.

"I believe that my sister has some childish notion in her head and is trying to force it to come true."

Hetty raised her eyebrows, bewildered, "Childish notion?"

A wry half-smile, "Yes, she was always inclined to — whimsy, even as a child and was fond of playing tricks on people — it frequently landed her in trouble. I'm beginning to suspect that she has a notion to find me — a bride."

Hetty's mouth fell open, but she quickly snapped it shut again in case she looked foolish, "A bride?" she repeated, wishing she could sound a little more intelligent.

Torquhil smiled at her, "I believe she is matchmaking."

In case she just continued to stupidly echo his words Hetty decided it was safer to keep quiet.

He watched her expressive face, "I think that my sister has chosen you to be my betrothed."

She could feel her heartbeat thumping in her throat and colour staining her cheeks; she found she had entirely lost the powers of speech.

"I can see that you are a little shaken by the thought. I can imagine that it must be something of a shock."

"I — I cannot begin — to understand — why she would — when she doesn't know me — when you are — I'm at a loss for words. It makes no sense."

Those hooded eyes darkened like a fast-approaching storm, "Doesn't it? You sound very averse to the idea — not that I can blame you."

Feeling desperately nervous that she might give away the fact that she found Eirwen's preposterous fancy strangely appealing, Hetty forced herself to smile as though the whole thing was amusing but baffling, instead of surprisingly alluring.

"Oh, goodness gracious, how is one supposed to react to such an absurd suggestion? Poor Eirwen if she thinks that we would be a good match! We are so dissimilar."

The usual silence ensued but was so long this time that Hetty began to wriggle uncomfortably and wish she'd just kept quiet.

"You think that husband and wife should be similar in character to be compatible? That's interesting."

She thought of her grandparents and how mismatched they had seemed and yet how devoted they were to each other. They'd been inseparable although Grandpapa had told her they'd regularly fought because of Grandmama's volatile temper and his exacting nature but that it had never made any difference to their marriage because whatever happened their love had been strong enough to withstand any adversity.

"It must surely help? You and I are like fire and ice. Dark and light. I would soon drive you to distraction with my irrational nature and uncertain temper! And you — "

"Yes? You would find me too cold and detached?"

She knew she was digging herself into an ever-deepening hole but seemed unable to prevent words from tumbling unbidden from her mouth.

She took a breath to agree with him but before she could utter a sound, she felt a strange sensation in her fingers that were still holding onto Eirwen's hand.

"Torquhil — ?" she whispered.

"What is it?"

"My hands — they're *freezing*."

He reached out and covered their hands with his.

"I believe she's making her opinion known," he said.

Hetty leant closer to her, "Eirwen, you cannot *force* people together — !"

The hand in hers began to tremble violently and Hetty looked up at Torquhil in alarm. Then the whole of Eirwen's body began to shake and the bed creaked and quivered as though made of nothing but frail kindling instead of solid oak.

She felt him tighten his grip on their hands as though trying to hold them steady and she looked at Eirwen's blank face and suddenly something snapped inside her.

She threw off their hands and jumped to her feet, "Eirwen! That's quite enough! We will *not* be coerced into something just because you think you can scare us into it! Now, kindly wake up and talk to us reasonably about this! And you can forget about trying to control us with your thoughts! I'm quite sure that your brother feels the same way too. This is becoming silly and dangerous. I could have died out there in the snow. Torquhil might have died. You can't just toy with people's feelings because you're bored. So, unless you want me to leave Galdre Knap immediately — you had better start behaving in a rational manner."

Hetty felt cruel saying this to the poor helpless girl, but she couldn't bear the idea that Torquhil might feel obliged to act upon Eirwen's playful schemes in order to pacify her.

Immediately the shaking subsided. The bed was still again, and the fragile body ceased its wild trembling.

"There now, I think you finally understand me. So, from now on we shall have a bit more cooperation please and then you will get better all the sooner. *And* you're going to start eating and drinking again."

Torquhil looked back at her, "Well, you've certainly made your feelings quite clear, and cowed Eirwen into obedience for good measure. That hasn't often happened, I assure you."

Filled with remorse, Hetty took Eirwen's hand again, "I'm so sorry! I truly didn't mean to be overbearing, I should learn to think before I speak!"

Eirwen's hand no longer felt as though it were frozen although Hetty was having to studiously ignore the painful tingling in her fingertips as she accidentally touched Torquhil.

Eirwen had been staring blindly into space but as Hetty and Torquhil touched hands, she seemed to focus, her mouth opened and she emitted a long, hissing sound like the sharpening of a scythe blade with a honing stone.

Torquhil smiled wryly and shook his head, "I shouldn't waste your breath Hetty. She's made up her mind although I'm sorry the idea is so abhorrent to you. I fear we must just endure her meddling while she is trapped in this state. Perhaps, it gives her something to think about while she is caught in this half-world and perhaps it will give her a reason to fight her way back to us."

"This is really all quite absurd, you know — " began Hetty indignantly then, seeing the look in his eyes, she swallowed her words and nodded, "Yes, indeed, Torquhil," she murmured, her voice unnaturally flat and placid, "It's possible that I may have been a little hasty — I should think before I speak. Pray forgive me, it's my unsteady temper, you understand!"

"Easily forgiven, Hetty. You've had a good deal to bear these last few days. You cannot be blamed for being a little waspish — "

"*Waspish!* No, really, that's going too far!" she exclaimed furiously but his guarded expression stopped her in her tracks, and she cleared her throat and continued, "Oh, but I forget that you're such a tease! I daresay I shall become accustomed to it eventually."

"I'm sure you will. You're certainly not slow to learn," he commented, and she could have sworn his eyes were laughing at her.

"Still, it's late and I expect you're tired. You must still be feeling the effects of your adventure in the snow. Why don't you go to bed, and I'll sit with Eirwen. I'll call you if anything occurs."

Hetty was trying to read his thoughts, but it was impossible, so she sighed and capitulated, "Whatever you think is best. Although I'm wide awake now."

"You fall asleep with childlike ease even in the most trying circumstances so I've no doubt you'll be dreaming of leaves catching in your hair within minutes of your head touching the pillow."

This pointed reference to their night at Friday's Acre was too much for her; she bid Eirwen a swift goodnight and swept off into her bedchamber with only a passing glare at her exceedingly irksome companion.

Twelve

It was with some relief and a generous helping of contrition that Hetty, respectably washed and dressed and her hair fiercely braided and pinned up, went into the Chinese Bedchamber at six o'clock to find, much to her secret disappointment, Aggie on duty and no sign of Torquhil.

Agatha said that she'd taken over from Mr Guivre at five o'clock and that he'd been in a much more cheerful mood, which was a pleasant change. He'd apparently told her not to disturb Hetty unless absolutely necessary.

Agatha was a little surprised that Miss Swift seemed to take umbrage at this, muttering, "High-handed!" to herself as she bustled about the bedchamber preparing for the morning's work.

Together they washed, changed and tidied Eirwen, who, Hetty was delighted to find, felt warmer to the touch. After a chat about what had happened overnight and what Mrs Ashby was preparing for dinner, Hetty sent Agatha away to help in the kitchen and settled down with a book beside the bed. She had found it in the library, recommended by her grandfather, and was just beginning it.

She looked at Eirwen lying in the bed and then back to the book, "I have no idea if you're interested in books at all, Eirwen but I believe you have a very vivid imagination so I'm going to read this story to you. I shall leave out any unsuitable parts and you only have to say if you would like me to stop reading. It's called Gulliver's Travels and it's by a writer called Jonathan Swift, which by chance is my surname too!"

There was no response, not that she'd really expected one, so she began to read.

After a while she realised it was probably not really suitable for young ears because it was a bit dull in places and she ended up making the story more fitting for a sixteen-year-old by removing parts and adding others. She doubted Eirwen was listening anyway but thought that the sound of a voice might be comforting.

She was just reading about the tiny Lilliputian people when she got a strange sensation like cold dripping water running down her spine. She turned to look behind her, expecting to see someone standing there but there was nothing to see. The casement shutters were open and the cold blue light from the snow-covered garden filtered in through the feathery frost on the windowpanes. The corners of the room were still shadowed, and the light made everything look different. The feeling refused to abate so she carried on with the reading but at the same time kept an eye on the rest of the room.

She reached the end of the first chapter and looked up.

Something was moving stealthily in the far corner of the bedchamber.

Gooseflesh rose on her arms. Edging forward very slowly and deliberately she looked out from behind the high wing of her chair.

She peered into the darkest corner behind the monumental Elizabethan linen press.

She waited.

Then, when nothing happened, she began to relate her version of the story again but this time with an eye firmly fixed upon the edges of the bedchamber where the shadows were deepest.

Slowly, slowly, creeping out of the dusty shadows, came a something. She found it was hard to focus upon it. She had stopped reading but kept speaking words softly, making up a nonsensical story so she could watch the intruder without giving away that she was aware of anything untoward occurring. She made no sudden movements and kept her voice low and colourless. Suspecting it might be something as harmless as a mouse or even, heaven forfend, a rat, she thought that she'd better bring Thistle up to deal with it later.

Whatever it might be, it was being extremely cautious, inching forwards but still keeping to the shadows. It had no shape or form that she could recognise, and it seemed to her to behave like smoke, drifting and swirling without actually being anything in particular; she couldn't give it a name and yet she found that she wasn't in the least afraid.

She was getting a crick in her neck but continued to observe it and gradually she stopped talking until there was only the sound of her own surprisingly even heartbeat and Eirwen's gentle breathing.

The whatever-it-was slithered to a stop and for a moment, while Hetty held her breath, it didn't move at all and if she hadn't known better, she would have thought it had stopped to consider its next move.

She was wondering what to do, whether to wait and see what happened or to call out for help.

A slightly irrational thought suddenly occurred to her, and she began to tell the story again, about the Lilliputians and the giant Lemuel Gulliver with his hair pinned to the ground by threads and she related how they kept him restrained until they were certain they could trust him.

"And then the Lilliputian emperor asked Gulliver to help them defeat their enemy in Blefuscu and Gulliver kindly agreed to help them."

Hetty eyed the shadowy thing and only when it began to change shape in a more dramatic fashion did she feel the need to stand up.

As it grew in size, she rose from her seat as though it would be easier facing it eye to eye — if it *had* eyes, she thought frantically.

She was about to move forward towards it when something touched her arm, stalling her, and she looked down to see that Eirwen was holding onto her, her fishbone-thin fingers biting into her flesh until Hetty winced in pain.

The pale eyes were still blindly staring, expressionless.

The hairs on the back of her neck prickled and Hetty glanced over her shoulder and had to bite back a gasp of horror, for standing just behind her was some sort of figure. It towered over her. She would have liked to have retreated but the chair was blocking her way.

Turning slowly to face the intruder, Hetty braced herself. Eirwen's fingers continued to dig into her arm remorselessly.

She may not have been afraid to start with, but she certainly was now. Part of her brain was trying to work out whether to flee and leave Eirwen to her fate or stay and fend this thing off, whatever it might be.

Looking at it with a critical eye and wondering if such a thing *could* be fended off, she tried to work out what it might actually be and how best to deal with it.

It was about two feet taller than she was and appeared not to be corporeal. She thought, with some astonishment, that it mainly consisted of dust and grit, small stones and the odd rock but not as in the solid structure of a sculpture but as though it were being held together by no more than an eddying wind. Its edges were fluid, solidifying and dissolving and swirling as though all the matter that made up its transient form was caught in a violent whirlwind but at all times retaining its overall formation — that of some kind of female. A woman in Roman attire, holding in her hands, what looked like, three apples.

Hetty suddenly knew precisely what this was. The apparition was the embodiment of the little stone carving she'd found on her pillow.

It appeared to be a kind of Roman goddess and even though Hetty was deeply alarmed by the sight of an ancient Roman deity scattering grit into the air just a few feet away from her, she felt strangely confident that it meant her no harm. She didn't know why she thought that, but she believed it wholeheartedly. The goddess was benign and had not come to inflict evil upon them. However, it still didn't make the situation any easier to endure. Hetty was shaking with fear and was having to clench her teeth together to stop them chattering noisily.

She prised Eirwen's fingers from her arm and held them firmly in hers, giving them a reassuring squeeze meant to convey her conviction, although she wasn't sure that Eirwen would even understand such a gesture.

Resolutely gathering her thoughts, she decided that she should treat this visitor as she would any other visitor to her home, with warmth and courtesy.

She released Eirwen's hand and approached the goddess cautiously, trying to avoid the flying debris, and schooling her face into what she hoped was a friendly smile — although she was slightly concerned that it would be more a grimace of fear and uncertainty.

At first the spiralling figure, apparently made entirely from dirt and air, seemed to take no notice as Hetty moved slowly forward, and then as she drew closer, the goddess gradually retreated further back into the shadows.

Hetty stood quite still.

And waited.

She wanted to see what would happen next and knowing how she disliked being harried herself, she tried to convey the impression of someone who wanted to welcome her visitor with a nice cup of tea and some plum cake, so as not to cause any undue dismay. The very fact that the goddess had backed away showed, Hetty felt, that there must be some kind of basic emotion within the swirling sandstorm. It wasn't just a phantom whirlwind she was hoping to reason with, it was, hopefully, a moderately sentient *something* — although how that could be, she wasn't quite sure. She had always thought, because of her grandmother's careful and extensive teaching, that she was fairly broad-minded, but this was really pushing her to her absolute limits.

The dust goddess was now half concealed by the darkness in the corner of the room and Hetty thought she seemed unsure about what to do next.

She never quite knew why, but she began to tell the story of Gulliver and the Lilliputians again, recounting how the tiny people of Lilliput had fed the giant on tiny roasted animals and how he'd gobbled down dozens of little loaves and drunk many barrels of their best Burgundy. She noted that as she talked the spinning of the dirt and grit became slower and the goddess eased herself back towards the centre of the room again, back into the light. Hetty continued just making up jolly things for Gulliver to do in Lilliput, eventually teaching the Lilliputians to play the harp, to sing and dance and make garlands out of flowers.

She occasionally glanced back at Eirwen to make sure she was all right but otherwise just set herself the task of winning the trust of the goddess.

The floor was now strewn with gravel, grit and drifts of grey dirt and Hetty thought it was going to be exceedingly difficult to find an explanation for Aggie, who would no doubt be landed with the job of sweeping up the resulting mess. She was also wondering why, as the goddess lost parts of her form, she didn't appear to shrink in size, the constant shedding of matter seemed to make no difference to her overall appearance.

Hetty was torn between wanting someone to come so that they could see this phenomenon and confirm that she wasn't losing her mind and not wanting to scare her away.

But she had reached a point where she couldn't go forward or backwards and was ostensibly just stuck entertaining a creature so far beyond her comprehension that her mind seemed to have frozen.

She suddenly thought of Torquhil, his face coming into her mind unbidden and once there, she found it hard to dispel the vision of his sloe-black eyes and crooked smile. She wished he was there in the bedchamber with her, in all the madness and whirling dust, because he would make her feel instantly calm and would probably have an idea of what to do about their uninvited guest.

As she was thinking of him, with a slightly distracted smile, she couldn't help but notice that the wild spinning was decreasing further still, until, apart from the odd piece of gravel skittering across the floor, the goddess became almost motionless.

Breathing a sigh of relief, Hetty smiled warmly at her.

"Goodness, that must be truly exhausting — all that swirling and trying not to unravel like a ball of wool! I think you're terribly skilful. I wonder if you get dizzy at all. Um, if it's not too impertinent may I ask — where you come from and why you're here — in Eirwen's bedchamber?"

She watched the goddess twitch and flicker as though she suffered from Saint Vitus's Dance; the dust and grit slowly compacting into a more substantial form, her edges solidifying and remaining fixed so that Hetty could finally make more sense of her shape.

She was a true to life version of the tiny carved stone figure she had beside her bed, and she was proffering three apples, all carved from stone, her tightly bound hair was in the Roman style, as were her garments. Her face, grey-brown and rigid, was nonetheless delicately carved and even though hewn from cold stone, it seemed to be rounded and feminine, the expression not in the slightest bit threatening.

Hetty was transfixed by the sight before her. She knew her mouth was hanging open in a silent O but couldn't seem to close it.

She looked back to Eirwen again, but she was still just staring into space seemingly unaware of the extraordinary visitor in her room, although Hetty was fairly certain that, at first, she had been holding her back or holding on to her, and therefore must have been conscious in some way that the goddess was in her bedchamber.

Confusion was the emotion uppermost in Hetty's mind, mixed with a generous helping of curiosity. She supposed that it was her grandmother's teaching that kept her from fleeing or scrambling under the bed to hide. She remembered Grandmama telling her that there were peculiar things in the world that were almost too hard to comprehend, but if you were patient and didn't panic then sometimes those things could become part of your life and turn out to be a blessing.

Hetty couldn't help but think about Torquhil in that context.

She realised, to her dismay, that he fit her grandmother's description perfectly and that he had indeed become, quite unexpectedly, a blessing.

She saw that the goddess was slowly drifting towards her and appeared to be holding out one of the stone apples.

Hetty took a tentative step forward and reaching out a trembling hand, received the apple. It was strangely warm and as heavy as a cannonball.

She wasn't quite sure what she was supposed to do with it, but she sort of curtseyed — she didn't know why.

"Thank you, er — Goddess. How kind. Am I supposed to do something specific with it? It's obviously — deeply significant."

The goddess drifted closer to her, and she had to admit that it was rather intimidating having her looming over her; she desperately wanted to back away but forced herself to stand firm, despite her shaking knees.

She watched in astonishment as the stone figure leant towards her, reaching out what could be described as arms as though to embrace her. Touched by this gesture of friendship Hetty took a step closer. She could feel the odd heavy stone colliding with her skirts and pieces of sharp grit stinging her skin as they still continued on their hectic orbit around the strange vision.

She felt an urgent desire to be yet closer still and began to feel a little dizzy as though she'd lost her bearings and her balance was out of kilter. She was just about to take the final step when the door opened and Torquhil was standing on the threshold.

"*Hetty!*"

Not stopping to ask questions, he was across the room in a heartbeat and, unceremoniously hoisted Hetty off her feet and hauled her back towards the bed.

He put her down with very little regard for her dignity and stood as a barrier between her and the menacing apparition.

"What the hell were you thinking?" he exclaimed, glaring down at her, his usually expressionless face showing undisguised fury.

The sound of his voice, hard-edged with anger, woke Hetty from her trance.

She tried to push past him but found herself forcefully restrained, "No, *no!* Don't scare her away!" she cried, distraught and tearing at his protective arm.

Torquhil took her roughly by the shoulders, "Hetty! Stop this at once! You don't know what you're doing!"

"She doesn't mean me any harm! She's not dangerous!" howled Hetty as though in an agony of pain.

"She's extremely dangerous! You have no idea how close you came — ! Stop fighting me! Hetty! She wants to take you away. You must resist her!"

The dawning comprehension in her eyes showed that finally she had registered his words and he turned back to the intruder, whilst still holding Hetty firmly out of harm's way, and began to speak in deliberately calm tones to the uninvited guest.

"Salutations, *Sulis Minerva*. This girl is under my protection. I have bound her to me, and you shall not take her as you did my sister. If I allowed that she would be lost to us, and I cannot countenance such a thing. Truly, I am sorry for your suffering but taking another hostage will not help your plight. I promise we'll do all we can to return you to the other *Suleviae* where you rightly belong. It may have been foretold, but that doesn't mean it cannot be changed. You can surely sense that Henrietta Swift is pure of heart — she can do so much good — you're the goddess of healing, *Sulis* — you're one of the Three Mothers — you should understand. I entreat you to leave this girl here with me."

Hetty, feeling rather sick and dizzy with trembling legs that refused to hold her up any longer, slumped down into the chair, all fortitude eroded. She no longer understood what was going on; she had thought just moments earlier that she understood the Roman goddess. She was certain that she'd felt a kind of profound connection with her and was ready to do her bidding, but she couldn't now make sense of Torquhil's confusing words.

She remembered feeling a little peculiar, as though she were sleepy and unable to marshal her thoughts properly, but she'd been so certain that this *Sulis Minerva* meant her no harm. She had felt an overwhelming need to go with her; as though nothing else mattered.

"Torquhil," she whispered, "Why is she here? What does she *want?*"

He was still shielding her, his fingers gripping her arm, but he turned to her when he heard her quivering voice.

In the murky corner of the room, *Sulis Minerva* was almost still, apart from an occasional adjustment to her form, as little landslides of dust and grit shifted and settled. Hetty thought she was listening, in some way, not as a human might, but in some mystical way.

"She wants you. She seeks revenge for being forcibly separated from the other two *Suleviae* Mothers. Many centuries ago, while still in corporeal form, she was removed from her sisters and buried in the Galdre Knap Long Barrow as punishment for not being able to heal a local Anglo-Saxon warlord — his tribe were merciless and unforgiving. He's buried alongside her. She should, by rights, be in the Bath's Sacred Spring — *Aquae Sulis,* with her sisters but has unfortunately been trapped beneath Galdre Knap all this time."

"But how is she *here* with us now?"

"I can only surmise that she has at last found the fuel she needed to reanimate her long dormant powers by having both you and Eirwen so close."

"So, she's just been waiting — for centuries — for this to happen?"

"Time is probably not the same for her. It is more of a distant and obscure concept rather than the physical passing of hours and months as we know it."

"So, this has something to do with Eirwen's condition?" asked Hetty, with one eye on *Sulis Minerva*.

"A few years ago, before all this trouble was stirred up, Eirwen's childish curiosity got the better of her and she broke into the tomb while I was in London."

"So, that's why — ?"

"That's when I first noticed that she had begun to change. She became distant and unable to focus on anything. Uninterested in life. She gradually lost her natural high spirits. It was as though she were being erased. Something happened to her in the tomb, and I believe it was to do with *Sulis Minerva*. I believe the goddess has come here to find you because she didn't manage to take possession of Eirwen. She needs to find some way of escaping from the tomb and returning to the other *Suleviae*. She was imprisoned against her will and finally sees a way to escape — through you. It may be that she's tried before, with other people, and been unsuccessful, we cannot know for sure — but I will not allow her to take you. She's broken Eirwen and I don't know if we can save her. I cannot and will not risk that happening to you."

"But she doesn't mean to hurt us! She's only trying to free herself — which is hardly surprising," said Hetty, utterly mystified by what was happening and still feeling thoroughly disorientated.

Torquhil glanced at the goddess, who seemed to be patiently waiting for something, some conclusion or action.

"Yes, I understand that. One cannot blame her for wanting to escape a fate that by rights has nothing to do with her — she was treated unjustly. I shouldn't have brought you here, but I had no choice. I've put you in danger and it may all be for nothing."

Hetty put a rather unsteady hand on his arm, "It won't be for nothing. And even if you *had* warned me — I'd still have come. Even knowing all of this, I would have come — for

Eirwen's sake if nothing else. What should I do now? Do you think she'll leave now that you've arrived? Will she try again?"

He looked down at her hand as though slightly surprised to find it resting on his sleeve, "It's hard to tell. She doesn't think like we do. She cannot feel the same emotions as a human being."

"Then, we must show her, that if we are united, she cannot succeed. We *must* be stronger if we're together."

"So I am led to believe," said Torquhil quietly and put his hand over hers.

The tingling began again in earnest, but Hetty was learning not to flinch when it started although the peculiar sensation was hard to ignore.

She wriggled her hand into his, so they were palm to palm, feeling his warmth and a welcome flood of comfort as his fingers curled around hers. She wished, rather forlornly, that it might have been in different circumstances, but was content, nonetheless, to just be holding his hand. She moved to stand right beside him, side by side, and turned to face *Sulis Minerva*.

She peeped up at him with a wry smile, "Unwanted guests can be so very tiresome!"

He smiled and she felt a small thrill that even in such a fraught moment that she'd managed to win a smile from him.

The next thought was that she was an utterly ridiculous creature for even thinking of such a frivolous thing when there was so much hanging in the balance and there was an unpredictable Roman entity hovering in the corner of the room displaying a good deal of menace.

Hetty took a steadying breath, "*Sulis Minerva*, I just want to say that although I'm deeply flattered by your interest, I think we're going to have to find another way to return you to your Sacred Spring — you see, I don't want to leave Eirwen and Torquhil. I really rather like it here at Galdre Knap and although you've quite obviously been done an enormous injustice, it's not really our fault — so, I'm afraid that for the time being you're going to have to return to the Long Barrow until we can come up with another more reasonable solution."

Sulis Minerva slowly rose up from the floor and began to advance towards them, dangerously spitting gravel again as she moved.

Hetty, thinking perhaps that she'd angered the goddess and was likely to be punished for her temerity, drew closer to Torquhil and unthinkingly slid her other arm around his waist and after a moment's pause, he responded by pulling her closely to his side.

The dust stopped swirling and the goddess sank back into the shadows and then, with a last defiant scattering of debris, she vanished, leaving only a cloud of clay dust spiralling behind her in tiny vortices.

As Hetty and Torquhil watched the dust settle and the air slowly clear, they didn't move, seemingly transfixed by the now empty space in front of them. Hetty was still tingling, from head to toe, and realised that she now had no legitimate reason to be clinging on to her companion as though he were all that was keeping her upright. She knew she should step away, release herself from his embrace and thank him for arriving in the nick of time. But she couldn't move a muscle and blamed the shock of having to confront a malevolent goddess made of dirt. That was clearly why she was still feeling quite shaky and in desperate need of reassurance. Almost without her own volition she tilted her head slightly and rested it against his chest and at once felt his arms tighten about her. In some remote part of her mind, she was concerned that she might possibly come to regret this uncharacteristically immodest behaviour but found that for the moment she just couldn't seem to care.

The tingling continued, but she also had some other odd sensations, which she quickly examined; she was feeling slightly short of breath but she put that down to being extremely distressed, with a quickened heartbeat, which, again must be because she was feeling so anxious, and a pleasant sort of fluttering in her chest like moths were trying to beat their way out, which, she couldn't account for at all.

Later, she would wonder how long she might have happily remained like that without regaining her sense of propriety, but she didn't have to make that decision herself because at that moment a sound from behind them made them both turn to see Eirwen looking at them, not just looking vaguely in their direction, but looking right at them, her gaze quite clear and direct.

Hetty practically jumped out of Torquhil's embrace and flew to the bedside, "Oh, my goodness! Eirwen!" she cried and put her arms around the frail young girl, "Are you all right? We're safe now, *Sulis Minerva* has gone!"

Eirwen blinked, the pale, wide-apart eyes flitting over Hetty's face, seemingly taking in her features, looking first at her eyes then her mouth and then flickering up to the bright copper hair. Hetty felt Torquhil beside her, as he came to perch on the edge of the bed. He reached out and took Eirwen's hand in his.

"Little sister," he said and Hetty could hear that his voice was husky with emotion even though his face, as usual, showed very little. "We've been waiting and hoping — "

Eirwen opened her mouth as though to speak and Hetty held her breath, watching the delicate features and praying for a word to come from between the colourless lips.

No sound emerged.

But for Hetty it was as though the Universe suddenly tilted; she felt a strange pressure in her head, as though someone was trying to crush her skull between their hands; the floor beneath her feet no longer felt solid. The air around her pulsed and rippled, the waves hitting her forcibly enough to practically knock her off balance. She closed her eyes for a moment and pressed her fingers to her temples.

"Hetty? What's the matter?"

She shook her head, "I don't know. My head is — oh, dear — it hurts most dreadfully. Like my skull is being battered." She bent forward, her head in her hands, the pain threatening to overwhelm her.

"Eirwen! Stop this at once!" commanded Torquhil, his voice harsh.

The aquamarine eyes slid to his and then back to Hetty and then to her brother's hand on hers.

"You cannot punish Hetty. She's done nothing but try to help you."

Hetty raised her head, her face screwed up with pain, "It can't be Eirwen — "

"It is I'm afraid and I think I know why. I must ask you to indulge me for a moment because I'd like to test a tentative theory."

"I'll do anything if you'll only make this agony stop! It's getting worse!" whimpered Hetty, beginning to feel faint.

"All right — " said Torquhil, and gently touched her hand.

She looked up at him, a little startled, and then smiled wanly through the pain and nodded, understanding and closing her eyes again. She didn't open them when she felt him lift her hand, pressing the softest kiss into its palm. She repressed an involuntary shudder of pleasure and tried desperately to concentrate on coping with the increasing discomfort in her head.

"Do — whatever you have to — " she said through clenched teeth.

"I'm so sorry," he murmured and tilted up her chin with one finger and she let out a little gasp as his lips lightly brushed hers. Her eyes opened very wide and found his face was still close, his gaze fixed on her, and she read in their midnight dark, a hidden message. She blinked several times to clear away the pain-induced tears and tried to convey without words that she understood his reasons for his surprising behaviour.

Torquhil looked at his sister and then back to Hetty who was obviously still suffering a great deal of pain. He pulled her gently to her feet and drew her into his arms. Hetty went willingly and allowed herself to lean into him and to take some illicit pleasure in the embrace. She knew why he had to do it and she realised that there was a perfectly logical and yet sadly absurd reason behind his actions, but she wished, so very much, that it wasn't just to get rid of her headache and placate his demanding sister.

She thought she'd try to make it easier for him, because she could sense his discomfort and realised that his natural reserve was being stretched to breaking point by the strange events at Galdre Knap.

She tilted her head and looked up at him encouragingly. He bent his head and quickly kissed her.

They both heard a soft sigh, like feathers falling.

Hetty felt him start to retreat and without conscious thought, she put up her arms and slid her hands under his long dark hair, her fingers clasped behind his neck and pulled his head back down to hers— and she kissed him back. The warmth of his lips against hers, the feel of his hands pressing the small of her back, the closeness —

She was torn between a sudden and powerful desire to keep kissing him and profound shock at her own shameless behaviour. But she didn't have a chance to decide because his arms tightened around her and she was pulled up onto her tiptoes and the kiss changed, becoming unexpectedly fierce and, to her delight, rather passionate. She wasn't quite sure if it was her doing or his. She could feel his breathing alter and the tingling intensified until it became almost unbearable. Then, just as he had suspected, she suddenly realised the pain in her head had stopped. She made a little moan because that was all she could manage, and he pulled back a little so that he could look down at her. His eyes were inky black, and he was breathing heavily.

"The headache — it's gone," she whispered.

They both turned to look at Eirwen, who was lying just as before but there were tears running down her cheeks and into her silver hair.

Thirteen

Hetty mopped Eirwen's tears with her sleeve and cried herself, sniffing and making sad-happy hiccupping sounds. She stroked the girl's hair and smoothed it away from her forehead. She didn't dare look at Torquhil in case she saw something in his eyes she really didn't want to see.

But however, she felt about that fraudulent kiss, Torquhil's theory had been proved correct. Her headache had been caused by nothing more than a petulant child toying with other people's emotions in order to get what she wanted and, as far as they could tell, what she wanted was simply a bride for her brother. It was inconceivable. They were at the mercy of the whims of a capricious child. It seemed to Hetty that the Universe was determined to be perverse and was leading them down a rock-strewn and dangerous path into the unknown and what promised to be an unsettling conclusion.

Hetty was in a state of bewildered bliss. On the one hand, she had just experienced her very first kiss and she could still feel the traces of it on her lips, but on the other hand, although it had been for a worthwhile reason, it had not been the *right* reason. Her heart was filled with joy because it had been the right man kissing her, but whereas the kiss had been thrilling and memorable, she knew deep down that unfortunately, on Torquhil's side, there was no love, whereas on hers, the love was, she now realised, strong and very real — if a little hard to understand. He had merely been hoping to find a cure for her pain and had now confirmed that it had only been Eirwen making a nuisance of herself because she'd nothing else to do, like a spoilt child making mischief to gain attention and to fill the hours of boredom. Hetty was having trouble stilling the erratic beating of her heart and the imaginary moths in her chest, which were behaving in a frenzied fashion.

The biggest problem for her was the shattering idea that it would probably never happen again. She was forced to imagine a life without any sign of affection from Torquhil; he could not, after all, continue with this pretence forever — it would not be feasible to keep up such a charade even to placate Eirwen.

The instigator of these particular troubles had ceased her weeping and seemed satisfied with the outcome of her machinations and, exhausted from the effort it'd taken to make it come about, was slowly falling asleep again.

Hetty watched as the blue-veined eyelids drooped down over her now unfocused eyes and her pale and emaciated face began to relax.

"She's asleep," whispered Hetty and surreptitiously wiping her own eyes, she adjusted the bedclothes and stood up, still not daring to face Torquhil.

"I think I shall go and make sure that Grandpapa is all right, I haven't seen him this morning as I was rather distracted by — events," and she turned away from the bed whilst trying to hide her embarrassment.

There was a pause and then Torquhil stayed her with a hand on her shoulder, "Hetty, I cannot apologise enough — I was really only trying to make Eirwen stop hurting you. It was too much to bear. I didn't mean to upset you — "

Hetty managed to glance up at him with a falsely bright and cheerful expression; she could feel the insincerity of her rigidly fixed smile, "Oh, don't worry! Of course, I didn't take it seriously! I knew precisely what you were trying to do! I must say it was very ingenious of you. And goodness gracious, it worked immediately, didn't it? How on earth did she manage to do that, I wonder — cause the headache?"

He hesitated, his hand still lightly holding onto her shoulder, "You didn't take it seriously?"

"Good heavens, no! Of course not. I realised immediately that you were just giving Eirwen what she needed to see. She needed to believe that you and I — you — that we — were in love. Perfectly understandable. I was not the least bit concerned. It was all in a good cause in the end."

"Hetty — " began Torquhil, but whatever he was about to say was left unsaid and hanging in the air between them because the bedchamber door cautiously opened, and Agatha poked her head in.

"Sir? Is everythin' all right? We're startin' to fret downstairs as neither of you have come down for breakfast," her gaze took in the unusual sight of a bedchamber covered in dirt and some rather substantial stones, and with a nervous glance at the ceiling to make sure it wasn't about to collapse onto their heads, she smiled and began to back out again muttering, "I'll just go an' fetch a broom — "

"I can explain Aggie!" Hetty called after her, but the maid had already clumped away. She looked anxiously at Torquhil, "How are we going to explain? She'll need a wheelbarrow to take all this away! Oh, dear, my life never used to be this — so complicated!"

"I think Agatha will just prosaically accept that strange things happen at Galdre Knap. The villagers have always talked about the peculiar occurrences up here apparently, long before I arrived."

Apprehensive that he might allude to what had just happened again, Hetty crossed the room, keeping her head down, and murmuring something about her grandfather, she went out quickly before anything more could be said.

What he didn't see was that on the other side of the door she came to a faltering standstill and covered her face with her hands and made some muffled sobbing sounds before setting off along the corridor, impatiently smearing tears away with the heels of her hands.

He may not have seen, but he had excellent hearing and the stifled heartbroken sobs were clearly audible even through the heavy oak door.

* * *

"But, Grandpapa, I had no control over her! She just appeared and there was nothing I could do. I couldn't abandon Eirwen, and it was difficult to call for help."

Roland Swift had finished his breakfast but was still sitting at the table writing letters to his attorney and a few of his old tenants, with whom he still corresponded, despite having removed some seven miles. He had been a fair and generous landlord and employer and remained so despite no longer being lord of the manor at Swift Park.

"My dear girl," he said and her heart quailed because she knew that tone of voice well, "I have always credited you with possessing a modicum of intelligence, but to hear that you've just come face to face with such a — thing and tried to cope with it without seeking assistance, makes me wonder if I've been very much mistaken in my way of thinking. What kind of fool would try to reason with an unknown spirit of any kind, let alone a wrathful ancient goddess with a penchant for abduction! You should have called for help immediately."

"But I didn't get the chance! Anyway, I couldn't have left Eirwen even had I been given the chance to make my excuses and run for help. *Sulis Minerva* was difficult to ignore. You should see the mess in the Chinese Bedchamber! The floor is covered in grit and dirt and some of the larger stones have actually dented the floorboards. Poor Aggie, she's going to have to shovel it up. I must help her, although she never seems to be fazed by anything, which, I have to say, is a great advantage working here."

Her grandfather raised an eyebrow, "It's futile trying to divert me, Henrietta. This might have ended very differently had not Torquhil arrived at that precise moment! We're in a strange situation — things are not always what they seem. You simply must take more care. There are ungovernable forces at work here and they are not to be trifled with. I wish Anne were here — she'd know what to do for the best."

"You don't trust me to do the right thing?"

"It's not that, my love, but you're so young. You've not had the experience that your grandmother had, and you've not yet learnt how to cope with such extraordinary incidents, and you have yet to learn the art of listening to the voices that matter."

Hetty huffed indignantly, "I jolly well heard Grandmama out in the snow! And I have the ridiculous tingling in my fingers, especially when Torquhil — " she stopped mid-sentence and turned quite pink.

He looked at her with an amused frown, "When *Torquhil* — ?"

Flustered, she hesitated, "I — when — I mean — he — oh, dear — " and to her own great surprise she burst into tears.

He put out his arms to her and she stumbled into them, "Hetty? What has he done?"

She sniffled loudly into his sober grey coat, "Nothing! I swear! He was only trying to stop me having a headache!"

"You've piqued my interest! You'd better tell me all."

"He — Torquhil — "

"Yes, I guessed as much," said her grandfather with a wry chuckle.

"Old Pa! I'm trying to *tell* you!" sobbed Hetty.

Chastened, he schooled his expression, "I apologise. Do please continue."

She wiped her eyes on her sleeve and he dug into his pocket and pulled out an enormous white handkerchief and she blew her nose and dabbed at her puffy eyes, "He — you see — oh, it's so very hard to explain, but he thinks this is all because Eirwen wants me to marry him!"

"Well, upon my soul!"

"And he thinks that all that business in the snow was her trying to — stop me leaving and force us together. And this morning after *Sulis Minerva* had left and we — Torquhil and I — had sort of — um — embraced after the worst was over. Then she unexpectedly woke up! But then when we separated, I think she became a little vexed and somehow gave me the most terrible headache. I thought my eyes would pop out of their sockets it was so very bad. Well, Torquhil thought that if we — er — um — were close again that she'd be happy for a while and would stop forcing us together to get what she wanted — *oh, Old Pa!*"

He stroked her back and rocked her, "There, there. It'll all be all right. So, what happened then?"

A few more sniffles followed, "So — he *kissed* me — or I kissed him — it was nice — I liked it. But then his plan worked, and the headache stopped and Eirwen was awake, and she was crying!"

"That all sounds very successful then. A definite improvement on what went before. I cannot fathom why you should be carrying on so."

Hetty emitted a wail of grief, "Because he only kissed me so that Eirwen would stop trying to control us!"

"Are you absolutely certain?"

"Yes. He doesn't feel the same way — "

"That you do?"

Silence.

"You've fallen in love with Torquhil?"

"I *may* have," grumbled Hetty.

Her grandfather smiled at her fondly, "It's no bad thing. He's a very agreeable young man. Eccentric — that goes without saying of course, but intelligent and he has a good heart. You could do a lot worse. In fact, you've already had a close call as far as marriage is concerned!"

"You're not *listening*, Old Pa! He kept *apologising!* As though it were torture for him!"

He shook his bewigged head, "My dear child you're not making any sense at all. He was only apologising to you for what he felt he had to do — had no *choice* but to do. The act of a gentleman in extraordinary circumstances. And when, exactly did he suggest that kissing such a beautiful girl might be torment?"

She glared at him through the tears, "He didn't — not in so many words. He's far too polite. But he said he hadn't meant it — the kiss. He said he was just trying to stop Eirwen from hurting me."

"I think you're being rather short-sighted over this. Anyway, why don't you just talk to him? Most problems can be solved with a nice chat."

Hetty sprang up and paced to and fro across the library, "No, no! He must never know! It would be too humiliating. I couldn't bear him to feel sorry for me."

Seeing that his granddaughter was becoming even more agitated, he sought to calm her, "Of course, if that's what you really want. But you must promise me that you won't push him away because you feel a bit embarrassed. I know what you're like Hetty! If something frightens you, you run away from it and try to shut it out of your mind. You mustn't do that to Torquhil. It would be unkind when he has so much to concern him already. Is there some way you might help him find a way to free *Sulis Minerva?*"

Hetty stopped her fraught marching and looked at him askance, "How can I possibly do that?"

For a moment the old man sat in silence just regarding her, "Oh, I think you already know the answer to that," he said quietly.

She rolled her eyes, which were still reddened from crying, "But I'm *trying!* I can hear Crow! And Grandmama and *Sulis Minerva* — well, I could tell what she was thinking — almost."

"You couldn't tell that she wanted to abduct you, which might have been advantageous."

"You have to give me a chance! I've only just found out what I am — that I'm supposed to be — *different*. Rome wasn't built in a day," declared Hetty sulkily.

"It's you who are impatient, Hetty. I suspect that you hear those inner voices but dismiss them out of hand because you're afraid."

She threw herself down into a chair by the fire and contemplated her grandfather pensively, "It's true. I *am* afraid. You truly think he's got a good heart?"

He smiled at her fondly, "Indubitably. I know a good man when I see one. And if you have decided to love him then he must have some splendid qualities because you're notoriously fastidious. Look at poor Mr Scroggs. Rejected out of hand when he's such an earnest young man and thought you to be the answer to his very earnest prayers."

That drew a reluctant laugh from Hetty, "Sadly, Edwin's a nincompoop."

The door opened and Agatha ambled in, bearing a large tray and apologising for being late, "Sorry, but I was clearin' up the Chinese Bedchamber — what a *mess!* I filled two big pails with the dirt. I'll just remove the breakfast things if that's all right?"

"Perfectly fine, Aggie. Thank you. I'm so sorry about all the extra work."

The maid grinned, "Ah, no! Don't mind me! I like somethin' proper to do. No point in just flittin' about with a feather duster!"

She had left the door open and at the sound of hurried flapping, she looked over her shoulder, "Should've shut that door. Sorry."

Crow swooped dramatically into the room, circled and settled onto the back of a chair, with a definite snap of his sharp wings. He eyed Hetty but said nothing, scratching nonchalantly under his chin with one claw.

They watched while Agatha slowly removed the covers and bore the laden tray out of the room. Hetty closed the door behind her and turned to look at the jackdaw.

"I can tell you're just longing to say something, so do go ahead. Don't hold back out of politeness."

Crow finished preening and cocked his head.

It sounds like it's been quite a morning.

Hetty folded her arms across her chest.

One can't help eavesdropping when one is cursed with supernatural hearing.

"And what exactly have you overheard, Crow?"

Ah, well, I may have heard a thing or two — about a visitor.

"You've been spying. Oh, of course! I've only just realised! How slow-witted of me! That's how your master finds out about everything, isn't it? Fancy trusting a jackdaw to relate the truth."

A little offensive. I'm not a spy. I simply deliver information for nothing more than some food.

"Purveying information. *Spying*."

You sound a bit cross. Has something upset you?

Hetty pursed her lips but said nothing.

You can tell me anything. I won't say a word.

"I may not be able to hear you Crow, but I can see from my granddaughter's expression that you're about to be ejected out into the snow. I should tread lightly if I were you," said Roland Swift, intrigued by the one-sided conversation, but anxious about the belligerent glint in Hetty's eye.

"The jackdaw just admitted to spying on us and has somehow already heard about *Sulis Minerva* and — *and* the other more personal matter no doubt. Which, as I cannot trust him, I find exceedingly vexing."

Crow clacked his beak.

I resent the insinuation. Magpies and jays are untrustworthy. Jackdaws are merely — a trifle mischievous.

"So, is this meandering discourse leading anywhere Crow or are you just bored and in need of someone to provoke?"

I thought I might offer my services. I could be more helpful to you if I was allowed out of my prison.

"What could you do?"

I could carry messages. Call for help. Poke out eyes.

"Ruin the furniture."

I'm not a goose! They're uncontrollable. Untrainable. The mess!

"So, if we allow you the freedom of the house, you'll help by being a messenger?"

In a nutshell, yes. Do you have any nuts by the bye?

"I can probably find you some walnuts. Didn't your master feed you this morning?"

He's a bit distracted at the moment.

He dipped his head and quivered his tail.

I could tell you why if you're interested?

"Well, I'm not. Thank you. If you come with me now, I'll see what I can find for you to eat in the kitchen. But you must stay with me and not pester or frighten the staff."

I swear I'll behave. Are you sure you don't want to know?

"Positive," snapped Hetty. She held out her arm impatiently and the jackdaw stepped onto it, being particularly careful not to dig his claws in as he could sense that Hetty was not her usual carefree self. Of course, he knew everything that had happened having listened outside the door and was constantly dumbfounded by the stupidity of humans.

"Grandpapa, will you be all right for a while? Would you like me to send Mrs Waverley to keep you company?"

"No, don't trouble her, I have my book to read. You run along but remember what I said and — "

"I know! *Listen!*"

* * *

The kitchen was buzzing with excitement after news of the morning's events had reached them; it seemed that everyone had heard about the havoc left in the Chinese Bedchamber and they could talk of very little else, making wild suppositions about what might have caused it and blaming everything from ghosts to deathwatch beetles.

Mrs Ashby was gutting some rabbits Sam had caught in his traps, which made Hetty avert her eyes as she was squeamish about the preparation of small creatures, furred or feathered, and would often weep as she was forced to prepare them for the pot. Aggie was clattering away at the sink scrubbing the breakfast things, making everyone wince as she carelessly banged the pots; Sam sat at the end of the long table blacking a pair of fine top boots; Jacob sat next to him mending a broken bridle and Finn was in his usual place by the fire, puffing thoughtfully on his pipe.

Hetty paused in the doorway, Crow perched upon her shoulder, and waited.

Mrs Ashby looked up and caught sight of the jackdaw, her mouth tightening into a thin line, "What's *he* doing in here? He made a mess in the corridor."

"I'm sorry for that — it won't happen again. He's hungry. Mr Guivre forgot to feed him with all the — disruption this morning. I was going to find him some nuts or something for his breakfast."

The cook shrugged her large round shoulders and made a disparaging face, "Whatever you say, Miss. But I don't hold with wild animals in the kitchen."

Unless they're dead and having their guts ripped out.

Hetty pretended not to hear him, "I quite agree, Mrs Ashby but I suppose you could say that Crow is a sort of pet — like Thistle. And he's very well-behaved, for the most part. I don't usually allow him to roam free in the house. If I promise to be responsible for him, may he please come into your hallowed domain, just while I find him something to eat?"

Pets are mindless slaves.

Hetty concealed a smile.

Making disapproving tutting noises and ripping the skin from the rabbit with unnecessary zeal, Mrs Ashby nodded reluctantly.

Hetty and Crow disappeared into the pantry and came out bearing a bowl of scraps that the bird had thought looked appetising. She put it down by the back door and Crow hopped down and attacked his breakfast with gusto.

Hetty sat down at the table to lend a hand with the chores.

His heart is good, you know.

She didn't respond but her cheeks burned as she began to shell roasted chestnuts for Mrs Ashby's rabbit stew.

She listened to the chatter going on: Sam talking happily about how the new horses were settling in and passing on news about her geese and chickens; Aggie remarked upon the damage to the Chinese Bedchamber floor and asked if Finn might be able to repair it. Finn made his usual response, a combination of a shrug and a grunt, which Agatha took as tacit agreement.

Hetty found the sound of their voices kept fading away as she reflected upon the morning's strange happenings and, despite the dramatic appearance of *Sulis Minerva*, her thoughts soon became desperately entangled in a haunting wilderness of sensations, fuelled by the fearsome goddess, Torquhil's dark eyes and the feel of his lips upon hers.

She heard the sudden creak of wings as Crow flapped up to alight on her shoulder again and saw that he was about to wipe his beak on her gown.

"Don't you dare!" she hissed and grabbed a rag from the table and held it up for him.

The old man is right. You need to talk to my master.

Hetty compressed her lips.

He leant his smoky grey head against her neck.

He's surprisingly intelligent — for a human.

She shushed him.

Finn looked up at them and frowned, "You want to be careful Miss Hetty — some creatures are fair devious."

"I know, Finn. But I do believe that, despite his sometimes-poor behaviour, he may actually have our best interests at heart."

Crow clacked his beak and pressed his head further under Hetty's chin. It was warm there and comfortable and he concluded that there were very few humans who were worthy of his admiration and loyalty but this one, this flame-crested girl, was one of them. He couldn't explain why he thought this; it was just a feeling he got when he was with her. But even though he thought her rather remarkable by his normally rigorous standards, he was concerned that her emotions were going to make her take the wrong path and that would bring a good deal of unhappiness to Galdre Knap. He found that when humans were happy, they were far more inclined to be generous with their food and kindness, upon which he depended.

He knew things he'd rather not know, and he knew there were bad things coming and that this disorderly flock of humans would need all their wits about them in order to survive. He would do his best to help them, but he wasn't convinced that even the grandmother's powerful skills could have helped them, had she still been alive. This girl hadn't yet managed to awaken her own buried abilities; she was untried as far as those essential inherited talents were concerned. If they were going to rely upon her to save them, it was bound to be an extremely risky venture and people would die. There would be carnage and he had inconveniently developed a soft spot for her; he didn't want her to get hurt.

He gave himself a reproving shake and settled down on Hetty's shoulder for a quick nap.

* * *

Mrs Waverley was finding the general conversations in the house difficult to follow and wondered if she'd missed something important. There seemed to be an undercurrent she couldn't name; a ripple of anticipation and excitement as though anticipating Christmas or someone's birthday and everyone was in on the secret but her. The talking would either awkwardly dwindle away or just stop dead as she entered a room and there would be glances, raised eyebrows and mysterious smiles. She was not possessed of a particularly curious nature, but even she would admit to finding it all rather intriguing. There was something odd about that jackdaw as well — he had a way of looking at you as though he understood what you were saying. It was, she concluded, an exceedingly unusual household.

As she'd walked into Eirwen's bedchamber that morning she'd passed Agatha coming out carrying two large pails of what looked like garden waste, soil and stones, and she noticed that the floorboards had been dented in places. The patient seemed to have come out of her stupor and her eyes were following people with an encouraging amount of interest, which was a definite improvement. It seemed that, while Mrs

Waverley had been peacefully asleep in her Lilac Bedchamber, the world at Galdre Knap had changed considerably and she found she was quite keen to know why.

There was, she noticed with a gleam in her eye, a palpable quiver of excitement between her employer and Miss Swift; words left unsaid and charged glances. She watched with fascination as what appeared to be an innocent comment would set Miss Swift's cheeks afire and drive Mr Guivre silently from the room. She saw Mr Swift's quick frowns and overheard the murmured words of advice to his granddaughter and was surprised by her truculent responses. Yes, there were some things going on behind closed doors that she couldn't fathom, but it certainly made for an interesting life; observing the aftermath and trying to decipher what was going on drove away the tedium of being confined to the house by the weather. She was getting paid a superior salary for very little actual work and was more than happy to help out wherever she could whilst being so royally entertained. She had never had so much fun. She was having the time of her life.

* * *

Hetty was overjoyed to find that Eirwen's health was slowly but steadily rallying. Over the next fortnight her appetite gradually improved, and she grew stronger day by day. After a week had passed, she was able to prop herself up with only a little help and hold a cup in her hand, and another few days saw her greet Hetty in the morning with a smile, her wide-apart eyes holding an expression of decided warmth. She still wasn't able to talk much, but Hetty was hopeful that her speech would eventually return to normal of its own accord and she didn't try to force her.

Hetty chatted away to her, filling the air with nonsensical news about her poorly behaved pigs and anything that might have happened in the house or village: how Sam and Jacob made regular forays out into the snow, to the village or just to hunt for rabbits and pigeons and what a nuisance Thistle had been that day leaving a half-eaten mouse on Mrs Ashby's chair. She read to her every day and would sometimes just make up fanciful stories to entertain her.

She had decided early on, as she didn't seem to be able to rid herself of him, to allow Crow to accompany her during her visits to Eirwen but had watched carefully to make sure that his presence didn't upset the patient. In fact, he seemed to enchant her, and she generally focused on him rather than anything or anyone else, so Hetty concluded that he was a positive element in Eirwen's recovery, and Crow himself was quick to assure her that he was indispensable.

As Eirwen's face began to slowly regain some of its childish curves and her cheeks a slightly healthier colour, Hetty thought she'd seldom seen such a beautiful creature. She lost none of her ethereal qualities, still apparently created from something gossamer like frosted cobwebs or the wings of damselflies. She possessed an unearthly aura and, as Hetty observed her gradually returning to the real world, part of her believed that everything would be all right, now that their patient was recovering so well, and she allowed herself to relax.

Then, early one morning, she was still pushing her arms into her wrapper and making her way into Eirwen's bedchamber when she stopped in the doorway and stared in astonishment.

Eirwen was sitting on the edge of her bed, her birdlike legs dangling down, and she was clumsily attempting to braid her own hair.

She looked up and saw Hetty and smiled, "Hetty!" she whispered, her voice thready and barely audible.

Hetty practically shrieked with excitement, "Oh, my goodness! *Eirwen!*" She rushed to the bed and began fussing around, but the girl put out a tiny cool hand and stilled her. Hetty grabbed her hand and held it, "You're sitting up! And *talking*. This is absolutely marvellous. But you mustn't tire yourself. I'll finish braiding your hair and then you must pop back into bed and stay warm. It's so cold, I don't want you to catch a chill." She sat down beside her and combed her fingers through her hair and then began to plait it. Eirwen allowed her, with a gentle smile.

"I think that in a few days Aggie and I might be able to wash your hair for you. She's made some lovely rosemary water which smells delightful and then we could get the proper copper bath up here and you could have a nice soak."

"Torquhil?" she asked quietly.

"Do you want to see him? Shall I fetch him?" asked Hetty eagerly.

Eirwen shook her head, "Together now?" she whispered.

Hetty understood exactly what she was asking and wanted to emphatically refute the implication, but she also realised that these were the first truly meaningful words Eirwen had spoken in many months and therefore they must be important, and she would have to find a suitable answer for her.

She looked at Eirwen directly and spoke decisively, "No — *not* together," she replied. "One cannot force people to love one another just because you desire it. And I must tell you that I do not appreciate your methods in trying to make it so! You hurt me very badly — my head ached for days."

Eirwen began to weep soundlessly and Hetty, already sorry for being so exasperated with her, gathered the girl into her arms and just let her cry, knowing that being trapped for so long inside a slowly deteriorating body, unable to communicate, would undoubtedly have taken a heavy toll, but she also knew that she couldn't allow such a powerful child to believe that she could manipulate anyone into doing her bidding — it could lead to disaster.

"Although, to tell the truth, I've no idea why you would wish us to be married anyway because, as you know, he's such an odd soul and anyone with any sense at all would run away rather than fall in love with him and I am not exactly going to ever be the perfect wife for anyone! I had the chance recently to marry a perfectly sensible young man who would have established me as a respectable wife in a respectable house and we would have attended church every Sunday with our respectable gaggle of children. Mr and Mrs Scroggs — respected pillars of the community."

Eirwen pulled away and Hetty saw that she was laughing weakly through the tears.

"I'm sorry for all that you have been through, but it is not an adequate excuse for inflicting pain on anyone. You must get back into bed now before you get tired and cold. I shall call Torquhil. He will want to see you. He loves you very much, you know!"

Eirwen nodded and then leant back into Hetty's arms and stayed like that for several minutes until Hetty, fearing a relapse, managed to persuade her to get under the covers again, promising that they would soon try to take a few steps to begin to build up her strength.

As she stood up to go, Eirwen caught her hand in hers, "Forgive me," she said.

Hetty kissed her cheek and tried not to break down herself; then went quickly to find Torquhil, followed out of the room by a blur of sooty black as Crow followed, having tactfully remained in Hetty's room while she talked with Eirwen. He followed her everywhere now, a constant companion, either hovering nearby or perched upon her shoulder, making scornful remarks about everyone and clacking his beak indignantly — he frequently made her laugh when she was feeling at her lowest. She very quickly found that she couldn't do without him.

Fourteen

Hetty at last found some time to visit her much loved livestock, which were now being very well looked after by Jacob and Sam. The path that had been cut through the deep snow, from the kitchen door to the stable yard, having been well trampled, was now readily passable and although the weather was still bone-achingly cold, once wrapped up in her grandmother's shawl and her grandfather's coat, she found she was able to tread carefully around the house and across to the stables, shadowed of course by Crow, who dashed off for an exuberant flight around the hill to stretch his wings and, being incurably nosy, to see what was going on in the vicinity. She waved to Sam who was hard at work, as usual, mucking out, and found Jacob in the barn, building some new nesting boxes for the hens.

He grinned at her despite having a mouthful of nails, "Miss Hetty, nice to see you," he mumbled out of the corner of his mouth, "Come to check on your beasts? They all be doin' just fine. Geese are a bit irritable being penned up all the time but as soon as the thaw comes, we'll let them out into the orchard."

"Oh, Jacob, bless you for taking such good care of them. They're always tetchy even when allowed out — it's just their nature, I'm afraid. I doubt the pigs have tried to escape though — they'll be more than happy to be tucked up in their warm sties."

"Good as gold. Hens are fine too as you'll see if you want to go up. Mind yourself though." He nodded to the upper loft.

Hetty couldn't resist and hitching up her skirts and tucking them into her waistband she clambered up the wooden ladder to the mezzanine level under the eaves where Jacob was building a splendid home for her chickens. They had access by ramps to the yard and the orchard behind the barn, but because of the extreme weather were being kept inside for the present. They all looked to be in fine fettle, and she stroked them and told them what was going on outside and listened happily to their contented crooning; it was so soothing that she wished she could sleep up there with them. She was just about to back down onto the ladder when she heard voices below and stopped to listen, not wishing to needlessly expose her ankles to a stranger.

"Henrietta Swift! What in God's name are you doing up there?" asked Torquhil abruptly.

She peeped over the edge at him, "Oh, good morning! I was just talking to my hens. I haven't seen them in a while, and I missed them."

"Well, you should have said, and I would have made sure you had easier access to the barn. Let me help you down."

"No, thank you. I can manage perfectly well."

"I have no doubt that you can but as I'm here — "

Hetty sighed, not wishing to quarrel with him in front of Jacob, and eased herself towards the top of the ladder, gathering her skirts about her to cover herself as best she could, she swung her legs out and placed her borrowed boots on the rungs and began to descend carefully.

She reached the halfway point and then out of sheer perversity she turned on the ladder and launched herself into the air with reckless abandon.

Even as she fell, she wondered what on earth had made her do such a madcap thing. She was seldom impulsive for fear of accidental injury or embarrassment. Torquhil had no choice but to prevent her from crashing to the ground and injuring herself, but the unexpected impact overbalanced him, and they tumbled backwards into a pile of straw.

She laughed out loud at his surprised face and then realising that she was, rather indelicately, lying on top of him, she became very still and gazed up into his eyes, the laughter dying slowly.

She bit her lip, "I told you I could manage," she murmured.

"And you are true to your word," he responded, and she felt his hands tighten about her waist, "Some word of warning would have been helpful so that I had time to brace myself for the impact."

She giggled, "I'm sorry. It was just a silly impulse."

"You can be surprisingly impetuous."

Her cheeks flushed hotly as she recalled how she'd kissed him, "I — I just didn't think."

"Oh, I'm not complaining," he said, and their eyes met and Hetty's breath caught in her throat, and she made a small choking sound.

The sound of Jacob's discreet cough brought them back to reality and Torquhil lifted her bodily and put her down on the straw beside him. He then stood up and held out his hand to her to help her up. Taking it, she allowed herself to be hauled upright and didn't object as he absent-mindedly picked straw from her hair and clothes.

Recalling him to his surroundings with a warning glance, Hetty untucked her petticoats and skirts, gave them a shake and stepped away from him.

"That ladder can be a mite tricky at times," remarked Jacob mildly.

"Indeed," said Hetty, "Perhaps that's what caused my fall."

"It may well have done, Miss. I did warn you to take care though."

Hetty grinned at him, "You most certainly did Jacob and I must declare that I think I would have been quite safe had not Mr Guivre interfered."

Mr Guivre cast her a fulminating glance but said nothing.

Enjoying herself immensely, Hetty smiled innocently at him, "You did provide me with a very soft landing though. I hardly felt a thing."

There was a decided gleam in his eyes as he replied, "I, on the other hand, probably have several broken ribs."

Again, she laughed, "If, by that snide remark, you're insinuating that I am heavy enough to have caused damage to your person — "

It may have been her imagination, but she could have sworn there was appreciative laughter in those dark eyes.

"May I suggest," she continued, warming to her subject, "That you might want to eat a few more of Mrs Ashby's hearty pies so that you have the strength to catch me next time without the prospect of injury!"

"Next time?" he echoed.

She smiled up at him, "One never knows what may happen and I am of the opinion that one should always be prepared for the worst."

"Or — the best."

"Oh," she said, wondering if he meant what she hoped he meant but rather doubting it. She searched his face and as usual found very little evidence of anything she would dare to pin her hopes upon.

Jacob, who was feeling rather sorry for his employer and Miss Swift because they were clearly finding it difficult to express their sentiments, would have liked to have told them about the first time he'd met his much beloved wife.

He'd seen her, scrubbing out a wooden pail in the rain, without a care for her appearance and she'd looked up at him and smiled and that was it, he was in love, and he told her so there and then. Of course, she'd merely laughed at him to begin with, but he'd worn her down with his persistence and in the end, she told him crossly that she'd marry him because she couldn't bear him constantly whining in her ear.

They'd been married for seventeen years and although his new job and the snow were keeping them apart more than either of them would like, every time he was able to get back to their cottage on the outskirts of the village, it was like their first meeting all over again. She'd look up and smile and say what fine brown eyes he had, and he'd ask her to marry him.

And they'd laugh together, and their three children would roll their eyes and tell them to behave themselves.

He secretly observed Mr Guivre and Miss Swift and although he thought it to be a rather odd pairing, like a rook and a goldfinch, he hoped they'd be able to come to some mutual agreement before something else came to stand in their way and prevent their happiness. He could quite clearly see their delight in each other. He watched them as they made their way out of the barn and into the snow-bright stable yard. The cold light caught the golden glints in Miss Swift's hair and Jacob smiled to himself, remembering her grandmother's stubborn refusal to cover her spectacular hair. It was as though she were deliberately throwing down a gauntlet to anyone she met and it had caused some of the worst scandalmongers in the district to sneer behind her back, but she had quite clearly never thought anything of their opinions because she carried on just as she always had, seemingly without a care in the world, her fiery hair a conspicuous beacon of defiance, until it had naturally turned silver as she aged. Her granddaughter was obviously cast from the same defiant mould and as he returned to the construction of the hen house, Jacob offered up a hopeful little prayer for a happy outcome for the pair of them.

Hetty heard the sound of Jacob's hammer beating out its confident rhythm again and stopped for a moment to look around at the disguised world surrounding Galdre Knap, the softening of the sharp edges and veiling of the distant landscape. It was magical and mysterious but at the same time, slightly sinister. She wasn't sure if she loved or hated it. There was still no sign of a thaw; the heavy layer of snow remained unchanged, pristine, apart from where Jacob and Sam had dug paths and carefully stacked the snow into neat banks on either side.

Seeing that Torquhil was halfway across the yard already, she dashed after him, with a decided skip in her step. As she caught up with him, he fixed her with such a considering look that she faltered to a standstill beside him.

"What is it?" she asked breathlessly.

"I'm not really sure. The sound of your boots on the snow — they sounded joyful — if boots can sound joyful. I've not been subjected to — much exuberance or joy. Eirwen and I were brought up by strictly religious parents, who condemned any kind of unnecessary signs of enjoyment. Skipping was expressly forbidden. They would have considered it an unforgivable slight against God to be seen to be too happy. I'm afraid they would have most certainly frowned upon you with your obvious passion for all manner of things, whether it be hens or raspberry leaf tea — they would have found you quite alien to their way of thinking."

Hetty studied his face, so still and impassive and she wondered if all his reserve came from his rigid upbringing and considered what he might have been like had he been brought up by more tolerant parents and without the added worry of having a sister with such extraordinary problems.

"Do *you* find me so?"

He continued to look at her for a moment then turned his gaze away to the tall twisting chimneys which reached up into the white sky like gnarled and ghostly fingers.

After a short pause he said, "Quite the opposite."

Flustered but pleased, Hetty stared hard at the snow-covered toes of his boots and willed her face not to turn a revealing scarlet, "Oh. Really? You see, I think that because I'm so scared of everything; particularly of familiar and much-loved things changing — I was sure I must seem rather a pitiful sort of creature."

He smiled, "Hetty, you are far from pitiful. You've had to move from your snug farmhouse home to an isolated and forbidding mansion where you've braved an irate Roman goddess, my possessed sister, you've been stranded in a deadly snowstorm, discovered that you have special powers — and then, of course, there's the upstart Crow, who would try the patience of even the most saintly amongst us. And, rather remarkably, you've confronted everything with determination and humour — which, as you readily admit that you're not naturally a courageous person, I think proves you're even more stout-hearted. Someone who feels no fear at all cannot truly be called a hero."

"Gracious," said Hetty, thoroughly overwhelmed and thrilled in equal measure but finding herself rather at a loss for words. There were all sorts of things she wanted to say to him but her natural reticence meant that she could voice none of them. She was only able to further scrutinise his boots and wonder what might have happened if she'd been able to express her feelings without worrying about what could very well be humiliating consequences. Her grandmother had seldom held back, believing that it was far better to say what was on your mind rather than bottling it up and then exploding without warning. The only time that Hetty had been disappointed in her uncharacteristic lack of veracity was when she found her grandmother had deliberately withheld the truth about their abilities. She did however realise that she'd been told no actual lies and accepted that her grandmother had merely committed the sin of omission, which in such unusual circumstances, could probably be forgiven.

"It's true. I've removed you from your nice safe life and brought you to a place riddled with unknown dangers and am now asking far too much of you."

"Nonsense," said Hetty adamantly, "I'm truly glad I came, and Grandpapa is more than happy to be here. He really didn't like the idea of me being at Friday's Acre because he blamed himself for our altered circumstances, although of course it wasn't his fault. I swear Torquhil, you have no need to be concerned for me. It is, without doubt, quite an odd life here at Galdre Knap, but I can assure you that it's preferable to living in a cold dark farmhouse and having to muck out the pigs in the snow! And I will admit that I was becoming rather tired of eating dandelion roots!"

"If you're sure — "

"I am *absolutely* sure. I don't want to leave — " Hetty just managed to stop herself from finishing the sentence as she'd meant to and quickly added, " — *everyone* here as I've become exceedingly fond of them." His curious gaze searched her face, but she was too embarrassed to meet his eyes. As the silence grew between them, her toes began to freeze and she hopped from foot to foot and blew on her fingers, which were white from the cold.

"Come with me," said Torquhil suddenly, "I'll show you the Observation Tower," and he gestured to the incongruous octagonal structure in the corner of the building, "There won't be much of a view sadly because of the weather but — "

"I'd love to see it — only how do you get into it?"

"There's a door around the side of the house, but there's also an entrance from the inside, a hidden door under the main stairs that leads to the tower's staircase."

He strode away down the snowy path and Hetty quickly followed.

The door was tucked away around the side of the house, small and inconspicuous, disguised with a thick covering of ivy. Torquhil ducked under the low lintel, pushed the door open and stepped aside to allow Hetty to enter.

She brushed past him and into the darkness and waited while he paused to light a lantern and then he led the way up the twisting narrow staircase.

As they climbed, the warm light from the lantern illuminated the walls and Hetty was astonished to see they were painted with a mural that depicted the English countryside and its softly rolling hills at the bottom and then as they ascended, there were tree tops and clouds, birds in flight, and then the night sky above studded with silvered stars, a crescent moon and hidden amongst the dark shadows were angels with indigo wings riding glistening winged serpents. She kept tripping up the steps as she tried to focus upon the beautiful painting and not get left behind by her companion at the same time.

By the time she reached the top behind Torquhil, she was completely out of breath and, as he ushered her across a dimly lit landing, through double doors and out onto the observation deck of the tower, she was trying not to pant inelegantly.

Hetty stumbled to a halt as she took in the extraordinary architecture; the ornately carved pillars supporting the roof, the stone parapet with writhing Wyvern dragons holding up the balustrade, the tiled floor with its exotic gilded patterns and then the view, which although restricted by the hazy white mist, took what was left of Hetty's breath away. She tried to say something but failed to find any suitable words as she staggered to the edge of the deck and clung onto the balustrade for support.

She could just see across the snow-laden roofs and treetops towards the elm avenue and although everything was misted and blurred, she knew that from their high viewpoint she would, on a clear day, probably have been able to see the chimneys at Friday's Acre and even some of its fields and outbuildings.

Wide-eyed, she turned to Torquhil who was leaning against a pillar, his arms folded across his chest, "What was the tower actually built for?"

"I suspect that it was initially for the ladies to observe from a distance as their menfolk hunted and also, in more dangerous times, for observing the enemy as they approached, I expect."

"The enemy?"

"Friend or foe. An early warning would always be useful in war or peace."

"This house must have seen a good deal of both over the centuries. I can imagine it having been used during battles, as a stronghold, a sanctuary and a lookout."

"Indeed, there are many tales of deserting soldiers from both sides forcing the owners to hide them in the cellars and shots being fired from this very tower at marauding armies, brigands and even angry tenants or jilted lovers. You can still see the bullet holes in the walls. It has a very chequered history. These walls could tell us quite a story if only they could talk."

Hetty raised her eyebrows, "I wouldn't be in the least surprised to find they *could* talk! Coat fastenings blink, Roman goddesses appear, jackdaws — "

Speak of the Devil.

A flurry of sooty wings and Hetty was looking into Crow's curious white eye as he peered at her from his perch on her shoulder.

He rubbed his head against her jaw.

Did you miss me?

"Not in the slightest," said Hetty, "It's peaceful without your constant prattling. Where have you been all this time?"

Just having a look around.

"And what did you discover?" asked Torquhil.

Food is scarce and there are mutterings in the village.

"About?"

Crow cocked his head.

You probably won't want to know.

The charged silence that ensued made the jackdaw shrug his bony shoulders.

There's gossip. The locals have little else to amuse them because of the snow.

He eyed his master uneasily.

They were bound to wonder. Humans tend to be suspicious of things they don't understand.

Hetty looked from the bird to Torquhil in confusion.

"What are they gossiping about?" she enquired anxiously.

Torquhil remained quite still but his eyes were on Hetty's face, "As Crow says, there was bound to be talk — it was inevitable. You and your grandfather moving to Galdre Knap will have certainly baffled some people. They have no reason to trust me — I'm a stranger to them and they probably view me as being a sinister and dangerous interloper, a foreigner, and I've given them no reason to think otherwise."

"You're *not* — !" began Hetty impulsively, "I mean — why would they talk about Grandpapa and me moving here? We're only here to help. I'm in your employ — it's just a job after all, no more or less than say, Agatha or Mrs Waverley. Surely, there's nothing wrong with you hiring domestic help?"

This should be interesting.

"Keep your thoughts to yourself, Crow," said Torquhil coldly, "Hetty, all they can see is that I've taken in a young, attractive and, more to the point, *unwed* girl! They will discount her grandfather, because he is, in their eyes, too old to properly protect her — so, in their eyes, she is also unchaperoned, her innocence under constant threat."

Whilst inwardly overjoyed that he considered her attractive, she shook her head, "But that's just outrageous! It makes me sound as though I can't fend for myself! That I do not know my own mind! And it makes you sound like a — like a — *libertine!* It's completely ridiculous. It couldn't be further from the truth. We must set them right immediately!"

Torquhil smiled but it didn't reach his eyes, "It will go no further than talk. They will soon become bored with the idea and move on to the next scandal."

"But it's not *true!* Someone must tell them. *I* will tell them. I shall go to the village this afternoon. Oh, this is unbelievable. Your reputation — !"

At this he actually let out a short, mirthless laugh, "*My* reputation? I have no reputation of which to speak. It's you I'm concerned about. Perhaps you should announce your engagement to Mr Scroggs. That might just halt the gossips in their tracks and give them something else to talk about."

Hetty made such a wild gesture of dismay that Crow, taken by surprise, lost his balance and took off, flapping about the tower, finally landing rather indignantly upon the balustrade.

"*Mr Scroggs!* Are you quite *mad?* I could *never* even consider marrying such a man! I can't believe you even suggested that!" She turned away from him in fury and held onto a nearby pillar to steady herself.

"I wasn't suggesting that you marry him — just that you announce your betrothal *ad interim,* in order to put a stop to the whispers."

"Oh," said Hetty, "I see. I'm afraid no-one would believe me. He's not much liked in the village, and they mostly know of my lack of enthusiasm for him. We had better think of some other solution."

I have one.

"Crow. It's time for you to leave," said Torquhil, a sharp edge to his usually calm voice.

"No, wait! He might actually have a good idea. He's really quite clever sometimes!"

I'm flattered. I was just thinking that you could still announce a betrothal.

"A betrothal? I don't understand — " She suddenly glanced back at Torquhil, her face colouring, "Oh — you can't mean — don't be ridiculous! *Crow!*"

"Don't pay any attention to him. He just likes to meddle. He's a mischief-maker." said Torquhil in soothing tones.

"Well, he's not getting any treats from the kitchen today!"

Crow remained silent and began testily preening his feathers.

"You know, it's not such an absurd idea, if you think about it logically," said Torquhil slowly, "It would put an end to any salacious talk, give you some much-needed protection and of course the main advantage is that it might help appease Eirwen until she's well enough to be reasoned with."

Hetty sighed, she was feeling mixed emotions, part fear, part elation. "It seems more than a little hare-brained to do something so momentous just to ameliorate a situation that could easily be resolved by me having a chat with some of the villagers."

"I'm sorry Hetty, I'm loathe to admit it, but I think the jackdaw might be right. This would solve some of our immediate problems and it might make you feel more at ease."

"I already feel perfectly at ease so there's no need — "

"Well, if you're dead set against the idea, we can forget about it."

Hetty's heart skipped a telltale beat, "I didn't say I was *against* it — I just — I thought you might not like — being coerced into a betrothal with a — a redheaded farmhand!"

"I can think of nothing I'd like more," said Torquhil, his eyes bitumen black.

Should I leave?

"Oh, do be quiet, Crow!" snapped Hetty, beginning to panic.

Crow shook his wings and turned his back on them.

Hetty lifted her chin and faced Torquhil, "I think you might be a little mad."

"Perhaps," he responded with his crooked smile, "But rest assured, I meant it. If nothing else, think how happy Eirwen would be. It might distract her and give us a little breathing space so that we can find another way of convincing her to stop her incessant and dangerous meddling."

She looked up at him anxiously, trying to read his now impassive face, "If you think it would be good for Eirwen — then I suppose that I *must* agree."

"Must? I don't think I want my er — betrothed to be so obviously unwilling. It doesn't do a great deal for a gentleman's ego."

"But I'm *not* unwilling — I would very much like to help in any way I can."

"So, it's agreed then."

"If you say so," she said, her heart thumping as loudly as Jacob's hammer.

She felt as though she had at least three hearts beating at once inside her chest and found it hard to keep her breathing steady. Even as she spoke, she was silently berating herself for being so spineless and just giving in, but as it was exactly what she'd been dreaming about, she couldn't bring herself to decline the offer despite well-founded misgivings. She realised deep down that it was very unlikely to end well and that she'd more than likely have her heart broken and be turned out of Galdre Knap, but it was a risk she was willing to take. She thought she was probably being selfish and more than a little foolish, but there was something pushing her to do the things she was doing and suspected it might be Eirwen or her grandmother egging her on because this was not what she considered to be her normal behaviour. Usually she did her utmost to avoid embarrassing situations which is why, of course, she had become embroiled with Mr Scroggs in the first place — she had not had the heart or the mettle to tell him that she had absolutely no interest in him whatsoever, even though she had known perfectly well that he never could be the man for her; she had therefore prevaricated too long and become ever more tangled up in Mr Scrogg's assertive scheming. She had been too afraid of offending him to tell him the truth.

And here she was, heading for certain trouble again.

"I think I shall go and discuss this with Grandpapa before giving you my definitively final answer. He will know the best thing to do."

Torquhil nodded but said nothing, silently observing the emotions crossing her expressive face.

Crow hopped onto her shoulder but was unusually quiet.

She couldn't meet Torquhil's gaze as she passed him and made her way quickly to the twisted staircase and then realised that he had the lantern, so had to stop and wait for him. He led the way and at the foot of the stairs showed her through the door which led into the main hall. The door was concealed within the intricately carved wainscoting and hidden under a heavy tapestry depicting deer running through a forest to escape the huntsmen.

He showed her where the mechanism for opening it was so that she could enter the tower whenever she pleased. She thanked him stiffly for the guided tour and they parted awkwardly, Hetty going to the library to find her grandfather and Torquhil to the kitchen to talk with the staff.

Crow, not wishing to have his beak tied, wisely kept his own counsel.

Fifteen

Roland Swift watched his granddaughter pacing the room again and sighed, heartily wishing his wife were there to help him disentangle the mess they found themselves in — she would have known exactly what to say and do. He had been hopeful that things were becoming less complicated and that Hetty was at last finding her feet at Galdre Knap. It seemed though that she now found herself in yet more of a quandary than before. She was wringing her hands and chewing her lip and even Crow had abandoned ship for fear of serious damage to his person, retreating to the safety of the top shelf to watch the proceedings from afar.

"I think it's unfair to blame Torquhil for the scandalmongering, Hetty! That is purely down to those weak souls who choose to spread such malicious gossip. I'm certain his reasons for suggesting this false betrothal are perfectly sound and that he has only your best interests at heart. I cannot really understand why you find this so difficult. This is surely what you have been wishing for."

She took a few more steps until she reached the wall and leant her head against it in despair, "But, don't you *see?* I may have wished for exactly this — but not in this manner! Not merely as a measure to stop people talking about us. Not to force him into something he doesn't want. I wanted — I wanted — " She stamped her foot in frustration, "What if I have somehow brought this about?" Turning to glare at her grandfather she held out her hands, "What if these hands have in some way cast a spell on him and made him think that a betrothal is the only solution? What if I have somehow influenced him — forced his hand without even knowing that I'm doing it?"

He shook his head, the lappets of his old wig swaying like the ears of an elderly spaniel, "I don't believe for a moment that Torquhil is so easily influenced, my dear. He seems to me to be a man who knows his own mind, but, at the same time, is perfectly aware of his own shortcomings and is therefore reluctant to pressure you into anything. I am fairly sure he has some potent powers of his own and would not unwillingly succumb to your wishes however magical they might be unless he truly wanted to. I think you are underestimating him."

"I wish I could believe that! If only he would talk to me and tell me what he's thinking. He's so — *guarded!*"

"The easy answer to that is for you to talk to him and ask him what his views are on the subject. Otherwise, you're just going to keep banging your head against walls. If you really want my opinion on the matter, I think he's finally come to some kind of decision and has thrown the gauntlet at your feet. Are you going to leave it lying upon the ground or pick it up?"

"I don't know! It's all very well you saying all of this but it's not that simple for me! I cannot just march up to him and declare that I'd like the betrothal to be real."

"I don't see why not. I think he'd be glad of some plain and honest speaking. He's been fighting to save his sister for so long — not knowing what would happen and he's had no time for himself, no time to think of what he might want or need — about his own future. It seems to me that he's a lost soul in search of something to anchor him — to give his life some purpose and it's just possible, strange as it may seem, that thing is *you*."

"But what if it isn't and I make a fool of myself!" wailed Hetty.

"Then at least you tried to resolve the matter and you will not have to spend the rest of your life looking back over your shoulder and regretting that you did nothing at all and stupidly lost him anyway."

Ouch.

Hetty buried her face in her hands and made a muffled groan.

"*You* make these problems for yourself Hetty. Your mother was the same. She shut herself away from anything that might be painful or difficult to deal with and became a sad shadow of the person she had once been and your poor deluded Father disguised his fears by being reckless and in doing so, ruined everyone's lives including his own. I fear he was always inclined to give in to his basest desires even as a child and then blame others for the predicament he found himself in afterwards — he never took responsibility for his actions. Naturally, you have some of their best and worst traits. But I know that what your grandmother said about you is true. Despite your volatile temper you are good and kind to your very core and when you love, you love with all of your heart. Whatever happens, if love is at the centre of it then it cannot harm you. You must just be brave."

May I say something?

"If you must," said Hetty with a mournful sniff.

Your grandmother would say that you already know the truth.

"Everyone seems to be very keen for me to say yes to Torquhil's proposal!"

So, you think she would want you to say yes? Interesting.

Hetty sent Crow a reproachful glance and compressed her lips into a furious line, "Oh, stop being so unbearably smug! It's infuriating."

"What does he say?" asked her grandfather, his eyes twinkling.

"He says Grandmama would have wanted me to say yes to the betrothal."

"My Anne was a very perspicacious woman and Crow is obviously more intelligent than he looks."

"But he *can't* know what she thought!"

Nobody said anything, neither jackdaw nor human.

Hetty went back to leaning her forehead against the wall.

"I must go and sit with Eirwen now. Mrs Waverley will want her tea. I shall speak with Torquhil about everything — tomorrow."

"Don't make promises you have no intention of keeping, my child. Tomorrow you will have found more excuses not to say anything. Try not to think about it too much. It's like taking medicine or pulling a tooth — get it over with quickly. You'll feel better once it's finally been decided."

"Yes, Old Pa," replied Hetty meekly.

"That attitude does not fool me! And don't forget that he's just a human being too. He's really no different to us — despite his exotic attire and oddly reserved nature."

"I am beginning to understand that he has good reason for the way he is — his upbringing was apparently sadly lacking in affection and horribly strict — his parents were intolerant and unforgiving." She straightened up and with a heavily theatrical sigh she went to the door, opened it and said over her shoulder, "Whatever his reasons may be, I cannot see how it can warrant such a bizarre suggestion and I shall certainly tell him so. Stay with Grandpapa Crow — I'm not speaking to you."

The door shut behind her.

* * *

Mrs Waverley was contentedly embroidering while Eirwen sat propped up on a pile of pillows, sipping chicken broth from a small cup. She looked as pale as ever, with dark shadows under her beautiful eyes, her face gaunt, her cheekbones sharp — sadly unlike a normal healthy girl of her age. It broke Hetty's heart to see her still looking so frail.

She smiled wanly at Hetty over the rim of her cup, "No jackdaw?" Her voice was still no more than a whisper as though she had not the strength to make a louder sound.

"No, he's in my bad books at the moment, so he's been banished. When you've finished your broth, I thought we might see if we could get you into a bath and perhaps even wash your hair, would that be all right?"

Eirwen nodded happily and Mrs Waverley immediately lay down her embroidery frame and began to organise the bedchamber to accommodate the copper hip bath and stoked the fire energetically.

"I'll have the room nice and warm in a trice, Miss Swift. Will you go and warn Agatha that she'll need to start boiling the water?"

"Yes, and I'll get the rosemary water too. And a fresh bath sheet from the linen cupboard. I won't be long. You finish up that broth Eirwen, it'll give you strength," and she dashed out of the room.

Eirwen looked at Mrs Waverley, her eyes alight with mischief.

Mrs Waverley shook her head, "You're playing with fire Miss Eirwen and no good may come of it. You cannot control people against their will my dear without there being unfortunate consequences. If you are patient and leave things to Nature it may very well all come about just as you want it, of its own accord. And, should anything go awry, God forbid, you could not be blamed. This way — *your* way — might very well lead to all kinds of unforeseen complications."

The girl smiled slyly and allowed Mrs Waverley to take the empty cup.

"Well done. If we feed you well enough, you'll get better much sooner. We need to fatten you up first and foremost. Now, we have to get you into a bathing shift and brush your hair. Are you ready?"

Eirwen nodded enthusiastically, "Hetty," she said softly.

"What about her?"

"My sister. My family."

"Well, of course, she would be — if it should all turn out the way you want it — she would become your sister-in-law and a very nice one too. But Eirwen, you must be so very careful — it would be easy to cause absolute mayhem by meddling with things you don't truly understand."

Eirwen closed her eyes, her mouth pursed in sulky defiance.

"Come," said Mrs Waverley kindly, "Let's get you ready, Miss Crosspatch, shall we?"

* * *

Down in the kitchen, Hetty helped an uncomplaining Agatha carry pails of water and retrieved the flagon of Rosemary Water from the pantry. Agatha was already putting the great pans of water onto the fire to boil and Hetty silently marvelled at how much the housemaid managed to get done despite being so sluggardly — she was slow but steady and seldom stopped to rest.

Within the hour they had carried up enough hot water for the bath and the bedchamber was fragrant with rosemary and misted with steam clouds. Between the three of them they managed to help their patient across the room in her modesty shift and lift her gently into the bath. As she entered the warm perfumed water, she let out a deep sigh of contentment and lay back with her eyes closed.

Agatha collected the empty pails and left the bedchamber and Mrs Waverley discreetly returned to her embroidery while Hetty set to washing Eirwen's long silver hair, chatting the whole time about anything that sprang to mind. She felt that it was a massive step forward and was sure that it would mean an improvement in her general well-being. After the bath Hetty dried Eirwen's hair then braided it again as she perched on the edge of the bed, quietly pleased that her patient's cheeks were tinged with the faintest pink.

"Right, let's get you back into bed young lady and I'll read to you if you like while Mrs Waverley goes to have a nice cup of tea, which is long overdue."

Eirwen reached out and touched Hetty's hand, "Thank you," she murmured, her eyes shining.

Hetty took her hand in both of hers and dropped a light kiss onto the pearly white skin, "I'm happy to help. After the terrible ordeal you've been through, you deserve to have a more rewarding life and I'm determined that you shall have one."

Eirwen's tears spilled over and made silvered ribbons on her cheeks. Hetty thumbed them away, tenderly cupping her face in her hands, "Please don't cry. Everything will be all right. We'll look after you. You know, I've been thinking, it would be so very helpful if the snow were to go away — it makes everything so difficult — although it is exceedingly pretty."

Eirwen made a slight shrug of her emaciated shoulders and then taking Hetty's left hand, she pointed to her fourth finger.

Hetty glanced at her ringless finger, and the girl nodded.

"Oh, for heaven's sake! You don't mean — ? I wish you would at least *try* to behave! You're still young but one day you'll understand that you can't always get what you want — however much you may want it. It's not that I don't want the same thing, you understand, it's just that in order for such a thing to come about there must be an agreement between *two* people."

Eirwen smiled wickedly, "Two. You. Me."

Hetty couldn't help it, she laughed. It was all so utterly ridiculous that she found herself just giving into the sheer absurdity of her companion's childish scheming.

She was still giggling helplessly when Torquhil came in.

He looked from one to the other, "Have I missed all the fun?"

Hetty sent Eirwen a warning glance, "No, not really, I was just — telling Eirwen about some of Crow's funny antics."

"The jackdaw is somehow both amusing and annoying," said Torquhil, not looking entirely convinced. "So, which particular antics have made you laugh so merrily, Hetty?"

Hetty felt a telltale flush of colour rising and fixed her eyes on the fastenings of his dark green velvet coat: turtles fashioned from gold, with emerald eyes. She had never been good at dissembling and had seldom even tried to evade the truth because she knew she would always be found out — her face would give her away.

"And answer came there none," he remarked mildly.

"I — we — Eirwen and I, that is — we were only talking about the — snow — we were wondering if it might thaw soon!" She looked to Eirwen for support, but she was grinning mischievously, "Oh, that's just *so* helpful!"

"May I just say that my sister, even before all of this, was an abominable rascal and not to be trusted."

"You might have mentioned that before," muttered Hetty crossly.

"So, she was trying to persuade you to accept my offer?"

"I cannot possibly say."

"I think I have my answer."

"You're being rather presumptuous."

They looked at each other, Hetty glaring indignantly and Torquhil, faintly amused.

"It may be an expedient measure but if you think about it in a purely practical sense, you'll agree that it would be advantageous to halt the gossip and as quickly as possible. I think you're beginning to see the full extent of my sister's Machiavellian plotting — I'm afraid we are entirely at her mercy."

Hetty was silent. She was feeling extremely anxious but at the same time something deep inside her was rejoicing. It seemed to her that he was quietly determined that they should become betrothed, and she was beginning to feel that as the gods were conspiring against her that perhaps she should just give in gracefully and accept what they had decided for her. Of course, she told herself, the fact that being betrothed to Torquhil was fulfilling her most heartfelt wish had absolutely nothing to do with anything.

"I suppose," she said hesitantly, "In order to appease the villagers and to make Eirwen happy — "

"Those are indeed legitimate reasons, although — " he paused and fixed Hetty with a look that made her feel a little light-headed and she wondered if he shared his sister's power to beguile people or whether she was coming down with some winter affliction. "Although," he continued with the slightest smile, "The reasons are not important. What is important is the result."

"And the decision can always be reversed at a later date without anyone questioning it?"

"If you wish."

Hetty took a deep breath, "I don't know what I wish."

"That's perfectly understandable. Perhaps if you think of it as being purely to keep the patient happy, you'll be able to find a way to come to terms with it, even if it's only for the interim. I wouldn't ever want to cause you any harm, Hetty."

"I know that. I just don't want you to — " she faltered.

"If I swear to you that I am more than willing, would that help you make up your mind?"

She frowned at him and said softly, "I've already made up my mind."

"I know," he replied.

Hetty studied his face for a long moment and was strangely reassured.

"All right," she said, "I so desperately want to believe you."

"Then please, I wish you would."

"Please," whispered Eirwen.

"Outnumbered and outgunned," sighed Hetty.

"So, in that case, Miss Henrietta Swift, may I formally ask for your hand in marriage?"

Miss Henrietta Swift, her heart thumping fiercely, listened to the voice inside her head and took an unaccustomed step into the unknown.

"I'm much obliged to you, Mr Guivre and I have great pleasure in accepting your kind — but somewhat deranged offer, sir," she said, with an embarrassed little laugh.

Torquhil took her hand in his and bowing elegantly, raised it to his lips and pressed a light kiss onto it, "You do me a truly great honour, Miss Swift and I shall endeavour to ensure you never come to regret your decision."

Hetty, whose fingers were prickling painfully, allowed her hand to remain in his for a moment longer than she felt she ought and then wriggled her fingers out of his and hid her hand behind her as though it were guilty of something unforgivable.

"Are you happy now little sister?" asked Torquhil.

Eirwen smiled naughtily and Hetty giggled, "I have the feeling we just lost a vital skirmish," she declared, wiping away a tear.

Eirwen closed her eyes, "So happy," she said.

Hetty wasn't quite sure how she felt, mostly an odd combination of anxious and elated, but there was also a feeling of something having slipped gently into place, like a missing piece of a treasured ornament, found hiding under a blanket chest; it's that moment when you hold the fragment up to the aperture and it slots together perfectly, and the break doesn't show at all.

She wanted to look at Torquhil but didn't dare, knowing that her face would betray her great joy. There was an awkward silence while she tried to think of something to say; after all it was a momentous occasion, someone should say something memorable.

"Family," sighed Eirwen.

Hetty watched as one of the golden turtle fastenings on Torquhil's coat twitched its flipper and wondered if she had perhaps lost her mind. This man standing beside her was an enigma to her and she thought that her innate common sense should be telling her to keep well away from him and the darkly strange world he inhabited but something was encouraging her to take the risk and it spoke with her grandmother's insistent voice. It was barely more than a whisper, a breath of wind caressing meadow grass, but she heard it nonetheless, quite distinctly. She knew with absolute certainty that somehow, she didn't understand how, her grandmother was still able to communicate with her across the barriers between Heaven and Earth.

She wasn't sure what she believed in anymore — her previously obdurate beliefs were being sorely tested. Perhaps she only really believed in her grandparents, the friendship of those at Galdre Knap and a jackdaw. It didn't seem like much, but it was enough for her, for now. She had never had ambitious plans for herself, being more concerned about caring for her grandparents. After the catastrophe her father had unwittingly caused, bringing about the ruination of the entire family and setting them all upon a path towards an entirely different destiny, she felt that it was somehow her responsibility to make amends. And now they were all being drawn helplessly down an uncharted road towards God only knew what. She was both excited and terrified. The main thing was that Torquhil was there with her, on the same course and whatever was waiting for them she felt that if they could meet it together, all would be well. A small but persistent voice, which she was confident did *not* belong to her grandmother, reminded her that their pretended union was but a delusion, a fabrication created merely for the sake of appeasing his wilful sister.

She took Eirwen's hand in hers, "Sisters," she said, "Forever and always — whatever else may occur."

She felt Torquhil's gaze and looked him directly in the eye, determined that she would no longer hide from the things that frightened her.

* * *

Mrs Waverley, observing those around the table, and listening to the awkward, telling silences, tucked into the delicious Buttered Chicken and Roasted Parsnips with a good appetite, wolfing down a large portion before gladly moving on to the dessert of Madeira Cake served with Madeira Wine. Mrs Ashby was an exceptional cook and was making her stay at Galdre Knap even more enjoyable; she had seldom had the privilege of living in such luxury and was determined to savour it. She was, by the end of the meal, both comfortably replete and feeling rather benevolent. Mrs Ashby had outdone herself and there was nothing like a good repast to make one feel generous towards one's fellow man.

She noted that Mr Swift was a little weary and quietly suggested that after his traditional game of after-dinner chess, that he should retire early and catch up on his sleep. He readily agreed and she suspected that he rather obviously curtailed the game with Mr Guivre and, after kissing his granddaughter on her shining curls, he wished everyone a very good night and went to his bed.

Conversation continued as they sat beside the fire sipping their hot toddies. Hetty seldom drank alcohol but had been assured that she would enjoy a cup of Hot Spiced Rum and she found this to be true; it tasted mainly of orange and cinnamon, but she could also taste the rich addition of butter and sugar on her tongue as well as the intoxicating but mellow heat of the rum.

In a pleasant state of rum-induced sleepiness, she listened to Torquhil and Mrs Waverley discussing the merits of travelling by coach compared with the faster and more dangerous curricle. It clearly amused Torquhil to discover that the seemingly sedate and restrained Mrs Waverley rather fancied driving across the country at breakneck speed in a smart curricle. It was becoming quite obvious that Mrs Waverley was not quite as prim as she first appeared and, as she finally rose to retire to bed, she addressed Hetty in her steady tones with their curling Scottish burr.

"Miss Swift, you have been looking a little drawn of late and I have been wondering if you might benefit from one or two proper night's sleep well away from the Chinese Bedchamber. You must sleep very badly, keeping one ear out for Miss Guivre at all times. One cannot thrive without enough sleep. I would not have you wither and fade when I could be of service."

"But, Mrs Waverley, you have already been invaluable! I — we — could not have done without you — it's most fortunate that you were able to remain here to help us. I cannot think how we would have otherwise managed."

"I believe you would have coped admirably — you have inner resources that very few girls of your tender age possess. I do not think I know anyone who would have faced such daunting trials with so much spirit and good humour."

"I agree," added Torquhil, "She's indomitable."

"Oh, goodness gracious!" exclaimed Hetty, quite overwhelmed by the praise coming from both Mrs Waverley and her employer. It seemed entirely unwarranted and embarrassing because she felt she was doing no more than the job for which she was being so handsomely paid.

"I have a suggestion. Why don't we swap bedchambers for a few nights? Miss Guivre is getting so much better day by day and will soon hardly need such constant nursing."

Hetty said nothing.

"What an excellent idea," said Torquhil poking the fire with a fire iron.

Hetty glared at his back, "I am absolutely fine. There's no need for you to put yourself out."

Torquhil straightened up and turned to face her, "I'm afraid I agree with Mrs Waverley. And as your employer — "

"Oh, that's wholly unfair!"

"That's debatable. I shall ask Agatha to prepare the rooms."

"Poor Agatha," muttered Hetty crossly, "It hardly seems right that she should bear the brunt, when it's completely unnecessary."

She met his implacable gaze and shrugged, compressing her lips and making an indignant puffing sound which made Torquhil smile and shake his head.

"If you are to continue in my employ, I think it would be prudent for you to heed some good advice and not argue for once." He raised an eyebrow, "Although I perfectly understand that it is in your nature to dispute. I will admit to sometimes feeling exceedingly sorry for your grandparents."

Hetty rolled her eyes, "Well, as I am said to be very much like my grandmother in all things, particularly temperament, I don't suppose they even noticed what a terrible trial I am."

"I didn't say you were a trial," said Torquhil, "Far from it, in fact. I think you're quite remarkable."

"That isn't necessarily a good thing. I would really rather just be ordinary."

"That can never be, Hetty."

Mrs Waverley finished her toddy in one decisive gulp and stood up, "I shall go and alert Agatha and help her with the beds. This really is the best thing for everyone, Miss Swift. Over thirty years as a nursemaid tells me so."

Hetty looked from Mrs Waverley to Torquhil and sighed, "All right, I capitulate but I would like it be known that it's not of my choosing."

Much to her discomfort, her employer gave her a horribly disarming smile and with her heart pounding uncomfortably, Hetty stuck her chin in the air, "Very well but I think that smiling like that is unprincipled," she said, nettled. She followed Mrs Waverley from the room but heard him laugh quietly as she closed the door.

Sixteen

Her pillow was filled with rocks, the mattress broken branches, the counterpane stitched with brambles and rose thorns and the bedlinen made from shards of ice. She'd been more comfortable on the hard little truckle bed at Friday's Acre.

Hetty tossed and turned, until her nightgown was twisted into a strangling knot about her legs. She lay staring irritably at the lilac curtains on Mrs Waverley's bed and thinking that she really didn't like the colour lilac. In fact, she hated it. It reminded her of bruises and of the overpowering smell in the church at her grandmother's funeral, the aisles having been adorned, by well-meaning villagers, with drooping swathes of lilac from the garden at Swift Park. The cloying scent still haunted her, as did the sound of her usually stoical grandfather, choking back heartbroken sobs in the pew beside her.

The wallpaper was, for her tastes, vastly over-embellished and even in the candlelit gloom, it sparkled in what she considered a rather sinister manner. She was not, however, in the least surprised Mrs Waverley had waxed lyrical about it, describing how it was a balm to wounded spirits and inspired peaceful sleep. The swirling flowers made Hetty feel slightly queasy, and she closed her eyes and tried to block out the hideous room and go to sleep.

After ten minutes of furiously squeezing her eyelids together, she let out a growl of vexation and opened them again, to stare once more at the canopy above her.

For all Mrs Waverley's good intentions Hetty felt that she'd merely been consigned on the flimsiest excuse to a back room, a backwater, where she felt as though she was out of touch with her charge. It made her feel impotent and somewhat ill-used and, at that precise moment, as though she'd never sleep easily again.

Eirwen had been strangely happy for her to be removed to this distant part of the house; she had, in her own concise manner, made it quite clear that she agreed with both her brother and Mrs Waverley. Hetty was a little hurt by this and had left in something of a huff. She had snatched up her night things and her comb and stamped away down the corridor to the rear of the house. She had slammed the door and leant against it, trying not to see the revoltingly floral wallpaper and furnishings.

"It's only for a few nights," she reassured herself. "Then everything can return to how it was before. I like things to remain the same." She laughed and shook her head, "So, I chose to move into a haunted house to care for a child who can make snow with her mind and manipulate people into doing her bidding. Not the wisest choice of occupation or new home now I consider it carefully. Perhaps I should have thought a little more before rushing into it." She looked around her and winced at the extravagant silver fronds which caught the light of the candle flame. "I miss my woodland counterpane."

She blew out the candle and closed her eyes again.

"Oh, for heaven's sake!" she grumbled. "Just go to sleep, you ridiculous creature."

After struggling for another few minutes, she sat up impatiently. She had never had trouble sleeping, not even in the most worrisome times; the moment her head touched the pillow she was asleep, the only welcome trait inherited from her father who never allowed any of his transgressions to weigh heavily upon him or cause him enough disquiet to alter his sleeping pattern.

Now her head was so filled with conflicting thoughts, tumbling over each other in order to gain her attention, that sleep was bound to be elusive, lost in the persistent clamouring of her battling worries and hopes. She wondered if it was being in a strange bedchamber that had triggered her restlessness or if it was anxiety about the peculiar situation she found herself in.

She hugged her knees and stared into the darkness.

It seemed as though the harder she tried, the more difficult it became. She found the tinder box and lit the candle again, glad of its gentle warm glow. She reached out to pick up the book she was reading, and her hand touched something resting upon it. Something cold and hard. And small.

She closed her fingers about it gingerly, picking it up as though it might bite or burn her.

She held it up to the light.

A ring. Made of gold. The back of it being constructed from two clasped hands. She twisted it this way and that and the candlelight highlighted the decoration on it. She peered closer, frowning. It wasn't mere decoration but lettering on the inner surface — some kind of script she didn't recognise. Odd shapes like dark sticks laid out by a child in the dirt to form naive shapes. Like stick men. But as she looked at them, she realised that they must have some kind of meaning — that they were true letters, of some unfamiliar alphabet, communicating what she presumed to be an important message from the giver of the ring to the receiver. She had no clue what that message might be. She ran the tip of her finger over the indentations.

Then, without thinking, she slid it onto her finger. It fitted perfectly just as though made for her.

She held out her hand and regarded the way it seemed to have been deliberately shaped to fit her finger. On closer inspection she could quite clearly see that it was an ancient relic and most probably very valuable. Her grandmother had told her about magical runes and how some objects could be harnessed for good or sometimes questionable purposes. She had warned Hetty that one had to be extremely cautious when dealing with everyday items that may have been bewitched and then she'd laughed lightly as though she'd only been making a light-hearted joke and Hetty had forgotten all about it until she'd touched the ring.

She knew the moment her fingers had come into contact with the metal that there was something not of this world about it. She didn't know how or why, but in the same way that her touch told her immediately that Torquhil was important to her, that Eirwen meant no real harm, it also told her that the ring on her finger was vital to her future in some way.

She turned it round and round, watching the engravings on the outer surface emerge into the light and disappear around her finger into the shadows again. The lettering inside intrigued her but also made her uneasy. She wanted to know what the wording meant and where the ring had come from; she was certain that it had not been there when she first came into the room and placed her book on the table beside the bed. So, it very definitely didn't belong to Mrs Waverley.

It had appeared since she had arranged her few belongings upon the table.

And no one had been in the room apart from her.

Examining the ring once more she suddenly felt inexplicably fearful and tugged at it to remove it from her finger.

She couldn't dislodge it.

She scrambled out of bed and hurried to the bowl of water on the side table and plunged her hand into it and began twisting and pulling at the ring.

After a few moments she realised that it was firmly stuck.

Clenching her teeth in fury she quickly dried her hands on a cloth.

Taking a panicky breath, she looked about the room and spotted three small pots carefully lined up on the top of the cabinet on the other side of the bed. She crossed the room, gathered up the pots and placed them on the bedside table, arranging them in the light. She removed the lids and peered into each pot. In the second one she found a kind of scented ointment. Sticking her finger into the vessel, she scooped out a dollop of the cream and rubbed it around the ring and her finger before continuing with her struggle to remove it — to no avail.

"Damn it," she said.

For a long moment she stood staring crossly at the offending relic and breathing hard.

Then, just as she was thinking to herself that it would have to wait until morning, when she could ask the advice of Finn or Jacob, she felt an all too familiar trembling in the floorboards under her feet.

"Oh, no, not now!"

She steadied herself by holding onto the carved post of the bed, hooking one arm about it and watching the items on the table quivering as they made their way across the polished wood like possessed automatons. The curtains shivered and somewhere glass chimed musically. Dust, dislodged from the elaborate decoration on the ceiling, drifted down in grey veils; she could taste it in the air.

The door latch rattled and Hetty eyed it nervously; it sounded as though someone angry were trying to break in. She could feel the vibrations beneath her bare feet and her skin prickling, as the edges of every solid thing in the room became liquid, rippling as though under water. She began to feel a little dizzy and closed her eyes for a moment, but that had the effect of making her lose her balance and she had to cling onto the post.

"This is utterly ridiculous," she muttered irritably. "Eirwen, if this is you, just stop it! It's not funny."

The unsettling shaking continued unabated.

Hetty concluded that either Eirwen wasn't the instigator, in which case it was something more dangerous causing the minor earthquake in her bedchamber, or she *was* responsible and was urgently trying to get Hetty's attention for some reason.

Hetty put her wrapper on, pulled a warm shawl around her shoulders and taking up the candle in its holder she stepped out into the cold, dark corridor. She was pleased to find that it seemed to be only her bedchamber that was affected by the quaking.

Tiptoeing through the house she was reminded of the times when she was a child and enjoyed raiding the pantry at Swift Park while everyone else was asleep, happily snuggling with the kitchen cat by the embers of the fire and eating the last of the orange tarts leftover from supper. She had felt secure and loved and her childhood home was a place of safety for her. Now, she wasn't quite so confident; this house was not exactly a friend to her — she wasn't yet familiar with every nook and cranny and hadn't had the time to visit large parts of it. She felt like a traveller in a strange land and although she was not usually frightened of the dark, she was filled with trepidation as eerie shadows cast by her candle, made sinister dancing shapes on the walls.

As she approached Eirwen's bedchamber, she wondered what she hoped to achieve by sneaking about in the middle of the night; she just knew that she wanted to check on her charge to make sure that the trembling floorboards were not a desperate cry for help.

She listened at the door and hearing no sound from within, she opened it cautiously and peeped in.

A candle was still alight in its sconce and the room was dimly illuminated by it. Hetty could make out the bed but as the curtains were partially drawn, she couldn't see its occupant. The door to her own adjoining bedchamber was wide open and she could hear gently refined snoring coming from Mrs Waverley.

The floor was thankfully steady.

She remembered where the creaking boards were and carefully avoiding them, she advanced towards the bed.

Stealthily parting the curtains, she took a peek inside.

Eirwen was sleeping peacefully.

With a relieved sigh, Hetty stepped back and looked around. Everything was as normal. Nothing unusual at all caught her attention.

Reassured, she left the room and stood for a moment in the corridor.

The candle flame wavered as her uneven breathing disturbed the air.

Taking a couple of steps towards the back of the house, she suddenly had the distinct impression that someone was watching her.

She stopped and looked over her shoulder, fully expecting to see another apparition standing right behind her, but there was nothing but the wavering shadows. She scolded herself for being unnecessarily anxious and resolutely marched away down the corridor, but after only a few yards the back of her neck prickled, and she looked nervously over her shoulder again. As she peered down the corridor, trying to see what was making her so uneasy, she noticed a faint shimmering light at the end of it.

She fervently wished she hadn't banished the jackdaw from her presence; she'd have to forgive him in the morning because she found she was far less jumpy when he was at her shoulder making disparaging comments. She felt he was keeping his beady eye upon her and, in his own self-centred way, looking out for her interests and when he was with her, she was unable to dwell on the things that would otherwise be scaring her. He was not only a guardian but also a strange, yet welcome companion and he gave her insights into things she might in other circumstances have not completely understood. He was insufferably know-it-all, which she had found irksome in the beginning, but she was slowly becoming accustomed to it. She hadn't wanted to admit the truth to herself and was piqued that anyone, or anything, had been able to see through her so easily. He had intimated, in that artful way he had, that she was eager to wed Torquhil and she'd found it exasperating because she hadn't had sufficient time to carefully consider the notion herself.

She considered the light, wondering what it could be. It had a cold blue tinge to it and wavered as though its source were struggling to maintain its strength like a guttering candle flame. It was quite vague and faded at the edges and she couldn't think of anything in the house that might make such a strange glow.

She found that she was walking slowly towards it and stopped herself.

"Wait, you halfwit, remember *Sulis!*" she chided herself, "This might be yet another devious trick."

Pondering what to do for the best, she watched it warily. No candle or lantern would cast such a light — perhaps only the moon might create it. But there was no moon, only a heavily overcast, snow-laden night sky.

There was a brief moment when she couldn't help yearning for her simple old life at Friday's Acre and remembering how uncomplicated things had been not so very long ago. As she edged gingerly towards the short flight of stairs that led up to the other bedchambers, she tried to recall what her grandparents had told her. She closed her eyes and concentrated hard upon all the words of advice which were clamouring for attention in her head. She could hear all the voices quite clearly, but the messages were desperately muddled. After a moment trying to decipher a single clear instruction, she gave up and opened her eyes again.

"All right, that's enough of that, Hetty Swift, it's not getting you anywhere. Obviously, things are a little confused at the moment."

She eyed the eerie light and came to a conclusion.

"I shall not be intimidated by another phantom intrusion. It cannot hurt me. It's just light after all. A little bit of light cannot harm me."

She approached it cautiously but with a defiant tilt to her chin that her grandmother would have recognised.

As she drew nearer, she decided it looked unthreatening. It seemed to be hovering in the middle of the passageway like a patch of early morning mist lingering over frosted fields, which made her feel for some reason that it was probably benign rather than malevolent.

It became decidedly chillier as she got closer to it, and she pulled her shawl tightly around her for warmth and protection. She felt a little vulnerable wearing only her nightclothes.

She had no clue what she was going to do when she reached it but had an idea that something should be done as it had made an appearance in their home. She couldn't just leave it lurking in the house unmonitored and unchallenged.

Holding up her candle she examined the phenomenon closely and found she could see right through it to the corridor on the other side, which gave her hope that as it was transparent it must surely be ephemeral and would soon be gone.

"I don't know what you are or why you're here but I don't think you belong here so I suggest that you return to wherever you're from and then I might be able to get some sleep."

Nothing happened.

Without further ado and very little thought, Hetty reached out and pushed her hand into it and watched in astonishment as it turned an odd shade of green and her fingertips faded a little at the tips. She snatched it back and was relieved to see it was still securely attached to her arm.

"That's interesting," she mused, studying her hand, which although really cold, was otherwise unaltered. "And, I would say, encouraging. Perhaps now we can find out why you are here."

She was just contemplating sensibly calling for assistance when everything changed, and she had any choice taken from her.

Before she could even think of doing anything to save herself, she was suddenly enveloped in the clinging mist. It was bitingly cold, burning her skin and making her bones ache. She felt as though she were floating and glanced down at her bare feet and saw that they weren't touching the ground anymore. She opened her mouth to cry out but couldn't make a sound and even as she struggled to shout for help, everything was changing around her. It was as though she were looking out of the window of a fast-moving carriage at the blur of the passing scenery.

She was no longer in the corridor but somewhere she didn't recognise. Somewhere even darker. Colder. Her candle flickered and went out and she found herself floating in what smelt like some kind of subterranean chamber and Hetty knew, with absolute certainty and a rapidly sinking heart, that she had somehow been transported into the Long Barrow beneath Galdre Knap. She tried to remain as calm as she could, although her first instinct was to give in to the rising panic that was coursing through her and just scream as loudly as she could. There was no chance of escape as her feet were only in contact with the chilly air and, with no candle, she was blinded, lost and suspended, helplessly at the mercy of some unknown force.

Even as she was thinking this, the light changed and brightened a little around her and she was able to make out the walls and ceiling that were confining her.

Her breath was making clouds in front of her. The dank smell was overpowering; cold wet earth and ancient stone, mould and decay, long forgotten air, imprisoned and dying. The mysterious light illuminated the wall nearest to her and she could just make out a beautifully rendered fresco painted upon it; the colours still as bright as the day it was created, and the subjects clearly depicted.

It looked to her as though it was describing some mythical tale. There were fanciful dark birds and winged beasts and what looked very much like a snowstorm and every so often three figures appeared together, one silver-haired, one dark and one with flames coming from its head. She peered closer. Not flames. It was a naive depiction of someone with bright orange hair flying like a pennant behind them.

It was, without any doubt, a likeness of her.

She shivered.

Another figure, obviously female, had long silver hair trailing along the ground behind her and was haloed by a scribbled white aura and, standing off to one side, partly concealed by darkness, was an imposing but faceless figure in dark flowing robes. The fresco stretched along the wall and disappeared into the shadows beyond. Hetty tried to see how the story developed but wasn't able to move her feet as they were dangling forlornly in mid-air. She wiggled her toes, but nothing happened. She was trapped, as though in aspic. Nothing she did made any difference.

She frantically looked around and seeing the low corbelled ceiling just above her head and the walls sloping in, she began to feel panicked; her heart began to race even faster, and she had a desperate urge to escape the underground tomb. She couldn't catch her breath. The ceiling seemed to be pressing down on her and stealing the air from her lungs.

"I must — get out of here — " she gasped.

And, even as the words left her lips, she was crashing onto the floorboards of the corridor, where she'd been standing only a few moments earlier.

The floor was unforgiving, and she landed awkwardly on her hip and let out a yelp of pain. She felt sure that from the way that she was propelled so violently from one place to the other that someone was angry with her. She lay for a moment nursing the ache and then struggled to her feet.

The strange mist had gone and there was nothing but the ordinary passageway and the ordinary dusty shadows. She inhaled the faint scent of beeswax polish and the reassuringly familiar smell of a place of relative safety.

With a sigh of relief, she touched the oak wainscoting like a talisman, to convince herself that she was no longer at the mercy of someone else's capricious whims. Her feet were very firmly upon the gloriously solid elm boards of Galdre Knap although she was without her candle.

"Well, thank heavens that's over!" muttered Hetty, as she turned away and headed back to her bedchamber on shaking legs that barely held her upright, feeling her way slowly along the passage and loving every solid, reliable inch of the old house.

She had hardly reached Eirwen's bedchamber when the house began to shake again like a storm-tossed ship trying to break free from its moorings. Hetty staggered and clung onto the doorframe to steady herself.

"Curse it — " she said crossly, "This is becoming rather tiresome."

She held on for a minute and then when the quaking didn't lessen, she took a tentative step back along the corridor. She wasn't quite sure why she was going that way but had decided to pay attention to her instincts, which, she assumed, was what her grandmother was referring to when she spoke about listening to voices. She was beginning to understand that it wasn't anything specific she had to listen for, not actual spoken words nor advice in any recognisable form but more something in the air, or in the blood; a change in the wind, a flurry of snow, the call of an owl — it could be anything and nothing and she had to be on her toes at all times in case she missed something of importance. With things as they were, so precariously balanced, she could not afford to miss anything. The fresco in the Long Barrow had told her that. It seemed that she was to somehow play a key role, whether she liked it or not; there was no doubting it now — she'd seen the evidence with her own astonished eyes.

She could no longer deny what her grandparents had told her. She could feel it in her bones, in the way she could hear the thoughts of a jackdaw, had seen the evidence of a haunted house and witnessed what a possessed child could do.

In that moment, with the house shaking, as she staggered along the corridor like a drunken sailor, Hetty, rather belatedly, realised that she'd *always* heard things, had always felt connected to wild creatures and her own animals and the people around her in a way that she couldn't explain. Her grandmother had tried to tell her this, had tried to prepare her for what she would eventually discover, but she had not wanted to hear her then, so keen was she to be ordinary. Perhaps she'd been too afraid of the change it would inevitably bring, or perhaps the stars just had to align before she could understand what was required of her. She still had no idea how she was supposed to help but at least she could brace herself for what was surely coming.

Hetty made her faltering way along the unlit corridor, not quite sure where she was going, one hand firmly on the raised edge of the wainscoting, as a guide. It was like a lifeline, and she didn't dare let go.

She could no longer feel her toes, they were so cold.

She did feel them however, when she stubbed them into the bottom step of the short flight of stairs that led up to the other bedchambers. She hopped up and down until the pain subsided and then continued to limp up the stairs. She was forced to stop every so often and cling to the bannisters as the house tried to shake her off.

"I will not be put off. You're just a house. A very fine one but mere stone and mortar and cobwebs, lots of cobwebs. You don't frighten me with your childish temper tantrums." She reached the landing and coming to the first door, she tapped upon it and waited. There was no response, so she went in.

Seventeen

The stump of a candle still burned in its holder on the side table, and she carefully tiptoed across the room to the bed, pulled back the hangings and peered in.

"Torquhil? Please wake up! I need you," she whispered urgently.

"I am awake. You banging your toe was enough to wake the dead."

"Oh, sorry. My candle blew out and it was dark — I couldn't see — but anyway, I thought I ought to tell you what just happened — I think it might be important."

"If you could just wait a moment, I shall make myself presentable and then you can tell me what's troubling you."

Hetty, seeing that he was preparing to get out of bed, quickly moved away and turned her back in some confusion, while he pulled on his breeches and threw on a long coat over his nightshirt. He invited her to sit in the chair beside the fire and efficiently stirred the dying embers back into life, "Now, tell me all, Hetty."

"It's hard to know where to begin but I can see that you can't feel that the house is shaking at the moment. It began after I found this — "

She stuck out her hand for him to examine the offending item, "It appeared on the table beside my bed." He took her hand in his and she felt his fingers explore the ring and her skin began to tingle.

"That's interesting. It seems to be a *fede* ring — from the Italian *mani in fede.*"

"Which means?"

"The hands are said to be clasped in faith."

"A sign of religious faith?"

"Or love. Kindred or romantic."

"Oh, I see. Why do you think it was left there?"

"It's a message, I suspect, for you."

"Who do you think left it there?"

"I can't even begin to surmise. Perhaps someone who loves you."

"Well, that would certainly narrow the field considerably," said Hetty wryly.

"I don't think you realise — " he began.

"I can't remove it. It's stuck on my finger."

His fingers circled the ring, gently turning it. "It may not actually be stuck. It may just not want to be parted from you. A different proposition altogether."

"You think it's *possessed?*" whispered Hetty anxiously.

"Not possessed but perhaps — *possessive*."

"I fail to see the difference."

"It doesn't want to take you over and possess you, it only wishes to be with you. That seems quite — understandable to me."

"Oh," said Hetty slightly overcome.

"So, there's the ring — anything else?"

"Well, there's the quaking of course, which, it appears, only I can feel — and there's the strange light in the corridor — "

"Light? What kind of light?"

"After I'd been to check upon Eirwen, I saw this peculiar blue mist hovering in the corridor — like moonlight but — not."

"Is it still there?"

Hetty swallowed nervously, "Not exactly, you see, I — approached it and it sort of swallowed me and — I found myself in the Long Barrow — "

"Good God! Are you all right? You weren't hurt?"

"No, I'm fine, a bit cold, but I'm not sure if I was there physically or just imagined that I was there. I wasn't able to touch anything — I was floating — for want of a better word.

But, while I was there, I saw something — a fresco on the wall — "

Torquhil sighed, "I was afraid you might have seen that." He crossed to his bed and removed one of the covers and wrapped it around Hetty's shoulders.

"Thank you. What does it mean? The fresco. I couldn't see all of it. It didn't make sense."

"I believe it to be a pre-Roman prophecy. It must have been added to the original barrow at some later date. No one knows who created it — although it's suspected to have been one of your very own flame-haired ancestors who was perhaps a seer. The warlord was buried there and, as I explained before, *Sulis Minerva* was wrongly imprisoned with him — causing some serious repercussions over the intervening centuries. One of the most recent being the worsening of Eirwen's condition. Now you're unfortunately becoming enmeshed in all of this and I'm truly sorry for involving you, but as you must have seen in the fresco, all three of us were quite clearly predicted to be involved from the very beginning."

"You believe the other figures are you and Eirwen?"

"I do."

She paused, taking in his words.

"But how was I transported into the Long Barrow?"

"Your grandmother was convinced that you were — a *wegfarende* — or in other words a *swefnracu*."

"Good gracious. I'm not sure I like the sound of either. They sound like mythical fire-breathing dragons."

He smiled, "It's Anglo Saxon and extremely difficult to pronounce. They refer to people who are able to dream at will, specifically one who can appear in the dreams they conjure."

"I'm not sure — "

"You're a kind of sibyl — one who can rove at will, which is highly unusual."

"Ah, — so much clearer."

"It's quite straightforward really — you're someone — someone very special, I might add — who can make things happen just by thinking about them and can transport herself at will. Even your grandmother was not able to master that. It seems that you're unique even within your already rather unique family."

"That sounds scarcely credible and exceedingly alarming."

Torquhil studied her for a moment in the glow of the reinvigorated flames, "I want you to stay here for a moment while I go and investigate and make sure everything is as it should be. Why don't you hop under the covers to keep warm, and I'll be as quick as I can."

She nodded and watched him leave.

After staring at the closed door for a few moments she stood up and walked slowly to the bed.

She was very cold indeed. Her toes were aching after being stubbed on the stair and she was shivering from exhaustion and fright.

She gave a little shrug and clambered onto the bed and pulled the still warm counterpane over her and snuggled down to wait, thinking how odd her life had become and wondering what Mr Scroggs would make of her being tucked up in the mysterious Torquhil Guivre's bed — whether he would still be quite so eager to make her his wife. She laughed to herself and closed her eyes for a moment, thinking that being a "sibyl" or whatever she was, was turning out to be exceedingly wearisome.

* * *

Warm and surprisingly comfortable, Hetty nestled her cheek into the pillow and wondered what could be keeping Torquhil for so long. Just one more minute, she thought, and she'd go and look for him.

Opening one sleepy eye and seeing it was still dark, despite the bed-hangings being open, she tried to focus her weary eyes upon the room.

"Go back to sleep."

Hetty struggled to sit up, "You're back," she said, happily.

"I've been back for over an hour. You were sound asleep. Everything is as it should be. Go back to sleep."

"But where will you sleep?"

"Here, by the fire."

She sat up, "Certainly not, I shall go back to my own bed — well, Mrs Waverley's bed," she said firmly.

"No, I'd rather you were here, so that I can keep an eye on you. I'm not entirely happy about the state of things at the moment. Is the house still shaking?"

Hetty considered for a moment and shook her head, "It seems to have stopped."

"I'm coming to the reluctant conclusion that it's you who causes it."

"Oh! That's unjust and unkind and not true!" She frowned, "Although, of course, now I think about it, it might actually be true — I have no idea. Apparently, I can float through medieval walls, so I might very well be capable of creating earthquakes, who knows! Although, I cannot quite see what I could possibly gain from making it impossible for me to walk in a straight line because of the wobbly floor. It seems illogical because it doesn't benefit me at all — in fact it only hinders *me* and nobody else."

"A fair point. We'll discuss this later. Why don't you go back to sleep, and I'll wake you in plenty of time to return to your room before tongues start wagging and I'm forced to defend your honour in a duel."

Hetty giggled, "Who would you fight? Grandpapa? Finn? I think they're probably on your side anyway. Oh, it might be Mrs Ashby! No, on second thoughts, she loves you. Everyone here loves you."

"Are you sure? Everyone?"

Hetty pulled the counterpane up to hide her pink cheeks and wished she would learn to stop chattering before she got herself tied into embarrassing knots.

"Why, yes!" she declared brightly, "Even Mrs Waverley seems to have a soft spot for you, and she keeps her heart hidden safely behind her battlements. Although, I must say that she's been really quite kind-hearted recently. I don't think she's as strict as she first appears."

"Henrietta! Will you please go to sleep."

"Don't call me that. It makes me think I must have done something wrong like when I was a child."

"I can imagine you were quite a trial to your family."

"I was good and obedient and a credit to the Swift name."

"I don't believe that for a second. You are far too wilful and reckless. Who else would march into a snowstorm to find raspberry leaves or willingly walk into a ghostly mist or trust a deadly Roman goddess?"

"I didn't walk into the mist — it sort of engulfed me and the goddess tricked me!"

"And the snowstorm?"

"But it wasn't snowing when I left the house! It could have happened to anyone."

"It seems to happen to you though," he replied but Hetty heard the smile in his voice and wasn't offended.

"I'm sorry. If I'd had a choice in the matter, I would still be at Friday's Acre, looking after my hens and geese — and the pigs and Thistle. Safe with Grandpapa. Maybe a little bored — "

Her companion fell silent, and she watched him stare into the fire until she began to feel drowsy again, her eyelids drooping.

"I think I might just — sleep for a while — if you don't mind — I'm so very tired. You could come and sleep here too — there's plenty of room. I wouldn't mind at all."

"Go to sleep, Miss Swift."

"Yes, Mr Guivre."

For a while there was no sound but the crackling of the fire, but it was only when Hetty's breathing showed that she had fallen asleep, did Torquhil rise and approach the bed. He stood for a moment looking down at her and then pulled the counterpane up around her shoulders and tucked it in. Returning to the chair by the fire, he made himself comfortable, stretching out his legs and keeping a watchful eye on the sleeping figure in his bed.

*   *   *

Hetty was awoken by someone gently touching her shoulder. Almost instantly she remembered what had happened and opened her eyes to see Torquhil leaning over her.

"It's probably time you were up and about, Hetty. I trust you slept well?"

She blinked up at him a little blearily and smiled, "I slept very well, thank you. You stayed in the chair all night?"

"I did but it was surprisingly comfortable so don't worry. And, rest assured, there were no more incidents during the night either."

"That's a relief. I was wondering if the Long Barrow is properly secured so that no one can wander into it by accident? It's been worrying me."

"After Eirwen managed to get in there, I had some invincible locks put on and added some extra precautions of my own. It's an impregnable fortress now. Unless of course, you've been blessed with special powers."

"Cursed," said Hetty gloomily.

He laughed, told her to make haste before someone found her cosily tucked up in his bed and left the room.

Hetty knew very little about the opposite sex and knew even less about the fine details of what went on between a man and a woman apart from what she had unwittingly witnessed in the farmyard at Friday's Acre. Her grandfather's advice had hardly been helpful either, as he would himself own; he had rather conservative ideas about how a gentleman should act and was loathe to explain to his innocent granddaughter just how babies were created. She had started to have her own suspicions though and although somewhat bemused, she had a healthy interest in what happened behind closed doors. There was no trusted female in her life she could ask or confide in once her grandmother had gone but she paid close attention to what the villagers discussed and gradually was able to form an idea of what married life might be like.

She had formed her unworldly views on gentlemanly etiquette and what was required from any man, high-born or otherwise, on what her grandfather had taught her by his own rigidly genteel example. Her opinion of Mr Edwin Scroggs had been severely influenced by Mr Swift's well-balanced approach to life and even though he had been, for a while, in favour of Mr Scroggs as a suitor she was also certain that, had he known the full extent of his protégée's lack of moral fibre and his casual cruelty, he would never have supported his repeated requests for Hetty's hand.

Men, she had decided — whilst in fact only knowing a handful as anything more than slight acquaintances — were almost always disappointing. The very first time she could remember being disillusioned with someone in her life was when she'd finally understood what her father had done. It had wounded her irrevocably and made it difficult for her to trust anyone other than her grandparents. Until the shocking truth about his exploits had been revealed to her, she had had a child's resolute belief that her parents were without fault, incomparable and unblemished in any way. To discover that they had critical flaws had been, almost without her noticing, the end of her childhood and she had been compelled to give her love and trust elsewhere.

She had cheerfully lavished her affections upon her grandparents and her animals: on any wild and injured creature who stumbled unwarily into her path and all the livestock she lovingly cared for. She had adopted them all into her rather scant family, named them, nurtured them and grieved for them when they inevitably died.

Her grandparents had been steadfast in their determination to take responsibility for her upbringing when her own parents had failed her so catastrophically, and they had supported her and loved her without question, never once letting her down. But they had never considered explaining to her the particular things she really needed to know in order to prevent embarrassment and a depressing future as a lonely, unloved spinster.

As she hastily padded back to her temporary room at the rear of the house, she wondered who she could possibly ask for advice. She knew it was thoroughly immoral for a young, unwed girl with her background to be thinking of such things, but there was a moment when Torquhil was by the fire, and she was in his bed when she had desperately wanted to be worldly-wise enough to be irresistible to him yet had only succeeded in sounding like the naive child she was. Why would he ever be interested in her: a horridly red-headed and lowly farmhand with a dark family history brimming with shameful secrets and nothing to recommend her as anything but a member of his staff and a bit of a nuisance.

She had never had any kind of urge to be closer to Mr Scroggs — in fact quite the opposite. She had never been filled with a strong desire she couldn't name and was astounded to hear herself invite her employer to share his own bed with her. She wasn't entirely sure what sharing a bed entailed, but she had thought that perhaps sleeping next to Torquhil might be quite pleasant and had not really thought her words through before she uttered them. She blamed the unusual events she had been forced to endure for the ensuing exhaustion and confusion.

The disappointing part was that he had so politely refused her offer, as though she were merely a disobedient child — she had been abruptly dismissed. It was quite clear that the kiss they had been inveigled to share had meant nothing to him and it wasn't just because it had been instigated by his meddling sister.

She sat before the tarnished looking glass, impatiently tugging at her hair with the comb and trying to disentangle the knots which had appeared sometime during her overnight adventure. Her eyes were bloodshot and shadowed; she was even paler than usual and looked very unlike herself. As she reluctantly examined her own face, she couldn't blame Torquhil for rejecting her. She realised that she must stop being so foolish. It didn't matter that Eirwen was determined that her brother should wed her — his sister could hold no real sway over him. He would, in the end, do just as he pleased and once everything was back to normal, she and her grandfather would, most likely, leave and return to Friday's Acre and their previously uneventful life.

The thought made Hetty want to wail like a grief-stricken widow, but instead she gave herself an exasperated scolding, hastily secured her hair, washed and dressed and dashed along to Eirwen's bedchamber to relieve Mrs Waverley.

* * *

Despite Hetty's concerns, no one had heard the events of the night; no one even mentioned anything untoward. She had been thinking, erroneously, that everyone must surely have been aware of the disturbance. Mrs Waverley confessed she had slept right through the night and that her charge had been no trouble at all.

Eirwen, while Hetty was briskly helping her get washed and dressed in a morning gown for the first time since she'd returned to Galdre Knap, confessed she'd had a very strange dream about Hetty turning into a barn owl and flying too close to the moon so that her wings froze solid, and she plummeted back to Earth.

Hetty bit her lip and debated whether to share her bizarre night-time exploits with her because there was obviously some connection between what she'd been dreaming and what had actually happened. She didn't think the young girl had been the instigator this time but had somehow been aware of the event in her dreams.

As she discovered each new and marvellous thing about Galdre Knap and its occupants, and ultimately herself as well, she found she was becoming less perturbed by each new revelation. It wasn't that she was becoming inured to her situation — far from it. It was just that with so many inexplicable things happening, her instinct for self-preservation was being gradually worn away and her resolve was beginning to fray at the edges. In the old days she had been flustered by trivial problems like the hens not laying, blight on her potatoes or scab on the apples, but never had she had to confront talking birds, the menace of fiendish deities or discovering that she had the ability to wander through walls at will. She was beginning to understand that there had been aspects of her grandmother's character that she had managed to assimilate perfectly as a child and had remained largely untroubled by them, but there were others that had been so profoundly life-altering and disturbing to her young mind that she had had no choice but to tuck them away in some dark unvisited recess of her brain where they could be forgotten. She was also beginning to understand that ignoring something doesn't make it any less threatening — you just don't see the danger coming until too late and are likely to be caught drastically unawares and then have to suffer the consequences of being too slow to react.

This had been Hetty all her life: hiding under the bedclothes, covering her eyes, pushing away the truth if it might prove to be too painful, distracting herself with activities and noise, singing constantly to block out any foreboding and dashing hither and thither like a mindless chicken so that those with the ridiculous idea that the truth cannot hurt had no chance of catching her and sharing their awful, life-altering knowledge with her.

But now they'd finally caught up with her and she had no choice but to face the reality of her future, however absurd and fantastical it might appear to her. It was a bit like suddenly discovering that the evil spirits every child was regularly threatened with in order to encourage good behaviour were, in fact, terrifyingly real. The nursemaid, whose brutally strict regime Hetty was subjected to for almost a year before the woman's unsuitable behaviour had been uncovered and she'd been dismissed, had wholeheartedly believed that children should be seen and not heard and confined to the nursery wherever possible. She had filled the little girl's head with such dreadful nonsense that it had taken another year for Anne

Swift to fully eradicate it and restore her very impressionable granddaughter to a stable and secure state where she could grow up without being scared of every shadow, every imaginary *kobold* that the nursemaid had conjured to make her own life easier. Anne had spent many months gently soothing away the resulting night terrors and replaced every diabolical fiend, that fed Hetty's fevered imagination, with the gentle joys of herbs, benign magic and the wonders of wildlife until she was able to forget their darkly sinister presence and remember how to be joyful again. Anne had agonised over what to do for the best and eventually shared her worries about Hetty with her husband, deeply concerned that beneath the gossamer veneer of happiness the childhood demons still lurked and always would. Roland Swift had been quick to reassure her that their granddaughter was imbued with the same iron-hard core of courage and derring-do that she had, and he was absolutely convinced that whatever Hetty had to endure she would be able to conquer it with a good deal of panache and inherited red-headed passion.

"You were a barn owl. Frosty white — like a ghost," said Eirwen, apparently a little puzzled by the idea, "You were — transparent. I could see your heart beating inside your chest."

Hetty took her hand, "It was just a dream Eirwen."

"Was it? It seemed real."

"Well, as you can plainly see, I'm not an owl nor am I transparent," laughed Hetty.

"And your heart is hidden," murmured Eirwen.

"Hidden? It's not hidden."

Her companion just smiled. A slow half-smile that reminded Hetty of her brother.

"I don't hide anything." She thought for a moment. "Well, not deliberately."

"You're hiding something now."

As she couldn't really argue with that, Hetty said nothing.

She assisted Eirwen into her chair and tucked a blanket around her legs.

"I think you could go downstairs in a day or so if you felt like it. You are so much stronger now. With a little help on the stairs, we should be able to get you to the parlour. It would make a change for you."

"That would be nice."

Hetty chatted animatedly whilst changing the bedlinen and giving the counterpane a good shake out of the window. As she was doing so there was a loud caw, a shadowy flurry of feathers and Crow swooped over her head and into the bedchamber.

Hetty hauled the counterpane back in and closed the window and turned to frown at the jackdaw perching precariously on the shining surface of the blanket chest. He ignored her and kept his thoughts under lock and key just in case the little human wasn't supposed to find out he could communicate. He was rather pleased with himself over this as humans were usually so eager to point out what a selfish creature he was, with few redeeming qualities. He wanted to explain to them that when you're a wild beast of any kind you need to think carefully about everything you do because it could so easily lead to disaster or sudden death. There was a very fine line between appearing selfish and not dying. Humans didn't really comprehend what a tenuous grip birds had upon life. An unexpected fright could stop their tiny hearts from beating. A loud noise. A slight bang to their fragile chalky skulls. And, gone. Just like that. Caution was the key. Caution and a little selfishness.

The girl was staring at him. She had eyes rather like his. Pale as birch bark. She was odd even by his standards. He stared back.

"I can hear even your quietest thoughts," she said a little tartly.

Eighteen

Crow was looking decidedly uncomfortable for a creature who usually showed no signs of ever being abashed.

Hetty grinned at him, "Ah, Crow! Hoist by your own petard! You'll have to be very careful now. If you annoy her, Eirwen could make you fall in love with a goose!"

I'd sooner it were a pig. At least they have a scrap of intelligence.

"Well, you'd better mind your manners. Have you been lurking outside for long?"

Long enough for my eyeballs to freeze.

"You should have stayed inside then, like any sensible person — or canny bird. I haven't been deliberately ignoring you, although you've been exceedingly irritating lately. I've been otherwise occupied. With — a variety of inexplicable things, which have proved rather distracting."

So I've heard from my master.

"Actually, I hate to admit it, but I've missed you. In the middle of all the — chaos, I thought you might have been quite helpful. I'm not keen on nameless things creeping up on me and you would've kept an eye out and warned me if something nasty were stalking me or my loved ones."

A change of heart.

"More a change of mind."

Whichever it is, it's a welcome change.

"I'm delighted you think so."

I was beginning to feel persecuted.

"You're not treated well?"

Jackdaws have been abused for as long as I can remember.

"I'm rather fond of the crow family, on the whole. Clever and funny, if a little sneaky and occasionally inclined to — borrowing things and being unnecessarily rude."

That's us, in a nutshell.

He hunched his shoulders.

Although, if we had cheery red breasts, we wouldn't have been so tormented.

"Sadly, you're probably right. Although my cheery red hair has always set me apart and seems to invite much unkindness and insults. I really have no idea why, except that it is uncommon and therefore more noticeable. It is, after all, nothing more than an accident of birth, like blue eyes or lack of stature. Crows do have an unfortunately sinister appearance and some — not you, of *course* — behave in a rather untrustworthy manner."

Your red crest would stand you in good stead in the bird world.

He clacked his beak and shook his grey head.

But only if you were a male.

"Well, that's the same for us. King Henry VIII was famously a redhead and brave was the man who would mock him! His daughter, Queen Elizabeth, was no doubt glad of her red hair because it showed quite clearly to anyone who questioned it, who her father was and made her distinctive. But they were royalty and I'm just a lowly farmhand. It will always be different for those with money and influence. I cannot incarcerate *my* critics in The Tower — much as I'd like to sometimes! The most I can do is to set the geese upon them."

Robins are not to be trusted. Ruthless killers.

"You're making that up!" declared Hetty, wide-eyed.

"I'm really hungry," said Eirwen, tiring of their nonsensical banter.

"Then I shall go and find you some breakfast immediately, my lady," laughed Hetty, curtsying theatrically, "What do you fancy? Eggs? Breakfast Cakes? Mrs Ashby makes the best ones in the whole world — so light and delicious. Or bacon and sausage?"

"Porridge," replied Eirwen.

The food of the Devil. Glues your beak together.

"I must remember that," said Hetty, "It could come in exceedingly useful."

Eirwen giggled and hid her face under the blanket.

*   *   *

Mrs Ashby was in no mood to make anyone breakfast.

She was standing, stout arms akimbo, and her round, florid face twisted into such an expression of fury that Hetty started to back out of the kitchen before she was spotted.

"*Henrietta!*" bellowed her grandfather ungallantly not giving her the chance to save herself.

"Yes, Grandpapa? Are you in trouble?"

He sent her a warning glance, "We're in dire need of some urgent assistance. It seems that mice have made their home in the pantry and have decimated, amongst other things, today's supper." He looked uneasily at the cook, "Dear Mrs Ashby is really quite put out."

"Yes, I can see that. What can I do to help Mrs Ashby?"

The cook thumped her ham sized fist onto the table, making the cutlery and pots clatter alarmingly, "I *want* someone to get rid of those damn pests *once and for all* and find something for everyone to *eat!*"

"That sounds just like Hetty's sort of assignment," said Mr Swift helpfully.

She caught his wide-eyed plea and nodded her assent, "Of course! You know, Mrs Ashby, I can certainly try to sort this out for you. It may take a little while, but I will do my very best to find a solution."

Hetty had no clue why she was saying such a thing; she actually had a soft spot for mice and couldn't understand why the maids at Swift Park used to scream and jump up onto chairs when they saw them. As a child she'd always run to their rescue and happily caught and handled the little creatures and removed them to the relative safety of one of the distant barns. She could never see how they could harm you as they were equally, if not more, scared of humans. One kitchen maid had told her it was their tails that frightened her and Hetty had shaken her head and thought the idea utterly ridiculous.

She marched resolutely into the pantry and closed the door behind her.

Leaning against it, she looked around the room and thought there was certainly a tempting feast for rodents there, all laid out on the dark slate shelves. It was no wonder they were helping themselves, she could hardly blame them, especially when their usual provisions were buried under so much tenacious snow. Mrs Ashby's stores were easy pickings.

She sniffed the air and thought it did indeed smell a little mousey. She wondered where on earth Thistle was and why he hadn't seen the intruders off, he was usually such a good mouser. She could scatter cloves around or, if it were summer, peppermint leaves. She had a small bottle of peppermint oil she'd made at Friday's Acre and wondered if that might work as efficiently. Her grandmother had taught her that mice don't like the smell of peppermint.

She remembered how her grandmother used to talk to wild animals and birds as though it were perfectly normal behaviour. Of course, when Hetty was a child, she had taken it all for granted and thought that it was just what old people did. She had no idea that Anne Swift was actually having a proper conversation with the creatures.

But she did now.

She closed her eyes.

"Dear little mice," she said, feeling thoroughly foolish, "If I promise to put out some food for you in the barn, would you please leave Mrs Ashby's pantry? I'd be most terribly grateful."

She smiled to herself and rolled her eyes.

"Mad, quite mad."

She wondered where the peppermint oil had been stored.

Then she heard a dry rustling sound.

A pitter-patter of tiny claws.

And she watched in complete astonishment, her mouth wide open, as a small troupe of mice gathered by the back door and one by one squeezed under it and disappeared out into the snow. "Well I never," muttered Hetty.

And she laughed out loud.

"Are you all right in there?" called her grandfather.

"I'm fine thank you!" She opened the door and returned to the kitchen where she found everyone, the cook, her grandfather and Finn, who had just come in from the stables, looking at her enquiringly.

"Mission accomplished," she announced, trying to appear nonchalant.

"Really? Just like that?" Mrs Ashby didn't sound convinced.

"She's always had a way with animals," said Roland Swift, smugly.

"How do you know they've actually gone? They might just be hiding in the wainscoting."

"Er — I just know. And I can assure you that I'm just as surprised as you are!"

Thankfully, at that moment Agatha bundled in through the door, wrapped in so many layers of scarves and shawls she looked twice her normal size, an ugly old brown hat pulled right down over her eyes.

"Lor, but it's bitter out there! It ain't never goin' to thaw! I'll be right glad to see the back it — walking through it makes my legs ache something dreadful. I've just been down to see Ma and Bessie at home and chatted to a few folk. They be gettin' a bit suspicious about the snow now. It's been around so long they think it's a curse come upon them."

"Morning Aggie. What do you mean by "suspicious"?"

Agatha took off her hat, unwrapped several of the shawls and hung them on the hook behind the door, "There's talk. That's nothing unusual. You know what they're like. Anythin' out of the ordinary sets them off. Oh, Mrs Ashby, Ma's sent some clouted cream — I've left it outside to keep cool. She says she knows that Finn is partial to a bit on his scone after work."

Finn nodded in agreement, "Being from Ilfracombe, she does make the best clouted cream I've ever tasted."

"She does that!" said Mrs Ashby, "Your Ma is the finest dairy woman hereabouts."

Agatha looked around the kitchen, "Anythin' happen while I was gone? I'm always afraid I'm going to miss the excitement!"

"Not much," admitted Finn, "Hetty's rid the pantry of mice."

Aggie laughed, "That's a good job done then! I don't like the idea of them nibblin' my supper! And they piddle everywhere too!"

"Agatha Giffins! A lady wouldn't mention such things!" exclaimed Mrs Ashby.

"I'm *not* a lady! Never was, never shall be!"

"Well, you could at least *try!*"

"No point, Mrs Ashby! Nobody wants a housemaid who thinks they're above a bit of hard work and gettin' their hands dirty."

Mr Swift cleared his throat, "I believe the definition of a lady is someone who treats others with kindness and that you most certainly do, Agatha."

"You wouldn't say that if you'd seen me and Bessie having a right old squabble this morning, Mr Swift! Honestly, that girl could sour milk just by lookin' at it!"

"What's she been doing now?" asked Mrs Ashby, shaking her head.

"Oh, y'know! The usual. She took my best church-goin' gloves without askin'. She's been gossipin' in the village. Spreading nonsense about, like a farmer spreads manure. Being mean and spiteful. No different to how she normally is to be honest! If we ever get her wed, it'll be a miracle!"

"Don't say manure!" said Mrs Ashby.

"What kind of gossip?" queried Hetty anxiously.

"Bessie and that sly Joan Fowler have been talkin' about Galdre Knap and letting it be known that they think there's some odd things goin' on up here. Course, Bessie's just jealous."

"'Odd things' — such as?"

"She's been telling everyone that the house is all evil and cursed an' stuff and Mr Guivre an' his sister are — no better than 'foreign folk'! That's the worst thing she can think of to say about anyone! She says they have no business livin' here with good honest folk. She says Miss Guivre is locked away up here because she's crazy as a cornered goose and she's a danger to everyone around her. I told them she's neither crazy nor is she 'locked away'. I told them that Mr Guivre's as English as you or me. But I did have to agree that the house is a bit — eerie. Because it is."

"I'd have to agree too, Aggie. Ancient mansions, like this one, can be daunting and this one can definitely be unsettling at times. I understand their suspicions of course. We all have a natural fear of the unknown, but I do wish they wouldn't make such accusations against Eirwen — she's just an innocent child and she's never harmed anyone."

"I told them that, Miss. But they like to give themselves a thrill because otherwise their lives would be duller than the dirtiest ditchwater! Bessie's always been one for thinkin' the worst of everyone. She's been spoilt rotten because her face once belonged to an angel. It's not really her fault."

"I wonder what we can do to counter these rumours?"

"Nothin' Miss, they'll always make things up. As soon as Mr Guivre moved here to the village, he was a target for their poisonous tittle-tattle an' one day someone else will take his place I expect."

"Ah, well, I suppose it can't be helped. But please let me know if you hear anything else. I don't want it to get out of hand when I'm confident that I could quell their fears by just explaining how things really are."

Agatha nodded, her mouth pursed.

"Thank you, Aggie. Could you please take Eirwen some breakfast? She only wants porridge. I shall see if I can find something to replace what the mice have ruined, which in this weather isn't going to be straightforward. I must go and talk with Jacob — he might have some ideas."

Agatha went immediately to fetch the oats saying that she'd put some clouted cream and honey in it to fatten the poor girl up a bit.

Hetty found her overcoat and shawl and it wasn't long afterwards that she was stamping her way across the stable yard to find Jacob.

"I can easily show you where the crate is, Miss Henrietta," said Jacob, "I put it away in the root store. As to the other things — I can give you a good idea where they might be hiding, and Sam can dig them up for you."

"Oh, I'm very much obliged to you, but I can dig. I'm thoroughly used to it."

"I'm sure you are, but the ground will be frozen solid and the digging nigh on impossible I shouldn't wonder. The soil up here on the hill is harder than down in the valley."

"All right, if you insist! I'll ask Sam. But — "

"No arguments. I'll have Mr Guivre after me if I allow you to go and dig all by yourself."

"Really? Why?"

"He asked me to keep an eye on you when you're out of the house. After the snowstorm incident I think he's become a bit wary of allowing you to roam freely anymore!"

"How — unfair — "

"But — right though?"

Hetty made a face at him, "Oh, very well, yes — *right*. But I don't know what makes him think that he can just tell me what to do!"

"Well, I should think the fact that he employs you might have some bearing on it, for one thing and for another I think — " he paused and looked out across the yard to the house, "I think it's good that he's taking an interest in something other than the business of rescuing his sister. I understand that it's obsessed him for a very long time. I would say that he's certainly changed for the better since you arrived. He never used to say a word when I saw him about in the village. He's more inclined to talk now and I've even seen him smile once or twice recently."

"I never knew him before I came here. Our paths never crossed until now. You really think he's changed that much? How strange."

"Not really. It's just Nature's way, isn't it? Even the strongest tree will slowly bend and change its shape if constantly harried by a strong wind."

"What are you saying, Jacob?"

"It would appear that you're a rather persistent breeze, Miss," he chuckled.

* * *

Sam, armed with a newly sharpened spade, hacked at the ground but they both quickly realised that it was futile. He could barely get the blade in more than a hair's breadth and after ten minutes work had made no impression upon the frozen soil in the kitchen garden.

"It's no use, Miss! I can't even make a dent! I'll never get these roots up. Not until it thaws, which, at this rate, may be never! Those roots will be ruined before we can get them out of the ground. Never seen snow that stayed around so long. It's like God's forgotten what comes next in the season. Do you want me to try in another part of the garden? Maybe nearer the woods where it's a little more sheltered?"

Hetty frowned and looked about at the disguised vegetable patch. Not even one stalk stood proud above the blanketing snow. It was a job to tell where any of the wintering plants might be concealed. She sighed, "No, thank you Sam. But — wait — hand me the spade please."

"Miss, there's no point — "

Hetty took the spade and jabbed at the area of soil from where Sam had cleared snow and a thick layer of protective straw away. It practically bounced off the surface, jarring her arm.

"You're quite right. As hard as Mrs Warren's plum dumplings. I think — " she began pensively, and leant on the handle, "If only — " and even as the thought occurred to her, she felt the spade slide slowly down into the ground. She glanced in surprise at Sam who was looking completely dumbfounded.

"Well, I'll be — " he muttered. "Seems the talk hereabouts is about right then!"

"Oh dear," said Hetty, as she levered the suddenly soft-as-duck-down soil out of the way and dug her way easily down to last year's waiting beets.

* * *

Two hours later, a little weary, and chilled to the marrow, she returned to the kitchen bearing a large basket laden with all the hidden treasures: beets and parsnips, some stalwart kale, bundles of Jack by the Hedge and Horse Parsley, a dozen wrinkled crab apples, some unappetising looking but nevertheless tasty Wood Ears from the elder trees and a few Grey Oyster Mushrooms, and she'd found enough rose hips still clinging courageously to their branches to make a decent quantity of jelly. She'd also delved her cold fingers into the sand-filled crate she'd insisted upon bringing in the cart from Friday's Acre and was pleased to find that the carrots she'd stored away last season had survived well and were still edible.

She thumped the basket down onto the table and Mrs Ashby examined the contents with a critical eye and then patted Hetty on the shoulder.

"You're a marvel. You must have magic in those fingers of yours."

Hetty couldn't help laughing, "Sam and I just dug some holes and grubbed about in the ditches and bushes a bit. I'm not sure what you can make from this odd little harvest but if anyone can create something delicious, it's you. The chickweed was a bit frosted and squashed by the snow, so I didn't pick any."

"I think you've managed to gather plenty here, Miss Hetty. I can make my Parsnip Pie for one thing."

"That sounds good — what goes into that?"

"Lots of spices and egg yolks, ginger and honey and usually fresh lemon but all I have are some lemons I preserved last summer, which won't be quite the same but will do. And then I top it with a nice crisp pastry crust."

"Oh, goodness, that does sound so good! Do you have enough eggs? Some of my older ladies are still deigning to lay one or two eggs a week, but the others have put their feet up for the winter."

"I wouldn't say no to a few more if there should happen to be any. I have some preserved in salt so can make do and mend. Perhaps I should just do Buttered Parsnips instead, it would be easier I suppose!"

"No, don't change your mind! I'm already looking forward to the pie. I shall go at once to the hen house! Goodness, you mustn't give up now! I'll be back in a trice."

She pulled her shawl around her and marched back out into the snow.

"Don't get lost again!" Mrs Ashby called after her.

* * *

As Hetty crossed the stable yard to the barn, Thistle appeared, daintily tiptoeing his way along the packed snow in front of her; a brawny feline ballet dancer, greeting her with a loud chorus of his happiest sounds, mewing and purring at the same time and making excited little chirruping noises. He wound himself around her, tail arched and when she crouched down to give him a cuddle, he was quite clearly gratified, vigorously bumping his head against her knees.

"Where have you been, you naughty fellow? You're supposed to be in charge of scaring the mice away! You'll get dismissed if you don't turn up for work. Please do not bring more shame upon our family." He followed her to the barn and while she searched for eggs in the henhouse, he sat and lazily observed a small hole at the base of a wall, his tail twitching spasmodically.

Hetty found just two eggs but praised her chickens enthusiastically anyway.

She balanced them on the low wall by the little gate to the vegetable garden and went to pay her respects to her pigs and geese. After making sure they were all happily going about their business, she stood and looked out over the grounds, down the hill to the woods which encircled them; she could only see maybe half a mile before the haze veiled the view of the valley, but she could quite clearly make out the odd curling plume of smoke from farmworkers' cottages. It was a reassuring sign that all was well with the rest of the world, even if things were a little askew up there at Galdre Knap.

The air was crisp and cold, hard-edged and made her chest ache a little as she breathed in deeply, filling her lungs with the day's freshness.

She decided that she would try to coax her grandfather out of the house for a short perambulation around the garden where Sam and Jacob had been busy clearing more paths through the never-changing snow. It was, away from the inevitable but necessary human tampering, as pristine as the day it had first fallen from the sky. Usually after a few days of being earthbound, natural snow would be shrinking at the edges and looking tired and a little grubby, but this magical snow was still absolutely perfect, smooth as a dish of junket and glittering with countless sparks even without the benefit of sunlight.

At night it glowed as though lit from within by a dozen moons and its unearthly light illumined the house both inside and out. She had always loved how snow changed everything. It made the familiar and the unremarkable into something other-worldly and mysterious; she glanced back at the house — rather like the master of Galdre Knap, she mused.

"Oh, enough of this nonsense!"

She made her way back to the yard and went to the wall where she'd nestled the two precious eggs.

But they'd gone.

She looked around on the unmarked snow but there was no sign of them.

Furious that she'd been so careless, she kicked a mound of snow that had been shovelled to one side and watched it explode with some satisfaction.

She then marched angrily through the gate straight into the arms of Mr Edwin Scroggs.

As she bumped violently into his chest, she looked up, gasped in undisguised horror and quickly jumped away from him, but found herself backed up against the wall.

"Ah! Miss Swift! How fortuitous! Just the person I came to see!"

"What on earth — ?" she exclaimed, unable to keep the horror from her voice, "Why are you *here?*"

"I came to see you, of course! I would have thought that quite obvious. But then you never were very good at understanding my meaning in things, were you?"

"Wasn't I?" faltered Hetty, desperately wondering how she could get rid of him. She couldn't understand his sudden appearance, having sincerely hoped never to see him again, but here he was, smiling down at her as though nothing untoward had happened in the meantime.

She was unable to recall when they had had any conversation in which she'd been allowed to freely voice her opinions, so was doubtful there had ever been a time when such a misunderstanding might have occurred. Apart from the rather awkward proposal, which had been the only time, as far as she could remember, when he had been so taken aback that he had remained silent long enough for her to say what was on her mind without fear of interruption.

He had a habit of ignoring what she was saying and talking at the same time. Their meetings had mostly been chaperoned by either her grandfather or Mr Randall, the churchwarden, so their conversation had been limited anyway. He had always been a stickler for propriety and insisted that a young lady should always be accompanied by a companion or governess. As she was, at the beginning of their acquaintance, still living at Swift Park, before all their troubles began, with a houseful of staff, this was perfectly reasonable, but when they moved to Friday's Acre, things changed. Her life changed dramatically, and she had been quite content to forgo the conventions of the day — she'd really had no choice in the matter. He had made his disapproval very apparent and never failed to lecture her upon her wayward behaviour.

But here he was, in all his pompous glory, intruding into her new life again just as though they'd never had any disagreements and she just couldn't even begin to understand the reason why.

"Mr Scroggs — *please* — let me — "

He put a hand firmly upon her shoulder, squeezing it hard, "Miss Swift, you must be reasonable in this! There has been much wild conjecture in the village recently and I feel it is my duty to do my best to convince you that your reputation is in grave danger of being ruined forever. Even, I, with my good standing in the district, will not be able to save you!"

"But I don't want — "

He continued without pause, "I have been thinking about this for the past few weeks and have concluded that you must return at once to the farm with Mr Swift. I will speak with the parson about arranging the earliest possible wedding we can. It is the only solution. Even though it may tarnish my own unblemished character, I am willing to risk the possible damage to my own good name because I am quite determined to take you away from this diabolical place and the ungodly people who are holding you here. I am very willing to marry you to shield you from inevitable dishonour. I feel it's my duty to prevent your bringing even more disgrace upon your family — "

"It's not your business — "

He paid no attention to her feeble interruption and ploughed on in much the same vein, " — although it's highly regrettable that you only have your grandfather now, as the rest of your highly unreliable family are no longer with us — and who knows how long *he* may last after all these dramas! It could very well be the death of him. But he must be accustomed to being ridiculed after everything that your father did and now that he must endure the sight of you fraternising with such inferior people, it must have brought all the old scandals to the fore again — the villagers are talking of little else. I felt, in such trying circumstances, that it was up to me to step in and do what I can to try to restore the honour of the Swift name — in order that the Scroggs name will remain unsullied by association. It goes without saying that my mother isn't going to be at all pleased about our families being joined especially now that Swift Park has been sold, but I expect if you demonstrate that you are duly grateful and make it clear that you have learnt your lesson — "

"Oh my *goodness!* You really should just *go away* Mr Scroggs!" said Hetty in failing accents.

He didn't hear her, quite decided upon his rescue mission, "You are, on the whole, an amiable female with a surprisingly superior mind and if it weren't for your obvious flaws, you would be an ideal mate. I shall not mention again the most glaring of these flaws because it is easily overcome — a wig for the present and, in the end, age will surely take care of it! I'm sure that I shall learn to tolerate it when we are fully distracted by our own family and life together has become commonplace. Your more outstanding imperfections will be less noticeable, I am absolutely certain."

Hetty's sharply indrawn breath went unheard, "Well, Mr Scroggs, as you refuse to leave, I shall damn well go instead. I bid you farewell!" And with that she tried to duck out from where she was pinned against the wall, but as she tried to slide past him, he grabbed her arm and held her fast.

"No, Miss Swift! I will brook no argument! You will not escape me again. I am quite determined in this. You are returning with me to my mother's house where you shall be safe from the scandalmongering. My wonderful and most beloved mother will take you under her wing until the day comes when you and I shall leave to begin our new life, as husband and wife."

Hetty tugged at his hand, but his fingers were digging into her sleeve, and she couldn't release them, however much she prised at them.

"Let me go at *once!*" she cried furiously.

"I don't think you understand, Miss Swift! You *will* be coming with me and there will be no argument. Stop struggling! I have a cart to transport you, which I unfortunately had to leave at the bottom of the hill but once we reach it, we shall be back in the village before anyone discovers that you're missing. Now, come along — " and he pulled at her arm, dragging her forcibly down the path to the wider track that led to the main gate.

For a moment, as she was being unceremoniously hauled along behind him, Hetty's mind just stopped working, she went quite blank and although she was still moving, albeit reluctantly and very slowly, she felt as though it wasn't really her.

She looked down at his hand, at his stubby fingers biting into her arm and she wondered what was happening to her and puzzled over where the eggs had gone.

She just didn't seem to be able to marshal her thoughts into any kind of order at all. She felt as though she had just woken from a dream and was in that strange state of confusion when reality slowly mixed back into illusion. But she wasn't waking up, she seemed to be stuck in the part where she was stupefied and frozen.

Her legs began to shake unhelpfully and her head pound. She closed her eyes again and felt the cold air on her cheeks, heard the crunch of the snow beneath their boots and a dull stabbing pain in her arm.

That's all there was. The cold, the sounds and the pain.

Nineteen

Cold, sounds, pain.

The cold was fierce, pinching her face and even through the thickness of her grandfather's old coat, she could feel each of Mr Scrogg's fingers gripping her arm as though they were biting directly into her skin.

The crackling of frozen snow. Snapping beneath her feet like the breaking of tiny brittle bones.

Her feet seemed to be moving without her own volition. She looked down at them scuffing through the snow, with some astonishment. As she found herself being dragged down a steep incline, her teeth clashed together, and she bit a chunk out of her cheek. The blood tasted like copper. She wondered idly how she knew what copper tasted like — had she ever licked something made of copper?

Inside her eyelids there were sparks and rippling coloured lights like exploding stars.

She heard the gate open, felt the slope of the ground and the bitter cold of the exposed hillside beyond the sheltered garden.

Time was slipping by too fast, and she was getting further from Galdre Knap. Further from….

She forced her eyes open and blinked blindly into the piercing brightness.

Somehow, she had to stop him. Somehow, she had to save herself.

Her assailant was taking no notice of her, she might just as well have been a sack of potatoes.

She didn't seem to be able to string together any useful thoughts at all, her mind was blank. It was as though it were happening to someone else and not her.

She needed her grandmother to talk to her, to tell her what to do.

Hetty saw the cart ahead of them. There was another man waiting beside it.

An accomplice.

"Ah, there's my brother. He's come to assist us. Lionel! I have her!"

Mr Lionel Scroggs came to meet them, clearly a little younger than his brother and looking decidedly dubious, "Edwin, are you sure — ? She looks rather reluctant to me!"

"No, no! Just the proper maidenly concerns. Perfectly reasonable. She'll be grateful when she understands what we've done for her. Help me get her into the cart."

Hetty, feeling a wave of anger rise up and threaten to overwhelm her as the peril of her situation suddenly became all too clear and her revulsion for her kidnapper engulfed her, without warning, dug her heels in.

"I will *not* go," she declared loudly.

"Yes, you will. You have no choice. You're coming with us."

She looked pleadingly at the brother, hoping for succour from that quarter at least, but could see that he was in awe of his sibling and was going to obey orders regardless of how he may feel about what was happening.

"You're taking me against my will! I want to stay at Galdre Knap! I don't want to get in the cart, and I most certainly do *not* want to marry *you,* you ridiculous blockhead!"

She grabbed hold of the side of the vehicle and held on grimly.

Edwin Scroggs tried to bodily lift her, but she made herself stiffly uncooperative and he had to instruct his nervous brother urgently to help him.

Lionel Scroggs took her by the other arm and when she tried to shake him off, they wrestled for a moment before she felt her feet lose contact with the snowy ground.

"Let *go* of me!" she shouted at them, "I'm staying with the Guivres! I love them! I *hate* you!"

"She seems exceedingly averse to accompanying us, Edwin!" said Lionel Scroggs, anxiously.

"Take no notice. She's been bewitched!"

"I have *not!*" snapped Hetty indignantly, "in fact, you stupid, *stupid* man, I'm betrothed to Mr Guivre! We're going to be married and when he finds out what you've done — !"

And, as the first large snowflakes began to dance past them, spiralling down from the darkening sky, Hetty laughed out loud, "Now you're in trouble! You should never anger Miss Guivre, she's very volatile, you know! This snow won't stop until you release me."

"I have no idea what you're talking about, but a bit more bad weather will not detain us."

Hetty looked back to the house, which was fast disappearing into the swirling snow.

She wanted to use her skills, to harness them to do her bidding. She thought about Eirwen, who was obviously already aware of the kidnap attempt, and she pictured Torquhil and the jackdaw, the impertinent, exasperating, *wonderful* jackdaw.

"I think you'll find it will," she murmured happily.

Then, as she was manhandled towards the cart and the snowfall continued to increase in velocity, she heard a familiar and most welcome sound — a raucous battle-cry.

One glance up into the otherwise white sky told her that help was on its way. Tears of relief started to her eyes, and she stopped fighting the two men, knowing their plan was doomed.

A jagged grey shape blurring against the colourless curtain of snow, Crow slashed through the storm so fast it was hard to focus on his flight and behind him and around him, a ragged battalion of his kind.

Mr Edwin Scroggs followed Hetty's inappropriately amused gaze and noted in some alarm that they were about to be attacked on all sides by an aggressive looking flock of birds, like a deadly volley of arrows loosed from archer's bows.

"What *are* they?" shouted Lionel Scroggs above the rush of wings and strident bird calls.

"*Crow!*" yelled Hetty in delight.

Crow, swooped, circled them and flew, with unmistakeable menace, straight at Edwin Scroggs, who, seeing the weapon-like beak coming right at him, released Hetty and threw himself to the ground to protect his face. Crow cackled triumphantly and feathering his wings to halt his flight, twisted in the air and landed with a flourish on Hetty's shoulder.

I'll leave the other little worm to my friends.

Once Hetty had found her bearings again she slowly began to retreat back up the track until she was at a safe distance from the roisterous scene of battle, and she watched with some satisfaction as the band of jackdaws mobbed the two hapless humans. The unfortunate brothers somehow managed to scramble into the cart and Edwin Scroggs, his bedraggled wig tilted over one eye, whipped up the now very skittish horse and with his wailing brother still hanging half off the side, drove away as fast as the deep snow would allow him, chased by a seething dark cloud of chattering birds.

Hetty and Crow silently observed the cart disappear into the snowstorm and then she turned and began to unsteadily trudge back up the hill.

"Thank you for coming," she said a little breathlessly. "How did you know?"

The pale one. She knew. She always knows.

"Of course. She just seems to sense — and naturally you were with her. Mr Scroggs really is horribly tiresome. An absurd buffoon. Full of his own imaginary importance and so eager to make me his prisoner for life. Imagine being married to him!"

I'd rather not, thank you. I have high standards for a jackdaw.

As they approached the house, the snow eased until it was just a few wandering forgotten flakes trying to find somewhere to settle.

They were greeted at the kitchen door by Torquhil, who cast Hetty a concerned glance and stood back to allow them to enter the house.

"Are you all right?" he asked her.

"Absolutely perfect, thank you."

The slightest crooked smile, "I wouldn't argue with that," he murmured. "Although I did think you might be trying to escape."

She stood utterly still and looked up at him from wide violet eyes, "Then, I'm sorry to say, you're as much a fool as that *gargantuan* fool, Mr Edwin Scroggs."

"Is he a fool?"

"He tried to abduct me. He thought I'd want to leave with him — to leave Galdre Knap. I had to tell him that I was already to be wed — to you. He wasn't at all happy about that."

"I can imagine."

"He was even unhappier about being attacked by murderous jackdaws."

"I can't blame him. It shows good sound sense."

"Torquhil! You're not taking this seriously!"

"I can assure you that I am. The brothers Scroggs will be made to pay for this day's work."

"Oh? Really? How exactly?" demanded Hetty with unladylike interest.

"I have not yet decided, Miss Bloodthirsty."

Hetty chuckled, suddenly quite over her horrible ordeal and wondering what punishment might be meted out to her attackers.

"Are you sure they didn't hurt you, Hetty?"

"I shall have a rather bruised arm but other than that — no injuries. I just — " she faltered to a stop.

"Just?"

She took a deep breath, "I couldn't — do *anything*."

He glanced at the servants who were surreptitiously listening and taking Hetty by the elbow, he led her away to the library, Crow still balanced on her shoulder.

He closed the door.

"Now, tell me."

Finding that her legs were actually no longer steady enough to hold her up, Hetty collapsed into the nearest chair and Crow flew up to his usual place on the shelf and prepared to be entertained.

"When he grabbed me — I thought at first that it was a silly mistake and that he would come to his senses, but he wouldn't listen to me — he *never* listens to me! And then — then I sort of froze — not because of the cold or because I was frightened — but because I knew I should be able to *do* something! After all, I have abilities! Or at least, I'm *supposed* to have abilities. They just wouldn't — I couldn't — "

"You couldn't use them to save yourself?"

"Precisely. It was very frustrating."

"That's often the way with such things at the beginning. You'll find a way to make it work. For Eirwen, being little more than a child, it seems to be dramatic emotion that guides her: anger, jealousy, fear, love — in this case, it was obviously her love for you. The fear of losing you gave her usually rather erratic powers some direction and with that incentive she's able to make significant things happen. In the early days we had to contend with the rather hit and miss results of her childish passions getting the better of her — it was dangerously chaotic for a while. Things were broken, people were hurt — accidentally, of course, but once she learnt the principles of controlling her rages and channelling her thoughts — fewer things were destroyed, and life became more ordered. It was a trying time for all concerned.

Life became a constant struggle for her. She ran away and unfortunately ended up in the asylum. Ordinary folk do not understand her. Doctors believe she's possessed and want to experiment upon her, to dissect her. They see her as something inhuman, something that needs to be cured, changed — destroyed. Priests want to cast out the Devil in her and even if it kills her, they say she will, at least, be with God.

I had to use alternative methods to rescue her. I am always reluctant to invoke anything other than what's considered normal to attain what is needed. One of the first things you have to learn is that any power must be reasonably governed or it can become uncontrollable. It can transform and spread, like a plague, and what may have seemed perfectly reasonable at first can quickly destroy all that it touches. You will learn how to control it. You'll find a way to make it a force for good like your grandmother did."

"I'm not nearly so confident. I *tried* to conjure something but there was nothing. No tingling. No voices. Nothing. Even though I was being dragged away from Galdre Knap and everyone I — love — I couldn't stop them."

"It's not something you can analyse or measure. There's neither rhyme nor reason to such things. It would be like trying to capture mist in a butterfly net. It's ultimately unfathomable. You cannot blame yourself for not being able to master it immediately."

"What if I can never control it? What if — ?"

"Stop. There's no point in trying to make sense of any of it. For some reason my sister and I have — well, as I said, one must just accept what has been decided."

"You mean like the fresco in the Long Barrow? Because it's been depicted, it must be so?"

Torquhil turned away to look abstractedly out of the window.

Hetty waited for him to say something.

Crow lifted a claw and flexed it.

Then after what seemed like a very long and weighty silence, Hetty began to wonder if she'd said something inappropriate. Perhaps she shouldn't have mentioned the fresco. Perhaps he was tired of the scrapes she constantly got into or perhaps now that Eirwen was finally on the mend, she was not needed anymore. Perhaps he didn't know how to tell her.

"Do you believe in prophecies?" he asked quietly.

"Prophecies?"

"Foretelling the future."

"I know what it *means!* I don't know. I — don't think I do."

"What if you had conclusive proof that a prophecy was coming true?"

"Well, I'd be astonished, and I suspect, a little doubtful. I would have to see the evidence of course. It's not that I don't believe in such things. I'm probably quite gullible by nature, but I suppose that I've learnt to be cautious. My father, you see — "

"I completely understand. Discovering that someone close to you is seriously flawed and, more to the point, untrustworthy, must be hard to bear and must inevitably change the way you perceive the world, which in turn must make you inclined to be sceptical."

"He betrayed his own family. They didn't deserve all the trouble he brought into their lives. It most certainly hastened my mother's death." She frowned, "You see, I just cannot understand why Grandmama couldn't have used her skills to do something about my father. She would surely have had the ability to change him in some way, enough to save him — to save them."

"It doesn't work like that."

"How inconsiderate. How thoughtless and cruel."

"Yes. You haven't really answered my question."

"I did. I said that I don't think I do believe in prophecies. But you haven't said if this prophecy is predicting something good or bad. Not that it would make any difference to how I feel about it. How can anyone tell what will happen in the future? It's not possible."

"You must be beginning to see that anything is possible."

"I am — I can see — but it still makes no sense. I think I'm essentially a practical sort of person — I like something solid that I can understand. A chicken or a basket of apples. A turnip."

"You're still feeling a little unsteady after your adventure," he said with a wry smile.

"I'm just a little tired. There was much walking in snow, which is quite hard, and also being dragged — it was — not easy. I must say I'm looking forward to *not* being abducted tomorrow!"

"I heartily concur with that."

"Oh, gracious!"

"What is it?"

"The *eggs!*"

"I'm afraid I'm none the wiser. What eggs?"

"I was collecting eggs and left them on the wall by the little gate and they just disappeared. Mrs Ashby needs them for supper!"

"I shall go and look for them in that case. Although I expect they're long gone by now. Rats probably — or a jay."

Sneaky beggars, jays.

"I shall be in such trouble. There'll be no supper."

"I'll put in a good word for you. You do have an extremely good excuse."

Hetty managed a weak laugh, "I'm afraid that Mr Scroggs may try to stir up more trouble in the village now that he knows we're betrothed. He could make things very awkward if he was so inclined. Perhaps I shouldn't have told him."

"I'm delighted that you did. It's set in stone now. It'll make it harder for you to back out."

She fixed him with a frosty look, "What makes you think I want to back out?"

"Good instincts."

"Well, Mr Guivre, I must point out, with the utmost respect, that you're very much mistaken. I have entered into a binding agreement with you, and I intend to honour it. Unless *you* — ?"

"Unless I change my mind? That's highly unlikely. It will solve a good deal of our problems, I think." He went to the door and opened it.

"Torquhil?"

He looked back at her.

She shrugged, "If you *should* change your mind — "

"Hetty, you have to believe in something."

"I do. I believe in Grandpapa. And hens. They're reliable."

"But you don't yet trust me enough?"

She gazed back at him for a moment in silence.

"No, I *do.* Although, I cannot for the life of me think why I should. You're not exactly a commonplace kind of employer or suitor."

"Should I be?"

"Oh, no! I like — I wouldn't want you to change."

"A fish out of water."

"Well, I suppose that would only really be a problem if you were the only fish."

This is worse than listening to geese talk.

"Pay no attention to him. He's still got the battle in his blood," said Torquhil, holding the door open.

"He came to my rescue."

"You weren't really in any danger, you know. Mr Scroggs is mostly bluster with very little to back it up. That kind of bullying man is easily diverted with even the slightest show of resistance."

"Are you suggesting that I didn't show resistance?" asked Hetty, affronted.

"Don't be ridiculous. I was just saying that a man like that is nowhere near as powerful as he thinks he is. You shouldn't be afraid of him. In fact, he should be more afraid of *you.*"

"I couldn't do anything to stop him."

"But you did. You thought of Crow. You called the jackdaws. Eirwen was aware. I was on my way. You had, without knowing, already sent for assistance."

The clarion call.

Hetty looked from jackdaw to her employer and shook her head, "It would have been quite helpful to know that at the time, rather than find out afterwards when it's too late. It's all too haphazard. I like things to be far more ordered."

You've come to the wrong place then.

Torquhil smiled at her and without saying anything else, he went out.

Hetty quickly turned away from the barrier of the closed door and began to straighten books that required no tidying.

Crow watched her for a moment with beady-eyed interest.

I can never understand why humans do not just say what they mean.

"Like you do? I suppose we are lectured from cradle to grave about the importance of concealing all emotion and above all, that good manners must be maintained come what may. We are creatures of habit — just as you are, but we humans are imbued with a rigid sense of propriety, which cannot, in any circumstances, be overcome, even if it causes unbelievable heartache. We cannot step outside those rules and regulations without endangering our very souls." She laughed as she said it, but the truth in his words had struck home and her amusement was not sincere. Once it was pointed out, this particular human foible was revealed to be utterly senseless.

My master is not subject to such restraints.

Hetty frowned, "He's certainly no ordinary man. But is he not restrained by his very nature? He's naturally diffident and remains aloof from those around him as though set apart. I'm not entirely sure why this should be. Their uncanny abilities — how did he and Eirwen acquire them — ?"

As you did. Inherited.

"From whom? I've heard nothing of their parents or any other family — "

That doesn't surprise me.

"I wish I understood."

A great great grandmother who was burnt as a witch.

"Oh, no!"

And parents who denied her very existence and tried to eliminate any signs of those offending skills in their offspring.

"They didn't succeed!"

No amount of denial or beatings could ever quash such a powerful gift, but it didn't stop them from trying.

"It's no wonder they are so very — different and that he's so reserved."

You might be surprised to hear that he is, unlike the damn snow, beginning to thaw a little.

Hetty blushed and lowered her eyes, "I have no idea why —"

Crow cackled.

Denying it will not make it any less true.

She shook her head, "We are only betrothed to stop the gossiping."

Is that so?

Hetty said nothing.

It seems to me that there were other more straightforward solutions.

She remained silent. Her mind sluggishly uncooperative. Crow cocked his head.

I was instructed to watch for you even before you came to the village.

She looked up at that, her eyes flashing, "You were watching me? Why? Under Mr Guivre's instruction?"

The bony blades of the jackdaw's beak clattered together.

We had been looking for someone with your red crest for some time.

Hetty's eyes widened, "Oh! I think I'm beginning to see. The prophecy. The fresco in the Long Barrow. He truly believes in it! But how can that possibly be? Something made so long ago — it cannot have any influence over the future. It's just not conceivable. Oh, I know that I've inherited some of my grandmother's more unusual qualities, but even though I've seen conclusive proof, I still have difficulty believing that such a thing is possible. I think I have a very unimaginative and ordinary mind. I like things to make sense and dislike surprises very much. I suppose I'm quite a dull person really."

You underrate yourself. Don't forget I've been observing you since your family's unfortunate downfall. You've comported yourself with dignity and relentless good cheer.

"Crow! Stop being so obsequious! It's making me nervous."

Perhaps you would rather I drew your attention to the fact that someone is approaching the house?

"Oh, no! Who can that be? I hope it's not Mr Scroggs come back again!"

They listened to the sound of a horse whinnying and blowing after a tiring journey up the steep hill to Galdre Knap, the knocking on the great oak door and the sound of Finn walking in his usual unhurried manner to answer it.

A few minutes later, Finn entered the library and made his announcement.

"There is a gentleman come, Miss Swift. He is waiting in the hall. Shall I show him in, or shall I call Mr Guivre?"

Hetty wasn't at all sure what to do in the circumstances and looked to Crow.

You're the lady of the house now.

"Thank you, Finn. Please show him in."

Twenty

The vigorous young man who entered the library, still sporting his many caped great coat and fashionable curly-brimmed beaver and wearing snow-stained top boots, strode in with an eagerness entirely undimmed by being travel weary, but his precipitous entrance slowed to a standstill as he became aware of a startlingly red-headed female staring at him with wide violet eyes and then out of the corner of his eye, a jackdaw, perched upon the back of a beautifully carved chair.

He removed his hat, smoothed his slightly disordered periwig and made an elegant leg to Hetty who, suddenly remembering her manners, found her smile and went forward, hand outstretched, to greet the stranger.

"How do you do, sir. I am Miss Henrietta Swift. Welcome to Galdre Knap."

He bowed again, "Miss Swift, how do you do? Adam Deering at your service. I'm sorry to intrude without warning."

"Oh, please don't apologise! I'm delighted to meet you. We are sadly lacking in visitors. The snow has been very off-putting. Have you come far?"

"From London, Miss Swift. And prior to that, France."

"Oh, good gracious, I suspect that you are the opera-loving gentleman?" exclaimed Hetty, light dawning.

He smiled most charmingly at her, "I believe that I am that fellow! Am I to suppose that my dear friend has mentioned me?" He looked about him, "I was hoping to find Torquhil at home."

"He has indeed mentioned you and with great affection. He'll be back shortly — he's just gone to find some eggs."

Mr Deering laughed, "He must be much changed then. Eggs! How unusual. It would appear that he's rather taken to animal husbandry now he's returned to Galdre Knap!" and he eyed the jackdaw warily.

"That's Crow, he's a — family pet. And, to explain, I carelessly mislaid the eggs earlier in the stable yard and Mr Guivre has kindly gone in search of them to save me from cook's wrath."

"Still as chivalrous as he ever was. That will never change."

"Mr Deering, please do remove your coat and have a seat. I am forgetting my manners. We are very out of practice with receiving visitors. Can I send for some refreshment for you? You must be hungry and thirsty after your journey."

Her guest shrugged himself out of his coat and threw it over the back of the chair before waiting for Hetty to sit down and then he too sat and let out a heartfelt sigh, "I must say, it's a relief to just be out of the cold and not be on my horse any longer. I'm not as young as I used to be. Travelling long distances is not for the faint of heart. Especially when I finally reached your part of the county with its oddly unrelenting fall of snow. Ten miles or so away, it's just the usual mud and deeply rutted roads — you seem to be the only area in the southwest to be suffering this strange weather. It had the ostlers at the inn all shaking their heads and wondering if the county had somehow angered God."

Hetty gave him a cautious smile and prayed Torquhil would come quickly before the conversation became anymore awkward. "I agree, it's most peculiar, but I expect it will thaw soon. Will you be staying with us Mr Deering? We would be delighted to have you."

"If it's not too much trouble. I hope that Torquhil will be delighted too — although I suspect he'll find my unannounced arrival rather irritating. We did not part on particularly good terms. I let him down very badly."

"Oh, I am sure that you did not! I'm quite sure that he understood you had good reasons for leaving. Being with Miss Guivre under such trying circumstances cannot have been easy for any of you."

"How is Eirwen? Is she here?"

"She is. Torquhil brought her here to recuperate and she is beginning to recover slowly from her strange affliction. She's no longer confined to her bed and can readily converse and thankfully her appetite has returned so she is looking more herself."

"That's excellent news. Does she have someone to take care of her?"

Hetty felt her cheeks heat up and she nodded, "Of course, Mr Guivre needed a companion and nursemaid for her, and I was happy to accept that position."

The young man raised questioning brows. She tried not to panic, "Mr Guivre kindly invited me to live at Galdre Knap. My grandfather also resides here. We moved in a few weeks ago from the village. There is also," she added quickly, "Mrs Waverley, the nursemaid, who escorted Miss Guivre from the — hospital to Galdre Knap. She has been indispensable. And all the household staff, of course."

Mr Deering smiled his rather boyish smile, acknowledging the list of reliable chaperones being offered up to reassure him. "I can see that you're quite clearly never left alone for even the briefest moment with your scandalous employer!"

Hetty couldn't help but chuckle as it was exactly what she had been trying to imply. "I can assure you that my reputation is perfectly safe with the Guivres."

"Oh, I have no doubt. Torquhil is, above everything, an honourable fellow. Curious, but honourable."

Feeling that it perhaps wasn't appropriate to be talking so freely about her employer with his friend, she deftly changed the subject, "Please, allow me to find you some refreshment, Mr Deering. I'm sure you would welcome a change of clothes and a chance to wash the mud off as well. I shall go and find the housemaid and ensure your bedchamber is made ready."

"Nicely done, Miss Swift," said Mr Deering with a wry look. "Although, I swear I would never say anything too outrageous about my dearest friend. It would be a relief to spruce myself up. I fear I'm trampling the outside into your home."

Hetty rose and casting a surreptitious glance at Crow, who was behaving with unusual restraint, she told Mr Deering she wouldn't be long and took a few steps across the room.

Too late. He's here. This should be interesting.

The door opened and Torquhil came in.

Hetty didn't know whether to be pleased or nervous, "Oh, there you are! I was just coming to find you. You have a visitor, Torquhil."

His gaze slid past her and met the candid, hazel eyes of his old friend, "Adam! What an unexpected surprise! What on earth brings you to Gloucestershire? I thought you said when last we saw each other that you would never return to England."

"You know I was only joking! We've been friends since school, through thick and thin. The trip to Vienna was quite demanding and I suppose I wasn't really prepared for all that it entailed."

"I can only apologise."

"It was hardly your fault, dear friend. I'm glad to hear that Eirwen is recovering well. As you know I found her condition deeply troubling. It made me feel helpless and I found it difficult to comprehend what she was suffering from. It all seemed to be — so far beyond anyone's area of expertise and very much beyond my limited understanding. Still, I'm here now and I've met Miss Swift, who managed not to wince when I said I would be staying — if it's not inconvenient?"

"Miss Swift, you will no doubt discover, is made of stern stuff. Very little confounds her. And it's entirely convenient. We'd be happy to have you."

"I understand that Miss Swift looks after Eirwen."

Torquhil glanced speculatively at Hetty, "Is that all she said, I wonder?"

"Oh yes, she became decidedly discreet when I began to talk rather too loosely about you!"

Hetty edged towards the door, itching to be gone.

"So, she didn't mention that she and I have recently become betrothed?"

Mr Deering's face was such a picture of pure astonishment that Hetty very nearly laughed out loud. He clearly found the idea preposterous.

"Betrothed? Are you *sure*?" he demanded.

Hetty was at the door and wishing she had already left the room.

"I am absolutely sure, Adam. Henrietta has done me the singular honour of accepting my offer of marriage. You may well look surprised but it's true, is it not, Hetty?"

Hetty fixed a smile upon her face and turned to face them, "It is. We are recently betrothed."

"Good God! I never believed you'd find someone willing to wed you Torquhil! And, if I may say so, such a rare beauty too."

Hetty saw Torquhil stiffen and, feeling distinctly discomfited, she fled the room unconcerned about the poor impression she might be giving.

* * *

She halted her flight for a moment outside the kitchen and leant her hot forehead against the cool panels of the door.

Somehow, the arrival of Mr Deering was making her take a good look at what was going on in her life. A stranger in their midst, intruding into their secluded world and bringing the outside in. She didn't want things to change. She was used to this new life now and she hated change.

She could hear voices in the kitchen. Reassuringly familiar voices. With a sigh of relief, she opened the door and went in.

* * *

"Mr Deering's bedchamber is spick and span, cobwebs gone, didn't take me long. An' Mrs Ashby's making him something nice to eat," said Agatha, wondering why Miss Swift was not quite her usual cheerful self.

"Thank you. I don't know how long he'll be staying. I don't know why he's here really — "

"He seems like a nice sort of fellow though, don't he? I caught a glimpse as he came in."

"He seems very pleasant, but I just wish — "

"Of course, Miss, I understand."

Finn, who was listening as he filled his pipe with raspberry leaf tobacco, looked up at them, "It would appear that the new arrival is causing some concern?"

Hetty shrugged, trying to look untroubled, "He's a good friend of Mr Guivre's so I'm quite sure that having him here will give us all some cheer. He does seem to be a good sort of fellow. It'll be nice for Mr Guivre to have someone else to talk to."

Agatha grinned at her, "An' quite handsome too. Well turned out. Polite. Lovely smile. Just about perfect I'd say! As long as he's got some money in his pockets!"

Hetty laughed reluctantly, "You've obviously been studying him closely, Aggie!"

The maid snorted, "I only took a quick peek, Miss. It's only natural! A fine figure of a man. Brawny but not stout. Tall but not so tall that you get a crick in your neck looking up at him. Kind eyes. Good teeth."

"You make him sound like a horse! Good teeth, indeed!"

Mrs Ashby limped into the kitchen from the pantry, "Nothing better to do than stand about gossiping!" she complained.

Hetty noted the cook's rather drawn face and frowned, "Tell us what you need, Mrs Ashby and we'll jump to attention." She went to her side and murmured, "Do please sit down and rest your leg. You've been standing up too much because of all the extra work. I'll stay and help."

Mrs Ashby nodded gratefully and plumped down into her chair, "It is aching me a bit, I admit. If you could lend a hand with the supper, I'd be grateful."

"I'd be happy to."

Mrs Ashby gave her a knowing look, "Avoiding the visitor, are we?"

Guilty as charged, Hetty just shook her head, "I like cooking," she said defensively. "What are we making?"

"Pork and prunes. I've a nice big piece of pork. Sam brought it from the village yesterday from Mr Warren who had to slaughter one of his pigs and with his two boys gone now, he had too much left over. Sam has offered to do some chores to repay him. He wouldn't take a payment. And Mrs Warren sent some bottled prunes, which are surprisingly good! It'll make a tasty meal for Mr Deering this evening. Aggie's going to take a tray in for him in a minute, a nice bit of suet pudding and a tankard of mead to fortify him after his journey — tide him over until supper. He'll sleep well tonight."

"Not in that bedchamber, he won't!" said Agatha, gleefully.

"Oh, Aggie! You haven't put him in the Wild Beasts Bedchamber! That's a bit cruel! Poor man."

"Well, we're running out of rooms! I didn't have much choice really. It was either the Wild Beasts or the Lilies and Roses."

"I see your point. But if he is assailed by appalling nightmares and runs screaming into the night, I shall not defend your choice! For all we know, he may be a devoted horticulture enthusiast and would have been very much at home in the Floral Bedchamber, hideous though it may be!"

"That room would give anyone nightmares," grunted Finn from his chair by the fireplace. "Why they can't just have plain whitewashed walls, I don't know. It's just showing off. Parading their wealth and plastering it up for all to admire. It's a mere frippery fashion anyway and is most likely fleeting, thank the Lord."

"But they're such exquisite paintings, Finn! I love my bedchamber, with the trees and toadstools. It's beautiful, just like being in a forest."

"The master chose that bedchamber for you," said Finn, "Long before you arrived here."

Hetty didn't acknowledge this interesting piece of information but kept her eyes firmly fixed on the jar of prunes Mrs Ashby had put on the table. She pulled it to her and removed the cork top, sniffing appreciatively at the sweet caramel aroma that it exuded. She longed to pop one of the wrinkled black fruits into her mouth but didn't dare as Mrs Ashby was watching her. She'd never tasted prunes before but the smell of them was mouth-watering.

She was beginning to see that she had long been expected to arrive at Galdre Knap, well before she herself had been informed of the latest change in her circumstances. It seems she was the last to know.

* * *

After a couple of hours helping in the kitchen, Hetty traipsed, leaden-footed up the stairs, thinking that she wouldn't be able to avoid supper with everyone without seeming rude and had therefore better change out of her work-worn gown and into one more suitable for company. She delayed the inevitable by going first to see Eirwen who was out of bed and sitting on the window seat, wrapped in several blankets, a shawl about her shoulders and head. She looked like a swaddled baby and Hetty couldn't help but grin as she went to sit beside her.

"Oh, Hetty! At last. I'm so *bored!* I've missed you — " a furtive glance at Mrs Waverley who was peacefully dozing in the best armchair by the fire, " — even though I've been guarded all day. I hear you've had quite an adventure."

"It's certainly been a busy day. I would much rather have been here with you having a nice peaceful chat. I cannot thank you enough for sending the jackdaws to help. I don't know how you do it, but it was timely as I was having a little trouble with a certain gentleman — as, of course, you already know."

"I *know!* Hateful Mr Scroggs! Isn't he just *awful?* Trying to take you away! How *dare* he! I'm so glad you're going to marry

Torquhil instead — you'll be safe with him. We'll be sisters then. That's what I've always wanted, a sister."

"Well, I'm not sure that we shall actually — I mean, it's really only a temporary measure — to stop the villagers being scandalised by our odd situation. It may not come to marriage in the end, dearest. Oh, do not look so despondent Eirwen! I shall still be able to keep you company, very little will really change."

Eirwen's mouth turned down at the corners, "It won't be the same. And if you do not marry, then Torquhil will not be happy, and I cannot bear that thought."

"I should think he would be very much relieved," said Hetty, a touch bitterly.

"Then you don't yet know him. He never does anything without good reason and a great deal of soul-searching. He's always been a devoted brother and he tried so terribly hard to be a dutiful son. We had hard times when I was very young. Being much older, he took care of me and protected me when our parents — my father particularly, was determined to rid us of any inherited likeness to our much-despised ancestor."

"Ah, yes, your great great grandmother, wasn't it? I've been told about her. It seems that we both have some oddities in our families. Do you know much about her?"

Eirwen closed her eyes for a moment, the pale lashes almost invisible against her snow-white skin, "Torquhil told me that she was silver-haired from birth, like me, and fair-skinned too. He said an account was written by the local priest about her and his part in her eventual death. The priest was, of course, triumphant that they'd successfully put her to death. Torquhil didn't want me to know, but in the end, he was forced to tell me to stop me from revealing my own abilities. They're jolly hard to control." She looked slightly abashed, "I'm afraid I didn't take heed of his warnings."

"You were just a child and children cannot be expected to understand the true gravity of such a situation. You cannot blame yourself. It must have been very difficult for you, knowing what had happened to her."

"Matilda Guivre. She was apparently able to alter the weather too and had visions and was able to make predictions which came true. Although her visions came during terrible seizures apparently, which could happen anywhere, without warning. It made her vulnerable. That's how she accidentally revealed what she was. I'm fortunate, I've been blessed with foresight that comes quietly. I can keep it hidden — unless, of course, I become *too* vexed and then it's exceedingly hard to conceal — and accidental damage can occur!"

"So I've heard."

"My father enraged me because he would punish Torquhil for *my* sins. Torquhil never retaliated — never used his powers to stop Father or silence Mother. He could have done, you see? He could have caused havoc. But instead, the only weapon he chose to use was his silence. As soon as he could, he left the family home to establish his own residence and just when I had begun to think that I'd been entirely abandoned, he came back for me, and we never returned to that place."

"I'm so sorry, Eirwen. It must have been very frightening for you, thinking you were all alone. Thank you for explaining — it accounts, in some degree, for your brother's behaviour and helps me understand him a little better. May I ask how he acquired his wealth?"

Eirwen shrugged, "There was an unexpected inheritance from Matilda and Reynold Guivre, handed down in a trust fund, I think. Probably, in some way, to make up for what she knew we would have to endure. Guilt for setting us on this tormented path. She, of course, could see things. Torquhil invested the money well when he came of age. He said that Matilda had left a letter for us with our family attorneys. She suggested that one day we would need control over our own finances and a place of safety."

"So, he bought Galdre Knap with the inheritance?"

"Oh, goodness no, he has not yet found his true place of safety — this house belonged to our great great grandparents! It had been much neglected for many years and then it was occupied by various people; all arranged by the attorneys to keep the house from becoming derelict and sliding down the hill."

"I am slowly discovering it's rather an exceptional house! Not at all usual. Did Matilda realise there might be problems for the residents?"

Eirwen nodded, "She did. She mentioned in her letter that due to some unforgivable human errors the house might become unstable at times, especially if, as she put it, '*the Red Wicche had come amongst us*', but she added, '*for only then will Galdre Knap and the Guivres be saved.*' She really was quite histrionic!" She paused for a moment, "Have you ever considered how odd it is that one can have such very commonplace relations as well as the more — outlandish types? Our parents were so ordinary, without any saving graces at all and yet my father was descended from someone as extraordinary as Matilda! It hardly seems possible."

"They say that certain traits often skip a generation. They certainly sound as though they did in your family. No doubt my father wished they had skipped right over him for he was not at all keen on the idea of carrying on the Swift family traditions. He would have much rather it had ended with his mother, my beloved grandmother. I must say that I cannot find it in my heart to blame him. It's a heavy burden for one person to bear. And it's not as though one can just ask someone's advice! Most people would think you'd run mad —"

"And lock you away — like they did with me! You know, I often think that it's because I look different. I cannot hide."

"You may well be right. People are always afraid of anyone who doesn't look as they do. I think it's probably why there are so many wars! I will admit that having such dreadful red hair has always been the bane of my life because it seems to be a deliberate provocation to anyone who passes by. It's an open invitation for insults. I can see that you might have had the same problems."

Eirwen grinned, "Icicle! Moon face! White witch! My favourite was — you look like a goose quill!"

"The not very original — carrot head! Oh, is it autumn already? I beg your pardon, Miss, but I think your head is on fire!" added Hetty, laughing.

Mrs Waverley awoke to the sound of muffled giggling and with a nursemaid's ability to go straight from asleep to awake, she sat up and looked at the two girls leaning on each other helplessly convulsed with mirth. But before she could ask what was going on, the door opened, and Mr Guivre entered the room. He stopped for a moment on the threshold to observe his sister and her companion.

Mrs Waverley noted a change in his usually impassive expression, a gleam in his dark eyes that she had not seen before. It made her think.

She put a hand up to straighten her lace cap, "What are you young ladies finding so amusing? I hope I wasn't talking in my sleep!"

Eirwen's mischief-filled eyes opened wide and Hetty started guiltily.

"We were just comparing the insults we've had about the way we look. When you repeat them, they actually sound quite funny, and it takes away the sting of the words. And no, you don't talk in your sleep, Mrs Waverley. I'm sorry we woke you. Oh, goodness, Torquhil!"

"Have you been leading my little sister astray, Miss Swift?"

Hetty blushed fierily, "No, indeed, I have not! We were only laughing — "

"And a joyous sound it was too," said Torquhil softly, "This house has not heard much laughter — it will light up the dark corners."

Eirwen looked at her brother with a roguish twinkle, "Well, if Galdre Knap has been like a tomb, that's almost entirely your fault, Torquhil. You seldom smile, let alone laugh!"

Hetty gasped.

Mrs Waverley thought, "Oh, my goodness," to herself and sank back to hide behind the wing of the chair.

Torquhil crossed the room and sat down on the bed, his face unreadable.

"You know, Eirwen, speaking as your dour older brother, I'm not at all sure that I didn't prefer you when you were comatose."

"Torquhil!" exclaimed Eirwen, "That's so discourteous!"

"And suggesting that I am humourless and am somehow to blame for the lack of joy at Galdre Knap *isn't* discourteous?"

Eirwen stifled a snort of laughter, "Not in the slightest because it's true. Ask anyone! Ask *Hetty!*" She turned to a horrified Hetty, "Tell him! You are to be married to him so speak now or forever hold your peace."

Hetty swallowed nervously, "I really don't think — "

"No, please don't feel you must spare my feelings," cut in Torquhil. "It's far too late for that."

"Oh dear," murmured Hetty, mortified. "I'd really rather not say."

"In that case I fear I stand damned by your silence."

She looked at him anxiously, "I can't tell if you're being serious or not! It's very frustrating."

"He's *always* serious. So, serious!" said Eirwen, "If I were you Hetty I'd marry Mr Scroggs, you'd certainly have more fun!"

"There's absolutely no chance of *that* ever happening," declared Hetty. "I cannot imagine a worse fate."

"So, marrying me would be the next best option?"

Hetty longed to say that for her it was the *only* option. That she could never consider marrying anyone else.

"May I just remind you — *Edwin Scroggs!* You really have no idea just what a terrifying notion it is to picture myself married to him! I could never even contemplate such a dire future and would rather stay a lonely spinster for the rest of my days."

"That would indeed be a pity. And would contemplating marriage to me also be so terrifying?"

Hetty considered all the ways she might answer this that would preserve her dignity.

But she replied very deliberately, "No. It would not." She heard a little squeak of surprise from Eirwen and continued, "It would be more than acceptable."

Torquhil's face creased into a slow smile, "That is extremely good news. I had begun to worry that I may have forced your hand."

"Well, to be perfectly frank, you did — but once I considered it rationally — I realised that I really had no objections whatsoever to your proposition."

"Damned with faint praise now."

She frowned at him, "I think you're teasing me."

"I may well be. However, I can assure you that I'm delighted to hear that you're not dreading becoming my bride."

The word and all that it entailed jangled in her head, and she took a shaky breath, "But only because my options are so severely limited!"

And Torquhil Guivre laughed out loud.

Twenty-One

The dining table seemed uncomfortably crowded to Hetty, as she entered the room. The gentlemen rose to greet her and Torquhil pulled out her chair for her.

She took her place at the end of the table with Mr Deering on one side and her grandfather on the other. Mrs Waverley was also there, wearing a celebratory ostrich feather in her severely arranged hair.

And there, sitting beside her brother, was Miss Eirwen Guivre, looking as pale as moonlight but resplendent in a gown of aquamarine silk, a slightly darker shade than her eyes and rather too big for her reduced frame. Her beautiful silver hair was just braided and arranged in a simple coronet because Hetty had not wanted to tire her out with too much fussing.

As soon as she was suitably dressed Torquhil had carried her downstairs, Eirwen having been forced to admit rather forlornly that her legs were trembling too much to walk so far. Hetty had dashed to change and then made her way quickly to the kitchen to make sure that Mrs Ashby wasn't feeling overwhelmed by the added work.

The cook glanced up as Hetty flew into the room and, taking in the gown she was wearing, nodded approvingly, even though she could see that it was not fashion of the first stare, "Green suits you, Miss Hetty. That's such a pretty neckline too. You'll need a shawl though — the dining room is always a little chilly, even with the fire lit."

"Thank you, Mrs Ashby, but it's a very old gown. I haven't really had the need for anything new — not since we left Swift

Park. We didn't exactly hold many soirées at Friday's Acre! And don't worry, I have a perfectly serviceable shawl of Grandmama's — I hung it over the newel post. I always get them in such a tangle, they end up dragging along the ground and Thistle thinks the dangling edges are purely for his amusement! I've come to see if you need my help in preparing supper."

"Certainly not!" said Mrs Ashby crisply, "As though I'd allow you to get that lovely gown messy! Everything is under control. Aggie is doing surprisingly well. She's turning out to be quite adept at cooking."

"Well, if you're really sure! I'll go and try to be affable all evening. Wish me luck!"

"You don't need luck, my dear. There's a gentleman in there who doesn't seem to care if you're affable or not."

"You mean Grandpapa?" said Hetty, twinkling.

"No, I do not! You know very well who I mean."

"Oh, I *see*," laughed Hetty, over her shoulder as she skipped blithely out of the kitchen, "You mean the handsome *Mr Deering*."

* * *

Mr Deering was in truth a very welcome addition to the table. He debated chess strategy, opera and poetry with Mr Swift, embroidery and herbal infusions with Mrs Waverley, land management and the unusual local weather with Torquhil and was happy to discuss the merits of the latest novels with Hetty and, much to everyone's surprise, asked Eirwen if she'd like to join him in a song at the pianoforte after dinner. Eirwen was clearly charmed by the suggestion but regretfully demurred because she said she wasn't really feeling quite strong enough and that her voice had not yet fully regained its previous strength. Mr Deering had gently acquiesced but promised that he would, as soon as she was feeling up to snuff, be delighted to accompany her because he remembered hearing her sing and had been very taken with her angelic voice.

He somehow managed to include everyone in the conversations and was knowledgeable about many diverse subjects. Hetty could tell that her grandfather was rather unsubtly trying to find out about Mr Deering's background and his reasons for visiting and rather wished he wouldn't be so blatantly inquisitive. He wasn't able to find out more than the bare minimum as his victim had a deft but polite way of diverting questions he didn't want to answer and avoiding giving away too much information about himself. What she did manage to glean was that he was entirely fancy-free, without a career of any sort — not even the Army or the Church — although trained in the Law Courts, and a music and opera devotee; there was very little else to be discovered from his cautious words. She thought he seemed to be trustworthy and had excellent manners. He was also handsome, in a robust sort of way, with laughing eyes and a ready smile. He was, considered Hetty, on reflection, everything any female, but particularly any young impressionable girl, could wish for — and Hetty could see that Eirwen was fascinated by him. Hetty, on the other hand, realised that although she found him to be perfect in every way, that he did not hold the same fascination for her, and despite her constantly struggling not to, she kept glancing up at Torquhil and thinking about the odd conversation they'd had earlier, which had ended on the rare sound of his laughter.

Her betrothed took very little part in the conversations, unless directly addressed. He seemed, to Hetty, to be more than usually distracted. Not that it was ever easy to tell what he was thinking. She eyed him surreptitiously and wondered what was so clearly bothering him. She wished she weren't sitting so far away because she wanted to find out why he was not engaging with his companions. She hoped that it wasn't something she'd said or done that was making him look so pensive.

For a moment she found herself wondering what it might be like to be his wife and found herself covered in confusion at the thoughts that filled her head. She lowered her eyes and concentrated on her plate of pork and prunes, which she was sure was delectable although she was unable to appreciate it.

After supper was finished and everyone was just idly chatting, Hetty noticed that Eirwen's energy was flagging. She knew the child was unlikely to admit it because she was so thrilled to be downstairs for the first time. Hetty caught her eye, and they exchanged a meaningful glance. After a mute struggle, Eirwen gave a reluctant little nod and Hetty rose to her feet and, during a pause in the conversation, informed everyone that it was time for Eirwen to return to her bedchamber as she was still not fully recovered. The gentlemen stood and wished her a good night and while Torquhil gently scooped his sister up into his arms, Hetty reassured Mrs Waverley that they would be able to cope and that she should continue to enjoy her evening, and then went out after the others.

Torquhil put Eirwen down onto the bed and, after conferring with Hetty to see if she needed assistance and hearing that she didn't, he left saying he'd be back in a short while. Hetty swiftly got Eirwen undressed, washed and into bed, by which time the girl was fighting to keep her eyes open.

"You looked lovely tonight Eirwen, and you managed your first expedition with such poise! I think everyone was very impressed, but you are bound to be exhausted after so much unaccustomed exertion. I'll stay here with you while you go to sleep." And she sat beside the bed until she was sure that Eirwen was sound asleep and then she allowed herself to slump a little and consider the evening.

She didn't have long to do so because Torquhil came back into the room, and she was faced with the main object of her thoughts.

After a few moments of silence, Hetty peeped up at him, uncertainly.

"What is it, Miss Swift?"

"Why, nothing at all," she replied airily.

"Henrietta?"

"Oh, please don't call me that!"

"It's a lovely name."

"For a chicken."

"We'll agree to disagree on that. Why were you watching me covertly throughout supper?"

"I wasn't!" muttered Hetty, unable to meet his searching gaze.

He said nothing.

She shrugged, "Well, all right, perhaps I was — but only because you seemed — a little — preoccupied."

"Did I? You were worried?"

She blinked at him; at the back of her mind wondering if she would ever feel entirely at ease with him, "I hoped that it wasn't something *I'd* done — "

He raised his eyebrows, "What could you have possibly done to cause me concern?"

"I don't know but — I do know that I have a tendency to fall into scrapes and can be, as Grandpapa would put it, a bit wilful at times — and of course, there's the small problem of my unfortunate ancestry and me being a — well, *whatever* I am! It cannot be easy for you. I've brought chaos into your life."

He smiled, "My life was already chaotic — quite frankly, you have no idea! You've brought light and warmth to Galdre Knap. To Eirwen. To me. And I suppose — a little chaos as well. But I'm used to that." He glanced at his sleeping sister, "The last few years have been something of a trial to us all."

"But she's getting better — surely when she's fully well again, things will return to how they were before — ?"

"They may well do, but even after she and I were reunited and came here, things weren't as they should be. Life was fraught, there were so many complications with Eirwen's condition — and then regrettably she found her way into the Long Barrow — and it was disastrous, sending her into a spiral of destruction. With options being so limited, we went to Vienna in search of professional help for her — it was a desperate last resort that I pinned all my hopes on."

"You did all you could."

"It wasn't nearly good enough."

"I think you are a wonderful brother. Quite exceptional," said Hetty, hoping she wouldn't blush with embarrassment.

"Are you all right?"

She looked puzzled, "I'm fine."

"You seem unsettled."

"I was anxious — about you. At dinner I thought you were — unusually inattentive."

"Then I'm heartily sorry, I had no intention of worrying you. Although," and he studied her flushed face, "I do find it encouraging that you were so concerned."

"Of *course* I was — why wouldn't I be? I'm naturally interested in all of the Guivres and, in fact, your entire household."

The corner of his mouth twitched, "That's reassuring."

"Well, it's true."

"Hetty, are you sure that this is what you want? It's not too late to change your mind. You could still choose a more sedate and secure life."

She considered him for a moment, "Are you trying to back out of our agreement, Mr Guivre?"

"Certainly not."

"Good, because if you dared to even try, I would bring all my haphazard powers to bear upon you and because they're not yet fully functional, I fear the result would probably be very messy. Let my red hair be a warning to you, sir! Do not toy with me unless you're prepared to suffer the consequences."

She had the pleasure of hearing his quiet laugh again and it made her feel a little heady as though she'd had rather too much of her grandmother's mead, and she thought to herself that beneath his dark and mysterious exterior was someone who had become lost to the simple joys of an everyday life; through no fault of his own he'd been forced to shoulder immense responsibilities, which were not really his problem, and having to deal with his sister's unusual condition must have been a heavy burden to bear for one so young and naturally reticent. He had missed out on having the kind of life most gentlemen of his ilk were expected to strive for and desire. A life with a carefully chosen wife of equal standing and probably one who would bring a large but, on the whole, unnecessary dowry with her, and children — lots of sloe-eyed children to fill the nursery and carry on the family name. He'd have been well-respected throughout the county and part of the upper ranks of the local landed gentry.

He was watching her intently, "What are you thinking?"

"I was just thinking that due to circumstances entirely beyond your control you've been deprived of all the privileges that would be considered to be yours by right and it seems to me very unjust. You've had no support from your parents and have therefore had no choice but to bear burdens that must have been enough to try the patience of a saint."

"I am no saint, Hetty," murmured Torquhil with a slight smile.

"Well, that's perfectly obvious," she said and desperately tried not to think of the kiss they'd shared in case she revealed her feelings.

"Now what are you thinking?" he asked in a bland voice.

Hetty tossed her head, "Of Mr Deering!" she said audaciously, "And what a nice, polite, charming young man he is, to be sure!"

Torquhil's eyes gleamed, "As I said, it's not too late to jump ship! Perhaps you and Adam would be well suited. He's solid and dependable. He would never let you down or frighten the locals. You'd be in very safe hands."

Hetty stared at him, "There you go again! Trying to worm your way out of our agreement. It's not the behaviour of a gentleman!"

"Ah, but surely you must blame my neglectful parents for that? As you just so pertinently pointed out, I cannot be held accountable for my actions."

"Well, now you're just being silly!" said Hetty, laughing.

"I don't believe anyone has ever accused me of that before."

"I'm not surprised — you don't come over as being precisely light-hearted."

He raised his eyebrows, "What are you implying, Miss Swift?"

"I'm not *implying* anything — I'm saying that you're quite a solemn sort of fellow, but you do have a mitigating excuse." She smiled at him gently to soften the blow of her words, "But, you can be a little — intimidating."

He said nothing.

Her eyes searched his face anxiously, "It's not that you're — menacing or in any way dangerous. It's just that you're inclined to brooding at times and that can be a little daunting."

The silence stretched out and Hetty waited.

The fire settled, sending a shower of sparks dancing up the chimney.

Eirwen turned in her sleep and sighed.

The candle flame grew steadily longer in the unruffled air.

Hetty had a sudden desire to sing to break the silence but pressed her lips together to prevent any sound from escaping.

And she just waited.

She put her head on one side and contemplated him and wondered what he might be thinking.

"You remind me of a robin when you do that," he remarked just as though they hadn't been talking about anything else.

She took a breath, "You see, these silences you fall into — it can be quite perturbing. One never knows what you might be thinking — "

"I'm thinking how your eyes are so very revealing."

"Oh dear," said Hetty.

He smiled, "That's one of the reasons I knew."

"Knew what?"

"When Crow eventually found you, at first I couldn't be sure — I could not see how you could possibly be the answer. But when I was able to observe you more closely my doubts were instantly dismissed."

"So, you saw the fresco in the Long Barrow and just set out to find someone with long red hair?"

"In a nutshell, yes. We had a few missteps and that wasted precious time. But in the end the Fates were kind and in a circuitous fashion, because of the actions of your father many years earlier, Crow heard about you and, to our great surprise and delight, discovered you nearby at Friday's Acre. It was as though it had been ordained that you should have ended up so close to Galdre Knap."

"And you were able to find me just because of what my father did?"

"You could say that. I suspect we would have found you eventually anyway, but because there was talk in the district it made the journey a little shorter. And of course, there's your hair — so rare — a fiery beacon."

"Can be seen for miles sadly."

"Luckily," remarked Torquhil, "You should celebrate the fact that it sets you apart, Hetty. Your hair is a thing of great beauty. A blessing. If not for its remarkable colour I might never have found you."

Hetty tried to imagine life without the Guivres and particularly without Torquhil and found she wasn't able to picture such an existence anymore. She wondered what might have become of her if she had remained on her previous path — would she have married Mr Scroggs in the end, worn down by his persistence and her desire to keep her grandfather safe in his last years or would she have struggled on, a forlorn spinster, probably ending her days in the workhouse.

She shivered as the full horror of the alternative future dawned on her, "I am glad of it then, in that case."

"Why?"

Hetty shrugged, "I — I cannot now contemplate any other life but this. It seems as though there's some truth in what the fresco depicts, and, for some obscure reason, I am destined to be here with you and Eirwen. Everything that has occurred, both past and present, is now beginning to make more sense to me — *almost* perfect sense — although the reasons behind it still elude me."

"You're not alone. It eludes us all. But somehow the creator of the fresco believed that you were going to be the key to solving the puzzle they became aware of many centuries ago. I know it's a daunting thought, but I shall be with you every step of the way."

Hetty pondered this rather pleasing notion and resolutely bit back the words she wanted to say to him. She found herself questioning her peculiar and growing addiction to him, thinking that he was hardly the usual type of gentleman to set a young girl's heart a'flutter. She was concerned that it was perhaps Eirwen's meddling that had caused this alarming partiality for someone who quite clearly would not be considered to be suitable husband material by anyone with an ounce of common sense. She studied his face and behind the stillness she thought she could perceive a faint glimmer of someone who had not been allowed to become the man he should have been. He had been stifled and restrained, forced almost to take on the duties of a guardian and selflessly set aside his own desires to ensure his sister did not vanish into madness.

She was beginning to understand that he had been pressed into a mould that had reshaped him until the original Torquhil had been almost entirely obliterated and even his own family would not have recognised him. She doubted that there had ever in fact been a moment when the boy he had once been had been able to express himself or steer his own course; even his strange and mysterious abilities seemed oddly subdued as though the enchantment he'd inherited from Matilda Guivre was beginning to wither away due to years of neglect.

"I am not entirely lost to salvation, Hetty," said Torquhil with a wry smile.

She laughed, "Oh, I was not thinking that you were, I swear! I — I was just a little sad that, because of unimaginable circumstances, your life has probably not turned out the way it should have."

"I can assure you that I no longer mourn that life. I may have done so for a short while when I was a callow youth, but the direction my path has taken, after a wholly unexpected turn, has led me to you and your grandfather and I now find that to be perfectly satisfactory."

"Oh, well that's reassuring. I was worried that you might be quite understandably resentful of my intrusion into your life. It must have been very disturbing to find the fresco and realise that something mysterious and dangerous was afoot and all the while you were having to deal with Eirwen and all that entailed and then there's Grandpapa and me — such a burden — and with no guarantee that I shall be able to help — it occurs to me that it's possible the path you've had to take is the wrong path — "

Torquhil reached out and took her hand and looked down at it with interest and Hetty felt the usual prickling sensation in her fingertips, and it gradually grew in strength, travelling up her arm to the back of her neck.

"You could never be the wrong path, Miss Swift. I knew from the first moment I saw you that things could never be the same again."

"Gracious, that sounds dreadful! I had no idea — I mean there I was just skipping through my life in complete ignorance — as though there was nothing more than pigs and chickens and turnips to contend with, and all the time there was this incredible world just up the hill. It was as though I had been asleep and only awoke when you found me. This whole thing is beyond belief and yet at the same time so enchantingly believable. May I ask you something?"

"Of course."

She hesitated.

He was absentmindedly stroking the mound at the base of her thumb, and she focused all her attention on the pleasurable feeling it was giving her.

Without looking at him she said, "I was worried — I need to tell you that I am very — inexperienced — in — well, pretty much everything actually — apart from perhaps herbal tinctures, which are not really helpful in this situation."

"Hetty?"

She held up her other hand to silence him, "I want to make it quite clear — you see? Nobody ever told me *anything*. My mother was more interested in herself, and her problems and my grandmother had many other important things to teach me. If we are to be wed — " She swallowed nervously and took a steadying breath, "I am going to need a good deal of tuition — "

The stroking stopped.

Hetty felt heat flood her cheeks, but she remained resolute. She was quietly determined to be heard — to state her case and clear her conscience — to make him understand that the deal they had struck was a little one-sided with him getting the worst of the bargain.

But then an unbidden thought occurred to her, "Oh, unless of course you only require a marriage of convenience? I had not thought of that — how very naive of me! Heavens! I'm such a fool." She covered her mouth with her hand as though to stop the embarrassing flow of words.

"No, don't do that," said Torquhil and he tenderly removed the silencing hand. "Speak to me. Tell me what you are thinking. I want to hear." He held both her hands now. "On one thing let us be quite clear — the betrothal may have come about because of necessity, but, if you are agreed, I am more than willing for a natural conclusion to our understanding. But, if you have any second thoughts, you must tell me. I wish only for you to be happy."

"Oh," said Hetty, in some confusion.

She could feel his fingers pressing gently on the inside of her wrists and her pulse drumming unsteadily beneath them.

The intoxicating excitement she was experiencing was entirely new to her and she didn't want it to stop, but such was her lack of confidence that she also wanted to turn tail and run. It was utterly bewildering.

Relinquishing control was something she'd greatly feared all her short life. A modicum of control was important to her peace of mind. It was imperative that she retained some tiny portion of command over her destiny because otherwise she would just be lost like one of those snowflakes falling listlessly to the ground, with no purpose and no hope.

"Talk to me," said Torquhil, an insistent note in his usually measured voice.

Her eyes slid away to the sleeping girl and then back to her companion, "What would you say if I said that I didn't want to wait?"

There followed the habitual deep silence, which she was gradually becoming accustomed to, and she waited impatiently, not daring to meet his intent gaze.

Something was changing.

She could feel it.

It was as though the tide had, without warning, changed direction and was heading back out to sea. A rising tide had unexpectedly turned into a falling tide, and she had barely noticed the undertow's urgent pull until it was too late to escape.

She heard a voice and listened to what it was saying.

She neither questioned nor argued.

The voice was not her grandmother's.

It was hers.

Twenty-Two

With one last glance at Eirwen, she rose to her feet and still holding his hand, she pulled him insistently towards the windowless passageway between the two bedchambers.

For a moment he resisted, a puzzled frown creasing his brow then he followed her into the antechamber.

Once in the concealing darkness Hetty paused and listened. She could hear, with an awareness she hadn't known she possessed, the muffled sound of distant laughter coming from downstairs and Aggie bashing pans in the kitchen, a door banging and somewhere, far away, a mournful owl.

"Here," she whispered, almost to herself, "Between worlds," and for the briefest moment she wondered what she was thinking, but no sooner had the thought entered her head, than she'd ruthlessly dismissed it. She was so tired of waiting for someone else to make the decisions that would, after all, she reasoned, exclusively affect her. She was impatient to try out her newly discovered wings and cease being merely a bystander in her own life.

He started to say something, but she gently hushed him.

"I really don't want very much," she said softly.

He looked at her enquiringly and she was glad he wouldn't be able to see the colour flooding her cheeks in that dimly lit space.

She soldiered on, determined.

"You see, I was just hoping that you might — be kind enough to — perhaps put your arms around me and — well, that's all really. I remember seeing my grandparents sometimes, when they thought no-one was observing them —

and I thought it looked rather comforting and I rather fancied trying it for myself so that I could see if — well, if we are truly compatible before — "

Torquhil said nothing but he still held her hand and even before she had faltered into silence, he took the other and drew her slowly towards him, the familiar crooked smile tilting the corner of his mouth.

She allowed herself to go to him, "You don't object?"

"Not in the slightest. Why would I? It seems to me that it's a perfectly sensible request. It wouldn't do at all to be tied irrevocably to someone who might possibly be the wrong person for you. At least this way, you will be able to run back to Mr Scroggs if I am found wanting."

The delighted giggle that tried to escape was cut short as she noted with some alarm that he was guiding her arms around his waist, and she tried very hard not to retreat in a cowardly fashion as her voluminous skirts enveloped his booted legs like the surging water of a rising tide.

And when he took her shoulders and pulled her even closer, she caught her breath and wondered rather wildly what she'd started.

As though reading her mind, Torquhil chuckled, "Impetuous! One day it'll get you into serious trouble I suspect — if it hasn't already!"

"Oh, do you think it has?" she enquired, straight-faced, whilst purposefully leaning towards him so that he had no choice but to support her weight.

"Miss Henrietta Swift — I believe you're rapidly becoming a shameless coquette."

"I'm afraid you may be right," replied Hetty and rested her forehead against his chest so that he couldn't see her face.

"It's too late to hide now, young lady!"

She mumbled something inaudible into his waistcoat and he laughed.

He leant back against the panelled wall, taking her with him.

As her stays dug uncomfortably into her midriff and the ornate silver buttons upon his waistcoat caught on the embroidery on her bodice, she began to tentatively hope.

The soundless darkness engulfed them.

Hetty gave herself up to his embrace and sighed with a strange combination of relief, contentment and a flutter of excitement.

Securely bound by his encompassing arms, confined and yet also sustained, she felt entirely safe and when he pulled his coat around her, enfolding her in its warmth, she felt as though she'd found her home.

"Hetty, are you crying?"

"Certainly not! What an outrageous slur!" sniffed Hetty as the tears coursed down her face and soaked into his beautiful waistcoat.

"Well, I must say that's a relief — I mistook the damp patch on my chest and the sounds of loud sniffling for evidence of weeping! It was never my intention to upset you. It would not be surprising if you were a little overcome by everything that's happened recently — it has been a very trying time for you — what with the charming Mr Scroggs and his misplaced devotion and then so carelessly losing the eggs — "

She smothered a reluctant chuckle under his coat, "Odious creature!"

"I'm sorry, I didn't quite catch that!" said Torquhil, the smile quite clear in his words.

She shook her head, "Insufferable!"

His arms tightened about her, "Look at me, Hetty."

But she was unable to and kept her face hidden. After a moment he reached around and tilted her chin up.

"In my defence this was entirely your idea. It would be craven in you to back away now leaving me embarrassed."

She blinked up at him through the gloom, "I had no intention of doing so! I'm just not at all sure how to proceed! I told you that I am very inexperienced. I've lived a very sheltered life. But, as you so kindly pointed out, I'm sometimes impulsive and that can cause unforeseen problems — like this!"

"You see this as a problem?"

She lowered her eyes, "I try to be decisive, but it always seems to twist itself into being ridiculously foolhardy. I don't really know what I think anymore." She shrugged, "I used to be so very sure about everything in my previous life, when I had so little to be certain about — but since leaving Friday's Acre I seem to have lost some of that certainty, and sadly become even more reckless. Of course, that confidence, I have since discovered, was built upon sand — its foundations were unstable and now with everything that my grandfather has told me about my unfortunate inheritance, it's a whole new world I have to contend with. I must come to terms with so much that is alien to me."

"I've a sneaking suspicion that you mean me."

"No, indeed — *not* you. I mean Galdre Knap and *Sulis Minerva* and snow that never melts and jackdaws who can talk and well, just magical things that have no rational explanation. *Not* you. You see, you need no explanation — for me."

"I'm not sure I believe you. I wouldn't blame you if you considered me to be somewhat outlandish because I know that I don't fit the mould of most conventional gentlemen of my age. I have been called many worse things in my life — mostly by Adam! He has always been keen to point out our very obvious differences because he found it amusing. I know he only meant it in jest, but it's the truth and therefore I see how you might view me in a different light to say, someone like Adam or your Mr Scroggs."

"I do wish you would stop alluding to Edwin Scroggs as though he were some treasured part of my life! He's infuriating! I want nothing to do with him. He thought I needed rescuing, first from my chosen life as a farmhand and then from you! He sees you as my abductor when, in truth, it is he who does the abducting."

"I must argue with that. Although, you have not yet realised it — it's *you* who steals hearts and souls."

She looked up at him enquiringly, "Now you're just talking nonsense!"

The crooked smile reappeared, "But it's true and I can't recall anyone ever accusing me of talking nonsense before. I am more often told that I am too serious — and am regarded with some pity because I have neither wit nor the capacity to be truly happy."

"Hogwash! Whoever told you that didn't know you very well!"

"My father."

"Oh," said Hetty blushing furiously. "I'm sorry — I didn't mean — "

He put a finger to her lips and stopped her, "Don't apologise! He saw only what he wanted to see and once he'd made up his mind there was no altering it. He considered both his children to be the Devil's work and told us so on many occasions. Mother invited a priest to cast out the evil spirits that had possessed us. That was when I finally decided that we had to leave before we too were infected by their prejudice and folly. It took longer than I'd hoped to arrange everything before I could rescue Eirwen and that remains my principal regret in all of this. Also, I'm sorry that I didn't consider escaping their clutches sooner. That unfortunate delay certainly affected Eirwen's state of health and I bitterly regret that."

"But you weren't to know! You cannot bear the responsibility for what your parents did. You've done your best for Eirwen ever since you took responsibility for her welfare. You found her and have ensured that she is cared for and regains her health. Nobody could have done more."

He buried his head in her neck and she felt his warm breath on her skin and couldn't help a shiver of delight.

"I couldn't have done it without you Hetty. You are the key — to everything."

When he straightened up again, Hetty was disappointed to lose that pleasurable close contact and wanted to tell him, but was unhappily still constrained by her natural shyness, despite a firm resolve to be less timorous. She was discovering that it was not quite as simple as that, to just change one's nature on a whim and was beginning to recognise in herself a certain awful likeness to jackdaws — outwardly ebullient but easily startled. Although, unlike a land-bound human, a jackdaw could take flight and escape into the sky whereas she had no choice but to stay and deal with the cause of her discomfort and embarrassment. She wasn't at all sure that she wanted to be the key to anything. Selfishly, she thought that she would much rather be the sort of person who was cherished and held in this rather unfamiliar and yet delightful manner.

"Torquhil — " she began but was interrupted by a muted thumping sound from the Green Bedchamber and she jumped like a startled deer and tried to pull away from him, "Torquhil! There's someone — " She was halted by a finger pressing against her lips. She swallowed her words and stared up at him in some consternation. She frowned, "Someone — " she whispered, but he bent his head and kissed her on her surprised mouth. It was brief and urgent, but before she had time to respond in any way, he was quietly steering her back into the Chinese Bedchamber where Eirwen was still sleeping peacefully. He gently pushed her into the chair by the bed and leant casually against the back of it.

They had no sooner arranged themselves than Mrs Waverley tiptoed into the room from the antechamber.

"Ah, there you are!" she said, "I have come to sit with Eirwen for a while, if you'd like. Your grandfather is still chatting with Mr Deering, and I suspect they'll be some time yet, so engrossed were they in the history of the house — consulting books and so on!"

"Splendid, Mrs Waverley! I should think that Henrietta could do with some sleep — she's been run ragged by my sister this evening and hardly knows if she's coming or going. I fear she's exhausted — she talks incoherently of lost eggs and has even started to believe that the jackdaw — "

"Torquhil! I beg you — !" Hetty faltered into amused silence when she saw the gleam in his dark eyes. "*Abominable!*"

Mrs Waverley, who was blessed with excellent hearing for a female of later years and had, during her long career as a nursemaid, had cause to put it to very good use, had entered the Green Bedchamber and inadvertently heard enough to convince her that her presence would not be appreciated. Realising that her arrival had not been noticed, she crept back out and then re-entered the room, shutting the door with unnecessary force to give them fair warning.

Despite being possessed of a practical and serene nature, she was at heart a romantic and thought that the still waters of her employer would provide a nice contrast and, hopefully, balance for Miss Swift's lively and yet inherently shy disposition. She thought of them as fire and ice and hoped that she would still be living at Galdre Knap to see the denouement of their odd relationship. She was keen to have a nice, neat conclusion. She had already witnessed the beginnings of change in Mr Guivre; he was noticeably more forthcoming and inclined to demonstrate a sense of humour nobody would guess he had from his general demeanour and she noted that he and Miss Swift were developing a rather nice raillery that was a distinct improvement and, as Miss Guivre's recovery steadily progressed, Mrs Waverley could see that life in the peculiar house on the hill was slowly but surely becoming more tolerable for everyone.

"Well then, an early night might be just the thing, Miss Swift. I'm sure Miss Guivre will be as good as gold. She's been sleeping so much better of late."

"Thank you, Mrs Waverley. I shall just go and say goodnight to Grandpapa and Mr Deering and then go to my bed."

After a perturbed sidelong glance at Torquhil, whose face was, unhelpfully, a bland mask, Hetty left the room.

* * *

Even though it was late, she found her grandfather and Mr Deering still in the library, poring over a gilt-edged tome of gargantuan proportions.

Mr Swift peered up at her over the rim of his gold spectacles, "Ah, Hetty, my love, come and see this! It's the architect's pattern book for Galdre Knap. So interesting and hugely unusual for that time. It's full of detailed engravings of proposed features for the building as well as strange additions of flora and fauna and indecipherable formulae, astrology and even the occult! Most extraordinary." He drew her closer to the table and carefully, tenderly turned several pages for her to witness for herself the beauty of the book. "See? Is it not utterly magical?" He looked at her face, "You are tired my child. We must not keep you any longer. I will show you the rest of the book tomorrow."

"It looks absolutely fascinating — I can quite see why you are both captivated by it. I only came to say goodnight as Mrs Waverley is sending me to bed like a disobedient child. Eirwen is already safely asleep, and Mrs Waverley is on guard for now. Thank you, Mr Deering, for keeping Grandpapa company — he's obviously had a splendid time. There is little he loves as much as books."

Adam Deering grinned, "It was my pleasure. I have learnt a good deal this evening and I must say that this book is enthralling! Some of the illustrations are hand painted and there are also letters to and from the architect to the original owners of Galdre Knap. It is a complete history of the house and the people who have been instrumental in its creation." He held up with his hands in a gesture of surrender, "But I am prattling! I shall not keep you this evening, but tomorrow we shall discuss at great length the contents of this miraculous book!"

Hetty beamed at him, he was so very hard not to like, "I look forward to it, Mr Deering. And we shall explore the house together to see what wonders we can discover! I have hardly seen half of the place since I came — there hasn't been the time but now Eirwen is on the mend, I'll be able to accompany you on your explorations."

"There are some intriguing drawings in the book of the foundations and, astonishingly, an undercroft like you might find in a church — much more elaborate than one might expect in a house of this era."

"You sound very knowledgeable," remarked Hetty.

"I have read a good deal about architecture and my brother is, in fact, studying to become a civil engineer and then hopes to become an architect. He spends his time making plans for the houses he will one day build and learning his trade under a local master mason."

"He sounds a paragon!"

Mr Deering laughed, "No, indeed, he is not! He's a dashed nuisance — always begging me for advice or extra funds!"

"You are fortunate to have any siblings. I have none and have always felt their lack."

"You may have some of mine then! I have three brothers and two sisters, and I am the eldest with all the trials and tribulations that brings. I am relieved to say that both my sisters are now married and are, at last, someone else's responsibility, but my brothers are still a great source of irritation to me. They believe it is my sole occupation to look out for their interests." He stopped and sighed dramatically, "I do apologise, Miss Swift! There I go again blethering away and preventing you from retiring."

Hetty just smiled at him, thinking that he would make an exceedingly agreeable brother — he was such an affable young man. Eventually she managed to say her goodnights and dropped a kiss on her grandfather's cheek, warning him not to keep Mr Deering up too late as the poor fellow had travelled a long way that day and would be desperate for a good night's sleep.

She went out into the hall and was immediately accosted by Crow who was lying in wait, having been ejected first from the library and then the kitchen, where he had been trying to snatch something to eat. He was perched precariously on the slippery newel post.

Have I missed anything important?

"Nothing at all," replied Hetty sternly, determined that he should know nothing of her time with Torquhil in the antechamber.

You know you can tell me anything in complete confidence?

She rolled her eyes, "I have nothing to tell and even if I did, I would not readily share it with you because you might be tempted to use it to your advantage."

That's unfair! I would never betray a trust.

"I cannot help but think that if bacon rinds were involved, you'd betray your own grandmother!"

Crow clacked his beak furiously, but the sudden movement made him lose his grip on the carved wooden finial and he took off, flapping around the hall in a flurry of irritation.

"What on earth has made you so skittish?"

The jackdaw landed on her shoulder, where he had come to feel most at home.

I don't know. Something is disturbing the air.

"You mean the weather?"

So literal.

"Well, perhaps you could give me a clue?" suggested Hetty, trying to keep calm.

If I knew, I would.

"Should we be worried?"

He pressed his head against the soft curve of her jaw.

It's hard to tell. But air is my element.

"So, what should we do?"

There's nothing to do but wait.

Hetty began to ascend the stairs and Crow, who wasn't keen on being bumped about, flew up to the landing and waited for her there.

There was no sign of Torquhil upstairs and a quick peep into the Chinese Bedchamber informed her that all was well with Eirwen and Mrs Waverley, so she made her way along the corridor to her temporary bedchamber, following Crow who was stretching his wings by flying the length of the corridor.

As Hetty made herself ready for bed, Crow, surprising even himself, diplomatically turned his back and pretended to be engrossed in watching a woodlouse making its way slowly across the floor.

"You will stay in here for the night then?"

Crow hopped down from his perch, flicked the woodlouse with his beak and watched it roll away into the shadows. They weren't very tasty anyway — fibrous and dry.

I can keep an eye on things while you sleep.

Crow watched with interest as the woodlouse rolled back into the light, spinning in wild circles by his feet. He cocked his head and eyed it with deep suspicion.

I'm staying. Things are a bit out of kilter tonight.

Hetty, while tucking her feet under the covers and arranging her pillows, looked at him quizzically, "Well, thank you for that encouraging thought! I shall certainly not sleep very well tonight!" She wriggled down and made herself comfortable, rubbing her feet very fast on the cold bedclothes, "I forgot to ask Aggie for a warming pan!"

Frankly, the least of our worries.

"Oh, Crow! *Please* stop! What is it that you think you can detect? Is it dangerous?"

It's a sour taste in the air. And a woodlouse.

"That makes no sense *whatsoever!* A woodlouse?"

Nothing makes much sense where this house is concerned.

"You think it's the house that's the problem?"

I'm only a jackdaw, how would I know?

"That's never stopped you before! You usually have plenty of opinions and are very free with them. Is there something wrong with the house?"

Crow hunched his shoulders in a careless shrug.

It hardly matters what is causing the disturbance — what matters is the disturbance.

Hetty glared at him over the edge of her counterpane, "No wonder Finn hates you."

He doesn't really hate me. He wishes he wasn't just a land-bound human.

"I'm going to sleep now."

You're not going to tell me about nearly being discovered in the antechamber?

Hetty made a growling noise and pulled the covers over her head.

Cackling unkindly, Crow ambled across the room, hopped up onto the window seat and settled down for the night.

Outside in the snow's eerie light, an owl called cautiously.

Twenty-Three

Mr Deering quizzed Torquhil over the breakfast table about the various parts of Galdre Knap that particularly interested him. The tower and the undercroft being high on his list of things to explore. His thirst for knowledge about all things architectural was unquenchable and he had an ally in Roland Swift, who was just as eager to uncover any mysteries the house might be concealing. Hetty noted that during the rather relentless inquisition, that Torquhil became noticeably, at least to her, reluctant to discuss the subject in much detail.

She was still smarting a little from Torquhil's demeanour as she and her father joined the others for breakfast, when he did nothing more than nod at her in the manner of a slight acquaintance. Deeply disappointed and seething with indignation, she realised that she had been looking forward to seeing him after their encounter the night before, but even though she realised that there were other factors, she reasoned with herself that he could at least have smiled.

Feeling very hard done by, she listened intently to the discussion about the mural and the carvings in the tower and deliberately provoked Adam Deering into asking even more unanswerable questions. She gazed at Torquhil haughtily and, when he raised an eyebrow at her, she tossed her head and turned her most enthusiastic and dazzling smile upon their guest, who was thinking what a bright, shining creature Miss Swift was — and by the end of breakfast he was already half in love with her.

Her grandfather cast her several enquiring glances over the table, whilst puzzling over her odd behaviour; she appeared to be rather on edge, and he recognised the telltale signs of her spoiling for a fight. He knew this particular version of Hetty, and it never bode well for those concerned. He wondered what on earth Torquhil could have done to make her so incensed with him. He would have to have a stern word with her about flirting so shamelessly with their handsome young visitor and encouraging him to believe that she might be interested in his friendly advances. Mr Swift was feeling a little disappointed in his granddaughter and would not hesitate in telling her so. They owed their host a good deal and he had no wish to offend him — he was enjoying his new life at Galdre Knap and very much looked forward to more chess and intellectual discussions with him for, despite his unusual appearance, Mr Guivre was a man of impeccable intelligence. Roland Swift knew that Hetty was secretly irked about something that she was probably blowing out of all proportion as was her habit and rather feared that the attachment she had formed for Torquhil was proving to be unrequited and hoped that if nothing came of it, as surely it wouldn't, that they would not have to move back to Friday's Acre to spare her blushes.

Having thought about it quite seriously, he decided that, in the event that should Torquhil declare his intentions, it could very well be an ideal solution for his granddaughter because, even though their characters were so disparate, they might, as he had with his own dear wife, find complete and unexpected happiness together — it wasn't beyond the bounds of possibility.

He had already grown quite fond of Torquhil, even though he'd a feeling that everything was not quite as it seemed beneath that unruffled surface. As he nonchalantly observed him this morning, he thought he could see a flicker of something rather hopeful beneath the habitually impassive facade. It seemed to Roland Swift that there was some undercurrent that was just evading his understanding. He listened to Hetty's rather forced laugh as Mr Deering remarked that he was looking forward to exploring with her. The young man made it sound a little indecorous, but she showed no signs of dismay, and her laugh rang out in all its insincerity and Mr Swift tried to catch her eye to make his own disapproval known.

Hetty studiously avoided looking at her grandfather because he had the same expression in his eyes as the time when she had shocked him by telling her fatally flawed father, after she'd discovered his gambling was ruining them, that she no longer considered him to be her parent. Even though she was still only a young child, her grandfather had made it quite clear that she had not lived up to his high expectations. She had felt utterly ashamed of herself and never forgot the lesson.

But, at this point, her temper had driven her to cast a little shade over the memory and she was able to allow her righteous indignation to silence any pangs of conscience she should have been suffering.

Mr Deering was enjoying himself hugely. He was quickly finding that Miss Swift was a rather delightful handful — she had so very clearly fallen out with his dear friend, and he was perfectly content to reap the undeserved rewards because she was turning out to be one of the most unusual females, he'd ever had the pleasure to encounter. He liked the way her eyes flashed with temper and then sparkled with laughter. He was perfectly aware that he was being blessed with her undivided attention because she was hoping to make Torquhil suffer for some perceived slight. His friend was renowned in their small social circle for causing consternation wherever he went, and it had been Mr Deering's unenviable task to try to ease the hurt he left behind because of his sometimes-tactless conduct. He had always made excuses for Torquhil, understanding that he'd never really had anyone to guide him when he was at an impressionable age and by the time he escaped into the world it was already too late and his character was unfortunately established.

When they'd set out on their mad quest to Vienna, he'd seen a side of Torquhil that had given him some hope for his future, an unexpected selflessness and a grim determination to save his sister. Adam hadn't been at Galdre Knap for very long but had already seen a significant change in him. The thing that had impressed him most though was the vast improvement in Miss Guivre. It was beyond belief, the difference, from the child they'd transported around the continent in search of a cure, to the magically transformed young woman he'd been delighted to meet again that evening. At the end of that nightmarish and ultimately fruitless journey he had given up all hope of her recovering and it had affected him very deeply. The waste of a young and promising life and the whole mystery of her affliction — even Torquhil was unable to explain it satisfactorily. Feeling entirely inadequate and overwhelmed by the seriousness of the situation, Mr Deering had made his excuses and, albeit reluctantly, abandoned his friend to save his own sanity. His cowardice had haunted him, and he had finally come to make reparation, but found that Torquhil in fact held no grudge against him. It was almost disappointing. He didn't know what he'd hoped for, but he felt he should have been made to suffer in some way — a fitting punishment to assuage his guilt. Instead, he was having a rather civilised and pleasant time in the countryside with wonderful food and excellent company — it hardly seemed just.

After breakfast Adam and Mr Swift went back to consulting the books in the library, promising that, as soon as they had established a few important facts, they would all meet in the hall before setting off on their exploration of the house.

Hetty thought that Torquhil was being ridiculously silent — it was quite obvious, to her, that he disapproved of the proposed tour of his home and wondered why he didn't put a stop to it. And she was beginning to suspect that last night had meant nothing to him as he had not exchanged one word or even a glance with her over breakfast.

She watched him leave the room without a backward glance in her direction and decided, on the spur of the moment, to follow him and confront him about his unfriendly behaviour, but just as she had risen to her feet, Mrs Waverley entered the dining room and immediately engaged her in conversation about Eirwen, which she obviously couldn't ignore.

"Agatha is giving Miss Guivre her breakfast — after her exertions last night she was far too tired to come down this morning, but I do feel that her overall improvement is so marked that it won't be long before she is able to re-join daily life. However, she was talking this morning, in a rather baffling fashion, which I didn't quite like."

"Oh? That sounds worrying, especially as you are usually so imperturbable."

Mrs Waverley smiled, "Scottish stock! It's true, as a rule I don't allow events to daunt me, but when it comes to my charge talking of, as she so succinctly and rather disturbingly put it, 'The inevitable fulfilling of the Galdre Knap Prophecy,' I must wonder what might be troubling her. She went on to say that unless something was done that it would be 'The End of Days!' Do you have any idea what she can have meant by that?"

Hetty tried to remain outwardly calm despite a sinking feeling in the pit of her stomach, "She is inclined, like most girls of her age, to be overly dramatic! I'm sure she was just allowing her imagination to run away with her. I'll have a word with her and make sure she's all right. She is bound to have been badly affected by all that she's gone through recently — how can anyone, particularly such a young and vulnerable child, have endured such traumatic times and not be changed in some way? In fact, it is astounding that she is as rational as she is given the circumstances."

Mrs Waverley nodded thoughtfully, "Just so. When first I took on her care, I must admit that I was not hopeful of a recovery of any sort, let alone such a spectacular return to health and I must admit that there have been few visible signs of the suffering she must have experienced. She is a quite remarkable child although I would say that she is not at all — usual. It seems that eccentricity runs in the Guivre family! She was telling me about one of her relations — in an attempt, I think, to explain how she had ended up where she did. Quite an extraordinary story, to say the least! Naturally we have all heard of the exploits of the Witchfinder General in the last century and those terrible tales must go in some way to prove that where there is smoke there may indeed be fire! I have never been one to readily believe that humans can possess supernatural powers, but one might be tempted to say that to believe in God is to believe in something supernatural and it is thought perfectly reasonable to do so. In fact, it is considered unreasonable to do otherwise! I suppose, in the end, it's a question of faith — faith in something one cannot touch or see, something that one cannot prove to exist. One just has to have faith."

Hetty listened with increasing disquiet. What on earth could she say? She had the proof. She could probably persuade Mrs Waverley to believe in the existence of Eirwen's mysterious ancestor by telling her about what those unwanted inherited gifts had been able to accomplish in the short time her charge had had sufficient control over them to muster them into some kind of order.

"She has certainly surprised everyone. When I first saw her — I was so afraid that she might never recover either her health or her spirits. She was little more than an apparition. You could practically see through her — she was so fragile. She must trust you a good deal, Mrs Waverley, to talk about Matilda Guivre. It must be so hard for her to understand what has happened."

"She seems to be quite *au courant* with everything."

"Yes, I daresay she thinks she is, but — she's very much still a child in all the most important matters, despite her superior understanding — and she does like to get her own way in things, swiftly becoming petulant if thwarted. It is hard to discipline someone who has had such an unfortunate start in life — one just wants to cosset them! It must be even worse for her brother because he has seen first-hand what she has been through and yet must sometimes feel the need to curb her wayward behaviour. She, naturally, will be eager to take advantage of everyone's forbearance. It's an exceedingly difficult situation."

Mrs Waverley's cool gaze went to the window, and she observed for a moment what she could see of the snow-covered garden, "This weather — it's almost as though it has followed Eirwen here. I would say, if I didn't know better, that she was, in some wholly unfathomable way, responsible for the peculiar nature of it. Of course, that would be absurd because only the Almighty has control over such things."

Hetty stayed silent, thinking that Mrs Waverley was slowly worrying her way closer to the truth and would soon resolutely ferret her way to the incredible heart of the matter. She wasn't sure how the nursemaid might respond if she found out precisely what was happening right under her nose. She might be phlegmatic by nature but the extraordinary abilities that Eirwen seemed to have at her disposal would be hard for anyone to understand and accept. Hetty had finally decided that she just had to resign herself to this astounding new world she found herself in. So keen had she been to make sure that her grandfather enjoyed his remaining years that she had gone in with her eyes firmly closed. She realised now that it may have been a little short-sighted to leave the comparative safety of Friday's Acre for the uncharted territory of Galdre Knap.

"I took quite a gamble when I agreed to accompany Eirwen on the journey here," mused Mrs Waverley as though she were able to read Hetty's thoughts, "It was a very deliberate decision and I'm glad I made it. I would not have missed all of this for the world. It is so much more interesting than my previous position where my charges, although tremendously nice, were as dull as ditchwater and I found myself longing for an adventure before it was too late, and I slid unnoticed into a lonely old age. I never yearned for excitement as a young girl, being content with the hand I'd been dealt, and I certainly had no inkling that I might be pitched into such a diverting state of affairs. It's been most enlightening but at the same time completely baffling. I expect that you will one day feel able to share the whole story with me. It would be nice to know what we're dealing with because I'm beginning to get the feeling that everything is not as it appears up here on this hill and my father, who was a lifelong soldier, said that you had to make sure that you gained the high ground to win the battle. He was invariably right about such things. Of course, I would understand if you felt you couldn't trust me — I'm a church-going woman and probably appear to be rather strait-laced and disapproving but I can assure you that despite the rather severe aspect I inherited from my dear father, my dour expression belies a somewhat frivolous nature!"

"I don't think you're dour at all, Mrs Waverley! Perhaps for a short while when you first arrived, but that was only from a fleeting first impression in exceedingly trying circumstances. One can be forgiven for being a little serious when the situation is so dire! My first opinions of Mr Guivre were very much the same but have now been tempered with an understanding of what he has been through and how that might have affected his demeanour. Nothing is set in stone. Mr Guivre, beneath that impassive mask, is not dissimilar to any other gentleman who may have been forced into a life that he hadn't planned. I suppose most people hide behind different disguises to cope with the vagaries of life. I pretend to be braver and bolder than I really am — my first instinct is usually to flee — and Mrs Ashby, I know, covers up her insecurities by putting on an act and I think that Finn's legendary choler is now firmly established — he's had so many years of practice!"

"As I understand it, he has good reason for his less than sunny nature. To lose all his family like that — to influenza — how could one survive the grief? He must have wished he'd not survived either. I cannot even imagine — "

Hetty looked at her in some astonishment, the nursemaid was proving to be a bit of a revelation with her insights, "No, indeed, it would have been enough to destroy most men to lose just one member of their family, but to lose so many at once — it would have been devastating. He has found a way to protect himself from anguish like a hedgehog curling into a ball to shield itself from its enemies, but that doesn't mean that Finn's not suffering inside. How could he not be?" She considered her companion's expression for a moment, "I think a lot of people are keen to hide their true natures from others in case they reveal too much and make themselves vulnerable."

Mrs Waverley nodded, "I agree with you, Miss Swift. Perhaps in this world, where appearances are everything, we are afraid that some shameful flaw might be exposed, but surely that is understandable when one considers how unscrupulous people through the ages have used such knowledge against their neighbours — one only has to think of those dreadful Witch Hunts to see how a little information can be twisted and used to destroy those who stand in their way. Matilda Guivre was unfortunate to have been one of them, but one cannot help but wonder what they saw in her that made them suspicious and frightened enough to put her to death. I can see the same kind of problems occurring again, here at Galdre Knap. I could not help but notice some strange incidents — I have, after all, been trained over the years, to observe my charges and protect them from harm — I'm able to watch without being observed myself; I blend into the background like most spinsters over a certain age and can become part of the shadows if needs be — to wear the darkness like a cloak and be a witness — "

"And — what have you witnessed — ?" asked Hetty anxiously.

A slight smile, "Well, I suppose I've been a witness to some extremely curious events — starting with weather that doesn't bear scrutiny, a house that seems to have a life of its own, a jackdaw I'd really rather not discuss and the birth of a romantic liaison that will confound most people."

Hetty turned a delicate shade of pink, "Romantic — " she faltered, "How — I don't understand — oh, gracious."

"There's no need for embarrassment, my dear, it is, after all, perfectly natural and I understand from those who know about these things that there's no use trying to evade what Life has in store of you. You can hide from everything but your Fate."

Hetty, thinking of the prescient fresco in the Long Barrow, went from pink to ashen. "I hope you're wrong. I truly do."

Mrs Waverley briefly rested her bony hand on Hetty's arm and gave it a reassuring squeeze, "I have no desire to alarm you, but I wanted you to know that whatever happens — I will be on your side!"

"Well, that's a comforting thought, Mrs Waverley, but I'm not at all sure what it is you think I might need rescuing from! And, as to the notion of something romantic — there is nothing — " For her pains, she received an arch look and she lowered her eyes in confusion, "Oh, you *heard* — in the antechamber!"

"It wasn't only that moment that convinced me that you and Mr Guivre were — interested in each other — one only has to see you together — the way he looks at you when you're not aware — it speaks volumes. All the signs are there and then there's your very illuminating reaction when he walks into the room!"

Hetty covered her overheated face with her hands and let out a soft groan of despair.

"No, no!" said Mrs Waverley, "Please! Do not be downcast! I have a strong feeling that all will be well."

"I wish I had your confidence!" muttered Hetty from behind her hands.

She was saved from further distress by the arrival of Mr Deering and her grandfather, enthusiastically bickering about exactly where to start their proposed tour of the house.

"I cannot think why anyone would want to start in the attics!" declared Adam, rolling his eyes expressively.

"Well, one has to start somewhere, and we may as well start at the top as anywhere! Thereby leaving what must be the best for last. The famous Galdre Knap undercroft! Surely that is our primary goal — to see the very foundations of the house and not the dusty attics, which are no doubt stuffed to the gunwales with unwanted furniture and mouldering rugs — perhaps even the odd missing relative — an elderly aunt who vanished without trace — "

Mr Deering laughed loudly and shook his head, "You are far too fanciful, Roland! There will be nought but a few dead mice and maybe a bat or two! But if it is your express wish, we shall start in the attics and work our way down through the house — finishing with a flourish in the crypt!"

"*Crypt?* Goodness no! According to the pattern book, it's a very fine example of a vaulted chamber — it's not a *church!*"

The door behind them still stood open and Torquhil appeared and leant against the doorjamb to listen to the rather heated but, at the same time, genial debate. Hetty eyed him a little warily, wondering what he might be thinking.

"Ah, Torquhil, dear fellow!" exclaimed Mr Swift, "Will you accompany us? We are just trying to agree upon a plan of action. You know the house intimately so you could enhance the expedition with your superior knowledge of the subject."

Hetty waited with bated breath. For some reason she couldn't quite fathom, it meant a great deal that he should want to show them the house himself. It suddenly seemed imperative that he should be with them.

"If you require my presence then of course, I'd be delighted," he replied, not sounding in the least bit delighted to Hetty, who was becoming sensitive to every syllable he uttered. "I would warn you to wear old clothes though as even with Agatha's war on dust, it's a very large and rambling building and some parts of it have been much neglected over the years."

It appeared that this had already been considered and both Adam and Mr Swift were sensibly wearing their outdoor clothes and when Torquhil cast an enquiring glance in Hetty's direction, she smiled and said, "All my gowns are for working in!" She looked down at the rather despised cornflower blue gown, "They are much used and battle-scarred from the farmyard already."

"You look perfectly lovely whatever their condition!" announced Mr Deering cheerfully. "You would embellish even the grandest ballgown!"

She blushed fierily, "I have no need for such garments anymore — not since we left Swift Park. There was very little call for satin and lace at Friday's Acre."

"That can soon be rectified," said the young man eagerly. "Galdre Knap has a more than adequate ballroom I understand! As soon as this dashed snow melts, we could give a ball and ask all the local gentry — it would cheer them up after this long winter! What do you say, Torquhil?"

Hetty watched his eyes flicker slightly and almost laughed.

"We could give a ball, Adam, *we?* What precisely will you be doing to organise this event?"

His friend had the grace to look slightly abashed, but nevertheless replied with his usual undaunted enthusiasm, "Anything that I'm asked to do! Do you not think that Miss Swift and dear Eirwen deserve some kind of celebration?"

"If that's what they wish, then of course."

"As noble as ever! Well, let us see what excitement we can uncover shall we and then apply ourselves to planning a ball that will set the county on its head!"

Catching Torquhil's eye, Hetty tried to smother a grin but failed and was pleased to see an answering gleam in his dark eyes.

"Come then, tally ho! Forward march!" cried Adam and led the way past Torquhil and out into the hall as though he were leading troops into battle.

Crow swooped down from his perch on the bannisters and settled on Hetty's shoulder.

I just love a mystery, don't you?

"Not particularly. Where have you been all morning?"

Here and there. Did you miss me?

"I don't miss your sharp claws digging into my flesh. It's really quite uncomfortable. Perhaps I should make you some little quilted satin slippers!"

Crow cackled indignantly.

They followed the little procession led by Mr Deering in field marshal mode, closely shadowed by Mrs Waverley then Mr Swift, a little more sedately and Torquhil as the rear-guard with Hetty.

Does anyone want to know what I think?

"No!" said Hetty and Torquhil in unison.

In the silent library the torquetum began to spin.

Twenty-Four

The attics, it turned out, were very much as expected, stretching out under the enormous, complicated roof, heavily criss-crossed with sturdy beams, on many different levels, each room overflowing with all the once precious things now considered useless and carelessly discarded. The dust was thickly textured as though embroidered in grey thread and it disguised everything under its drab cloak, beneath which the rejected furniture and objects slept, nibbled by mice and gnawed by woodworm. As the small band of explorers made their way through the endless dark spaces, armed with lanterns, they disturbed the ancient particles and the air quickly filled with motes, swirling in surprise as they passed by.

There were impossibly tiny staircases concealed behind the walls, cleverly hidden in forgotten corners and odd little passages and rooms that appeared to have no purpose at all, apart from probably amusing the architect who designed them. Under the eaves in one of the larger attics they discovered a small enclosed room that contained a modest-sized bench and Mr Swift and Mr Deering argued cheerfully about its possible origins, trying to decide if it was perhaps a priest hole, added at a later date to hide Catholic priests from Cromwell's army or, as Adam suggested, it was merely a cupboard with no practical function apart from providing a home for an unwanted bench and giving the mice somewhere peaceful to spend their days.

While the two gentlemen disputed every minuscule finding and poked about in the darkest corners of the upper floors, Mrs Waverley examined the abandoned treasures that were stored there, shaking out moth-eaten fabrics and admiring the faded, frayed embroidery, running knowledgeable fingers over broken things from earlier eras and mourning the lack of care and consideration they'd been shown in their old age. She and Torquhil came to an understanding that if she thought anything was worth the effort of repair that she could save it with his blessing, and he would instruct Sam and Jacob to transport the items to the stables where they could be mended and put back to work in the house.

Hetty wandered between the neglected piles of belongings and felt sad for them, as though the inanimate objects had feelings and were aware that they had been so callously forsaken. She found the attics unbearably oppressive despite the brisk chill sneaking in through the cracks in the mortar and was desperately keen to return to the lower levels of the house and friendly normality as soon as possible. The only thing that kept her from bolting was the tempting thought that she could spend an hour or so with Torquhil and hopefully satisfy her growing curiosity about Galdre Knap's baffling history. She watched Torquhil lift down a tapestry that had been draped over a crossbeam and spread it out for Mrs Waverley to inspect, he caught her eye but didn't smile at her. He just regarded her steadily across the shadowed, cobwebbed attic and she returned his gaze, her heart thumping a little too intrusively.

She was brought to her senses when she suddenly became aware of a strange noise. It sounded like a rushing wind, and it was coming closer and growing swiftly louder.

They all looked around at each other and there were puzzled frowns and questioning glances.

Crow took off with a loud squawk and flapped around unhappily.

The sound grew louder still and Torquhil, who had been staring down the length of the attics, sprang into action, unceremoniously pushing Mrs Waverley to the floor and throwing the tapestry over her; he then instructed Adam and Mr Swift to get down and in a couple of strides was beside

Hetty and pushing her back against the wall. She slid down onto the cold floorboards with Torquhil shielding her. He pulled his coat around her for added protection.

Hetty wriggled, not understanding what was happening but he just held her fast.

The noise that assailed her ears was indescribable and within seconds it engulfed them. She instinctively stopped struggling and ducked closer to her guardian — she couldn't help letting out a muffled gasp.

"Don't move," he whispered urgently somewhere near her ear.

She held her breath and waited.

The terrifying tumult continued, and she felt something bash into her arm and jumped.

"It's only bats," said Torquhil calmly.

He pulled her even closer until she could feel nothing but the safety of his embrace and the comforting warmth of him.

She could still hear the bats madly circling, the rustle of their leathery wings and the shrill calls they made. They must have disturbed them, sending the colony into a frenzy of senseless activity. Hetty, who didn't mind mice, was not quite as fond of flying rodents, her mother having told her that they would get caught in your hair and you'd have to cut them out.

That's just an old wives' fable. You should know better.

Crow had squeezed his scrawny body into the angle between the main beam and the roof, well out of the way of the storm of frantic beasts although he knew by instinct that he was in no danger of a collision — the tiresome creatures never actually collided with anything, not walls nor other creatures — it was nothing short of miraculous. Still, it threw off his balance to be surrounded by so much tireless movement; he'd stay out of their way until the crisis was over. However, the feathers on the back of his neck were refusing to lie down and those same instincts were telling him that whatever this was, it was something to be wary of — he was by nature wary, but he was sensing that there was something not quite right happening within the house — something was quickening, and he didn't like the feel of it.

Hetty was both disturbed by a misguided fear of the bats and by her craven willingness to just remain where she was, cradled against Torquhil and foolishly content with her plight.

Adam and Mr Swift were huddled down under a lopsided, three-legged table and Mrs Waverley sensibly stayed hidden beneath the dusty tapestry even though she wasn't afraid of any kind of being and was finding it rather airless in the makeshift tent.

Their collective stillness seemed to calm the flurrying bats and gradually they slowed their senseless circling of the attics and began to find their way back the way they came.

After a short while, the panicked rustling sounds ceased, and there was silence as displaced dust motes drifted back to the floor.

Hetty felt the tension ease out of the arms shielding her and she sighed with both disappointment and relief. Then the coat was removed, and she was gently released, allowing the cold of the room to find her exposed skin. She wanted to nuzzle her way back into his embrace, but her overriding emotion was that she needed to make sure her grandfather was safe.

For a few minutes the explorers were in a state of confusion. Freed from their hiding places and blinking in the light of the lanterns, they stared at each other, and nobody spoke until Mrs Waverley, absent-mindedly straightening her unusually dishevelled hair, smiled at her companions and said, "Well, merciful heavens! What an adventure we're having, and we've only just begun our journey!"

"Good God, Mrs Waverley! You do not think we should continue with this shambles after such an inauspicious start?" exclaimed Adam, ineffectually trying to brush cobwebs from his coat.

"I do indeed! A few flying mice and we weakly surrender? That seems pigeon-hearted! Surely we are made of sterner stuff, Mr Deering! I know as a Scot that I am ready to face whatever Galdre Knap has to throw at me! Surrender indeed! What nonsense!"

Adam Deering looked a little shamefaced and bowed apologetically, "Pray forgive my mortifying want of courage — it was but a momentary aberration! Mr Swift, are you ready for yet more derring-do?"

Roland Swift had never been one to shy away from a challenge and the look on his granddaughter's face decided him.

"This has only whet my appetite for what is to come! Bats are a natural occurrence in any old building — they roost in any space available — attics, ruins, barns, church towers — it's nothing out of the ordinary. We startled them and they in their turn startled *us!* I suggest we finish our tour of the upper floors and then perhaps we could take a closer look at the Observation Tower?"

"Excellent!" declared Mrs Waverley, "Let us venture forth at once and see what other treasures we can discover! I hope to see this tapestry again later — it is only a little nibbled and is of remarkably fine quality — I could easily repair it."

Hetty was torn between a strong desire to go and hide in her bedchamber under the bedclothes and the need to stay with Torquhil. There was something hypnotically powerful pulling her in the latter direction, but for a brief moment she was certain that safety was the only choice, then a sideways glance at Torquhil convinced her that whatever happened she needed to stay close to him. It was imperative.

She was as certain of this as she was of the love of her grandfather.

Adam Deering put his hand under Mr Swift's elbow and gently manoeuvred him around the table and across the attic, back to a less cluttered part of the room.

"Wait a moment," said Torquhil, "There's another staircase we could use, which leads to the Tower. You may find it of interest," and he led the way through the interlinked attics.

"*On y va!*" ordered Mr Deering enthusiastically.

"About! Turn!" muttered Roland Swift and with an amused glance at Hetty he allowed the young man to lead him after their host.

As they made their way through the dark, confined spaces, Hetty rather wished she'd gone with her other instinct and run away.

She saw that Adam had taken on the role of guardian and thought at least her grandfather was being looked after. Mrs Waverley was clearly exhilarated at the idea of a longed-for adventure, and would no doubt have been a spirited standard bearer had they needed one.

Hetty couldn't help a small chuckle escaping and Torquhil glanced down at her, the lantern casting strange shadows over his angled features.

"Something amuses you, Miss Swift?"

"People always surprise one, do they not?"

"You most certainly surprise me at every turn."

"Heavens, do I? I don't see how. I am so fearfully ordinary."

"Ordinary?" he smiled crookedly, his eyes gleaming in the half-light, "You are the least ordinary person I have ever come across and that is taking into account that I am very well acquainted with Eirwen, who, you must admit, is hardly conventional. I do not say this lightly — you are extraordinary not ordinary."

She blushed with pleasure, but seeing the others disappearing into the shadows, she tugged on his coat sleeve, "We must follow, or they'll think we've been abducted or something!"

"They'll think we are lingering behind for a stolen kiss."

Hetty gasped, "Oh dear!" and she let go of his arm and rather hurriedly set off after the rest of the group. But she was abruptly stopped in her tracks as he caught her hand in his and pulled her back towards him. She looked up at him enquiringly, a little hopeful, but all he did was push back a tousled curl from her forehead and then he gently led her by the hand through the attics until they caught up with the advance party who had already reached the final chamber and were waiting for them to arrive with further instructions.

Torquhil, letting go of Hetty's hand, crossed the room and approached what appeared to be a plain beamed wall made from whitewashed lath and plaster. It looked unpromising and everyone watched him curiously to see what he was going to do.

He ran his hand underneath the beam until there was an audible clicking sound and then he pressed the panel and slid it sideways.

Adam stepped forward to examine the mechanism closely, "I've never seen anything like that! Astonishing! What a fascinating house this is! My brother would be in raptures over it!"

They ducked through the aperture, one by one, and into a narrow corridor that ran the length of the room under the eaves. It had been much neglected, and the cobwebs were hanging thickly in silvery hammocks and Hetty, not overly fond of spiders, dodged them nervously, batting at her hair with feverish hands. Her grandfather was enjoying himself, pointing out anything of interest as they made their way along the peculiar, cramped corridor. After following it for about twenty feet they turned a corner and continued into the next stretch, Adam noting loudly that the ceiling was even lower in this part of the house.

Torquhil explained that they were reaching the most forsaken section of the building and should keep a wary eye out for unsound floorboards as it had mostly been left to the woodworm and mice.

They trooped along until they arrived at a small doorway in the main, outside wall, incongruously arched and decorated with outlandish carvings of owls and flying serpents, centaurs and angels. Hetty thought it odd how someone had gone to so much trouble to make the entrance so eye-catching when it was only to be hidden away from sight.

Crow muttered darkly and Hetty had to reprimand him for holding onto her shoulder too forcefully.

"You'll ruin my gown! It'll have holes torn in it."

My apologies. In my defence, to spend the day like this would not be my first choice.

"You wanted to come. You could have stayed in the library."

I had no choice. You need me.

As Hetty had been thinking the same thing, she was unable to berate him further and reached up to stroke his beak, "I understand. Something is making me very uncomfortable and it's not just your sharp claws! Still, we'll soon have finished this viewing and we can return to the comfort of the less spidery areas of the house!"

Torquhil lifted the heavy wooden latch on the door and ushered everyone through into the Tower's interior landing and invited them to investigate the rest of the unusual edifice at their leisure, which they did, patently amazed by what they could see. They all stood at the edge of the viewing platform to stare out across the blank white landscape and remarked on the obdurate snow, the leaden sky and the lack of any sun or wind. What they could see from their high perch was unrelentingly faceless and offered no hope of an imminent thaw.

Hetty, having already seen the wondrous architecture on her first visit to the tower, stayed at the back of the platform, holding onto one of the spiralled pillars for support and watching the others enjoy the moment, a brief release from the imprisoning walls of the main building. The air was raw and bracing and she breathed it in to rid herself of the stale, mustiness of the attics, it made her lungs ache, but she was of glad of its purifying effect.

She surreptitiously observed Torquhil who, in turn, was keeping a watchful eye upon his guests. Crow, keen to be rid of the feeling of being caged, took flight and darted out of the tower for a quick reconnoitre of the grounds. He was feeling even twitchier than usual and was concerned that there was some unknown reason for this.

As Hetty observed the jackdaw tumble away across the sky, she smiled to herself. He was a pest, insolent and often ill-tempered and seemed not to care much for anyone but himself; he was probably not the ideal companion, but she found that she was a little calmer when he was around. She felt he was keeping his beady eye on things.

"He's won your heart," remarked Torquhil.

She nodded, "Sometimes I forget that he's a bird — he seems so human, and I picture him in my mind's eye as a thoroughly wicked parson in long black robes and a grey wig trapped in the bony body of a jackdaw. I have become rather fond of him even though he can be something of a trial at times."

"I'm discovering that it's remarkably easy to become fond of even the most maddening creatures."

Hetty smiled uncertainly, at once flattered by what she hoped he might be intimating but, at the same time, a little aggrieved that she should be in some way compared to Crow.

"Now what are you thinking?" he asked.

"I wasn't thinking anything at all!" lied Hetty, avoiding his interested gaze.

"Of course not," he replied gravely.

"Oh," she said, "I think you're being rather odious. Please do not say more — the others are coming!"

"Fearful of scandalising our guests?"

"*Our* guests?"

He said nothing as the rest of the party arrived vociferously extolling the virtues of the Observation Tower and what little they could see of the extensive grounds. Mr Deering enthused about the astonishing carvings and the ingenious structure of the four-storey tower itself.

"It appears to be built along the lines of those impressive towers that abound in Italy, but with an eye to English mythology and customs. If you allow, I'd love to bring my brother to visit one day to see it."

"Of course. He would be most welcome. Now, we shall descend via the main staircase, which will bring us back into the hall. Do be careful as the steps are narrow and the incline steep."

"And you may find you're distracted by the mural!" warned Hetty.

However, as they made their way down the precarious stairway, it was Hetty who found herself transfixed by the mysterious painting.

As she followed them, her eye was caught by the stars in the midnight blue sky — they seemed brighter than before and even as she stared at them, one shot across the dark expanse trailing a comet's tail and faded from view into the corner where the wall met the ceiling rafters. She blinked in surprise and continued down the stairs very much in danger of tripping over her own feet as her eyes never left the strangely busy mural.

The painted moon disappeared behind dark clouds.

A winged serpent slid menacingly over the canopy of the shadowed forest and vanished over the horizon.

Sinister flocks of birds scattered as she passed and one of the indigo-winged angels followed her progress, pursuing her as she descended, the beautiful face blank and the eyes dead.

Hetty, casting a fearful glance at the terrifying figure, almost fell in her haste to escape.

"Torquhil!" she squeaked.

He stopped and looked back at her and seeing her obvious distress he held out his hand and she grabbed it as though it were her only means of deliverance from the unknown corruption that seemed to be stalking her.

She was practically tumbling down the stairs after him, but she suddenly came to a slithering halt.

"*Crow!* Where is Crow?"

Torquhil shrugged, "I shouldn't worry he'll find his way back to you."

Hetty felt panic rising steadily.

"No, you don't understand! I *need* him! Why hasn't he come back?"

"He's no doubt been distracted by something more interesting. He'll get bored soon and return," he frowned at her, "What frightened you just then?"

She glanced up at the mural and shrank back when she saw the angel hovering on the wall just a little way from her.

"Do you see that?" she whispered and pointed to the baleful figure.

He examined the painting, "I only see what is always there. What do you see?"

"An angel. It's animated and rather threatening. And other things are moving too — the stars and birds — the clouds — it's as though it's come to life."

"It seems that there is something strange happening, but only you can see it. Have you witnessed any other phenomena today?"

"Only this. And the bats of course, but they were real, and everyone saw them."

A shout from the bottom of the stairs reminded them that the others were waiting for them.

"Come, we must catch up or we'll have a mutiny on our hands. Don't worry about Crow, he knows what he's doing, and the mural cannot hurt you — after all it's merely paint. Even if things are moving, they are not corporeal."

"*Sulis Minerva* is not supposed to be real, but she looked dreadfully solid and the mess she left behind was certainly real enough and had to be shovelled into buckets!"

They reached the hall and found their companions waiting for them.

"By heavens, you two have been an age!" said Adam impatiently, "We're champing at the bit!"

"The mural on the staircase is fascinating," remarked Roland Swift, "Was it here when you came?"

"It was. It came with the house. I have no idea who the artist is or why it was created."

"I must say it's rather melancholy. The angels are — not in the least comforting as one might expect them to be. And one wonders why dragons seem to be a recurring theme in the house."

Torquhil said nothing, but his eyes flickered, as though moonlight gleamed briefly on a darkened sea, and Hetty noticed a slight change in him, a subtle shift that made her worry even more. She was beginning to feel that he understood more than he was revealing and wondered why he should keep secrets from her when she was obviously meant to be involved — after all she was featured in the fresco. That had to mean something.

The fresco might just be the creation of an ancient and yet deranged mind; it might not have any bearing on what was happening or what might happen in the future. Even though she believed in everything her grandmother had shared with her and had seen with her own astonished eyes, the improbable things that had happened, *were* happening at Galdre Knap, she still retained a little scepticism, which meant that she remained decidedly uneasy. And Torquhil wasn't helping by being so reluctant to explain what he knew. She understood that he was probably trying to protect her and was grateful that he should want to do so — it showed that in some way he cared for her and that made her happy.

Adam broke her reverie, "What do we explore next? The bedchambers? I understand that they are quite something to behold. I must say that my room is certainly like nothing I've ever beheld before — Wild Beasts! And *such* beasts! My imagination could never conjure up such extraordinary sights — gryphons and serpents, wolves and sea monsters! It's enough to make one hide under the covers! The artist must have been quite mad by the time it was completed. Or maybe they were already mad before they even started it."

"Perhaps you should be in one of the more sedate floral bedchambers, Adam. I'm sure you could persuade Agatha to make up another bed for you."

"No, indeed! I have become used to them now and would probably miss their fearsome teeth and manic, staring eyes!"

After Mr Swift had found his ebony cane to lend him support, they slowly made their way back up the main staircase to the first floor, where they went from room to room examining the extraordinary wallpaper and admiring the hangings, all of which were richly embroidered, and the Tudor furniture, which was so beautifully embellished with intricate carvings.

They entered The Indian Bedchamber, intently studying the elephants and other exotic creatures depicted on the walls, the little groups of villagers and the semi-naked lovers hiding behind the trees. Hetty averted her eyes, but noticed that Mrs Waverley had no such qualms, holding her lantern closely to the paintings to see every minute detail.

"Not to your taste, Hetty?" murmured Torquhil.

She blushed, but nonetheless fixed him with her direct gaze, "It's very beautiful but rather — shocking, I suppose. I've led a very sheltered life as I've already told you. I think all the bedchambers are exquisitely decorated, but I must admit that I'm glad I'm not sleeping in the Wild Beasts bedchamber! I am heartily fed up with lilacs though and would like to return to my own room — I find sleeping in the woods very soothing." A thought entered her head unbidden, and she quashed it immediately, but not before it had shown on her expressive face.

Torquhil smiled, "You have already seen my bedchamber, Miss Swift."

Maintaining her outward composure, she replied, "I was so distraught at the time that I didn't notice the walls! It was dark and I was tired and a little confused after all the floating and the phantom light and the fresco and so on."

"I could show you if you'd like?"

Hetty glanced across the room to where the others were discussing the merits of hand-painted wallpaper and pointing out the various amusing scenes they had discovered.

A vibrant green parakeet darted across the painted sky, Hetty watched its energetic progress and for a moment was tempted — sorely tempted.

"I cannot leave them."

He said nothing.

"Even Crow thinks there is something afoot." She looked out of the nearest window, "I wonder where he can be? It's not like him to miss the excitement."

After the other bedchambers had been investigated, the small troupe returned to the ground floor and made a cursory visit to the few rooms they hadn't already become acquainted with during their stay.

"I'm just going to see if Crow's somehow managed to find his way into the library," said Hetty and hurried away across the hall.

Twenty-Five

She stood in the doorway of the library unable to form words.

The sight her eyes beheld was beyond her comprehension and all she could do was to turn and look back at Torquhil.

He went immediately to her side and looked over her shoulder into the room.

"So, it begins," he said darkly.

"What is happening?"

As she spoke, the armillary sphere floated past them and the *erdapfel* span across the room towards them and stopped a few feet from their faces, spinning wildly. In the middle of the library the torquetum held centre stage, the light glinting on its metal discs and around it hovered a flock of books, inkwells and other paraphernalia orbiting the ancient astrological device. Amongst the animate objects were lit candles and quills, rolls of parchment, a small sundial, a quadrant and several stringed musical instruments, all of them ignoring the basic rules of gravity and physics. Hetty reached out and snatched a pocket-sized astrolabe from the air as it sailed by, its golden chain looping behind it like a drunken snake. She examined it and then let it go again and it rejoined the crazed merry-go-round.

A steady thrumming sound vibrated her skin, making Hetty's hair stand on end and leaving her slightly dizzy.

She swayed and Torquhil took her by the arm and calmly drew her back into the hall, "Come away, it's too dangerous."

"But, how — *why* — ?"

He firmly closed the door behind her and for a moment they just stood and looked at each other as though that might anchor them in a world that seemed to be tilting off balance.

"I cannot tell you, Hetty. All I know is what the prophecy has foretold, but there's no logical reason why we should believe in such a thing." He took a deep breath and as the others spilled out of the corridor that led to the ballroom, he escorted Hetty towards them.

"Well met! We've seen where we shall hold the ball and very fine it is too — such chandeliers and paintings and tapestries!" exclaimed Adam happily, but he stopped halfway across the hall and frowned at his friend, "Torquhil — Miss Swift! You both look as though you've been ambushed by a squadron of ghosts! Are you quite well?"

"Perfectly well thank you, Adam. You found the ballroom up to your impossibly high standards?"

"It is magnificent and once filled with all the local *haut monde* in all their gaudy finery — and the chandeliers are sparkling and the candles all lit — why it will be unforgettable — they'll be able to tell their grandchildren that they were here, that they witnessed the most memorable Galdre Knap Ball there ever was!"

"You might be presuming rather too much, my dear friend. There are no guarantees — "

"I understand that and yet still I have hopes for a spectacular event that will make tongues wag right across England and beyond!"

"I admire your ardour as ever but must temper your enthusiasm with a warning that it is very possible that not everything will go to plan."

Adam slapped Torquhil on the back, "You worry too much! After everything that you've been through it's time you learnt to enjoy yourself. You must learn not to become weighed down by all the world's troubles. Don't you agree, Roland?"

Mr Swift, who had found an uncomfortable wainscot chair to sit upon to rest his aching knees while he awaited their decision about what was to happen next, didn't feel able to side with Mr Deering against his host, "I believe it must be up to Torquhil to decide. It would be quite an undertaking — the planning, the cost, the disruption to the household — you would need such splendid refreshments and musicians and extra staff — a daunting prospect indeed."

Mrs Waverley was listening with interest and trying to read between the lines. She could hear a faint humming sound coming from the library and could quite clearly see that Miss Swift was on edge and that even Mr Guivre, usually so enigmatic, was looking a trifle unsettled. She was fairly sure that they had just seen something untoward in the library and she wondered what on earth it might have been. She was not easily intimidated, having spent many years looking after some of the most unruly children imaginable and even worse, some of the unruly children's parents, who had been either unreasonably controlling or neglectful of their offspring. She was feeling somewhat frustrated that she wasn't able to assist in any way — being little more than a helpless bystander was proving to be quite exasperating.

"A ball would be the very thing! Should this snow ever melt, everyone will be wanting a little frivolity and we have much to be thankful for, what with Miss Guivre's miraculous recovery and Mr Guivre and Miss Swift's betrothal. The good news must surely warrant some kind of memorable celebration," suggested Mrs Waverley.

Adam nodded in agreement, "Thank you Mrs Waverley for your support! Obviously, it won't be for a while yet, but at least we have plenty of time to plan. Now my friends I believe we have one last part to explore — the famous undercroft. I must say I've been looking forward to this. The architect's pattern book was bursting with fulsome descriptions of its rarity and beauty. A chance of a lifetime."

Mrs Waverley saw the shared glance between Mr Guivre and Miss Swift and, on one hand, was encouraged by their improving communion, but, on the other, she could sense their reluctance. She could see their attachment and her romantically inclined hopes for them soared.

"Mr Guivre is perhaps otherwise occupied at the moment?" she suggested.

Torquhil gave Hetty another sidelong glance, "No, indeed, there is no need to postpone your visit — in fact, it is too late to do so now," he said cryptically.

Hetty's eyes widened, and she caught his hand in hers, entirely heedless of those observing them with varying degrees of concern.

"Too late? It cannot be! There must be *something* — "

Torquhil held her hand tightly, "You saw — in the library — there are things beyond our control — even Eirwen could do nothing to stop them now. It is an ancient prediction and, so far, everything depicted has come true."

"And you know the outcome because you've seen the whole fresco?"

"I have."

"Just tell me — what does it foresee?"

"There is no need for you to know Hetty. It will do no earthly good. Let me just explain — everything that has so far been set in motion can no longer be halted — and it has always been so from the very beginning — everything I have done to change the outcome — to outwit Fate — has been completely futile. In trying to correct a senseless decision made in the distant past, in order to mend the future, I have only further endangered those I love."

Hetty stared at him in dismay. Listening to this strange admission, from a man who seldom made any kind of emotional statement, was overwhelming, she didn't seem able to comprehend what he was saying.

Seeing his granddaughter's stricken expression, Roland Swift cleared his throat and addressed Torquhil, "We all need to know what is happening, dear boy. We cannot go in in total darkness."

Torquhil kept his eyes firmly fixed upon Hetty, "I am about to show you, but I must have your honour-bound word that none of you will try to do anything reckless. Adam? I must ask you to not be hot-headed as there is nothing you can do to change our plotted course."

Adam shook his head, "You have my word — but I think I can speak for everyone here — can you not tell us anything to satisfy our growing curiosity and alleviate our anxiety?"

"Torquhil?" whispered Hetty wretchedly.

"Adam, please would you guide Mrs Waverley and Mr Swift downstairs to the cellars — just follow the staircase and go along the corridor to your left and wait for us by the first arched doorway. We will be with you in just a few moments."

Just as Mr Swift was rising to his feet the door to the kitchens crashed open and Agatha tumbled into the hall.

"Aggie!" cried Hetty.

Adam went immediately to Agatha and taking her arm led her to the nearest chair, "Miss Giffins! Calm yourself and catch your breath!"

Hetty rushed to her side and knelt on the floor beside her, "What is it? What has happened?"

Agatha opened her mouth, but no sound emerged, she gulped, shook her head and pointed to the main stairs.

"Someone had better go and check on Miss Guivre," said Mrs Waverley serenely.

Adam looked around at his companions, "I believe I shall volunteer for this assignment. Please, stay here until I return — I don't want to miss out on anything," and he went dashing up the stairs two at a time.

Agatha made a hiccupping sound and clung onto Hetty's hands.

Mrs Waverley sat down on the austere monk's bench against the wall in order to watch the proceedings. She exchanged a glance with Mr Swift and smiled slightly when he raised his eyebrows at her. They were caught up in something nobody seemed to understand and could do nothing but wait for whatever came next.

"Aggie, can you not tell us what has overturned your usual calm? We might be able to help."

The housemaid could do nothing more than close her eyes and press her lips together as though trying to block out everything.

After a few minutes Adam came running back down, his face as white as the snow outside.

"Well?" demanded Torquhil.

"It's Eirwen!"

"What about her, Adam!"

Adam made a slightly panic-stricken gesture, "She's gone! No sign of her. The windows are closed. There are no footprints in the snow below her window and there's no sign of a struggle. She's just vanished."

Agatha let out a muffled wail.

"*Gone*," she sobbed.

"You were with her this morning?"

Agatha nodded, "Went to find her some stockings — she wanted to get up an' come downstairs — but when I got back — the room was empty — no sign — just *gone* — "

"Well, it's certainly not your fault Aggie!" said Hetty, "There are some rather peculiar things going on in the house today over which we have no control. You're not to blame yourself — we shall find her." She turned to Torquhil, her cheeks colourless.

He said nothing.

She patted Agatha's hand and stood up, letting out a frustrated sigh. She crossed the hall and stood in front of Torquhil, looking up at him, her fine eyes kindling.

"Torquhil, this is not the time for you to retreat into your melancholy silence again! I've been very tolerant I think of your habitual reticence, but the time has come for you to take charge and stop being such a fatalist."

He frowned, "You have indeed been — very forbearing where I am concerned. I can only apologise — "

"No, that's not what I want. Where do you think Eirwen can have gone? We must find her at once."

Torquhil took her hand, "I must talk to you first. I have to explain — "

"Look, I don't need explanations especially if you find it difficult — needless to say, I'm worried and frightened but most of all I need to know that Eirwen is safe."

"My sister's a law unto herself, so I expect that she's taken it into her head to interfere and, like any child, is intent on getting her own way come what may. She has always been obstinate." He guided her across the hall and into his study, closing the door behind them.

Mrs Waverley and Mr Swift settled back on their inhospitable chairs and prepared to wait. Aggie sniffled.

* * *

Hetty, her heart pounding, marched into the centre of the room and turned to face her companion.

"Well? You have something to say?"

He stayed where he was by the door, "Yes, but due to our circumstances — being overtaken by events beyond anyone's control — I cannot say what I perhaps should have said some time ago — when things were not quite so complicated and there was at least some hope."

"Is everything *so* hopeless now?"

A shadow crossed his face, "In the only way that matters to me — yes."

"And what is that?" She took a step back and leant on the edge of his desk because her legs were beginning to shake and she clasped her hands neatly on the folds of her blue skirts, to keep them still.

"When we first set out to find the third character — before knowing anything at all really about what we faced — I was hopeful that you would be the answer to our prayers. I hadn't taken into account various other elements. I hadn't taken into account the difference you would make here at Galdre Knap. I had entirely underestimated your powers."

"My powers? But I haven't used them yet — I still have no control over them — they are ungovernable as far as I'm concerned!"

"You're talking of the powers you've inherited from your grandmother — I'm talking about something entirely different."

She cocked her head, "I don't understand — "

"Crow found you — after a relentless search and then your bad luck became our good fortune because it brought you to Friday's Acre and we were able to keep a watchful eye upon you and your grandfather. No, don't look at me like that! It was not so much spying as guarding. We knew that you were in danger from the deplorable Mr Scroggs who was threatening to take you away and also due to the fact that you had no idea of your inheritance. Anything might have happened."

"And you knew what to look for because of the fresco?"

He nodded, "There were only three other possible females in this district who could have been our redhead. Then Crow heard about your family troubles, your father's exploits and then the sad death of Anne Swift made us realise that your pedigree was sound, and we focused entirely upon you. The moment I first saw you, I knew."

"Knew what?"

He just looked at her.

She felt the infuriating colour rise in her ashen cheeks and willed herself not to turn away to avoid his penetrating gaze.

"I knew that you were the one," he said.

For once it was Hetty who said nothing.

"That was what I wanted to say to you — before we go to the undercroft."

"I'm scared," whispered Hetty.

"I know. I wish — above anything that I could alleviate your fears — but I cannot."

"I fear for Eirwen — for you — I have only just found you both and I'm so frightened that I will be made to leave before — before — "

"Before what, Hetty?"

Torquhil approached her, moving slowly across the quiet room, his long coat like a shadow. He stopped just in front of her, and his gaze travelled over her upturned face, as though, she thought, committing her features to memory.

"Before — my courage fails me."

"And what do you need courage for?"

"To speak my mind."

"I can assure you that you do not need courage to do so. Whatever it is you have to say, I shall not dispute, nor will I retreat into "a melancholy silence" — I wouldn't dare now!"

"Oh, Torquhil! I am in a state of apprehension and cannot be held responsible for the terrible things that I say!"

"I cannot blame you for being honest. I blame myself for not being level-headed enough to remain true to myself — I allowed the weight of the responsibility I'd taken on to distort everything — my only defence is that I was but a callow youth who was forced to shoulder a burden that would not, in usual times, have been laid at my door — but having said that, I'd not have it any other way now. Eirwen is the only family I care about, and I'd do anything to secure a happy and safe future for her. And whatever happens, I'm still hopeful that she'll be able to have some kind of life without any more anguish — in her few years upon this earth she's had more than her share of trauma and has suffered unimaginable indignities and uncertainties. She's missed out on a traditional childhood, and it was my duty to make sure she had a chance of recovering from her ordeal and then hopefully have some kind of rewarding life. In my eagerness to rescue my sister, I had no choice but to involve you and your grandfather — something that I now bitterly regret."

"You regret meeting us?" asked Hetty rather mournfully.

"Good God no! Don't wilfully misunderstand me! I only regret that we could not have met under more usual circumstances — perhaps at a ball or after church on a balmy Sunday morning, the way most people meet. Even the way our betrothal has come about is not natural and must cast doubts upon our association in the eyes of those who are interested in such social niceties. The gossips will have gleaned much pleasure from our awkward situation."

"I don't care about such people. It doesn't matter what they think."

"I wish that were true, but you'll find that they can ruin lives."

"They can say what they like — I still wouldn't care," said Hetty mutinously.

He smiled, "Courageous."

"Not really. I've just realised that one has to fight for what one wants, otherwise life just happens, and you have no say in the matter. I want a say in what happens to me from now on."

"And what is it that you want to happen?"

Hetty took a deep breath.

But before she could answer him there was a sudden loud rushing noise from the chimney and a cloud of grey ash billowed out into the room, followed by an angry, dishevelled, dust-covered jackdaw, his feathers misshapen and standing at odd angles. He landed in a disgruntled heap in the hearth and struggled to right himself, opening his beak wide and making a hoarse coughing sound.

"Crow!" Hetty dashed across the room and quickly snatched him out of the falling soot and dust, placed him carefully upon the desk and tried ineffectually to brush the ash away.

"What a mess! You're lucky the fire wasn't lit this morning, you blockhead!" she grumbled, as she tried unsuccessfully to straighten the worst feather and smooth it back into place. "Why the chimney for Heavens' sake?"

I couldn't find another way in.

"Where have you been? You just disappeared!"

It may have appeared that way.

"But the chimney! So dangerous!"

As I said — I had a little trouble getting back into the house by normal routes.

"Why didn't you tap on the window like you usually do?"

I did. You couldn't hear me. Nobody could hear me.

Hetty looked back at Torquhil.

"It's entirely possible," he said, "Everything is in a state of flux and until it's sorted out, we shall be at the mercy of some ruthless and unpredictable forces."

"And this is all depicted in the fresco?"

He looked at her from hooded eyes, "Yes, someone has been able to predict the future with uncanny accuracy and so far, it's all come to fruition."

"But why would Crow be barred from the house?"

"Because he's also included in the fresco — as you no doubt saw — but he's a wild creature and not predictable in any way — he will always do as he pleases and is, for the most part, ungovernable. The seer who made the original predictions would not have been able to accurately anticipate his reactions and behaviour. He's an unknown quantity. A thorn in everyone's flesh."

"Good for Crow!" declared Hetty as she removed another cinder from his bedraggled tail. "You should really be put in a pail and thoroughly scrubbed!"

Over my dead body.

"It won't have done you any good breathing in all that soot so that may yet come to pass, which would serve you right!" she responded irritably, but, as she was stroking his head affectionately as she said it, he didn't take offence.

I knew as soon as I left the Tower that something was wrong.

He coughed raucously and shook himself, creating a small cloud of smoke around him.

The air didn't feel right. It was hard to fly in a straight line.

"What on earth do you mean?"

Like before a storm. The air crackles. The wind shifts without warning. It's like trying to fly through fast running water.

"So, what did you do?"

I tapped on windows, but it was as though I had become invisible.

"So, you decided the chimney would be the answer."

I had no choice. I had to be here.

Torquhil went to stand beside Hetty, "Why?"

The jackdaw, exhausted and quite mangled by his dramatic entrance, merely shrugged his ragged shoulders and leant his head on Hetty's arm.

"Crow? Why do you *have* to be here?"

To be a witness.

This made Hetty reach out to grip Torquhil's arm, "What would he be a witness to? This is absurd! What aren't you telling me?"

He put his hand over hers, "We must go down to the undercroft and then I shall show you — but you need to know that whatever happens, I do not regret one single moment."

"That's not exactly reassuring! What if we just don't go down there? What if we all just leave Galdre Knap right this minute?"

"The prophecy would still stand. We would still somehow be made to fulfil our part in it. The narrative might deviate from its course for a while, but it would always come back to its original direction."

"That sounds terrifyingly — final. Our Fate has been decided and come what may we're hurtling towards an outcome we cannot alter — even though none of this is actually our fault! We're being punished for something that happened many centuries ago. It's not fair!"

"I know — but it's been foreseen. There's nothing we can do. Come, the others are waiting for us — they'll be getting impatient."

Hetty studied his face for a sobering moment and seeing that there was no other way, she scooped up the depressed jackdaw and reluctantly followed Torquhil to the door.

I'd utter a clarion call if my throat wasn't so damn dry.

Twenty-Six

As they made their way down the narrow stairs into the cellars, the party of explorers were unnaturally silent. They had left Agatha and a grumbling Finn to keep an eye on things in the hall and Jacob and Sam had been instructed to guard Mrs Ashby. The house was in a state of readiness, although nobody knew what they were readying themselves for. Mr Deering has taken it upon himself to marshal the troops and make sure that all eventualities were covered as far as it was possible.

Eirwen's disappearance was mentioned to all of the staff, and they were asked to be sensible in their responses to anything that might occur. Finn had already been alerted to the strangeness of the situation because Thistle had squeezed himself under the heavy oak sideboard, only the tip of his twitching tail was now visible and Finn, listening to Mr Deering's polite but very firm commands, began to worry.

Mrs Ashby, by nature a stoical female, (unless rodents ate her precious supplies) started to prepare dinner, while Jacob and Sam patrolled the house and the stable yard, Jacob armed with his trusty old "fowler", which was primed and loaded and Sam, brandishing a pitchfork with youthful enthusiasm.

Finn sat bolt upright in a wainscoting chair in the hall, his aching knees preventing him from standing for any length of time; he held an ancient broadsword he'd taken down from the wall, while Agatha peered out of the window, her fists clenched and ready for a fight.

"The sky's darkenin'. It don't look good. Where d'you think Miss Guivre has gone?"

"No idea," said Finn unhelpfully.

"Quite excitin' though, isn't it! I didn't get nothing like this in the village. Bessie's goin' to be beside herself with jealousy when I tell her!"

Finn grunted and they lapsed into uneasy silence and waited.

* * *

Below ground, the flames of their lanterns and candles flickering, they trooped slowly along the first dark corridor, noting that the unpleasant smell of damp and decay was becoming increasingly pronounced.

Cobwebs and dust clung to their clothes and Hetty, with Crow perching on her shoulder, made sure that she followed closely behind Torquhil so that he could clear any spiders out of her way. Mr Swift was just behind her, then came Mrs Waverley and bringing up the rear was Mr Deering.

Just before they had set out on their peregrination, Hetty had begged a moment and leaving Crow crouching unsteadily on a chair, she raced up the stairs to her bedchamber, where she snatched up the stone apple that *Sulis Minerva* had given her and the little statue of the goddess and pocketed them without knowing why.

As she returned to her companions, the stone objects, concealed in the pocket hanging beneath her skirts, knocked heavily against her hip and she wondered why she had felt it imperative to retrieve them. If *Sulis Minerva* was as evil as Torquhil had suggested, the apple was surely no more than a symbol of the goddess's dark desires, a tangible link to her torment and grief.

She had to stay alert this time — to be wary of being lulled into a false sense of feeling secure and in control — to not allow herself to be persuaded, without convincing proof, that *Sulis Minerva,* or whatever was causing this disruption, was unthreatening and amiable. It could very well lead to tragedy, and she wasn't prepared to permit any kind of threat to her family — the Guivres were now her family.

Hetty picked up Crow again, taking care not to hurt him further.

I may never fly again.

"Was it just the fall down the chimney that caused your injuries?"

Trying to gain access to the house was hard on the beak.

"How did you know — ?"

There's something in the air — a bad taste and that woodlouse —

"Why are you so obsessed with a woodlouse?"

It's when creatures don't behave as they should — it's a warning.

"You never behave as you should!"

But you know that I'll always behave badly so in a way I behave as expected.

"And the woodlouse?"

It rolled back into danger when it should have stayed hidden.

"The world seems topsy-turvy."

A jackdaw's life is always topsy-turvy.

"But you have no advice for me about the best way to deal with this?"

The jackdaw cackled a little weakly.

Go straight through. Don't stop whatever happens. Believe your eyes. It's all true.

"What's true? What do you mean? This is no time to be talking in meaningless riddles!"

Life is a riddle — and then you die.

"Here we are," said Torquhil, standing before the arched door.

He took a key from the pocket of his coat, fitted it into the lock and turned it — it jammed. He took it out and inserted it again, gave it a little twist and the insistent clicking noises began. When they finally ceased, he opened the door and led the others into the next passageway.

"It's not far now. Mind your head Adam, the ceilings are low."

After negotiating the slippery stone steps, they came to another arched entrance that led into the undercroft. He lifted his lantern and surveyed the vaulted cellars, and all was as it should be.

Adam looked around him in astonishment, "By Jupiter! This is really something! Look at the floor — those tiles! Italian?"

"Reclaimed Roman, I believe."

"'Pon my soul! What a discovery! Thomas, my brother, would be in his element down here. Will you look at this fan vaulting! In an undercroft! A criminal waste of such architectural treasure! What do you think of this place Roland?"

Mr Swift had found a stone bench to sit upon as he was feeling rather weary, and the airless chamber was making him a trifle breathless.

"It's very fine just as we expected. The diagrams do not do it justice though."

Torquhil frowned, "Stay there, Roland, and rest for a moment. The air down here is poor, you must conserve your strength."

"I'll join you in a moment."

Torquhil rested his hand upon the old man's shoulder, "Take your time."

"Just be careful — "

Hetty dropped a kiss on her grandfather's forehead, "Will you be all right?"

"Of course, my dear. You go on ahead."

Mrs Waverley stepped forward, "I shall remain here with him, so do not worry."

"But you will miss the famous Long Barrow, Mrs Waverley!" exclaimed Mr Deering.

"I have no great desire to see it, to be perfectly candid with you. I would rather make sure that Mr Swift doesn't suffer from the ill effects of this poorly ventilated dungeon. I had not fully considered in my initial enthusiasm that it would be so very — different from the house itself."

"You're too kind — " murmured Roland Swift, gratefully.

"Well, in that case, Hetty, Adam and I will continue, if you're happy to stay here?"

"Entirely happy, thank you Mr Guivre," replied Mrs Waverley.

Torquhil glanced at Hetty, and she held her lantern aloft and saw the door on the far side of the undercroft. He reached it first and held it open for them to pass through into yet another uninviting dark passage.

Adam, looking pained, clutched his head, "It must be the foetid air down here but I'm getting quite a headache!"

"You'll get used to it," said his friend unsympathetically.

When they came to the entrance to the burial chamber itself, he paused by the intimidating portal stones and turned to Hetty.

Adam quickly pretended to be examining the dry-stone walls with great interest, his back to his fellow explorers.

"What is it, Torquhil?" asked Hetty, anxiously.

His face was eerily lit by the lanterns, making him look darkly sinister.

"If I could prevent any of this — I would."

"I know. You know what is going to happen don't you — which means that I'm at something of a disadvantage. I may as well be blindfolded."

Crow, who was trying to doze on Hetty's shoulder, opened his eyes and peered around at her face, fixing her with a baleful look.

Say what you mean before it's too late.

"I have. I *am*! Don't be so unkind Crow!"

He shrugged and tucked his head back under her chin. He didn't know what else he could say. It was too late anyway. And he liked her, so it was a shame. He wasn't sure how much help he could be especially as the challenge of finding his way back to her had almost incapacitated him — he was pretty sure one wing would never be the same again; he'd be lucky if he could fly at all and if he did, it would be with a decided list to one side — he'd probably only be able to fly in dizzy circles. He was ruined. There was no hope and all he could do was watch and, with any luck, stay alive.

Torquhil took a step towards her and reaching out, rubbed his thumb across her cheek, "He's leaving smudges of soot on you. You look like a chimney sweep."

She stared up at him through the gloom, "Torquhil?"

He moved suddenly, pulling her close so that she was crushed against him.

Crow complained at being jostled so thoughtlessly and clacked his beak crossly.

Hetty found herself being kissed so fiercely that it made her knees buckle and Torquhil had to support her insignificant weight as she happily slumped against him.

She heard him laugh softly as he lifted his head. She wanted to make him stay there and kiss her again, but as his mouth had covered hers, the voices had immediately started to jangle in her head, clamouring to be heard, each one with something important to tell her, each one believing they were the only voice.

She could hear her grandmother whispering; words of reason and comfort, telling her not to be frightened and that she knew the answer. Then her father, advising her to run away, to hide, to save herself. Hidden amongst their overlapping words were voices she didn't recognise, some of them sounded merely unfriendly and some — aggressive. It was like being caught in the middle of a large gaggle of geese when they had spied an intruder. The cacophony was overwhelming and rendered her quite incapable of rational thought.

For a moment she was thoroughly disorientated, her brain fogged with the confusion of noises in her head.

Only one thing made sense to her.

She closed her eyes and clenched her teeth, fighting to stay calm.

Her skin began to tingle wildly, and her hair stand on end.

She wasn't entirely sure if it was because Torquhil had kissed her or because they were in the undercroft, standing so close to the Long Barrow.

As she carefully considered this, the floor began to shake.

"We must continue," said Torquhil seeing her expression, "Adam, would you please stay here and wait just in case Mr Swift changes his mind and decides to follow without Mrs Waverley, I wouldn't want him to be alone and there is very little room inside the barrow itself."

"Of course! You be careful in there though and call if you need assistance."

"Thank you, my friend, and may I just take this opportunity to say what a good friend you've been?"

"Offering me Spanish coin, Torquhil! That won't do at all! Don't be long, I'm eager to have a look at it myself but am starting to feel a bit peckish! I don't want to miss my dinner!"

Torquhil shook his head, "Hollow legs, as ever." He then held out his hand to Hetty and she happily took it and held on tightly, following him through the aperture in the septal slab and into the dank tunnel beyond with absolute trust.

* * *

The moment she stepped into the Long Barrow, she knew.

She knew that all the answers were there.

She held onto Torquhil's hand as though it were a lifeline.

The clamouring in her head thankfully fell suddenly silent, but the stillness only lasted a second before she heard another voice, dominant and resolute.

A voice she knew only too well.

And she listened.

* * *

Torquhil with his superior height had to walk down the passageway with his head down, whereas Hetty was able to stand upright and marvel at the construction of the underground burial site. She marvelled and feared at the same time. It was all she could do to keep moving towards the centre of the barrow; the damp chill of the place penetrated her thick shawl and heavy skirts, and she began to shiver. Crow stirred and complained, and she nudged his head with her chin to reassure him, although it was she who needed comforting.

The barely adequate light from Torquhil's lantern glanced off the walls as though reluctant to illuminate too much. The ground beneath Hetty's feet was worn smooth but not being entirely level, was difficult to walk on without stumbling. She would have fallen several times had it not been for the firm hand holding hers.

They came to the end of the passage and entered the first burial chamber.

Hetty recognised it.

She'd been there before.

But this time her feet were firmly in contact with the slippery stones on the floor of the chamber. This time she could feel the warm, reassuring touch of Torquhil's hand. She had a connection with the real world that kept her from panicking.

There were metal candle sconces fixed to the walls, obviously a much later addition to the barrow, and Torquhil lit them so that the shadowed corners of the chamber came into focus.

On the far side of the chamber was a tidy stack of weapons, spears and swords, shields and the indestructible fittings from clothes: buckles and breastplates and a few decaying leather items. There were vessels made from glass and bronze, filled to the brim with coins and other sparkling treasures. A pile of working implements such as shears and knives, flint saws, sickles and stone hammers had been tossed carelessly into another corner. Hetty wished she could have a closer look at the extraordinary collection of objects — to touch things that were so ancient and last held by somebody who'd now been dead for a thousand years.

And there, in front of her, was the beginning of the fresco, its colours unaffected by time; she could make out the finer details on the first section and could see that it was the work of a very skilful artist. The roughly hewn walls had been treated with plaster first to provide a smooth surface for the painting and as Adam had helpfully informed her, it was a tricky job to have to paint onto the still wet plaster as was the custom.

"The fresco was obviously added at a much later date," said her companion, "The barrow itself being Stone Age and the fresco having been completed during the Roman occupation. It has often reminded me of the Giotto frescos I once saw in Italy. The rendering of the faces and figures is surprisingly lifelike, is it not?"

Hetty, who was not in the right mood to discuss the intricacies of the work, merely nodded, her eyes fixed upon the carefully rendered depiction of their unforgettable past and unavoidable future. She could see the creation of the Long Barrow by earliest Man, who had constructed it for whatever Pagan purpose it served at the time and then as the centuries passed, the changes around the hill and surrounding area were clearly shown.

Then it showed, after the collapse of the Roman administration, how the arrival of the Anglo-Saxon warriors and their tribes changed things yet again, leading to ferocious wars and centuries of tumult in the borderlands between the rival kingdoms, as they fought for survival in a brutal world.

At this time, three matronly females entered the narrative for the first time, the Celtic goddesses, the *Suleviae*, always together, sometimes bearing baskets of bread and fruit and other times holding babies in their arms while children clung to their skirts. It was clear to Hetty that they were benign and represented givers and mothers and she felt at peace with them despite her earlier encounter with *Sulis Minerva*.

The figure of the vengeful Warlord was a threatening presence in this part of the fresco — he seemed to cast a menacing pall over everything, until his death and subsequent burial in the Long Barrow.

This episode was closely followed by another death, that of the goddess, *Sulis Minerva* and she too was placed in the burial mound.

Frowning, Hetty peered closer at the painting and ran a curious finger over the figure of the goddess, removing the film of accumulated dust.

She recalled what Torquhil had told her of the formidable Warlord whose injuries or illness had unfortunately not been cured by one of the *Suleviae* and how his tribe had cruelly and unjustly taken their revenge upon her, killing her and burying her with the Warlord in the Long Barrow.

Something didn't make sense.

"*Sulis Minerva* is walking into the barrow. Why would she be walking? Surely — oh, dear God, that can't be the way it happened! They *wouldn't* — !"

She turned to her companion and her smouldering eyes demanded an explanation, a denial.

"I'm sorry but it's true. She walked."

"They executed her inside the burial mound?"

When he didn't respond, Hetty gaped at him in disbelief and then covered her eyes.

"They buried her alive didn't they!"

It took her a moment to recover from this horrific revelation and Torquhil made no attempt to comfort her.

Eventually, although still suffering from shock, she was able to turn back to the fresco and noticed the first appearance of some recognisable females with tell-tale flame red hair.

Torquhil was watching her as she made her way along the walls closely examining the painting. She stopped and looked curiously every time one of her ancestors appeared, keen to know about her own unusual history, keen to understand how she fitted in.

"As you can see, your family is hard to miss. You see how every so often the redhead was male? The skills occasionally skipped a generation and jumped across to the male line, as with your father, although they never lasted long — it seems that men were more likely to duck their Fate and the females were more steadfast and stuck with their responsibilities come what may. A strong stubborn streak runs through the women in your family. They had no choice but to be redoubtable because of the ordeals they were forced to endure." He smiled but it didn't reach his eyes, they remained completely unreadable, veiled by the heavy lids. "I need you to know that, whatever happens, it could not be stopped. Nothing could have stopped it."

"Please — you're scaring me — I cannot — *will not* allow you to speak so discouragingly! I want to see the rest of the fresco now," said Hetty resolutely and she headed towards the next passage.

He followed with the lantern and ducked past her, leading the way into the final burial chamber, where the ceiling was a little higher and the paving on the floor smoother. He lit the candles in the sconces and stood back, holding the lantern so that it shone on the last scenes of the story.

Hetty made herself look at the beginning without attempting to cheat by trying to see the end of the fresco.

She saw the wars and famine and sickness. The despair.

She then spied, painted so that they melded with the shadows, the arrival of a new group of people; tall, dark haired and faceless.

"First signs of the mysterious Guivres?" murmured Hetty.

Torquhil said nothing.

"The likeness is rather unflattering, don't you think?" she asked wickedly, thinking just how accurate it was.

She came upon the first deaths of some of the characters she was beginning to recognise. Some of the females, in both her family and also Torquhil's, appeared to have a particularly torrid time and few seemed to live a long and fruitful life of unbounded joy. Her very own red-headed clan and their arc in the painted history was mostly depressing — including, halfway around the chamber, what looked like the arrival of madness and despair and around the same time, for at least one of the Guivre women, a sudden and fiery ending.

"Matilda," said Hetty sadly and averted her eyes quickly but not before they had filled with tears.

And then, she was into territory she was more familiar with — the building of Galdre Knap, which seemed to stir up some particularly strange and fearsome creatures who populated the skies above the hill, the omnipresent flying serpents, dark angels and other mythical beasts. And the advent of what was quite obviously Torquhil, in his long dark coat and Eirwen trailing a silver comet tail of hair and glowing.

A small, shadowy blur appeared here and there but the presence of the vexing pest was reassuring to Hetty rather than alarming.

And snow.

One whole section of the fresco was just white, with deep, angry scratches gouged into the plaster, as though made by claws and, down in one corner, an apple. A small, green apple.

She looked beyond it, into the pitiless nothingness and her heart quailed.

Torquhil moved quietly to stand behind her and held up the lantern so that the wavering light illuminated the last piece of the story.

The sound that Hetty made was lost in the darkness.

A breath, a sigh from her broken heart. A whimper.

She turned slowly to look at Torquhil.

"You *knew* — all this time — you knew, and you didn't tell me."

The floor was shaking beneath her feet and the walls began to ripple, as though made from undulating black water. She put out her hand to steady herself against the wall, which disturbed Crow and he had to flap a sore wing to regain his balance.

"It's time," said Torquhil, observing her struggle to remain on her feet.

"It *can't* be! This cannot be allowed to happen! I won't let it!"

"There's nothing you can do. It's all right there in front of your eyes."

"We could just destroy it!"

"You cannot rewrite history or alter the prophecy."

Hetty turned back to the hateful fresco and looked at it desperately, searching for an answer, her breathing ragged, "There *has* to be a way! Otherwise, why was I brought into all this madness in the first place? What is my *purpose*? Am I just to stand by and do *nothing*? After all that's happened it can't be so futile — so unjust!"

"Someone must take her place. A sacrifice must be made. It has been foretold and, as you can see, her replacement has already been selected."

Hetty, overcome with rage and grief, flew at him and smashed her fists into his chest, wailing angrily as she pummelled him. The attack was so unexpected that caught off guard, he was knocked off his feet and staggered back a few steps.

Crow, unable to keep his tenuous grip upon Hetty's shoulder, took to the air and flapped feebly around the confined space looking for somewhere to land safely. He was feeling weak and disorientated and couldn't quite grasp what was going on. Being underground was having a detrimental effect on his usually impeccable navigational skills; no sun, no stars and no landmarks that he recognised to guide him. The air was pressing down on him, making it hard to stay airborne. He was feeling dejected and listless.

Hetty eyed him as he sat mournfully on the wet stone slabs, his head drooping and one wing sitting at an uncomfortable angle because it pained him.

"Crow, if you know anything that might help — now is the time to speak."

Crow opened one eye.

I've already given all the advice I have.

Hetty frowned.

"It wasn't very helpful," she said impatiently.

Wasn't it?

Hetty grabbed at the wall as the chamber began to rock to and fro with renewed violence.

"You must leave," said Torquhil.

She stared at him, "*We* must leave!"

He let out an exasperated sigh, "If you don't go — this has all been for nothing. You must find Eirwen and take care of her. I trust you to do that."

"Oh, thank you *so* much!" snapped Hetty, "You can't trust me with the fact that *you* — " she choked back hot tears, " — that I'm never going to see you again! That you're to be the ultimate sacrifice!" She thumped him feebly in his midriff, "You're so *stupid*! I can't think why I — " she faltered to a seething halt.

Just spit it out!

"Shut up Crow!"

Torquhil took her by the shoulders and began to push her inexorably towards the passageway and the way out of the Long Barrow.

For a moment her mind drifted, rudderless and she allowed herself to be guided across the chamber, but Crow sharply clacked his beak and jolted her out of her inertia.

She span around, twisting deftly out of Torquhil's grasp and dashed like a crazed wild creature across the chamber, to stand panting and confused in front of the last scene in the fresco.

"*What* did you say, you infuriating, maddening jackdaw?"

Crow eyed her with interest.

'Just spit it out'?

"No, not *that* — stop being so provoking — the *other* thing — before!"

'Go straight through. Don't stop whatever happens. Believe your eyes. It's all true.'

"That didn't make any sense to me — until just this very minute," declared Hetty, her skin prickling all over, cold chills running through her. "You could have been a little less obscure, you exasperating creature! One day I'm going to wring your scruffy neck!"

Crow shuffled back a bit, dragging his wing.

I don't even know what it means myself.

Hetty growled.

She turned back to the fresco, hands on hips, her face screwed up with emotion and determination.

"Go straight through," she repeated. "Don't stop whatever happens."

Torquhil made a slight movement behind her.

Without looking back at him she held up a quelling hand and stopped him in his tracks, "Believe your eyes. It's all true," she intoned as though under a spell.

Taking a step towards the wall, she felt the weight of the stone apple and the statue rolling heavily in her pocket and reaching into the opening in her skirts, she pulled out *Sulis Minerva's* gift, looked at it curiously and then examined the painting again, particularly the green apple tucked away like an afterthought in the corner.

She closed her eyes, "Go straight through. Don't stop whatever happens."

She put out her hand and thrust it towards the wall, expecting her fingers to bash painfully into solid stone and plaster but all she felt was biting cold, so painful that it made her cry out in shock; she looked at her hand and it was green and transparent.

And then everything changed.

Twenty-Seven

Hetty's first thought, as she looked about her, her mouth slightly agape, was that she was very much relieved to find she wasn't floating because the experience had not suited her and secondly and, more importantly, that the instincts that had brought her to this unexpected place, had been correct. She had no wish to be boastful but, finding herself in a hidden chamber, she could not help but congratulate herself a little.

Torquhil had been mistaken — the future did not have to be accepted as set in stone after all. Whereas their history was unalterable.

As before, she was cocooned in the mysterious glowing light, which helpfully lit the space she had entered so rashly and yet with such profound certainty. She was forced to wonder whether, if she'd had any choice in the matter, her first conscious decision to use her powers and rove at will would have been to choose such an unprepossessing place as this.

She found herself in another burial chamber — hopefully the *final* burial chamber, which had a corbelled ceiling, considerably higher than the others, a neatly paved floor and a much grander chamber obviously meant for a far more august dead person. There was a row of alarmingly familiar mounds on the other side of the chamber — unmistakably graves.

She shuddered and turned away from them to look at the walls of the chamber.

They had been carefully plastered and painted.

The fresco hadn't finished relating their story.

Hetty took a deep, rather shaky breath and stepped further into the chamber.

The mystical light enfolding her moved with her and as she approached the last part of the fresco, it grew in intensity so that she was able to see quite clearly the conclusion of the narrative, which was painted in such intricate detail she could see the bright blue sheen on the jackdaw's wing and a dark aura around the figure that clearly represented Torquhil; it seemed as though it were trying to obliterate him.

And there was the tiny figure of Eirwen, a shimmering silver unearthly being, who appeared to be little more than an elusive shaft of moonlight and, looking utterly forlorn, poor Crow, his damaged wing all too evident.

Galdre Knap, The Observation Tower, a flock of geese, *Sulis Minerva*, her beloved grandfather — they were all there. Even the craven Mr Scroggs and his brother being attacked by the mob of jackdaws and Friday's Acre caught in the snowstorm — they were all depicted with uncanny accuracy.

It was strange to see her own likeness in the fresco, the ever-present plume of coppery hair flying above her head as though she were emitting flames. She noted rather indignantly that her grandmother's red hair was always portrayed as being under control and realised that it probably had something to do with how they each dealt with their volatile temperaments and the difficulties they encountered. It was perfectly obvious to Hetty that the artist considered that she was not yet in command of her newly found skills and, until she learned how to manage them, was still at the mercy of her unpredictable passions.

Incensed, Hetty muttered to herself as she tried to make out what else was in the fresco.

The last section was even more difficult to decipher than the previous parts; it was almost impenetrable to her already bemused mind. It was as though the fresco's creator had premonitions that had come all at once and tumbled over each other, defying logic and adding to the general confusion.

And to make it even more baffling, the last scenes were practically obliterated as though someone had tried to wipe them away, leaving a washed-out smear instead, which was not remotely helpful.

Hetty took a step back to look at the whole from a distance and tried to make sense of what she was seeing.

"What is *that*? It looks like some sort of pond! Why a *pond*? What does that have to do with anything? And there, what is that fierce bright light? The moon? A star? I just can't fathom this at all! It's impossible to decipher."

Then, even as she railed against the painted prophecy, a low rumbling noise caught her attention and she span around to see what it could be.

Emerging gradually from the shadows in the corner of the chamber, a towering figure was rising up from the largest of the burial mounds, spewing soil all around.

Hetty flattened herself against the wall and found she was having difficulty breathing — she had not expected to be faced with this — a giant brute of a creature, dressed in chainmail, tarnished metal and rotting leather, his head completely disguised by a much-embellished iron and bronze helmet.

Her eyes never left the appalling apparition because she had no desire for him to creep up on her like *Sulis Minerva*.

She could feel the stagnant air in the chamber slowly distending and pushing at her in a very real and muscular fashion, as though displaced by the enormous figure barging his way out of the ground. An involuntary gasp of terror escaped her, and the strange vision turned its terrible head towards her, and she saw that there was no human face within the mask, only emptiness and desolation.

"Oh, my God!" muttered Hetty, starting to panic.

Eyeing what she assumed must be the colossal original occupant of the burial chamber fearfully, she contemplated fleeing forthwith, but was halted mid-thought by the stone apple, still gripped tightly in her trembling fist, growing steadily warmer until she was prompted to glance down at it in bemusement.

It was glowing with an eerie inner light, as though it had somehow swallowed a star.

The Anglo-Saxon Warlord was now standing at full height and shedding dirt from every part of him, from every crevice came a small landslide of hillside clay and small rocks, cascading down as though he was entirely composed of earth.

Hetty was bleakly wondering what she ought to do when an unbidden thought occurred to her.

What if everything that had happened since the very beginning was linked in some way to this murdering despot? What if it had all started with his black rages and evil deeds? His decline and subsequent death had been unfairly avenged by his tribe, probably at his deathbed behest, and *Sulis Minerva*, an entirely innocent soul, had been made to pay in the cruellest way imaginable for something that was not her fault.

It was no wonder the ill-fated goddess was so eager to leave the Long Barrow and return to — Hetty clapped her hands together in excitement — the Sacred Spring in *Aquae Sulis!* The pond in the fresco! Of course! Finally, it was starting to make sense, the threads were coming together and instead of being just a knotted tangle of loose ends, a definite picture was forming in her head, like a cobweb spun from glassy strands.

There was a sudden crash as a larger stone hit the paved floor and Hetty glowered at the encroaching Warlord.

She raised her hand imperiously, "*Stop!* That's quite enough! You're beginning to annoy me."

The Warlord juddered to a halt.

"Things are becoming clearer at long last, so I really haven't got time for all this nonsense." She cast a surreptitious glance at him and noted that he had thankfully come to a standstill, "I completely understand how you came to be so angry in the first place — you'd hoped to continue your reign as omnipotent military commander of your domain, but it unfortunately came to a premature end, and I truly don't blame you for being exceedingly vexed. I *cannot* see, however, how you could justify executing an entirely innocent and, indeed, thoroughly benevolent female like *Sulis Minerva*! That is wholly unforgivable! Of course, I'm only able to assume this, as there are no official records of your dreadful misdeeds and we have only apocryphal tales to rely upon and they, by their very nature, can be much exaggerated. But anyway, I digress! I can see from the fresco that there's still some way to go before a satisfactory conclusion to our predicament can be reached — and, as the ending has been defaced and is hardly legible, we'll have to rely purely upon conjecture. It's very inconvenient because I should have liked to have known the outcome before committing myself to any plan of action, you see? It's quite helpful to know beforehand that your efforts will not be in vain. Still, I digress again. It's a sad flaw in my otherwise exemplary character. So, taking everything into account, I believe we shall have to go forward as best we can and leave the rest in the lap of the gods. I am of the opinion that one can only do one's best — do you not agree? No, I don't suppose you do, having spent centuries doing your very worst!"

While she frantically dissembled, Hetty was desperately trying to come up with scheme to outwit the despicable Warlord and to thwart Fate, as they both seemed bound and determined to ensure that she should be lonely and miserable for her remaining years — if she was allowed to live at all! But she was having a good deal of trouble thinking of anything that might divert this monstrous spectre before her.

She made a swift mental list of things she had to accomplish to outwit Destiny: *Sulis Minerva* must be saved — this was of prime importance if she was not to spend all of eternity being sad, looking for revenge and causing more wanton destruction. The Warlord must be prevented from destroying all that she loved in an eruption of ancient wrath. Eirwen must be found — this was paramount. Torquhil must be tactfully steered away from his martyrish path and made to see that a lifetime tied to a redheaded farmhand would be punishment enough! And it was imperative that she find a safe way out of the Long Barrow because it was a singularly unpleasant place, and she had no desire to end her days there.

There was so much to do and so little time.

She weighed the stone apple in her hand. A small and yet remarkably heavy cannonball of limestone.

Why had *Sulis Minerva* given it to her? What can one do with an apple made of stone?

Its inner light grew suddenly brighter until it began to hurt Hetty's eyes, and she was forced to look away.

She considered the problem for a brief moment and then suddenly smiled to herself.

"It hardly seems polite, but I can think of no other use for you!"

She looked at the Warlord and tossed the apple up and down in her hand in a rather menacing fashion and then, before she could change her mind, she drew back her arm and threw with every bit of strength she possessed.

Miss Henrietta Swift watched with some satisfaction as her missile whipped across the chamber and, with deadly accuracy, smashed into the Warlord's impressive helmet, knocking it askew.

The visitant appeared to rock on his feet, which were not, at that time, visible, being still buried in the displaced earth from his grave. He put up a handless arm and with some difficulty rearranged his headgear as though he were suffering from concussion.

While he struggled, Hetty was able to look around with a view to finding something to assist her in her mission. There were no treasures or implements to be found and she became rather agitated wondering what she could do.

The Warlord had adjusted his helmet and was now facing her, looking even more threatening than before.

"It's just possible," admitted Hetty, "That throwing an apple at you was a grievous mistake and I should perhaps have tried reasoning with you instead — although you don't really look as though you're likely to be reasonable. So, I've been thinking that I might try a different approach." She reached into her pocket and pulled out the little statue of *Sulis Minerva*. It lay cradled in her hand, and she thought how matronly and amiable it looked and understood that it was perfectly forgivable rage at the injustice of her demise that had provoked the goddess to try to kidnap her, in order to find a way back to *Aquae Sulis,* where her sisters had been waiting for her for centuries.

A tingling at the back of her neck alerted her and she turned to look over her shoulder at the fresco.

And, straight away, she knew for sure that things were about to get a good deal more complicated.

"Well, that's just preposterous!" declared Hetty and she laughed.

* * *

Not very far away, in the middle chamber, Torquhil and Crow were waiting impatiently, although, as Crow had his head under his wing and was largely insensible to the current state of events, it was only Torquhil who paced the floor and stared in frustration at the wall that had apparently swallowed Hetty.

He asked for probably the tenth time what he could do and got no answer.

It was hardly conducive to his habitually serene condition to have the love of his life torn away by mystical forces no one understood.

"I was prepared," he complained to no one in particular, "But this is intolerable. What on earth was she thinking? Everything had been arranged."

You forgot to tell her *that.*

"I tried."

Someone's coming.

Torquhil ground to a halt and watched as Mr Deering emerged from the passageway.

"What the Devil!" exclaimed that fellow, in some consternation as he ducked under the low lintel. He glanced around and saw only his friend and the bedraggled jackdaw. The third member of the party was conspicuously missing.

"Where is Hetty?"

"That's a very good question," replied Torquhil.

"And what is the answer, pray?"

"You probably know as much as I do. One minute she was here and the next — vanished. She did it once before although I didn't witness it. She has the power to — move between realms — at will."

"Move between realms? Now I've heard everything! I was only just becoming accustomed to Eirwen's inexplicable behaviour and now you spring this upon me! What am I supposed to think?"

"I don't mean to insult you Adam, but I don't really care what you think. I'm only interested in getting Hetty back from — wherever she is."

"And how do we do that?"

Torquhil looked down at the pitiful feathered thing upon the floor.

"Crow?"

The jackdaw raised his weary head.

Be patient. She's nearer than you think — but she's been delayed.

"By what exactly?" demanded his master.

I have no wish to alarm you —

"Crow! If you think you're in discomfort *now* — " said Torquhil, towering menacingly over the wholly indifferent bird.

She's having some unexpected difficulty with an infernal warrior.

Torquhil abruptly turned away and strode to the wall where the details in last part of the fresco taunted him, every line of his slender frame taut with chilling fury.

"She's discovered another chamber? The one where the damnable Warlord is interred? Isn't that just like her! And now she is at his mercy."

Or vice versa.

Torquhil glared at Crow, "What do you mean by that?"

Only that, knowing her character, I would be more afraid for the unfortunate Warlord.

"Warlord?" exclaimed Mr Deering, joining his friend by the fresco and casting a casual eye over the painting. "You mean this poor fellow here? The one who looks as though he's being incinerated?"

Torquhil didn't answer.

Adam saw the expression that crossed his face and moved nearer to the fresco to take a closer look.

"Is this the — ? He's certainly tall and dark — no, wait — it cannot *be*! What *is* this?" He turned on his companion with dismay and disbelief, his face drained of colour, "Torquhil — I don't understand — this makes no sense at all — this figure looks very like *you*! What does it mean?"

"I hardly know myself. The fresco is Roman, as you already know — but we've no idea who may have painted it — or how they knew what would happen in the future. We only know that everything depicted in it has come true."

"*Everything*? But — that means — " faltered Adam helplessly.

"Hetty saw this — and became incensed."

"She will do anything to prevent such an outcome! She would never stand by and allow *this*!" He gestured to the likeness of his friend and put a hand over his eyes as though to block out the terrible image. "Wherever she is, she'll be trying to save you Torquhil — this much I know for certain. That girl — "

He never finished the sentence.

* * *

On the other side of the ancient wall, Miss Henrietta Swift held up the statue of *Sulis Minerva* and turned it to face the demonic Warlord.

"Do you see how gentle she is?" she asked him, "She never meant you any harm. She tried to heal you, but your condition was too serious for her medicines to cure. And for her kindness, you ensured that she suffered the worst death imaginable and after all this time she's still in torment. Frankly, I don't believe you deserve a second chance, but I'm willing to offer you one despite my reservations," she said without rancour.

She took a step towards the monstrous apparition, holding the stone carving out like a talisman.

"'Go straight through. Don't stop whatever happens. Believe your eyes. It's all true," repeated Hetty, wondering what it meant and why she should find it to be so important.

The Saxon Warlord appeared wholly unmoved and Hetty swallowed apprehensively and considered her next step carefully, whilst at the same time keeping an eagle eye on the immense obelisk-like form simmering with violence in front of her.

"Go straight through," said Hetty, wrinkling her brow. "Well, that could be taken in many ways, but I'm starting to wonder if I shouldn't take it quite literally! Perhaps I'm making this all too complicated — perhaps I should just listen to — to — " she glanced down at the little statue in her hand.

"Don't stop whatever happens."

Hetty bunched her skirts in her other hand.

"I'm putting my trust in a jackdaw! I must be deranged."

And without further consideration, she took off and hurtled across the burial chamber at the Warlord.

The resulting explosion was a wonder to behold and had Hetty not been intent upon the task she had so rashly settled upon, she would probably have much appreciated the shower of glowing red sparks and cloud of debris that ensued. It was quite spectacular and devastating to the Warlord, whose ashes returned once more to the soil beneath Galdre Knap.

As it was, her attention was taken by suddenly realising she was somehow in Bath, standing on the edge of a hot-water spring in what appeared to be a Roman Temple. She just had time to note the bright mosaic floor and the freshly painted frescoes on the walls, but fearing that her poor skills might lead her to being trapped in that place forever, she dropped a farewell kiss upon the head of the stone carving, "Now, please be at peace, *Sulis Minerva*, you've caused enough trouble," and she tossed it into the jade green waters; it made a soft splash and she watched the ripples grow and spread until they gently lapped the step at her feet. She had expected the water to boil and froth but nothing so dramatic happened. She waited until the water had stilled and become a smoothly reflective mirror again and then she closed her eyes and fervently hoped.

*   *   *

The middle chamber was in complete chaos. But Hetty had fully expected it. She had seen the fresco so she was as prepared as she could be.

The sight that met her eyes would have daunted even the most courageous of hearts, but she had no time to stop and consider how she should address the situation — she just flew at it, hoping wildly for the best.

It seemed that in rescuing the goddess she had unwittingly upset the balance and had tipped Galdre Knap into a state of mayhem. Even though she had been alerted to the possibility, it was still utterly shocking to her to see the prophecy in the fresco coming true before her eyes. Torquhil being sacrificed in *Sulis Minerva's* stead had gone ahead despite Hetty's frantic attempts to prevent it. She wondered briefly if she had been away in Bath for a longer time than she had first supposed.

As she hastily approached what she could only describe as an effusion of bright light such as a comet might produce, she heard Mr Deering cry out, but taking no notice of his shouted warning, she thrust her arm into the effulgent manifestation and just tried to grab hold of anything she could. She had no care for herself at all. The light pulsed and rippled as though the unexpected attack was an irritant, causing torn and gossamer areas to appear that Hetty could see through, and she gasped as she was able to make out the faintest outline of something that had nothing to do with the master of Galdre Knap as she knew him.

A jaggedly dark and fiery thing with eyes like glowing red embers.

Hetty closed her eyes and prayed.

It wasn't a very well thought out plan of action, but she couldn't think what else she could do, and she concluded that the *fede* ring had to mean *something*. She was finding that actions were more precious than words.

As her arm flailed around in the all-consuming brightness, she happened upon Torquhil's outstretched hand and she held onto it with every bit of strength she had, willing herself not to let go.

The moment their hands touched and clasped together, the light died and faded away and then there was just an aching silence and she caught sight of the ring, still firmly stuck on her finger — the *fede* ring, with hands so lovingly clasped — *mani in fede*. It was radiating light. A gift from someone who knew that at some point she would be in need of a helping hand — a gentle hint as to what might be required — or just a sign of love. She didn't know but it had been enough.

She looked up at Torquhil's pale countenance, making sure that it was really him and not some other unknown creature and, quaking from head to toe despite her bravado, she fell against him without coherent thought of whether he was in a fit state to support her or not.

"You idiot," she cried into his waistcoat, "As soon as this is all cleared up, we shall have words!"

His arms slid around her and she felt herself held tightly against his chest, his rapid heartbeat thumping beneath her cheek.

She heard distant noises from the others in the chamber, "Are you both all right?" she asked in a muffled voice.

Blinded by celestial light but mostly unscathed.

"Hetty! Where have you *been*? How did you — ? Did you *see* — just then — ? What in God's name *was* that?" demanded Mr Deering incoherently.

"Let us leave this dreadful place and then we can try to answer at least *some* of your many questions Adam!" replied Hetty with a rather watery smile.

She reluctantly leant away to observe Torquhil and saw that he was staring down at her with what she could only describe as a look of amusement.

"I cannot wait to hear your explanation," he said softly.

Twenty-Eight

As they trooped out of the undercroft, collecting a confused and very tired Mr Swift and a profoundly intrigued Mrs Waverley as they went, they hardly spoke, wearily climbing the stairs to the upper floors of Galdre Knap where they discovered Finn and Agatha waiting impatiently in the hall.

Finn averted his gaze from his master's coat fastenings and the, for once, subtle embroidery along the collar, which although plain by his usual outlandish standards, was animated with frenzied activity, the tendrils of vines snaking their way around his neck. Finn had never seen them so lively and wondered what on earth had happened in the undercroft to make them so restless.

"We must find Eirwen at once," said Torquhil as soon as perfunctory greetings had been exchanged.

"It's all right," Hetty replied soothingly, "I know where she is and she's perfectly safe."

She looked around and seeing all the familiar friendly faces watching her with a mixture of concern and burning curiosity, she had to swallow sudden tears and was glad of Torquhil's steady hand still holding hers. She noted that the tingling sensation she usually felt when they touched had considerably reduced in strength and thought it had perhaps been altered by the strange happenings in the Long Barrow or, she wondered, was it lessening as she became more in control of her peculiar gifts?

Torquhil tilted her face up for inspection and smiled at her, as though he knew what she was thinking. The look in his eyes making her catch her breath.

He then tried absent-mindedly to clean the sooty smuts from her face with the tail end of his neckcloth.

"You still look like a chimney sweep's apprentice but at least you now look less uncared for."

"Torquhil — ?" She wanted to ask him about what she'd seen but wasn't sure how — or if she really wanted to know the answer. Either way it made no odds to her.

"I think the library, don't you?" said that gentleman with his slightly crooked smile.

Hetty agreed and listened to him instructing everyone to gather there and wait for them. As she passed the looking-glass on the wall, she saw her hair had come free from its confines and was hanging in bedraggled curls down her back — with the remaining smudges on her face, she looked like a ragamuffin — she shrugged — it hardly seemed to matter now.

Torquhil opened the door of the library a little cautiously to peer in and when he found the orbs had stopped their demented spinning and the books were now lying reassuringly still, as though carelessly cast down upon the rugs with no care for the state of their pages, he allowed everyone to enter the room.

Crow was being carried by Adam, who gently helped him to a comfortable perch on the window seat. The jackdaw tucked his head under his wing and closed his eyes, he was feeling decidedly unwell, and his wing ached.

Agatha was sent to fetch Mrs Ashby, Jacob and Sam and when they had all been safely installed in the library to murmur in a bemused fashion to each other, Torquhil took Hetty's hand again and they ascended the stairs and went into the Chinese Bedchamber.

Eyeing the empty room, he cast a glance at Hetty and raised his dark brows questioningly.

Hetty chuckled, "I realise it doesn't look very promising at the moment, but I can assure you that I saw your sister in the last part of the fresco, and she was here." She approached the bed and drew back the hangings, which were obscuring their view.

"There you are, Eirwen!" she said cheerfully. "We've all here at last."

Eirwen snatched at her outstretched hand and grinned happily whilst tears coursed down her wan cheeks, "You can *see* me! I was here *all along,* but no one could see me! It was *dreadful*! I tried to make you hear, but it was as though I were invisible, or you were all blind and deaf! I was so frightened. I thought you'd forgotten me, but I could see what was happening — and I couldn't help."

"Oh, my *dearest* child — I truly believe you *did* help. You left the *fede* ring for me, did you not?"

The girl nodded warily and Hetty scooped her into a bracing hug, "Well, in doing so, you saved your brother! So, I cannot thank you enough! Things in the Long Barrow had become — rather difficult and I was in a quandary about what to do and the ring showed me the way!"

"But Hetty — I meant it only as a sign so that you would know that you were loved!"

Hetty shrugged, "It matters not *why* you left it — what matters is that it conveyed exactly the right message at just the right moment, and I was able to hold onto Torquhil — clasping our hands together like the hands on the ring — so, he's safe because of you!"

Eirwen smiled a little tremulously at her brother, "So, it *was* love that saved him. I am indeed glad of that then! I had meant it to persuade you to perhaps consider — "

"My love! Say no more I beg you!" cried Hetty in some embarrassment and on hearing Torquhil's quiet laugh behind her, she turned on him and glowered, "And you can just be silent, sir! You're already in a great deal of trouble! I shall attend to you later!"

He suppressed a grin and said blandly, "I'm not sure I can wait that long."

"*Oh!*" exclaimed Miss Swift, turning quite pink.

"Precisely," said her tormentor, regarding her with a dangerous glint in his hooded eyes.

At length she managed to utter, "*Odious creature!*" and she turned back to Eirwen who was watching them eagerly, her aquamarine gaze alive with childish glee.

"And don't *you* dare say anything either, Miss!" She pulled back the covers, "Now, no more nonsense, we need you to get up and come down to the library. There is much to discuss."

Eirwen looked at her brother and seeing his expression, she slid obediently from her bed.

* * *

In the library the others had immediately set about clearing up the disorder they had found there. They righted chairs, replaced books and cushions and Mr Deering returned the various, miraculously undamaged, spheres to their allotted positions whilst trying very hard not to think about how they came to be lying on the floor in the first place.

Mr Swift and Mrs Waverley were sitting side by side on the sofa not saying anything at all, merely observing the activity around them and Finn was busily helping to restore the smaller objects to their rightful places, his head down in fear of anyone mentioning the bewildering afternoon he had just spent waiting in the hall, carefully ignoring all the madness around him. Agatha had clearly had no idea that there might be something strange going on, but he, for some unfathomable reason, could hear the inexplicable sounds coming from the undercroft and he could see the carved wooden reptiles and animals on the banisters madly coiling themselves around the posts and slithering along the handrail as though they were alive. He had kept his gaze averted but was still aware of them out of the corner of his eye. He said nothing of this to anyone. It was easier to lay the blame at the door of Mrs Ashby's potent mead. He would have to cut down his consumption forthwith.

Mrs Waverley had listened to the extraordinary noises coming from the Long Barrow and had wanted to take a look to see what was going on but didn't dare leave Mr Swift alone. When the muffled explosion occurred, the floor and walls had rocked and she'd been certain the ceiling was about to collapse upon their heads and when it didn't and there came eventually the sound of shouting and she heard something like a loud roll of thunder, followed by a sharp hissing crack like a lightning strike, she had decided in that moment that although she'd been longing for adventure, she would, from then on, be thoroughly content with her mundane life as a nursemaid. She would happily leave such dangerous escapades to the foolhardy young.

Hetty entered the library, followed by Torquhil carrying Eirwen in his arms, he placed her tenderly in a wing chair by the fire and Hetty tucked a blanket around her before retiring to the little sewing chair beside her rather joyous looking charge.

Agatha came racing back, keen not to miss anything of importance, dragging with her Mrs Ashby, Sam and Jacob, who arranged themselves expectantly on the other little sofa on the far side of the room and looked about them curiously.

Torquhil stood before the fire, his fists thrust deep into the pockets of his breeches and surveyed those gathered there. He looked at Hetty and she smiled at him encouragingly.

A suspenseful air filled the room.

"I have a few things to say to you all before I allow Miss Swift to take up the telling of this tale." He ignored Hetty's horrified frown and the fervent shake of her head, "I will keep it as brief as I possibly can, but you will have to bear with me. This is not an easy task. I need you all to suspend your disbelief."

He paused, took a breath and began.

* * *

It was some while later that Hetty finally sank back into her chair, relieved that the worst was at last over.

The unnatural silence that followed her halting story enveloped her like a heavy cloak.

She wondered if anyone would ever say anything again.

Eventually, seeing that her audience was in an understandable state of shock, Mr Deering got reluctantly to his feet, stepped into the middle of the room and cleared his throat with obvious intent.

"Ladies and Gentlemen, I think it must fall upon me to say something at this juncture. I can see that there's a good deal of consternation and incredulity in this room, which is, of course, wholly unsurprising considering what we have just been told. I would just like to say that, as a witness to some of these extraordinary events, I'm more than willing to corroborate everything Hetty and Torquhil have said.

It may make no sense to us at the moment, but I believe that if you look into your own hearts, you'll realise that you too have seen things — unaccountable things — that you may have dismissed out of hand. If one only considers what the locals have been saying about Galdre Knap, probably for centuries, one can perhaps see that in order to save our own sanity we may push our suspicions under the rug in order that we may carry on undaunted — or as I did, when faced with Miss Guivre's affliction — or gift some may call it — on the way to Vienna — I'm ashamed to say that I hauled anchor and made for the coast, unable to come to terms with events I could not even begin to understand. It was cowardly and selfish.

I think we have all at some time believed in something that cannot be proven or had some slight inkling that someone possessed mystical qualities that could not rationally be accounted for. I now know those feelings to be real. There are some beings who are set apart from the rest of us — they are blessed or cursed with abilities that are beyond our understanding and perhaps may even be considered ungodly. In days of yore, I've no doubt they'd have been hunted down and persecuted by zealots, but we are thankfully not so suspicious and intolerant in these more enlightened times.

I could say, for instance, that Mrs Ashby might be considered to be just such a person — your skills as a cook are without equal — utterly magical!" This brought a welcome murmur of approval and amusement from his audience and Mrs Ashby's round cheeks reddened with pleasure. "And Eirwen has abilities none of us lesser mortals can even dream about! Then, of course, there's Miss Swift — Hetty, who as we've heard, has inherited her grandmother's talent for helping others in ways we cannot yet fathom.

There are those amongst us who conceal and suppress their gifts in order to remain undiscovered — those who may indeed be hiding their true natures and origins — " he paused, his eyes travelling around the crowded room until they settled briefly upon Hetty — and the conspiratorial look she shared with him, told him that she too had witnessed what he had down in the burial chamber. "But whatever anyone might be hiding beneath their necessarily deceptive mask, it makes no odds — just as long as they mean no harm to those who love them."

Hetty blushed and lowered her eyes.

Crow, who had been listening to this with listless interest, raised his head and clacked his beak.

And I'm *accused of talking in riddles!*

Every occupant of the room turned to see who had spoken.

Crow eyed them a little warily and shrugged his shoulders.

Well, that's never happened before!

Hetty laughed out loud as she watched the reactions on the faces around her — dismay, disbelief and amusement in varying degrees.

"That damn jackdaw!" muttered Finn.

"Well I never did!" said Mrs Waverley in mild surprise.

"I always knew that creature was up to no good!" declared Mrs Ashby, her face turning a deeper shade of beetroot.

Hetty was so consumed by slightly hysterical giggles that Eirwen cast a speaking glance at her brother. He inclined his head, acknowledging her unspoken sisterly advice and went to stand before Hetty.

"Miss Swift, I would like to speak to you alone, if you please."

She looked up at him in puzzlement, "I cannot think why —"

He held out his hand and she put hers into his, without thought or further argument.

Adam grinned at them and with great presence of mind began to usher everyone out of the library. Some left rather unwillingly, wishing that they could see the denouement of this exceedingly interesting day, but there were animals to feed and dinner to prepare.

Mr Swift went to Hetty and dropped a kiss on her forehead, "My love, your grandmother would have relished the way you have dealt so capably with all that Galdre Knap has thrown at you. What's more, it seems that you've won your very first battle in your own inimitable fashion, just as she predicted you would. I suppose we may never know the truth about what happened in the past, but it's enough to know that whatever happens from now on that you'll be able to cope. And Torquhil — I'd like to thank you for all you've done for us — no, do not argue with me! You will no doubt need me on your side in the very near future! I wish you luck, my dear fellow, you'll need it!" and still laughing, he went out of the library to find Mrs Waverley and ask her to walk with him in the garden as he had a feeling the sun was about to come out.

Adam lifted Eirwen and bore her away ostensibly to play the spinet for her in the parlour. She cast a glance at Hetty over his shoulder and her happiness was complete.

"That's it," she whispered, "The *answer*. Matilda you can rest now. The Guivres have at last found the answer."

"And what *is* the answer, Eirwen?" asked Adam, looking down into her shining face.

"Why, it's love, of course!" she exclaimed happily.

* * *

In the library all was quiet again.

Hetty could hear only her heartbeat.

She thought the silence was a little discomfiting and had an idea that it needed filling.

"Gracious! What an exhausting day that was! I must say that had I had any inkling of what was in store for us this morning, I may well have followed Adam's example and hauled anchor! I have an idea about Adam — do you not think he would make you the perfect brother-in-law! Oh, no don't frown so! I know that Eirwen is still far too young but in just a few years — I do believe they might make a match! He's so sensible and placid and she so volatile — he would provide a steady foundation for her, and she would enliven him! I think you'll find I'm right! I have exceedingly good instincts, you know!

I suppose all the trouble began when Eirwen saw what she believed to be the end of the fresco and that sent her into a spin! How could anyone, let alone a mere child, cope with seeing her beloved brother like that? It would have been devastating! And then you took Grandpapa and me in because of what you'd seen in the Long Barrow. I probably haven't said, but I'm very much obliged to you for doing so — it has given Grandpapa a new lease on life and I — well, I — have very much enjoyed our stay here," she finished rather lamely.

Torquhil said nothing.

She peeped up at him.

"I suppose, in a way, although the fresco has been proved wrong, it was, in fact, right," she continued in a rush, " — until one realised that Fate could be changed. Nothing is truly set in stone."

"One thing is very certainly set in stone," said her companion gravely.

"Oh? What is that, pray?" enquired Hetty, intrigued.

"Very occasionally one is fortunate enough to see something that one just knows will have some profound and lasting effect upon one's life."

"I know precisely what you mean! The moment I saw the rooftops of Galdre Knap above the trees from Friday's Acre,

I knew somehow that we had been destined to be here instead of Swift Park even though being forced to leave my home had broken my heart."

"And how is your heart now, Hetty?" he enquired.

"Oh, it is much repaired, thank you! You see, I had lost not only my childhood home but my beloved grandmother, who was more mother to me than my own mother. And all the memories I had laid down at the Park, being young and mostly happy-go-lucky — I spent my days gambolling after Grandmama through the woods or walking the dogs and fishing in the lake with Grandpapa. They were halcyon days for me, even now, knowing there were undercurrents of despair I couldn't understand, created by my father and his thoughtless behaviour — I can see how lucky I was. Then, when they had all — gone — finding I only had one relation left in the world — You see, perhaps, in some way the fresco was correct in what it depicted — although, it could not predict that what it foretold could be altered."

She looked down and realised that he still held her hands in his and she tried to release them from his grasp. He held them firmly for a moment and then let go.

She was briefly crestfallen and for want of anything better to do began to coil her dishevelled hair into some sort of order.

He stopped her, "No. Leave it."

"But I look a complete disgrace!"

He smiled his crooked smile, "Yes. You do. I prefer you this way."

"Torquhil! What will people think!"

"To be perfectly frank I have never really cared about what people think — until I met you. It's a new and oddly pleasurable sensation."

"But I look as though — "

"You look as though you've been bundled in a hay barn."

She looked shocked, "Hush! Someone might hear!"

"I seriously doubt you've ever allowed your virtue to be imperilled in a hay barn — "

"No, indeed," she interrupted in an embarrassed rush, "Mr Scroggs was extremely disapproving of hay barns in general! And anyway, he never once was overcome by romantic emotions — if he had any — even in the kitchen of Friday's Acre! He always seemed to me to be perfectly in control of his passions until the ill-fated kidnap attempt. And to be perfectly frank, I don't think it was any tenderness for me that drove him to act so rashly. I think he just didn't want me to — to — well, to be at Galdre Knap, where he would no longer be able to just turn up whenever he pleased, in order to hector me *ad nauseam* about my wayward behaviour and to make me feel thoroughly inadequate! It gave him power over me."

Torquhil lifted an enquiring eyebrow, "I cannot imagine anyone being able to hector you without getting a flea in their ear for their trouble."

"Do you think me such a martinet! That's unfair! I had no choice but to defend myself — I could not worry poor Grandpapa! And it seemed that Mr Scroggs believed he was doing me such a very great favour by taking an interest in me — especially as he thought me well below his station! A true gentleman and a lowly farmhand would never be a match made in heaven!"

"I don't believe that for a moment. No man in their right mind could see you without wishing you were his."

"His *property*?"

"His to love."

Hetty lowered her eyes, faint colour stealing over her soot-smeared cheeks, "Oh," she said indistinctly, "What an odd thing to say. I'm sure no one has ever felt that way about me."

"You sound very sure." he asked softly, "Are you intimating that you have no insight into my feelings for you? And here was I thinking that your inherited skills would have told you everything!"

She smiled wanly, "It appears that those abilities are only successful when used for someone else's benefit and not my own!"

"That is indeed unfortunate because it means that you are as much in the dark as I am."

"In the dark?"

"Miss Swift, I am assuming that you have not forgotten our rather hasty betrothal, which I realise was, at the time, supposedly to quell gossip — on *your* part at least. I'm beginning to think that it has rather muddied the waters. The best thing for everyone would be if I retract my offer — "

Hetty flinched like a startled deer, "*Retract!*" This was something she hadn't bargained for! "What do you mean, *retract?*" The rosy colour had faded, to be replaced by a shocked pallor beneath the remaining ashy smuts.

Torquhil's eyes gleamed darkly, "I have recently begun to suspect that you might perhaps like to be free to find a gentleman more to your taste, rather than one who was foisted upon you because of circumstances beyond our control."

Hetty blinked at him, "Free?" she whispered forlornly, "You think I want to be free of you?"

"Am I wrong Hetty?"

She fought to steady herself, "I can assure you that I have never wished for anything less!"

His sharp intake of breath was clearly audible, and she frowned, "I cannot think why — after what happened in the Long Barrow — that you would ever believe that I should be desirous of being rid of you. It just shows how remarkably foolish you can be!"

"Henrietta Swift! What are you saying?"

"You know perfectly well — so kindly stop teasing me! The *fede* ring must surely have given you a clue! You told me, when you first saw it, that the hands were clasped in love. When I saw you — being consumed by — whatever that was — there was no doubt in my mind — I already knew how I felt about you but at that moment — even though I think you were being unforgivably idiotic — I had only one thought — that I would not be parted from you before I could tell you — " she faltered and bit her lip.

"Tell me what exactly?"

"That I love you, of course!" she said crossly.

And, to her great delight, she found herself being pulled into a ferocious embrace and held against him; she was just able to tilt her head back to look up at him and the expression in his usually unreadable face told her everything she needed to know.

"You need to know something about me first, Hetty," he murmured into her tousled hair.

"There's no need to speak of it! I saw everything in the Long Barrow, and I have no objections whatsoever so there's no need for you to be in the least concerned. After all, you're foolishly taking on a red-headed sibyl! Anyway, you haven't hidden it really — it's all there in plain sight — even in your surname!"

"How very perspicacious of you! I think I may have to explain to Adam though — he was not unreasonably taken aback!" He held her away from him and searched her face rather anxiously, "You know, I only meant to retract my offer so that I could ask you again for the *right* reasons!" he informed her.

"Oh, that was cruel — you made me think you wanted to be free of me — that you wished to unburden yourself!"

"Never!" murmured Torquhil bending his head to kiss her with the smile still curling his mouth.

Hetty put up her arms and wound them about his neck and kissed him back with much enthusiasm and a great deal of long suppressed passion. When finally, he raised his head again she smiled at him shyly and said rather huskily, "The sooner we are married the better!" Her eyelids drooped as though she'd been drugged with opiates, and he seized her again and left her in no doubt of his feelings.

*   *   *

A little while later, she was comfortably arranged upon his lap, in a fireside armchair, her head nestled under his chin.

She stirred reluctantly and sighed, "I suppose we should go and make sure everyone is all right."

"I don't see why," said Torquhil unfeelingly.

"They may be worried about us."

"Again, I cannot think why we should care if they are."

"You're being very obtuse. I wouldn't want them to think —"

"Let them think what they like."

"It's easy for you to say that but your reputation has already reached its nadir and only by making an honest man of you will I be able to rescue your good character in the eyes of the locals. Although, I'm sure you will tell me that they can take a powder!"

"Such language and from a lady too," he kissed her behind her ear and trailed his lips down her neck, making her shiver with delight, "Although you're the *first* lady I've ever seen covered from head to toe in the ashes of a dead Saxon warlord."

She sat up suddenly and glared at him, "Oh, I'd forgotten! And you allowed me to —! I must go and change my clothes!"

He laughed, "If I have no objections to kissing an urchin grave-robber, I don't see why you should mind!"

She adjusted her clothing, tucking the crumpled fichu back into the neckline of her gown and slid from his knees to stand a little unsteadily before him.

He held fast to her hand, "I loved you the moment I first set eyes upon you, you know? I was riding by, and you were wrestling with a particularly disorderly pig in the meadow."

She looked at him lovingly, "Then the rumours are true — you are surely deranged!"

He dragged her remorselessly back into his arms and kissed her hard but with a stifled groan she tore herself away, "You *must* let me go! Eirwen should be chaperoned! And poor Grandpapa must be wondering where his dinner is!"

"You know very well that they will all be just fine," he said, his face alight with love and amusement.

She looked at him for a long moment and at length said, "I dare say, but I cannot — *must* not stay."

"Ah, I see! You do not trust yourself!"

"You've quite clearly taken leave of your senses, Mr Guivre. It is that I cannot trust *you*!" countered Hetty as she reached for the door handle.

"Quite right too! So, in the end, it turns out, Hetty, that you are to be my Fate," he reflected.

"Well, it serves you right! You get what you deserve."

"You are my place of safety," said Torquhil.

"And you are mine," replied Hetty.

She pulled open the door and looked back at him over her shoulder, and seeing the expression that crossed his face, she slammed the door shut again and ran back to him, flinging herself onto his lap to find herself held so tightly she could barely draw breath.

"Oh, Torquhil, I do love you so!"

There came the sound of impatient clacking from the other side of the room.

To think that if I fancied a mate, I'd only have to present her with a twig, and it'd be signed and sealed.

Hetty sprang back guiltily and Torquhil laughed.

And at that moment dense white fog obliterated the view of the garden and began to seep into the house like ghostly fingers, sneaking through the cracks in the mortar and the gaps in the windows and doors.

Crow shivered his feathers.

And so, a little warmth brings the thaw.

The End

HISTORICAL ROMANCE

BY CAROLINE ELKINGTON

Set in the years shown

A Very Civil War (1645)
Dark Lantern (1755)
The House on the Hill (1765)
Three Sisters (1772)
The Widow (1782)
Out of the Shadows (1792)

A VERY CIVIL WAR
1645

Con's life in the small Cotswold village, where she spent an idyllic childhood, is nothing out of the ordinary, which is good because she likes ordinary. She likes safe.

Her three boisterous nephews have come to stay for the summer holidays, and she's determined to show them that life in the countryside can be fun — she has no idea just how exciting it's about to get.

Whilst out exploring with them in the fields near the village, they find themselves face to face with a Roundhead colonel from the English Civil Wars and, due to some glitching twenty-first century technology, Con is transported back to 1645 and into a world she only recognises from books and historical dramas on television and finds hard to understand. She reluctantly falls for the gruff officer, who is recovering from injuries sustained in recent hostilities with Royalists but must battle archaic attitudes and unexpected violence in order to survive.

With no way of getting back to her family and her nice secure real life and unable to reveal who she really is, for fear of being thought a witch, she struggles to acclimatise to her new life and must fight her growing feelings for Colonel Sir Lucas Deverell and deal with the daily problems of life in the seventeenth century and the encroaching war. When she intervenes to save a dying man, suspicions are raised and she begins to fear for her life, with enemies on all sides.

Constance Harcourt discovers a love that crosses centuries and all barriers, but which could potentially end in heartbreak. Can the power of True Love overcome the power of the Universe?

This is a time-slip story filled with passionate romance, the very real threat of persecution and war, the charm of the Cotswolds and touches of Beauty and the Beast.

DARK LANTERN
1755

An unexpected funeral, a new life with unwelcoming relations and a mysterious stranger who is destined to change her life forever. Martha Pentreath has been thrust into a bewildering and perilous adventure.

Set in 1755, on the wild coast between Cornwall and Devon, this swashbuckling tale of high society and secretive seafarers follows Martha as she valiantly juggles her conflicting roles, one moment hard at work in the kitchens of Polgrey Hall and the next elbow to elbow with the local gentry.

Then as dragoons scour the coast for smugglers, she finds herself beholden to the captain of a lugger tellingly built for speed. Unsure whom to trust, Martha soon realises that everything she thought she knew was a lie and people are not what they seem.

With undercurrents of The Scarlet Pimpernel, Cinderella and Jamaica Inn, this is a story of windswept cliffs, wreckers, betrayal, secrets, murder and passionate romance.

Martha fights back against those who would relish her downfall and discovers the shocking truth about her own family. But she will find loyalty and friendship and a love that will surprise her but also bring her heartache.

THE HOUSE on the HILL
1765

After falling on hard times due to a family scandal, Henrietta Swift lives with her grandfather in a dilapidated farmhouse and is quite content to live without luxury or even basic comforts.

However, she's being watched.

Someone has plans for her and despite suffering misgivings she has no real choice but to accept their surprising proposition in order to give her beloved grandfather a better life.

It leads her to Galdre Knap, a darkly mysterious house, where her enigmatic employer, Torquhil Guivre, requires a companion for his seriously ill sister, Eirwen, who is being brought home to convalesce.

With her habitual optimism, Henrietta believes all will be well — until the other-worldly Eirwen arrives in a snowstorm. The house then begins to reveal its long-buried secrets and Henrietta must battle to save those she loves from the sinister forces that threaten their safety and her happiness.

In the process, she unexpectedly finds true love and discovers that the world is filled with real magic and that she is capable of far more than she ever thought possible.

Here be Dragons and Enchantment and Happy Ever Afters.

THREE SISTERS
1772

The prim and proper Augusta Pennington has taken over the management of a failing Ladies' Seminary with her two sisters, grumpy Flora and wild Pandora. Their elderly aunts, Ida and Euphemia Beauchamp, can no longer run the school and have been forced to hand over the reins. They are losing pupils, as they lag the fashions in female education, and are struggling financially.

Their scandalous and irascible neighbour, Sir Marcus Denby, is reluctantly drawn into their ventures by the younger sister, Pandora, who tumbles from one scrape into another, without any concern for her safety or her family's reputation.

With the help of Quince, a delinquent hound, Pandora befriends Sir Marcus's estranged daughter, Imogen, who has been much neglected by her beautiful but venomous mother.

Augusta, initially repelled by Sir Marcus's notoriety, tries desperately to resist the growing attraction between them. It takes a series of mishaps and the arrival of some unwanted guests to finally make Augusta understand that not everything is as it seems and love really can conquer all.

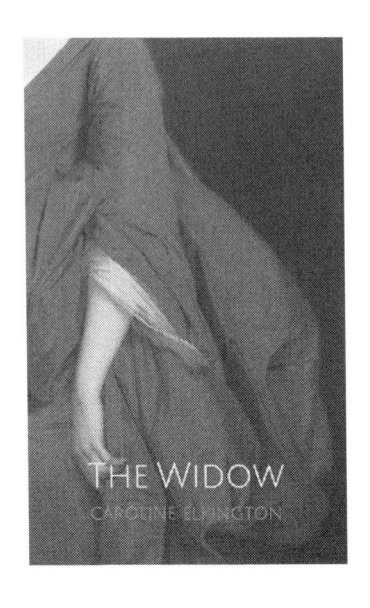

THE WIDOW
1782

Nathaniel Heywood arrived at Winterborne Place with no intention of remaining there for longer than it took to conclude a business proposition on behalf of his impulsive friend Emery Talmarch.

Impecunious, cynical and world-weary, he is reluctant to shoulder any kind of responsibility. Nathaniel was just looking for an easy way to make some money to save Emery from debtor's prison and possibly worse. He had no idea that he would be offered such an outrageous proposal by his host, Lord Winterborne, and find himself swiftly drawn into a web of intrigue and danger. He wants nothing more than to escape and be trouble-free again.

Above anything else he wanted his freedom.

And then he meets Grace.

OUT of the SHADOWS
1792

In this deeply romantic thriller, an inebriated and perhaps foolhardy visit to London's Bartholomew Fair begins with an eye to some light-hearted entertainment and ends with a tragic accident.

Theo Rokewode and his close friends find themselves unexpectedly encumbered with two young girls in desperate need of rescue. As a result, their usually ordered lives are turned upside down as danger stalks the girls into the hallowed halls of refined Georgian London and beyond to Rokewode Abbey in Gloucestershire.

Sephie and Biddy are hugely relieved to be rescued from the brutal life they had been forced to endure but know that they are still not truly safe. Only they know what could be coming and as Sephie loses her heart to Theo, she dreads the truth about her past being revealed and determines to somehow repay her new-found friends for their gallantry and unquestioning hospitality, but vows to leave before the man she loves so desperately sees her for what she really is.

Her carefully laid plans bring both delight and disaster as her past finally catches up with her and mayhem ensues, as Theo, his eccentric friends and family valiantly attempt to put the lid back on the Pandora's Box they'd unwittingly opened that fateful night at the fair.

About Caroline Elkington

When not writing novels, Caroline's reading them - every few days a knock on the door brings more. She has always preferred the feel — and smell — of a real book.

She began reading out of boredom as she was tucked up in bed by her mother, herself an avid reader, at a ridiculously early hour.

In the winter months she read by moving her book sideways back and forth to catch a slither of light that shone through the crack between the hinges of her bedroom door.

Fast forward sixty years and she's someone who knows what she wants from a book: to be immersed in history (preferably Georgian), to be captivated by a romantic hero, to be thrilled by the story, and to feel uplifted at the end.

After a long career that began with fashion design and morphed into painting ornately costumed portraits and teaching art, she has a strong eye for the kind of detail that draws the reader into a scene.

Review This Novel and See More by Caroline

Point your phone's camera at the code.
A banner will appear on your screen.
Tap it to see Caroline's novels on Amazon.

Printed in Great Britain
by Amazon